The Effect of Her

ALSO BY GERARD STEMBRIDGE

According to Luke

Counting Down

Unspoken

Unspoken: Downloadable Audio Version (read by the author)
Available at www.oldstreetpublishing.co.uk/old-street-audio-store

The Effect of Her

Gerard Stembridge

OLD STREET PUBLISHING

First published in Great Britain in 2013 by Old Street Publishing Ltd
Trebinshun House, Brecon LD3 7PX
www.oldstreetpublishing.co.uk

ISBN 978-1-908699-32-9

10 9 8 7 6 5 4 3 2 1

A CIP catalogue record for this title is available from the British Library.

Typeset by Old Street Publishing Ltd.

Printed and bound in Great Britain.

For Donal

'But the effect of her being on those around her was incalculably diffusive: for the growing good of the world is partly dependent on unhistoric acts; and that things are not so ill with you and me as they might have been, is half owing to the number who lived faithfully a hidden life.'

George Eliot, *Middlemarch*

1970

One: October 25th

Womb. Fetus. Unborn. Abortion. Francis Strong knew he'd have to look up these words, so he'd understand properly what Mr Moran was telling 6A.

He'd been daydreaming. The brilliant thing about his new classroom was that it was so high up he could see over the school wall to the railway station. The afternoon train to Dublin was taking off. Francis wished he was on it. He was in Dublin only once and that was in a car a year ago with Ian Barry, who was his best friend then, and his dad. Mr Barry brought them to RTE and a man called Gavin showed them around the studios. He was very funny. That was the best day, but it would be even better to take off to Dublin in the train, all on his own, and have an adventure, or a big mystery to solve, like in the last Agatha Christie book Francis had read, *Murder on the Orient Express*.

It was the freakiest coincidence that at that very second, he thought he heard Mr Moran say, 'Murder'. Immediately he turned from the window and looked at his new teacher. Had he really just said 'Murder'? If he had that would be a lot different to compound interest, or the mountains and rivers of Ireland, or subject, predicate and object.

Mr Moran was saying he was sorry if he sounded angry because he wasn't angry with any of the boys of 6A but he would make *no apology whatsoever* for being angry at what was going on in England right now, this very minute, as he was speaking. Francis wished that he'd been listening earlier. What was going on in England? Then Mr Moran said it again. Murder was a shocking word to use, but he would stand by it because that's what abortion was – no more nor no less than the murder of innocent babies, and let no one tell them any different. Even though he'd only been their teacher for a few weeks, he could tell that they were intelligent boys and grown-up enough to know about these things and, as far as Mr Moran was concerned, it was vital, *absolutely vital,* that everyone knew about the horrors of abortion so as to make sure it never *ever* happened here in Ireland.

Francis was sure he wasn't the only one in the class who'd never heard the word abortion before, because usually he knew more words than nearly anyone else, and this one was completely new. It sounded like an 'A' word. From what Mr Moran was saying, it meant murdering babies, but he'd look it up to make sure. The more Mr Moran talked the more annoyed he got. Not just annoyed. Perturbed. Agitated. Fretful. He kept stabbing his finger in the air at the class. Until now Francis had thought his new teacher was the most easygoing he ever had. At the start of the year Mr Moran even said it himself. 'I'm an easygoing kind of a man, boys.' And he showed them just how easygoing he was. He held his leather strap up high. 'See this yoke?' Then he pulled open a drawer and dropped it in. 'That's going in there and as far as I'm concerned, it'll stay locked away for the rest of the year.' Then he took out a key and locked the drawer. 'You see, I'm not one of those teachers that uses fear to make boys do their work.' The whole class knew he was talking about Brother Hedgehog. 'I believe that if I teach with a smile on my face you will learn with a smile on your face.'

But there was no smile on Mr Moran's face now. Francis tried to think of a worse word than scowl. Glare maybe, but worse than that even. Mr Moran was really raging about abortion. His voice had gone very low. He pulled off his glasses and pointed them at 6A. He said he knew what he was talking about, boys, because his wife had been a nurse in England and she had seen, *with her own eyes,* bins hidden away at the back of hospitals, full to the top with these misfortunate unborn children, hundreds of them torn from the womb, *every week,* in such a horrible way he would not even describe it because he didn't want to be upsetting the boys too much by telling them exactly how the fetus was *ripped* from the womb. Francis wished he would describe it so he'd have some chance of knowing what fetus and womb and unborn meant. Was unborn the same as not born? But if they were not born how could they be murdered? He'd just have to look up all these words when he got home. He said them over in his head to make sure he'd remember them.

Mr Moran couldn't seem to stop talking about abortion. The more he went on about babies being killed in hospitals in England the more Francis couldn't understand why such an awful thing wasn't on the RTE News every night, the same as the black babies dying in Biafra. Mr Moran said he wanted everyone in the class to tell their mams and dads what he'd explained to them. Abortion, he said, was something everyone should be talking about. How could they put an end to this terrible evil if people didn't speak out?

Francis hardly ever asked his mam anything anymore because, when he did, she'd just say 'What do you want to know that for?' And then there'd be a big rigmarole before he'd get an answer. If he got one at all. 'I haven't time to be answering your questions,' she'd say sometimes, or 'Ask your father.' But his dad talked in such a roundabout way that, by the time he'd finished, Francis would have nearly forgotten what he'd asked him in the first place. So when he got home from school he didn't say anything to his mam about what Mr Moran had told them or ask her any of the words he didn't know. His sister Marian was at her secretarial course, so he snuck into her room and borrowed her *Little Gem Collins English Dictionary.* He brought it into his bedroom and sat on the lower bunk. Abortion was easy to find. It was a noun.

'The premature ending of a pregnancy when a fetus is expelled from the womb, before it can live independently.'

There was nothing about murder. And what was 'pregnancy'? Francis also noticed the words Mr Moran had said weren't spelled the way he expected. He thought 'womb' would be 'woom' like 'room', but it was like 'tomb'. And he had been sure that 'fetus' would have two e's because it sounded like 'feet'. When he looked it up, he found another new word: 'embryo'.

'The embryo of a mammal in the later stages of development.'

He immediately went back to the 'E' words and looked up 'embryo'. Another noun.

'An unborn animal or human being –'

So there was such a thing as being 'unborn', but Francis still didn't know what that was and the rest of the definition didn't help.

'– in the early stages of development, in humans up to approximately the second month of pregnancy.'

That word 'pregnancy' again. It had to be important, even though Mr Moran hadn't said it. Francis went to the 'P' words. But under 'pregnancy', it just said 'the state of being pregnant'. Pregnant was just below it. It was an adjective.

'1. Carrying a fetus or fetuses within the womb.'

Francis was getting really annoyed. He hated it when the dictionary used words he didn't understand to explain other words he didn't understand and just went round and round in a circle. He noticed there was a second definition of 'pregnant'.

'2. Full of meaning or significance. A *pregnant* pause.'

It had nothing to do with the mystery he was trying to solve, but at least he understood the definition. He liked the sound of it. So, what did he know? A fetus was something unborn. Pregnant was carrying a fetus in a womb. Francis suddenly remembered the word womb was in the Hail Mary. 'And blessed is fruit of thy womb, Jesus.' He rattled off that prayer every morning in school. When he was very young and he thought about his prayers much more than he did now, he used to imagine that a womb was a kind of basket that Jesus had, with loads of fruit in it. But the truth was he hadn't a clue what it was. Now he was about to find out. He went to the 'W' words, almost at the end of the dictionary. Womb was a noun.

'The organ in the lower body of a woman or female mammal

where offspring are conceived and in which they gestate before birth.'

Something stirred in Francis' brain. Since coming back to school after the holidays his friend Ian Barry didn't seem to want to talk to him much anymore. He sat next to Padraig Leddin and preferred hanging around with him and Dave Flannery. They were always whispering in a corner and laughing. One day in the yard he saw them say something to Andrew Liddy who sat next to Francis. They laughed and Andrew laughed too, but Francis could tell he was only laughing because the others were. Later in class, while Mr Moran had his back turned writing on the blackboard, Francis asked Andrew what they'd been laughing about? He whispered, 'girls'. Francis wondered what about girls? There were no girls in the school, so why were they laughing about girls? Then Andrew told him that Dave Flannery said if a boy rubbed his mickey against a girl, *down below*, then a baby grew inside her.

'Well, would you look at Andrew Liddy and Francis Strong, whispering secrets like a couple of silly little girls.'

The rest of 6A had looked around, laughing at what Mr Moran said. Francis and Andrew went completely red and sat up very straight as far away from each other as they could.

What Andrew Liddy said had sounded so ridiculous that Francis had thought Dave Flannery must've been making an eejit out of him in front of Ian and Padraig. But now here it was in the dictionary. 'The lower body of a female.' Could such a mad thing be even half true? What was this other new word 'gestate'? Francis didn't even know how to say it. Was it 'G' like 'guess' or 'G' like 'gesture'? Both ways sounded right. He flicked the pages back to G. It was a verb.

'To carry a fetus in the womb from conception to birth.'

'Is that my dictionary?'

His big sister Marian was looking in the bedroom door. Caught.

'You know you're not supposed to go into my room without my

permission. How many times do I have to have to say it you?'

Marian came in and stood over him. The little brat had an awful cheek, he really had. What made him think it was his right to go wandering into her room and take her stuff? Why had he shut the dictionary so fast and why had he gone scarlet? Usually he loved boasting about the new words he'd discovered. Of course! Her eleven-year-old, know-it-all little brother was looking up dirty words. She wanted to laugh, but instead kept a straight face and asked him, really seriously, as if she wanted to help.

'So what were you looking up?'

Francis, his cheeks burning, looked away from his big sister's face. But now he was looking straight at her miniskirt. At the *lower part of her body*. Did his sister have a womb in there? He managed to mutter.

'Nothing. Just some words.'

'Really? Just some words? In a dictionary? That's an amazing thing to be doing.'

Francis couldn't look up at her eyes, he couldn't look down at the dictionary and he couldn't keep looking at Marian's miniskirt. He didn't know where to look.

'What words? Tell me, maybe I can explain what they mean.'

Marian enjoyed seeing Francis squirm and knew exactly how to torture him even more. She'd suggest that he should tell Mam what words he was looking up. That would really frighten the life out of him. It might teach him once and for all not to go into her bedroom without permission. But before she could say anything more, he dropped the dictionary on the ground and she heard him trying to hold in sobs and saw him rubbing his eyes. Marian felt guilty. Genuinely, she'd never meant him to get that upset. She reached down and picked up the dictionary, trying to look him in the eyes, but he buried his face in his hands.

'Ah Fran, I was only asking. You don't have to tell me if you don't want to. They're just words. There's nothing bad about words. You can borrow the dictionary anytime, but you have to ask first.'

Smart and all as he thought he was, her brother was still just a big baby. It was probably better to lay off him. Back in her own bedroom, Marian couldn't help wondering exactly what words he had been looking up that were so awful he was too scared to tell her. She could guess. How many years ago was it when, right here, sitting on the side of her bed, terrified she'd be caught, she'd looked up 'menstrual'? Dr Greany, so brisk and cold, had used that word to explain what was happening to her and she'd never heard it before. So innocent then.

As she was putting the dictionary back on the shelf amongst all her old Leaving Cert books, suddenly Marian felt a bit like crying herself. She didn't know why. No tears came, but she still couldn't get rid of this strange pang. What was the matter with her? This first week of the secretarial course had gone fine. Shorthand was going to be complicated, Marian could see that, but really interesting. Mrs McNamara said she seemed very adept at the keyboard and would have good typing speeds in no time. Her mam was so thrilled that she'd got into Mrs McNamara's course. 'There now, all that work for the Leaving Cert was well worthwhile,' she kept saying –as if Marian had thought it wasn't. Never once had it crossed her mam's mind that doing the Leaving Cert might have allowed her to go on to uni. The truth was she'd never really dared think that herself. How could they afford it with her dad's job? No one in her class was going to uni except Mary Considine, who got a scholarship, so what was there to complain about? She wasn't complaining, she knew how lucky she was to get on the commercial course…

Marian heard Francis sneak past her room very quietly and go downstairs. Didn't take the little baba long to recover. She immediately regretted such an angry thought. What was the matter with her!

Francis felt he was on the brink of solving an enormous mystery. He thought of how often grownups started whispering to each other so he wouldn't know what they were on about. Was all the whispering something to do with these words he'd just discovered, words he had never ever heard spoken out loud? Pregnant. Embryo. Fetus. Gestate.

In the back room, Eugene was fast asleep as usual in his cot. His mam was always saying thanks be to God he was a very placid child. She'd arrived home with him at the end of January after being away for about a week, in hospital Francis had been told, although his dad had never brought him to visit her. There was such commotion and excitement about this tiny baby; his new brother, everyone told him. Loads of people called at number 66: every aunt and uncle and cousin and neighbour and friend of the family. Even Granny Strong, who was eighty-seven, a great age everyone said, actually left her house to come and visit the new baby. His mam's sisters, Mona, Una and Bernadette seemed to be around all the time, helping out. Everyone who called in brought a present and drank a toast and talked and talked about baby Eugene all the time – what weight he was, his hair, his eyes, was he a Strong or a Casey?

Until now Francis had never thought even once about where this new little brother had come from. His mam had brought him home and there he was. The only important thing had been that all of a sudden, after ten and a half years, he wasn't the baby of the family. It had always been Ritchie and Gussy and Marian and Martin and him last, but not anymore. He liked that because it made him feel more grown-up

But now he was staring at his baby brother and thinking, fetus, gestate, womb –

'If you wake him I'll kill you.'

Francis didn't turn round to his mam. If she looked in his eyes she'd know what was going on in his head.

'I won't.'

'You'd better not.'

His mam went back into the hall, shouting up at Marian to come and help set the table. Francis tried to remember how small Eugene was when he first saw him eight months ago. He was tiny all right. And before that? Had he been even smaller? Had he been a fetus? When Francis heard his sister come into the back room he didn't dare look at her either. Eugene's tiny hands were clutching and opening and clutching again. And his little toes wriggling. Could it be? Did he really – he wished he knew the right way to say the word – gestate inside his mam? In her womb. For how long? Now he remembered something that happened about two months before Eugene was born, last November, at his brother Ritchie's wedding. Near the end of the ceremony the priest came down from the altar to where his mam was sitting, put his hand on her stomach, muttered some special prayer and made the sign of the cross over it. Francis had never seen a priest do that before. It was a bit weird. His mam was thrilled to bits. Now he wondered was the priest blessing Eugene, who was unborn, a fetus, gestating in his mam's womb?

Over the clatter of plates Francis heard his mam saying that the girls who did Mrs McNamara's course always got great jobs out of it and having shorthand and typing would stand to her all her life. Slowly Francis sneaked his head around to look at his mam and his big sister laying the table for tea. He stared at where the belt of Marian's miniskirt was pulled tight around her thin waist. His mam's lower body was bigger and rounder and when she leaned over the table her stomach bulged more. If Eugene had been inside his mam before he was born then that meant... it had to mean Francis was once inside her too. And Martin and Marian and Gussie and Ritchie? Could it be true? It was what the words seemed to mean.

*

If she hadn't got back from dropping the kids off at school when she did and hadn't heard the phone as she arrived at her front gate and hadn't managed to get the key out of her bag quickly for once and opened the door and picked up the receiver just in time, Mags Perry would have missed out on an unexpected day's work. That in a nutshell was the freelance life for which, over the last three frenzied years, she had never stopped thanking her lucky stars.

Ciarán, the news editor at the *Irish Press* wondered was there any chance she could get to the Four Courts by ten and fill in as court reporter at the Arms Trial of all things. Michael Mills, the political correspondent, would be handling the main front page story, but they were stuck for someone to do the basic five hundred words detailing the important exchanges of the day, at the usual daily rate for female reporters. Four quid was four quid and Mags was delighted to get it, even though she would have preferred to contribute a very different kind of article about the so-called Arms Crisis, one which would propose that the whole wretched circus was the direct result of men-only government. Like spoiled brats at a privileged single-sex school, government ministers behaved as if politics was some nasty playground game and, when the trouble started in Northern Ireland, the bullies in the yard had decided that playing with guns seemed like great sport. The article she'd like to write would contend that had there been even one woman in the cabinet – what a thought! – the alpha-male antics would never have reached this farcical stage with a government minister and his cronies arraigned in the high court, accused of illegally importing guns into the State. In short, the Arms 'Crisis' was all about machismo, testosterone, ego or, to put it more plainly, middle-aged men in suits throwing shapes like adolescent boys. Of course she knew there was as little chance of such an analysis of the great political scandal of the day being published in a national newspaper as there was of a woman being appointed editor of any of those same publications.

One slight problem: the kids had to be collected from school, but Mags knew her mother would be delighted to take them for the night, because apparently the only time those misfortunate neglected grandchildren were fed properly was when they were in her miraculous care. How Mags had ever managed to keep the poor mites alive for eight years in faraway England, was something that occasionally she'd been tempted to inquire of the Widow Perry, but reluctance to bring up her marriage at all usually meant she kept her trap shut.

Widow Perry got very giggly when she heard why Mags needed the favour.

'The Arms Trial? Well, say hello to CJ for me and thank him for the free travel.'

Unbelievable! In court for gun-running, but the Great Man had bestowed on pensioners the bus pass, and so deserved their eternal loyalty. Her mother started going on again about how the conductors on the number 12 would flirt with her when they saw her photo on the pass, 'Go 'way outta that. That must be your older sister. Come on, pay up, young lady!' Mags knew if she responded at all – Oh sure, Mam, being able to get that old bus into town, free of charge, makes up for all your years of unpaid housekeeping, child-bearing, child-rearing' – it would turn into a long rant – 'and imagine, the women are getting the same bus pass as the men, not two-thirds of a pass like the two-thirds of a wage that working women get right now compared to a man doing the same job. I feel so much better knowing that we'll all be equal when we're seventy' – But if she was to be at the Four Courts by ten, Mags realised she needed to hold her tongue for once.

There wasn't time to wait for the immersion to heat the water so she grabbed a lightning-fast cold shower. What was this fascination about CJ? It wasn't only grateful lady pensioners. Editors and political writers, husky men all, were just as obsessed in a way Mags had always thought creepily homoerotic. When a few months back the public had been informed that the Minister for Finance had an unfortunate fall from his horse and broken some bones, in the smoke-filled murk of Mulligan's and Bowe's and The Oval, the 'lads' from the *Press* and the *Times* and the *Indo* found themselves unable to utter the phrase, 'riding accident', without that particular emphasis on the first word which inevitably spawned sniggers galore, followed by a competitive sequence of double entendres. Carry on Journalist. Mags had even heard one reporter name a particular lady from whose bedroom window he had been assured – tap of nose and significant nod – the bould

CJ had to drop hastily that night, occasioning the 'riding' injuries that kept him in hospital for over a week. Oh he was a rogue, a rapscallion, a man among men. And now, it seemed, a gun-smuggler too.

Mags, shivering, scratched vigorously with the towel as she scooted about, gathering clean knickers, jeans and her favourite wine peasant top, not so much a uniform of protest as wanting to feel comfortable during what would be a long day in a stuffy courtroom. So, she wondered, was CJ the saviour of poor defenceless Catholics in Northern Ireland, or the instigator of a coup d'état in the Republic? Or, Mags added her own third option, just another self-regarding and mildly repulsive member of the State's male hierarchy? And such a stunty little creature too.

The Round Hall in the Four Courts was a humming hive sketched in grey and black. Mags felt her consciousness boil up that the very few other women present seemed to feel they had to encase themselves in their stiffest and dullest two-piece outfits, but her annoyance was offset by amusement at the feminine flutter of gowns and the bouncing curls of the learned gentlemen's wigs as they glided about, oozing camp pomposity. Even charismatic CJ wore a suit so anonymous that Mags spotted his entourage before she picked him out, squatting amongst them in an alcove. They whispered gravely, necks folding into chins as all of them inclined towards their Master. All except one. This one stood taller and certainly seemed trimmer around the waist. His other singularity was that he was not exclusively focused on CJ. He lent an ear to the little conference all right, but never spoke, and his eyes were always elsewhere. Those eyes had black depths that her mother would call moody-looking. Mags preferred saturnine.

As her task today allowed no comment, or colour, and therefore, no thinking, she had time to observe the particular brand of maleness that seemed to thrive in the courtroom environment. Its scent seeming almost to seep from the walls. Here was the lair of cerebral man, analytical man; that creature of cold disinterested logic. *Sturm und Drang* would not be welcome here, nor the sweaty towel-slapping vulgarity of the locker room. In physical terms, it was the home of flaccid man; from the judge's quivering *foie gras* chins to the wafer-thin skin hanging disconsolately from his tipstaff's long bony face, to the considerable paunches sagging ever nearer the groins of the senior counsels, to the assorted bent shoulders, twitchy faces, shiny domes, milk-bottle glasses and pigeon breasts of the all-male jury. Mags found it freakishly fascinating.

All four defendants were male too. Albert Luycks, a bewildered-looking balding Dutch businessman, John Kelly, who everyone whispered was IRA high command, Captain James Kelly, the dutiful army officer, and CJ, who, despite being the shortest of the defendants, strove to seem above it all, sitting with head back to ensure the tilt of his fine Roman nose looked as imperious as possible. Sizing them up in the dock, Mags thought the public should be grateful that this particular form of beauty contest didn't include a swimwear section.

They were all pleading not guilty. Three of them claimed that buying guns in secret and smuggling them into the country to pass on to beleaguered Northern Catholics was, albeit *sotto voce,* official government policy, so how could it be a crime? CJ's defence, as far as Mags could work out, was he that hadn't done it – but if he had done it he still wouldn't be guilty of anything. A mere female reporter on two thirds of a man's wages could never be expected to follow that level of cerebration.

The Minister for Defence, Jim Gibbons, was called and it was soon clear that his evidence would be as dull as his presence: 'No'; 'I did not'; 'I don't recall that'. Mags could relax. Her dodgy shorthand skills, an untidy makey-up jumble of Pittman and Perry, wouldn't be stretched. The man was a Fianna Fáil minister and knew his job. Deny, deny, deny. The party never, ever, ever, had a policy to give arms to Northern Catholics. Not officially, not by wink and nod, not at all. Not at all at all. As the minutes that felt like hours dragged by, the dogged simplicity of his answers easily trumped all the sophisticated stratagems and urbane cunning of the defence counsels. Mags was reminded of her younger child, Simon, who had recently discovered a boyish pleasure in catching people out, especially, it seemed, his mother and older sister.

'Mum, which is right – the yolk of an egg *is* white, or the yoke of an egg *are* white?

Mags had only been only half listening. 'Is white.'

Simon had hooted. 'Ha ha ha, you're wrong. The yoke of an egg is yellow. Ha ha! Caught you.'

Watching the antics in court this morning, Mags decided it might be time to start gently discouraging this tendency in her little boy. Was it a uniquely male characteristic, this delight in setting verbal traps, wrong-footing, making others look foolish? It was called one-up*man*ship, after all.

Saturnine Man provided the only distraction from the tedium. Mags had forgotten about him until he caused a minor upset in the public gallery, working his way a bit too noisily along the row towards the exit. A few minutes later he returned, creating another kefuffle. About half an hour later he left again. And once more before the lunch break. Weak bladder? Chain smoker? Or just frustrated, trapped for some reason in a place he didn't want to be, but had to remain? Mags could sing that tune. She didn't even have his luxury of slipping in and out. He was at it again early in the afternoon. The next time he returned, Mags gave up on the Minister's obstinate repetitions and transferred her curious attention to Saturnine Man. He was now sitting very still, arms folded, eyes fixed somewhere high above the action, giving no indication that he was in any way restless or ill at ease. But the mouth and eyes were the giveaway. No contentment there. It was hard to put an exact age on him. Was he ten years older than Mags? Definitely. Over forty-five but probably not yet fifty.

When he rose again, what surprised Mags was that she'd detected no prior warning, no change of expression, or exhalation of breath, or body adjustment. It was as if some powerful spring had unexpectedly ejected him from his seat. By now, the others in his row were clearly irritated by these comings and goings, but Saturnine Man didn't seem to notice or care. This time ten minutes passed without his return. Had he left for good? Quarter to four. Mags told herself that in the few minutes left before the court adjourned the chances of the Minister crumbling in the face of his tormentor's superior interrogation skills and crying out 'I did it. I authorised the gun-running!' were slim. Solving the mystery of why one of CJ's entourage kept leaving court number four was at least potentially more interesting.

He wasn't in the Round Hall, but outside she spotted him immediately, directly across the road, leaning over the low wall, looking down at the river. It would never have crossed the mind of a casual passerby that this man might be about to throw himself in, but having witnessed his behavior all day, Mags was less certain. He could heave himself up and over in a second and that would be that. At the very moment she'd decided that wandering over cigarette-in-hand to ask for a light was too obvious a ruse, Saturnine Man turned and, it seemed to Mags, stared directly at her. Then he quickly crossed the road towards her, but walked past without a glance. Then she heard his voice.

'Sorry, weren't you in number four?'

Was he talking to her? Mags looked round.

'Oh. Ah, yes. How did you know?'

'You were in the press box. You kinda stood out, you know…'

The gesture towards her clothes was as awkward as his tone.

'Right. Well… a clown at a funeral.'

'Not at all, you livened up the look of the place.' She couldn't nail his accent precisely but it had a flat, rural, hoarsely aggressive edge to it. Not deliberately unfriendly though.

'When I saw you heading out I thought they must be finished for the day.'

'They probably are, more or less. I just couldn't take anymore to be honest.'

'I'm with you there. What a load of bollocks – sorry, pardon the French.'

Mags was quite surprised to hear a CJ acolyte echo her own sentiments and in not dissimilar terms. A bit of a maverick then? Was he was the kind who might speak out of turn? Just then the doors of court number four opened.

'Ah here they are – well, nice talking to you. Who do you write for?'

'*Irish Press.*'

'Oh, one of Tim Pat's ladies. You're not your one… what's her name… Mary Kenny, are you?'

Mags smiled and shook her head. She couldn't help being a little flattered. Mary Kenny was at least ten years younger, with all that went with that.

'No, I'm freelance. Just filling in for the day.'

'What's your name?'

'Mags Perry.'

'You heading up to the Russell?'

Mags was well aware that the Russell Hotel on Harcourt Street was where to see Fianna Fáilers of a certain ilk disport themselves. The opposite was also true and it was a place to avoid if you did *not* want to see Fianna Fáilers disport themselves.

'No, I have to get my report in.'

'Well, we'll be there for the night I'd say so anyway. I'd better head.'

Had he forgotten to offer his name? Or deliberately not told her?

'And… what's your name?'

'Oh – ah… Michael Liston.'

She watched Michael Liston nudge his way toward CJ through the hordes of fans, more women than men, all demanding autographs and stretching to shake the hand not in a sling. As before, he hovered close by, but said nothing and looked elsewhere. Part of the entourage and yet somehow separate.

For Mags, entering the Irish Press building by the Hawkins

Street works entrance and flashing her NUJ card at the doorman still served as a reminder of her lucky escape from the respectable village wife role she had trapped herself in for so long. The rattle of the old lift, the clackety-clack of the newsroom it ascended to... Together they sounded a ramshackle fanfare for the shabby, uncertain, but transforming world of freelance possibility Mags had managed to reopen for herself. Her escape to survival had not been without cost. What a cost. But worth it.

Reducing the key evidence of the day to five hundred words of reportage didn't strain the brain too much. The political correspondent, Michael Mills, smiled his old-world-gent smile across his desk and Mags wasn't remotely offended that he couldn't quite manage to disguise the fact that her name escaped him.

'Thanks for filling in. A good day to be there. The most exciting so far.'

As so often with male journalists, Mags found herself wondering had she been at the same event. There was a pause and she heard herself asking Michael Mills if he knew Michael Liston.

'Do you mean CJ's Michael Liston?'

'Ah... yes.'

'Well, I've heard of him and seen him. Never spoken directly to him though. Not a great man for putting himself forward. That'd suit CJ of course. What do you want to know?'

Mags, not even sure why she'd asked about Saturnine Man, hadn't a clue what she wanted to know. Luckily Michael Mills was content to answer his own question.

'I think he's one of these people... I understand he knows a lot about banking and so on. You know the way CJ likes to gather courtiers around him, experts in this and that.'

Back on the street, waiting for the 48A, it occurred to Mags that the Russell Hotel was on her route home if she walked and, there being no kids to look after this evening, she had time on her hands. A quick gander at the goings-on in the famous Russell might be amusing. Couldn't do any harm.

*

Matthew Liston was scared he'd start crying if Father McCormick confiscated his Philips cassette recorder. Any other punishment except that: slaps or detention or anything. He couldn't let his classmates see red eyes and stained cheeks when he came back from Father McCormick's office. Why had he let Nailer dare him sneak the cassette recorder into study hall? It was his own fault for thinking he was so smart, Nailer wasn't someone who could make him do something he didn't want to. No one was.

'The wire for the earpiece went under his shirt collar and all the way down inside his shirt and pants and out again, so it was no trouble to connect it to the cassette recorder which was in his bag, right there at his feet under the desk.'

Matthew thought Useless sounded the tiniest bit like he sort of admired how clever the trick was, but Father McCormick just stared at the recorder with glassy eyes. No one ever knew if Father McCormick was angry or not. He never shouted or made violent gestures. But if he felt like it he'd confiscate the recorder quick as the blink of an eye and Matthew would never see it again.

'Clever of you to notice it, Father Eustace.'

'Well, to be honest, Father, there was little enough cleverness on my part. I don't think I'd have spotted it at all only that, whatever happened, the wire somehow got disconnected from the machine. Then of course the whole room heard the... ah... heard the noise.'

Matthew still couldn't believe how thick he'd been. He'd been making faces and rocking his head to show Nailer how brilliant the music was. Then – unbelievably thick! – he'd sat back and stretched his legs under the desk. Everything happened in a second. He remembered feeling the wire suddenly go tight, then loose, and next thing the song was blasting out and everyone was looking round. Useless was up out of his chair in a flash. If Matthew had only thought of trying to stop it with his foot he might have clicked it off before Useless spotted him. Instead, like a dope, he'd bent down to get at it.

Father McCormick wondered what to do with Matthew

Liston. His disciplinary record was reasonable, his exam results exceptional, but one always sensed a polite silent resistance behind the child's dark eyes. Four years at the school had certainly benefited him academically, but Father McCormick was concerned that neither he nor his brother priests had managed during that time to penetrate and guide his soul. St Ignatius was clear that the battle had to be won in the early years. The child's family situation was a not unimportant element. No mother and a surly incommunicative father who had looked at him like he had two heads when Father McCormick had delicately suggested that telling his child the truth about his mother's death could be cathartic for both father and son. Afterwards Father McCormick wondered had 'cathartic' been a mistake. Perhaps Liston *Père* wasn't familiar with the word.

Only the other night he had been reminded of the matter in quite disturbing circumstances. Watching the nine o'clock news he saw, during a report on that wretched Arms Trial business, the boy's father outside the Four Courts, looking as lugubrious as ever, one of a little group standing behind the accused ex-minister. Father McCormick had of course been aware of Liston's Fianna Fáil connections. There were very few boys at the school whose fathers were not immersed in the political or judicial life of the nation: two sons of cabinet ministers right now and numerous sons of TDs and senators. Most of the parents tended towards the opposition Fine Gael party, which happily accorded with Father McCormick's very privately held opinions. He had been particularly pleased that it was the Fine Gael leader who had brought this terrible gun-smuggling business to public attention. Thankfully none of the cabinet ministers involved were ex-pupils. Christian Brothers boys mostly. As he presumed Liston was. Clearly, the man didn't mind displaying his colours on national television, implicating himself in the whole scandal. Fortunately his child would not have been watching the nine o'clock news.

'Do you want to hear what he was listening to, Father?'

'What? Pop music I suppose?'

'Yes, but ah… well… I think you should have a listen and… ah… it's probably better if you use this.'

Father McCormick took out his handkerchief and cleaned the earpiece before inserting it carefully, wondering why Father Eustace had such a peculiar look on his face and seemed so determined that he hear whatever pop nonsense the child had been filling his ear with. He pressed 'play'.

Matthew heard a tiny crackle invade the deadly silence of the wood-dark room and knew exactly what part of the song was playing now. It was the bit where the singer was confused because Lola walked like a woman but she talked like a man. That was very funny. And it was funny that even though Lola looked like a beautiful woman she was strong enough to nearly break his spine with a hug. And it was *really* funny when she sat the man on her knee and the singer began to realise that Lola mightn't be a woman at all. Scared as he was that Father McCormick was going to confiscate his recorder, Matthew nearly giggled out loud when he suddenly realised that the old priest standing over him, was, like Lola, also wearing a dress. A long black swishy number. Imagine if he sat on Matthew's knee.

Father McCormick's shock was profound. He had gleaned from Father Eustace's face and tone that it wouldn't be 'All Kinds of Everything' the child had been listening to, but this… this was utterly perverted. Girls like boys and boys like girls! The nauseating implication of the man on his knees in front of this 'woman' was perfectly transparent. Father McCormick's unblinking eyes noticed the child's lips quiver. He hoped it was nervous shame, as it should be, and not the suspicion of a smirk, which it could be. Had one of the senior boys been caught listening to this – Father McCormick would not call it a song – excrescence, it would be shocking , but a child of – what? – was he even twelve yet? He pulled out the earpiece and had to exercise more than usual control to ensure that neither his face nor his voice betrayed any agitation.

'Where did you get this?'

'My father bought it for my birthday –'

'The song, the song, not the machine.'

'Oh, sorry Father. I recorded it off the radio. Larry Gogan.'

Father McCormick had heard him. One those silly cheerful pop presenters. He had seemed a perfectly inoffensive type. Was this kind of thing now being played on Radio Eireann?

You recorded it yourself, you say? No one else gave it to you?'

For a second Matthew was tempted to tell a ridiculous lie the way William in the 'William' books always did when he was in trouble. It'd be funny to make up some crazy complicated story. It would also be the absolutest best way to get his Phillips recorder confiscated. No one ever lied to Father McCormick. He always caught them out.

'No, Father, I did it myself. There's a microphone in the machine – there. If you press that button and that one at the same time and then just hold it against the radio, it records.'

'And what else have you recorded on this tape?'

'Just the top ten show.'

This vulgarity was in the top ten? Father McCormick despaired. He had fully supported the school taking an enlightened view of pop culture and the boys seemed appreciative. Father Colleran had enjoyed a very enthusiastic response from the junior choir when he introduced 'Let It Be' and 'I'd Rather Be a Hammer than a Nail' and other pop hits to the repertoire. Father McCormick would have thought that the hit parade on Radio Eireann was relatively safe for the boys to hear. Clearly he and his brother priests would have to be more vigilant. In the meantime how was he to deal with this child in a way that wouldn't see him retreat even further into private darkness? Father McCormick pressed 'eject' and the cassette leapt up. He held it in his right hand and the ear piece in his left.

'I am confiscating this and this. Frankly, Matthew, you deserve much harsher punishment, but instead, I am going to allow you an opportunity to show Fr Eustace and I that you are capable of, not merely obeying the rules, but using your intelligence and skills in a more positive way. I will allow you to keep your recording machine on one strict condition. That you do not use it, or allow others to use it, at *any* time, without first asking Father Eustace's permission. I am putting you on your honour,. You understand what that means?'

'Yes Father, I promise.'

'I will also ask Father Colleran to allow you to attend junior choir rehearsal and record some songs. I want you to make the best recording you can and bring it to me. I will assess it.'

Matthew could hardly believe he was getting off so lightly. He'd manage without the ear piece and he had plenty more cassettes. Recording Fr Collie-dog's choir wasn't like a punishment at all. It'd be a laugh. The main thing was he had the precious Philips in his hands again.

'Thank you, Father. Thank you, Father.'

It was the nearest thing to a smile that Father McCormick had ever seen on the boy's face. Good. Turning the punishment into positive action could prove a turning-point, a new beginning for Matthew. He might start to reach out, look for guidance, open himself to positive influence. Time would tell. Nonetheless, it was also time to have a serious conversation with his unpleasant father.

*

At long last Michael Liston was talking, but Mags couldn't hear him because he wasn't bothering to raise his voice above the general hubbub.

'What?'

He seemed to repeat what he'd been saying, but it was no use. At two in the morning everyone who crammed into the tiny space of the Manhattan was loudly drunk. Not least the two heads of hair squeezed next to them at the little table, who were bellowing odd words and phrases at each other. 'Rory Gallagher!' roared one head of hair and the other head of hair roared back, 'Oh man, oh man!' Mags couldn't see faces, just identical lank mousy shoulder-length hair and identical denim jackets. The only point

of difference was that one was attacking a rasher sandwich while
the other was rolling cigarettes. At least she presumed they were
just cigarettes. '"Catfish"!' Cigarette Roller roared and Rasher
Sandwich shook his hair violently. 'No. No way, Head. "Sugar
Mama" – dropping his sandwich to squawk a blues guitar solo,
his hair slapping around his neck.

By leaning forward and pressing a finger to her left ear Mags
managed, more or less, to tune out 'Sugar Mama'.

'Sorry, what?'

Now she could just about hear Michael Liston. Despite the
truckload of G & Ts she had seen him put away over the last few
hours, there wasn't even a hint of slurring in the dry truculent
tone, but the dark eyes glittered.

'I was livid, absolutely ragin' with CJ.'

After several hours talking and drinking, Mags still had no
idea if Michael Liston was a bachelor, or separated or widowed or
whatever. He had a house in Clontarf. That was about all she'd
discovered. Now his tongue was suddenly off the leash. Was it
the cumulative effect of so many G &Ts, along with the big plate
of deep-fried black pudding, rashers and fried egg that he'd just
gobbled?

'I said it to him too. CJ, I said, are you out of your mind? You'll
destroy everything we've been creating for the last four years. You
might as well set yourself on fire like your man in Prague last year.
Imagine, the best Minister for Finance the fuckin' country ever
had – sorry, excuse the French –'

Mags frowned. The Heads of Hair were now loudly performing
the same guitar solo, in different keys. The smoke from their
rollies drifted past her face; only cigarettes after all. She'd smoked
her last before arriving at the Manhattan. What had Michael
Liston just said?

'Sorry, what?'

He still didn't raise his voice, but leaned in a bit closer.

'I said, from the look on your face, you don't agree that CJ was
the best Finance Minister we've ever had?'

Mags answered carefully. She didn't want to say anything that would shut him up, now that he was in talking mood.

'Well, I suppose he has had his moments –'

'You're going to mention the free travel for the pensioners, aren't you?'

It had been on the tip of Mags' tongue. In honour of Brenda Perry and her precious bus pass. Michael smirked.

'Brilliant, wasn't it? Inspired. You know it costs a pittance and it'll guarantee the votes of every auld one in the country forever and a day –'

Mags could vouch for that.

'– but that isn't why I'm saying he was the best Finance Minister the country ever had.'

'Why then?'

Michael Liston leaned in even closer. Now he was so near her ear, his breath tickled.

'Because he was good for business. Look at what's been built in the last few years, look at the money that's sloshing around the place that was never there before.'

Mags really really wanted to ask, yes but who's getting all this money? She held back. Let the man talk. Their heads were so close now, anyone looking at them would assume he was whispering something romantic.

'Budget after budget we were putting things in place. Nice and quiet like. Nowhere near where we hoped to end up, but getting there. And winning the election last year gave us another five budgets to make sure that the right guys, the entrepreneurs, got the necessary room for manoeuvre, and the occasional leg up, yeah? Because, as we all know, once they make things happen, everyone wins.'

Michael Liston pulled back and popped a cigarette. He offered Mags. She was sorely tempted but Rothmans was a bit on the strong side. The glitter of his black eyes faded to regret.

'And then CJ goes and fucks it all away – sorry, excuse the French – and what for? What for?'

He lit up. Mags couldn't think of anything beyond the obvious.

'To protect the Catholics in Northern Ireland?'

'Ah pull my wire – sorry… You don't really think CJ gives a toss about the North do you? Neither does Jack, believe me. It's an annoying distraction and you know what? He's right. But he made a stick to beat himself with by appointing a few United Ireland loonies to the cabinet.'

The eyes blazed again. 'Nordy Neil, chief among them, sucking on his pipe, puffing smoke in Jack's eyes, prodding, nagging. "What's the Taoiseach going to do to stop the persecution of the poor Northern Catholics?" Oh a right pain in Jack's arse – pardon the French. Of course CJ gets it into his head that Neil is looking to take over as party leader, become Taoiseach. That's when he panics and makes his big booboo. He tries to get the better of Neil by acting like even more of a hardline Republican, so when Neil and his pals start going on about arming Catholics to help them protect themselves from Protestant Loyalist attacks, what does CJ do? Well… he has control of the public purse, doesn't he? If anyone can organise the moolah to buy guns, he can.'

A penny rolled and spun in front of Michael Liston. The Heads of Hair were leaning in to each other, almost making one curtain of hair, counting their cash, painfully working out if they had enough for a taxi. Michael's stare made Mags fear he might be about to crack those heads together. She tried to distract him.

'So, what did you say to CJ about that?'

Michael Liston now turned his stare on her. Just as Mags thought she wouldn't get an answer, he leaned in again.

'He never told me. That's what drove me spare. I'd have warned him not to go near it. I'd always advised him to be patient. As Minister for Finance, he was running the show anyway. I thought he knew how devious and twisted Jack was, for all his soft little voice and weepy eyes. He's a Corkman, yeah? Ask any auld fellah who saw him in his heyday on the hurling pitch. He never put the boot in on an opponent until he'd made sure the ref wasn't looking. Jack gave the impression he was dithering, but all the time he was watching CJ and Neil locking antlers, digging a big hole for themselves and – ah!'

Michael Liston jabbed the remains of his cigarette in a saucer and raised his voice so loud that Mags was worried everyone in the Manhattan would hear him.

'Jack was warned about the plan to bring the guns in *six months before it happened, for Christ's sake!*

He took control of himself and dropped his voice.

'He knew what was coming and did nothing to stop it. He just let the game play out. I visited CJ in hospital last May, the day after the famous riding accident – don't ask, I'm saying nothing about that – anyway, it was the first I heard about guns. Jack had already been in to tell him that Special Branch had informed him that CJ'd organised the whole kit and kaboodle. Jack mentioned resignation, but CJ said not a chance and for some reason seemed to think that was that. I says to him. "You don't really believe Jack is going to let it go at that, do you?" "What choice has he?" says CJ, "Neil and I are too powerful in the cabinet and he's a coward." Oh yeah? What happens next? Three days later the leader of the opposition gets an anonymous tip-off and the public are suddenly hearing all about two powerful ambitious ministers up to their necks in gun-running. Poor old Jack is awfully shocked. Oh he's flabbergasted altogether to hear of such terrible goings on and sure he has no choice but to sack the two ministers. In fact, it looks like they'll have to be prosecuted. But isn't it lucky for the country that Honest Jack is there to clear up this terrible mess – Lads, will you ever fuck off! Give us a bit of peace!'

Two heads of hair turned. Mags saw only noses and dazed eyes.

'Hey man, cool the head, stall a ball there, we're going, all right?'

If Michael Liston had hoped their departure would give Mags and himself a bit of privacy he was doomed to disappointment. A giggling couple, plates and mugs in hands, swooped immediately to grab the free seats.

'Isn't it just unbelievable at this hour of the night.'

'If they knocked that wall away they'd still fill the place.'

'But sure where else would you get it, rashers and sausages and black pudden served up to you at all hours?'

The girl shrieked delightedly as her boyfriend grabbed her knee under the table. Mags Perry suddenly felt very single and young – well, youngish – and out in the night-world. A chiding voice still whispered that, before dawn broke, a certain separated wife and mother of two young children would pay a price for the frivolity of several pints of Guinness and a big fry-up at an ungodly hour, but she ignored that killjoy and snatched the last half slice of bread to mop up what yolk and rasher grease was left on her plate. Michael Liston's glowering rage had cooled to saturnine silence again. Mags had a notion there was melancholy there too. He was an odd, uncomfortable man and yet, earlier on in the Russell, when Mags requested a pint of Guinness, he hadn't batted an eyelid and passed no remark, jokey or otherwise, about women and pints. When the lounge-boy had automatically placed the pint in front of the man, he had, without fuss or comment, just swopped the drinks round, before paying. His gesture and attitude had impressed Mags, unlike the pale teenager who, when she lifted the pint to her lips, had averted his eyes, as if she'd exposed her breasts.

'Imagine, it turned out to be CJ, not Jack, who was the stupid naive one. All our good work thrown away. And he'll never get back to where he was. Even if he's acquitted in court, even if he manages to hang on in the party, politically, he's a goner. And for what? For fuckin' Northern Ireland!'

This time he didn't even apologise for his French. Mags was struck by how, in the oddest way, coming at the thing from totally different angles, she and Michael were in agreement that the Arms Crisis was a big fat waste of space. He'd said it: stupid men, locking antlers.

Outside, the chill felt like winter already and the vomit she nearly stepped into dulled the Manhattan's late-night sparkle.

'I'll run you home.'

'No, no I'll get a taxi.'

'I'm only parked round the corner. Where are you?'

'Ranelagh. I could walk it from here.'

'It won't take me a minute to run you out.'

He was already guiding her towards Harcourt Street.

'All right but on one condition. You have to answer any question I ask.'

'Like what?'

'Well. Let me see.' Mags pretended to hesitate, even though she knew exactly what she wanted to know. 'Are you married?'

'No.'

'What, then?'

'I answered your question. You said "any question", singular.'

'Ha ha, you know what I meant. If you're not married, were you ever? Are you separated? Are you a bachelor? What?'

'All right. I'm a widower.'

'Oh. I'm sorry about that.'

'Don't worry about it.'

They drove towards the canal. She felt a little guilty now for having been so pushy. If he was widowed recently it wasn't surprising he didn't want to talk about it.

'I'm separated, hoping to get divorced but that's —'

'Divorced?'

'A UK divorce. We lived in England and my ex-husband is still there. I left him. I ran away with the children.'

Mags searched his face for a reaction. There was none that she could detect.

'I brought them back to Ireland three years ago. Since then I've been trying to work as a freelance journalist.'

Mags wanted to tell him more, but wasn't convinced he wanted to know. They passed the public toilet at the Triangle. There was something she really needed to ask.

'And that's it really. Have you children?'

'I have. Am I going straight on, or left, or right?'

'You're going right. Oh sorry, this one. Here!'

He spun quickly and just about made the turn.

'Sorry about that. On the left. Number 43.'

In the few moments, silence before Michael Liston parked in front of her house Mags made a final, final definite decision and felt that, in fairness to the man, she needed to make it clear.

'I won't be inviting you in. Is that all right? I mean, I'm not saying I wouldn't want to invite you in, it's just that…Well… not tonight anyway. Is that okay?'

That was fine by Michael, no problem. The truth was, he felt a bit relieved. It had been on his mind since she sat into the car: once they got to her place would he be expected to charm an invite out of her, play that game, no matter if he didn't want to? Not that he didn't want to. He did. At least he was fairly sure he did. But all of a sudden, like this? After how many years of nothing doing? She was smart and had a bit of go about her and the flamey hair was just the business. A pint drinker, he liked that too. So, yes, he was up for something. But… but… the whole evening had come at him out of nowhere and Michael had no difficulty admitting to himself that it wrong-sided him a bit, simple as that. He'd been out all day, hadn't washed since this morning, he didn't want to end up feeling smelly and exposed. Not to mention all the questions. Odds on there'd be plenty more of those if he got himself invited in. More questions as the kettle boiled, and then tea and more questions. And then the really awkward bit; how to move things on, drop the hand or whatever – no, no! He just wasn't up for it tonight. It was interesting though that she'd walked out on her husband. That showed a bit of grit. Something he should have done to that cow all those years ago. Before it got too late.

From the way Michael Liston wasn't looking at her, Mags figured he couldn't wait for her to open the passenger door and get out. Was he not even going to go through the ritual of asking for a phone number? What was the etiquette these days? Mags realised that she wouldn't mind meeting him again. There was depth in those black eyes. Older was interesting too, definitely completely different to Marcus. If he just said good luck now she'd be disappointed.

Michael knew that if he let this woman get out of the car with no more than a 'g'night so', he'd be raging with himself afterwards and it'd be too late. But it was up to him to find the words. Jesus! Dopey teenagers in every village in Ireland had no trouble asking young ones for their phone number these days.

'So, Michael, do you want my phone number or anything?'

'What? Oh – ah, yes. Yes.'

'Don't feel you – I mean only if you –'

'No, no, I do. I was going to…'

'Actually, the main reason I wanted to give you my number was so I could show off these cards I just got made up.'

'Cards? Very American.'

Mags rummaged in her bag. She rummaged deeper. Christ, typical!

'Sorry, I can't seem to – sorry, hold on. Won't be a sec.'

She hopped out and ran to her front door. Michael liked the go of her all right. She reminded him of someone but he couldn't think who. Not anyone he knew personally. Some actress? She disappeared into the black, leaving the door open like an invitation. Michael was tempted to follow, which surely was a good sign. What would her reaction be if he did? There was no more time to think about it. She reappeared, still on the trot.

'I get cards made and then don't carry them with me. What am I like? There you go.

Michael Liston tilted the card toward the streetlight.

'I went for Mags rather than Margaret. I thought about it, but in all honesty I couldn't remember the last time anyone called me Margaret.'

Except she could. The chilly 'Dear Margaret' in the letter from Marcus soon after her escape. His withering dismissal of her from his life.

'Anyway, goodnight. And thanks for, you know, the night and the lift…'

Neither of them was able to begin the move that would end in a simple goodnight kiss on the cheek, but Mags, closing the passenger door, stopped and stuck her head back in.

'You know, I get the feeling that you will call me.'

'I will.'

He watched her walk away and was glad she turned and waved goodnight before going inside. Michael didn't drive away immediately. He sat looking along the dark terrace of redbricks, Nice little properties these. Probably a lot of them in student flats. Great spot Ranelagh, though. Great potential. Did she own her place?

The children, had they been home, would have been silently asleep, but all the same Mags felt the emptiness of the house once she got into bed. It had turned out to be quite a night. She wasn't sorry to have kept it going and not sorry to have called a halt when she did. Michael Liston was interesting in himself, not just as a CJ acolyte. See if he called her. Take it from there. What was his story? What would he make of hers? That would probably depend on how much she told him and how.

Two: New Year's Eve

By the third song of the fast set Marian didn't want to listen to him anymore. All that talk about uni. Uni was savage. Galway was unreal. The Cellar was just crazy. He hadn't done a tap since October, but everyone said it was okay to go mad in the first term. There'd be loads of time after Rag Week to get it together for the exams. Rag Week was going to be savage altogether. Marian should come up for it. He'd find her somewhere to kip no bother, not that anyone would be sleeping. No one went to bed for the whole week. Mad stuff.

When she said thanks at the end of the fast set and turned to leave the dance floor, he acted like she was joking and held onto her hand. She had to pull it away. God, he was full of himself! After that Marian didn't dance for a while and only got up with her pals from the commercial course because she really liked 'Yellow River.' Then DJ Mike Rave spoke in an unusually serious voice.

'So, it's official, the Beatles really are no more. The end of an era. You're probably like me, thinking, it can't be, it just can't. This band was such a part of our growing up, it's hard to imagine a world without John, Paul, George and Ringo. But you know something, their spirit will always be with us through the music they have left behind. Music that will never... ever... be forgotten.'

The lights dimmed as the intro to 'In My Life' began. Marian heard sobs from two girls beside her.

'So as we say goodbye to 1970, let's say our own special fond farewell to the greatest band ever. Thanks for the memories, guys, we'll never forget you.'

When the boy came towards her and held his hand out, Marian couldn't see his face properly because his white shirt glowed so brightly under the ultra-violet tubes. She couldn't hear his exact words either but obviously he was asking her to dance. Everyone seemed to be getting up for this slow set because of the Beatles breaking up, so Marian let him take her hand. She was glad it felt dry. His grip was gentle. As he led her through the crush to the centre of the dance floor she noticed how blond his hair was. When he turned and came closer to put his hands on her shoulders, he was taller than she'd realised. His chin was above her head. His teeth glowed when he smiled. She put her hands on his hips and they swayed on the spot, turning slowly.

'What's your name?'

'Marian.'

'Stephen.'

When 'In My Life' faded into 'Something.' Stephen shifted closer, sliding his hands around to clasp them behind her neck. The dance floor was so packed now there was no room to turn without brushing against other couples. She could barely hear him. 'You go to the commercial college, don't you?' Marian looked up, surprised, and nodded. 'I thought I recognised you.' 'Do you go there?' Stephen showed his glowing teeth again. 'No, I was delivering the post and I noticed you.' As George Harrison's guitar solo climbed higher and higher, Marian felt Stephen's cheek graze her hair and she allowed her head to sink onto his chest. Looking off to one side she noticed the couple next to them weren't even moving anymore, just standing with lips locked together. The boy's fingers were sliding along the waistband of the girl's jeans. Marian felt one of Stephen's hands caress the back of her head and press her cheek harder against his chest.

When 'Yesterday' began, she saw more girls sobbing. The boys dancing with them touched their faces or kissed their foreheads to comfort them. Paul had always been Marian's favourite Beatle and, even though she wasn't the crying type, it did seem so sad to think they were no more; like the end of something. She could hardly remember a time before the Beatles. Smiling back at Stephen, Marian wondered if her teeth were glowing too. She wanted to see his face properly, especially his eyes, Stephen bowed his head until his forehead rested on hers and their noses were almost touching. His breath was arrowroot. His hands cupped her neck and his thumbs caressed her earlobes. She slid her hands around his back and he eased closer until the buckle of his belt pressed against her stomach.

For some reason the start of 'Hey Jude' made Marian hug Stephen tighter. Crushing her cheek against his chest, she felt his lips, gentle on the top of her head. As they turned and turned there were flashes of other bodies pressed together. Lips locked and hands roved everywhere, touching faces, inching down backs, caressing bottoms, and even – had she seen that right? – a hand sliding up a skirt. Fingers lifted her chin and Marian looked up at Stephen knowing the decision would have to be made in the next second or two. Did she want to kiss this tall slim blond boy with glowing shirt and teeth? Or not? Well. Who plays it cool, only a fool?

Na na na nana na naaaaa!

Stephen was a good kisser, his lips told her something. Marian wondered if he thought she was a good kisser too. When she opened her mouth to him she sensed a tiny moment of surprise before he accepted her invitation. Then all thought dissolved. She was no longer aware of where his hands were or her own, where their bodies were,

Jude, Judee, Judee, Judee, Judee, Judee! Yeow!!

*

Mags was still trying to persuade her mother to take one of the four copies of *The Female Eunuch* she'd been given for Christmas.

'Are you joking me? I couldn't even say the name of that book.'

'You don't even have to whisper the name, Mam. Just read it.'

At first Mags had been silently impatient with those friends who had bought it for her. 'I know you probably have this already.' Well why give it then? Mind you, who was she to talk, having bought six copies as presents? Women all over the world were probably doing the same this Christmas. It was a gesture more than a gift, a message to each other. A message clearly falling on deaf ears when it came to Widow Perry. Mags had bought it for herself back in October, as soon as it came out, and read it in two sittings. The thing she liked most about it – and envied – was that Germaine Greer was *so funny* about the condition of womanhood. Oh to write as wildly and stingingly and hilariously as Greer. No one she knew could. Well… maybe her pal Nell when she was really on form.

'I wouldn't even have it in the house, not with that disgusting cover on it. Which reminds me, I hope you don't leave it lying around for the children to see.'

Which reminded Mags it was nearly time to ring them in Marlborough, to see if they were enjoying New Year's Eve with their father. Simon more than Susan, she suspected. He still needed Marcus and no one else was going to take his place. Which was fine. Mags had no intention of presenting them with a replacement father and, luckily, Michael Liston showed no inclination to take on that role.

'Anyway, just because you have too many of them, don't think you can dump them on me. Throw them all in the bin. The proper place for them.'

'Give it a go. I promise you, Mam, it'll change the way you see the world.'

'The way I see the world is grand, thank you.'

Mags wondered was it embarrassingly dull, not to mention downright odd, to be happy spending New Year's Eve sitting in, half watching the telly, half sparring with her old mam? She was even glad the kids were in Marlborough because it was definitely a whole lot better than last year's disaster, with Marcus coming to Dublin, putting himself up in a hotel, calling to the house every day to collect the kids, then hanging around, acting the martyr when he brought them back. Would the kids mention Michael and his boy? Well, what harm? None of his concern. Thankfully the new no-fault law coming into force in England meant Marcus couldn't continue to refuse a divorce.

What would it be like to be unmarried again? Would it change anything about her daily life here? Certainly Mags wouldn't be diving into another commitment. This thing with Michael, whatever it was, seemed to suit them both. Each time they'd got together it was only for that time. And, so far, each time they'd both ended up wanting to meet again. The sex part was definitely a work in progress. The evening Mags had finally decided the moment was right, Michael of course had no protection. But, she had to hand it to him, his apologetic reaction helped save the situation. He was funny, explaining that he hadn't been abroad in months and anyway, to tell her the truth, it probably wouldn't have occurred to him to bring any Johnnies back. The way he said 'Johnnies' made him sound even more of a country boy.

'I'll sort something out, next time.'

His discomfort had probably helped encourage Mags to take the initiative. When she'd slid down under the covers his excitement was all too obvious. That he climaxed so quickly suggested it had been a long time since anyone had done him this particular service. Or possibly never? It wasn't so much the sheepish grin on his face afterwards that had been gratifying, as the spontaneous guffaw when she said, 'You have Germaine Greer to thank for that.'

When, a few minutes afterwards, Michael had tried valiantly to return the favour, with more enthusiasm than technique, it had to be said, Mags had laughed in turn at the muffled mutter from far below.

'Hank u Hewmaine Weew.'

'What's that smirk on your face about?'

For a second Mags felt a daughter's embarrassment. Only a second though.

'Hm? Oh I just remembered a funny comment I heard about Germaine Greer. No point in me trying to tell you, Mam. You wouldn't get it unless you'd read *The Female Eunuch*.'

She articulated the title with brazen relish.

*

Francis giggled merrily at cousin Eva's take-off of her mother. She had Auntie Mona down to a 'T'; the way she leaned forward and spoke ext-ra slow-ly when passing on an important bit of gossip, the look she gave over her glasses sometimes, and the special phrases she loved using.

'Imagine, Mammy's only after meeting this woman and she's telling her "I take people as I find them, but to me now, that fellah is little more nor little less than a layabout." She's giving out about the Lehanes from next door, and who do I see coming into the café at that very second but Mrs Lehane. I swear Fran, she's no further away than that wall, looking round for a seat and Mammy has her back to her. So I try to warn her quietly, you know. Well, of course you can imagine what happened then.'

And Eva did Auntie Mona's angry expression and made her voice very shrill.

'"Eva! Will you please not interrupt when adults are trying to have a conversation. How often do I have to tell you?"'

Francis thought it was really funny the way Eva then completely changed over to Auntie Mona's soft voice.

'"I'm very sorry, Mrs Hartigan. Where was I? Oh yes. Those Lehanes —" But now here's Mrs Lehane coming straight at us, so I try again. "Mammy!" Well! She turns on me, hissing like a… a… rattle snake. "Eva! I'm warning you. Don't think just because we're in the Stella I won't give you the slap you deserve. And sit up properly and fix that skirt, please!"'

Eva was brilliant. It was as if Auntie Mona was there talking to him.

'Well Fran, when Mrs Lehane appears in front of her, for the first time in my life I see Mammy stuck for something to say. "Hello, Mrs Durack, hello, Eva," says she "Desperate, weather, isn't it?" And Mammy looking up at her, her mouth open like a fish.'

Eva did the mouth and Francis hooted.

'But wait — this is the best bit. I mean you won't believe it,

Fran. As soon as Mrs Lehane goes off, she turns on me. "You dope! Why didn't you warn me? Will you try and think once in your life!" I mean, what could I say? I'm always in the wrong.'

When they stopped laughing, Francis thought he saw Eva look sad for a second. Even though his cousin was brilliant at telling the story in a funny way, it must have felt awful to be given out to like that in front of someone else in a café. Francis liked his Auntie Mona, but why was she always correcting Eva unfairly? Was it something to do with her being an only child?

Eva, smiling again, said she'd better go and see if Eugene was all right. Francis said he'd get more biscuits and Club Orange. Eva said tea for her, please. His cousin was always so polite and never treated him like he was a child even though she was three years older. As she tiptoed up the stairs, Francis accidentally saw up her dress, but not as far as her knickers. Did she have a boyfriend yet? Probably not. How could she, the way Auntie Mona kept checking her?

It was a strange New Year's Eve with no one at home. His mam and dad out with Ritchie and Áine at the Krupp's staff dinner dance, Gussie back in Killarney on duty in the Great Southern Hotel for their big New Year's Eve do, Martin at a party in his new girlfriend Veronica's house, and Marian off to the discotheque with her pals from the commercial course. Francis was glad Eva had been asked to come and mind Eugene. She was so good-natured, telling his mam her dress dance outfit was gorgeous. Francis had wondered was she was joking, because he thought his mam looked like a Knickerbocker Glory.

After they left, Eva had kept saying how well Auntie Ann looked and what great fun she was and how lucky Francis was to have a mother like her. He'd wanted to let her know that his mam could explode into terrible tempers sometimes and God help any of them that crossed her when she was in one of her moods, but he'd guessed his cousin didn't really want to hear about that.

Eva came downstairs and said Eugene was fast asleep, wasn't he such a dote? They ate biscuits and drank tea and Club Orange and played Beggar thy Neighbour and Lives, and had such a laugh that they forgot about the time until Francis happened to notice the clock on the wall read ten past twelve. He turned on the telly just to make sure. They had missed midnight.

'Sure isn't that a good sign, we were having such a laugh we didn't even notice the time. Well, happy New Year, Fran.'

And, to his surprise, she put her arms around his shoulders and hugged him tight. He put his arms around her. Being smaller, Francis' nose and cheek were nearly buried in Eva's chest. He was surprised at how soft it felt. Then he smelt something. What was it? He remembered the smell from somewhere but didn't know where exactly. It must have been a long time ago, and the memory was pleasant but scary at the same time. What was it? Before he could work it out, Eva let go of him and the smell and the memory just disappeared. Francis saw her eyes were watery, but she was smiling so it wasn't sad.

'Happy New year, Eva.'

1971

Three: March 6th

"If ye watch not, ye are doomed" What was that from? Shakespeare, was it? The line came into CJ's head as he looked down the table at Liston, shovelling hunks of lamb. The only one of any use to him now. Liston understood money and money was the prime mover. CJ had watched all right. And listened. He wasn't doomed yet, although despite the acquittal he'd nearly been dragged under at the party jamboree last month. Blaney and Boland, barking mad and going baldheaded for Lynch and his flock of sheep: Colley, 'de nephew' O'Malley, Paddy-boy. Cunts.

For a second CJ thought he'd said that out loud, but the uninterrupted chatter and clink around the table reassured him. He had buried his bile deep. If anything had kept him safe these last few months it was his silence. 'Give them nothing.' Liston's advice was always so simple. Head in the plate, scooping up his grub, he might never contribute to the hilarity of the table, but it was he CJ would usher to the snooker room later.

For some time fear and isolation had been his companions. Having survived the wreckage and watched, as from behind a rock, the storm toss debris everywhere, now, in the uncertain calm, he found himself naked and alone. All lost, all broken – that was from something wasn't it? *The Wreck of the Hesperus*? One of those storm at sea things. He could go under yet, he understood that all too well. No point in battling through the storm only to succumb to famine or contagion. Money. Money was the necessary condition.

After dinner, the lads set up in a corner of the ballroom. CJ loved the ritual tuning of fiddle and wheezing of bellows, and of course the laconic witticisms so characteristic of great traditional musicians. For the first few bars of 'Bímis ag Ól's ag Pógadh na mBan', CJ was transported. Then, catching Liston's eye, he slipped out and crossed the atrium to the back stairs. Loyal footsteps thumped behind, tumbling down to the snooker room. He poured two malts and chalked his cue. Great to be free of that sling at last, able to grasp with both hands. He broke. Nothing dropped.

'Well?

The bounce of light from the baize lit Liston's eyes like a cat in the dark. He had been presented with every bank statement and invoice, full disclosure of every incoming and outgoing. The humiliating frankness of the detail ought to have been a clear signal that CJ was fully prepared to hear the worst and be a wise, listening chieftain to his sharp-brained gilla.

'You certainly don't need me to tell you the basic problem. Your outgoings are so far in excess of your incomings that it's not a matter of a shaving here or a minor cutback there. I'm guessing I can be straight with you?'

'Of course.'

'Well, I've known you now five years and I have to admit, no more than many others, I had a certain curiosity about where it all came from. Turns out there's no mystery. You're up to your eyeballs in debt, which was no great problem while you were Minister for Finance. But you've been through the wars and ended up a backbench TD. Am I right in thinking your lenders aren't inclined to be as patient?'

If ye watch not, ye are doomed. Just say nothing. CJ held himself in check and didn't ram the thick end of the cue down on Liston's skull as he bent over the table.

'We both know there's only two ways to deal with your situation: spend less or earn more. I'm guessing you won't want to sell up here and live in a semi-d in Raheny, so the only solution is to drum up enough moolah to fund your lifestyle.'

CJ had to presume his gilla wasn't just being pointlessly insolent and had something more positive to contribute. Liston potted and a hint of a smile appeared on his sickly green face.

'If the whisper went out that help was required there's certain fellahs we both know would stump up straight off, no questions asked. Even if it was just for old times' sake and nothing more, these lads wouldn't be found wanting. That might provide a stopgap, but in the longer term, if you are to have access to – what'll we call it? – an appropriate regular income stream, then even your biggest fans'd want to feel they're funding something tangible… significant. Like seeing the country move in the right direction, for example. Which means they'd want you back where you were before. You see where I'm heading, CJ? Now I can source support, maximise the financial potential, all that old magic roundabout, but there's a big job for you to do as well. You've managed to hang in there, which is good. Now we need to convince friends that you're a viable future investment.'

The pause. CJ wondered why his brave gilla was suddenly looking so wary. What was he going to ask him to do, have Lynch and his cabinet topped?

'These fellahs are no daws and if I told them everything was going to be sorted in a few weeks they wouldn't believe me anyway. But they could be convinced by a serious plan with a practical long-range timetable. Remember they do like you, they respect you. You are their man, have no doubts about that. They want you back on top.'

As he should be. As he fucking should be! Liston was a wise counsellor and, more to the point, a resourceful gilla, not some sentimental ninny, but CJ wished he'd get on with it, tell him what he had in mind. Liston excused himself, went upstairs and returned, holding his briefcase like a ceremonial gift. He opened it, took out a folded-up paper, thrust the balls aside to make space on the billiard table and spread out a large map of Ireland.

'You see what I've marked out?'

'The constituencies.'

'Lynch thinks that joining the EEC will do him some good with the voters so there'll be no election until after that's sorted, but I think he hasn't a hope anyway. We've been in power since

1957 and, after the shenanigans of the last year, the voters have had enough.'

CJ nodded. This made sense above and beyond his pleasure at the notion of Lynch being dumped out.

'So, you'll be in opposition and some kind of coalition will take over by the end of say, '73. But, chances are, any deal between Fine Gael and Labour will collapse sooner rather than later, so you could be back in government as early as '76. Reasonable enough?

'Go on.'

'That's our timescale. If I can convince friends you have a decent shot at being a government minister again in five years, they'd be well pleased.'

Liston made it sound so straightforward, but his words were like a switch, sending a pleasurable current through CJ's body. He saw the stone roll back from Lazarus' sepulchre.

'Okay. See the constituencies I've marked? In each of these there's one of the old guard on his last go-round and a youngfellah looking to take over. I know some of them. Savage, they'd take the hand off you for a seat. They'd slice off their granny's ear. A few have done well locally in business over the last few years –'

'Thanks to me.'

'You know something? They realise that. They're looking for a champion. Someone important, who'll make them feel important. That's the card you have, CJ. You mightn't be a minister any more, but you could be a rallying point.'

The hunt. These young bucks seemed like interesting prey. CJ traced a pulsing finger over the map.

'Kildare, Westmeath, Longford, Roscommon, Galway, Mayo, Sligo? Country and western territory.'

'I won't lie to you, CJ, These lads are not urbane, more shithouse rat cute, but mark my words, they'll all get themselves elected and they'll be looking for someone to lead them.'

He pointed a finger directly at CJ.

'I think they can put you back where you belong.'

'And what are you not telling me?'

'Well, let's be straight, their support won't just fall into your lap. None of these lads I'm talking about is on your invite list tonight, and they won't be rubbing shoulders with you at an Abbey opening or one of your pals' art exhibitions. You're going to have to leave the estate and go down among them.'

CJ stared at the map. The midlands, the profitless bog where only a snipe could dwell. Great line from Kavanagh.

'The thing is, if you do they'll love you for it. In the saloons of Longford and Roscommon and Mayo you're already a bit of a folk hero, you're *real* Fianna Fáil. But more importantly, as far as our friends are concerned, once they see a plan being implemented and something stirring, once there's any sign that you're on the way back, then believe me, they'll want to be part of it. Are you on?'

CJ smirked. He could survive this penance.

'Well, Gilla, I put myself in your hands.'

*

Francis, in the back room with his mam and dad, was watching the *Late Late Show* and reading his library book *When Eight Bells Toll* at the same time. At first the book got more of his attention as it seemed much more exciting than a crowd of women on the *Late Late* complaining about their rights. As soon as Gay Byrne said, at the start of the programme, that tonight he was going to hand over the show to the women of Ireland, Francis was disappointed, knowing that meant there wouldn't be any famous singers on, or actors telling funny stories like Richard Harris who'd been a guest a few weeks before. He'd told Gay Byrne that, when he went to Hollywood first, the film studio put him up in a big fancy hotel in Beverly Hills and he couldn't believe the prices on the breakfast menu: a dollar for one boiled egg. Francis' mam had gasped when she heard that. Richard Harris said he noticed that two boiled eggs cost a dollar and fifty cents. So he told the waiter he'd like to order the second boiled egg. Gay Byrne nearly fell off his chair he laughed so much at that.

But tonight there were no funny stories, just giving out. Francis wasn't even half-listening at first because assassins had arrived to murder Philip Calvert and he'd coolly dispatched two of them. When he told Charlotte he was sorry he hadn't finished off the third assassin, she was angry at his sardonic *sang froid*, but then realised that Philip Calvert was only doing what any man would do to protect them, so she apologised.

Francis heard one of the women say, 'Under Irish law, married women are little more than chattels of their husbands.' He liked the sound of the word. Chattels. From the way the woman was talking it meant prisoner or servant. Francis wondered what his dad would think of that considering he brought his mam tea and toast in bed every morning before going to work, and his mam was always telling him what to do. He went back to his book, but the women in the audience were having their say now, and there was a lot more shouting over each other, so he kept getting distracted. One woman said that the most important thing was that the children's allowance should be in the mother's name not the father's, and another woman said, yes I agree, but – and then said something completely different about widows inheriting their husbands' property. Another woman interrupted her and said she agreed with the first woman, but that the real disgrace was the raw deal unmarried mothers got. Once Francis began to realise that there might be a big row on the *Late Late* he stopped reading his Alistair MacLean altogether. A woman who said her name was Mags Perry got a huge round of applause for saying that the most important issue was the free availability of contraception. Until women had control over their own bodies, there would never be equality. Loads of women in the audience cheered at that and someone else shouted out that women weren't going to be baby-making machines any longer. Contraception. Francis had never heard of it before.

'How can you read your book and watch the TV at the same time?'

Why was his dad asking him that all of a sudden? It was easy. He often did it.

'I just can.'

'Wouldn't you be better off reading upstairs?'

Con-tra-sep-shun. Francis guessed the word had something to do with having babies.

'Anyway, it's near your bedtime. You'll be able to concentrate better if you read upstairs.'

He really wished his dad would shut up and let him hear what the women were saying. He was distracting his mam too.

'Fonsie, I can't hear the programme properly with you talking.'

'I'm just saying he should take his book up to his bedroom.'

'I don't care what he does with his book. I just want to watch the *Late Late* in peace. I'm after missing what that young one, Nell, is after saying. I like her, she's not a bit afraid of anyone.'

His dad now stood in front of him. Francis couldn't even see the telly.

'Right, you heard what Mam said. Off to bed with you.'

Francis was raging that his dad was stopping him from enjoying the brilliant shouting match on the telly. Why was it suddenly annoying him so much that he was able to read a book and watch the *Late Late* at the same time?

'Do what you're told. You can read in peace in your bedroom. Come on now, off with you.'

Just then the ads came on. Francis knew that his dad wouldn't stop going on at him.

'All right, all right!'

He slammed his book as he got up and walked out, making a sighing sound to show how stupid he thought his dad was being.

After he had gone, Ann looked at Fonsie.

'Why were you at him? He was sitting there grand and quiet for once.'

'I didn't think he should be listening to… all that.'

Ann wasn't sure of what Fonsie meant by 'all that', but she wasn't bothered enough ask any more. As long as she could watch the row on the *Late Late* in peace, she was happy.

*

Dr Garret FitzGerald could contain himself no longer! He was more than aware of the very cogent reasons why close advisors and confidantes had impressed on him that, at times, he needed to restrain his natural enthusiasm for discussion and argument and his admittedly somewhat professorial tendency to share with everyone the fruits of his study and research on an astonishingly wide range of topics because they all insisted – and Dr Garret FitzGerald very much recognised and accepted the point – that from a purely political point of view, sometimes it was better just to listen to people, even when what they said was ill-thought-through, superficial and, depressingly often, factually incorrect.

Always keen to master a new skill, Dr Garret FitzGerald had taken this advice very much to heart when he went canvassing for election to the Dáil the year before. What he accepted in theory however was rather more difficult to achieve in practice. This was mainly because the voters of Dublin South-East were an impressively loquacious electorate, indeed in many cases almost as talkative as Dr Garret FitzGerald himself! Many were steeped in the legal profession and had many many opinions on many many subjects, so that, throughout the campaign he was placed in the extraordinarily frustrating position of having to stand silent at a doorstep or supermarket entrance, or outside a church, listening to someone ask a question which was not technically a question at all but, in reality, a tirade – usually unendurably long-winded! – on a subject about which the author of the tirade frequently knew rather less than he or she intimated, but on which he or she tended to have very fixed views! He was then constrained in his reply because his campaign team had virtually forbidden him from teasing out all the complexities of a given issue with each individual voter even though that voter might not, through no fault of his, or her, own have available the kind of detailed information that Dr Garret FitzGerald kept readily in his head and was more than happy to share with anyone who showed an interest.

During the four weeks of electioneering, he had learned so much about the art of listening that afterwards Dr Garret FitzGerald was of the strong view that his acquisition of that difficult skill would prove to be of long-term importance in his political career, even more significant than his immediate success in becoming a representative for Dublin South-East!

But, watching tonight's *Late Late* strained his determination to listen in silence to breaking point and, finally, beyond. It wasn't so much the inaccuracy of certain things the women on the programme said – although Dr Garret FitzGerald would have loved the opportunity to correct some of the more egregious factual errors, and in fact *did* correct them, albeit only for the benefit of his dear wife, Joan, as they viewed the programme – but rather what animated Dr Garret FitzGerald most of all – and had finally propelled him from his chair to roam about the hall in search of his shoes and coat – was the attitude of some of the individual contributors on the show to men in general. In particular, that very flamboyant and excitable young journalist, Mary Kenny, who had, only a moment before, thrown her hands in the air, very melodramatically, as was her wont, and proclaimed the most extraordinary generalisation that, in the matter of women's rights, *male politicians simply did not care*! That remark was the limit as far Dr Garret FitzGerald was concerned, and for two quite separate reasons. One, because, apart from his very healthy suspicion of generalisations *per se*, he thought that this one was entirely disreputable, especially as he could legitimately point to himself as a male public representative who was, very sincerely and very vocally, a strong advocate of Women's Rights, to the extent that he would not baulk at the term, male feminist! Two, in terms of balance and of fairness, because both panel and audience of tonight's *Late Late* were entirely composed of women, there was no one in the studio apart from Gay Byrne himself – who as chairman couldn't really take sides – to counter, not only Miss Kenny's groundless accusation, but other, more subtle implied criticisms of what was referred to several times as the *male hierarchy*.

Now he had his coat on and had located one of his shoes.

'What are you doing, Garret?'

'I'm going to RTE, darling.'

'Sorry?'

'I have to make some attempt to correct the impression that there are no men supporting the aims of women's organisations, while at the same time –'

'Oh Garret, sit down, it's only the *Late Late.*'

'No, it's terribly important. Naturally I also want to demonstrate that there is at least one male public representative who is on their side.'

At last, the other shoe. How had they ended up in two entirely different parts of the hall? Extraordinary!

'What are you going to do, leave a note at the reception desk?'

'No. I'm going to ask to be allowed on air.'

'Oh Garret, that's silly.'

The drive from Palmerston Road to the RTE studios took only ten minutes. The security man, recognising Dr Garret FitzGerald from his frequent television appearances, just smiled and waved him through. The lady at the reception desk was clearly bemused.

'Oh, good evening, Dr FitzGerald.'

'Please, call me Garret. I'd like to speak to one of the *Late Late Show* researchers please.'

'Of course, Dr Garret.'

There was no sound from the TV in the corner of the reception area, but from the way the shots cut quickly from one woman apparently shouting, to others also apparently shouting and then to Gay Byrne with his hands raised in an extravagantly pleading manner, it was clear to Dr Garret FitzGerald that the discussion had become even more incendiary. He suspected that, whereas there were some very fine, thoughtful feminist voices on the programme, such as his good friend Nuala Fennell, there were also others – those angry young faces on camera right now for example – with a far more radical agenda, who did not appreciate, or want to appreciate, that, in attempting to go too far too fast, they actually made it more difficult for genuine supporters, such as he, to persuade what was after all a largely conservative electorate, that women truly were discriminated against in this society.

'Dr FitzGerald. My name is Pan.'

'Please, call me Garret.'

The charming and very tiny lady researcher seemed to respond very positively to his brimming passion – ordinary people, in his experience, frequently did – as he explained what had motivated him to abandon his fireside and arrive here, unannounced and uninvited. It was, he conceded disarmingly, appalling bad manners! Not at all, Pan assured him, she appreciated his depth of feeling. As Dr– As Garret was probably aware, Gay was the producer of his own show so he made all the important decisions. The next ad break was just coming up, she would talk to Gay then, if he wouldn't mind waiting. He didn't mind at all. The ad break began just after Pan had left him and, much faster than he expected, she was back, beaming.

'Gay says he'd love to hear what you have to say. He'll bring you on straight after the break.'

Dr Garret FitzGerald's brain quickly enumerated and ordered the points he wanted to make. He also considered possible questions he might be asked and what informative answers he might give. Pan led him through the studio door into darkness and guided him slowly until he could see the steps leading to the guest entrance. She did a little mime to show him what to do next, which, had he not felt suddenly tense, he would have found quite amusing, as her dumbshow was entirely incomprehensible! He heard Gay's voice welcome viewers back and then announce that one of the audience's hated male legislators had actually arrived, 'entirely spontaneously, nothing to do with us *at all*', at the studio building and here he was, prepared to face them.

When his name was announced and Pan nudged him, Dr Garret FitzGerald stepped forward carefully. The shock he felt as he walked onto the set was not because of the sudden glare of studio lights, but the loud boos that greeted him.

*

Philip Calvert's gun was pointed directly at someone called Donald MacEachern. Francis realised he hadn't a notion how Calvert had got there. How long had he been reading and turning pages, but thinking about something else? Why hadn't his dad just let him alone? It was really exasperating. Why should it matter to him if Francis read his book standing on his head *and* watched the telly at the same time? He turned back a few pages to where Philip smelled Charlotte's perfume. He started again but the annoying image of his dad standing between him and the telly kept intruding. The maddest part was that his dad was usually the one *stopping* him reading in bed, telling him that it would make his eyes sore. It was infuriating.

Francis tossed the book on the floor. Why didn't his dad understand that he could read anytime he felt like it, but once *The Late Late* was over, he could never see that again. It was gone forever. Every so often he caught the tantalising sound of distant shouting from downstairs whenever the arguing on the telly got louder. There was nothing else in the whole world that Francis wanted more than to be watching *The Late Late Show*. But he wasn't allowed do that and he couldn't concentrate on his book and he wasn't sleepy at all. The only word to describe his feelings now was apoplectic

After what seemed like ages curled up and miserable, a familiar chainsaw buzz coming up the road distracted Francis. It had to be Marian's boyfriend Stephen bringing her home from the pictures on his Yamaha 125. His mam was always warning Marian not to go next nor near that bike unless Stephen had a crash helmet for her and promised not to go more than thirty miles an hour. Francis was surprised not to hear the front door open. The motorbike didn't take off either.

Curious, he hopped down from the bunk and went to the window. He inched back the curtain and saw the motorbike parked right on the corner with two people sitting against it, kissing. The streetlight was behind them and they were wrapped up in each other so it was hard to see exactly who they were, but Francis recognised the Yamaha 125 so it had to be Stephen and Marian. He didn't know how long they'd been kissing before he started watching, but they kept at it for ages. Finally they stopped and Francis could see two faces. Marian said something and Stephen laughed. Then she laughed. Then he laughed. Everything they said seemed to be funny. Sometimes they stopped talking and just stared at each other, smiling. They kept their arms around each other's waists. When they kissed again Francis noticed that the streetlight behind made a long shadow of their bodies on the road and it looked like one lanky person with a big head riding a motorbike.

Francis completely forgot his annoyance about *The Late Late Show* and being sent to bed. Even though nothing was happening for a long time, except for talking and smiling and staring, he enjoyed standing in the dark, watching, waiting to see what was going to happen, especially because he knew that Marian and Stephen hadn't a clue that he was there. He'd seen boys and girls kiss on the telly and in films, and remembered seeing Marian holding hands with some other boy, but it felt different, more tingly, watching her like this, at night, when she had no idea that she was under keen observation.

Stephen pulled her closer and stood up at the same time. He towered over her and, as they kissed, Marian kept leaning further and further back. Francis saw the Yamaha shake and Marian nearly fell off the seat but Stephen was able to hold on and stop her bashing off the ground. The two of them straightened up, laughing again. Marian hugged Stephen hard and her face disappeared into his chest. Then they both went completely still, holding on to each other. They stayed like that for ages. Francis wasn't sure exactly what he wanted them to do, but he wished they'd do something else.

By the time he noticed the muttering voices, his mam and dad were nearly at the top of the stairs. How come he hadn't heard the music at the end of *the Late Late Show*? He scarpered from the window and hoisted himself quickly onto the top bunk. His feet got tangled in the blankets but he shut his eyes and went still as the bedroom door opened. His mam's voice whispered.

'Will you look at the bedclothes. Kicking in his sleep.'

He felt the blankets being tugged gently from his feet and drawn over his body to his shoulder. He heard his book being placed on the dressing-table and then the door closed. Francis wished he had enough cool courage to hop down again and continue his secret surveillance. Instead he decided just to listen intently, but there wasn't really anything to hear. Long before the Yamaha zinged away from Rowan Avenue and the cautious click of the front door signalled Marian's safe and happy return home, Francis was fast asleep.

*

The women in the back of the cab were too busy venting their still-raw rage at Gay Byrne's handling of the show and the *nerve* of Garret FitzGerald swanning in like that, to notice Mags asking the driver to pull in quick. She had already paid him before the talking stopped and the others looked around. This wasn't Hawkins Street.

'C'mon. I'll explain when we get out.'

The other women followed. Another taxi passed and pulled in hastily a little further on. Mags waved and seconds later more women got out. She calmed the flurry of questions by pointing at a pub across the road.

'That's one of the pubs that won't serve pints to women. Let's go order a round.'

Tom Scanlon was, to say the least of it, bemused to see a gaggle of ladies piling in the door only five minutes before closing time. His pub was never what you might call a favourite with the fairer sex, although occasionally one of the regulars might have the wife in tow, which was fair enough. Tom could cope with that. But ten or so ladies, all – at a guess – in the thirty to forty age group, some of them not really dressed in what he would consider an appropriate ladylike way, looking for drink at this hour was not an ideal scenario. On the other hand a round of drinks that size was a welcome few bob, especially when he'd be calling last orders very shortly and turfing them out in twenty minutes or less. Tom Scanlon decided to be gracious and allow them one round. They were a giggly lot and maybe it wasn't so surprising they had only each other for company as a few of them would be hard put to attract any man, although, in fairness, the one doing the ordering was a fine-looking redhead.

Having warned them that they only had the bare few minutes, Tom poured the drinks swiftly. They certainly had money to spend: two double brandies and ginger, two double bacardis and coke – with ice, says she, and got her answer quick enough – two double gins and tonic, a Babycham, and a Snowball, and a Campari and soda. He couldn't recall the last time he'd opened that bottle of Campari. Tom had no trouble totting up in his head as he went, but found it hard to work out what the total, £2.17.6d, was in new pence. The ladies were all saying thank you and you're a great man and cheers as they splashed their mixers into their drinks. The fine redhead was smiling. She took out her purse.

'Now, what do I owe you?'

'Two pounds... ah... eighty... seven and a half pence.'

The fine redhead held up three pound notes.

'Oh, silly me. I forgot my own drink. A pint of Guinness, please.'

Well, that took the wind out of Tom's sails: a well-spoken lady like her looking for a pint? Of Guinness? She'd look much better with a Campari in her hand. Tom covered his surprise and explained the house rule very politely. No pints served to ladies, but he could do her a half pint. The fine redhead, still holding the pound notes and smiling, said she wasn't a lady and would prefer a pint. Now the gaggle seemed quieter all of a sudden and the ten pairs of eyes gawping at him weren't so laughy and pally. It was like that, was it? Tom Scanlon wasn't one of those publicans who loved lording it in his premises, always looking to bar anyone who looked crossways at him, but neither was he a pushover and, once it was put up to him, there was no man less likely to give way. Still polite, but with a bit of steel in the voice now, he explained the rule of the house once more. So. Would the lady like to order something else? Are you sure I can't have a pint? says she, and Tom thought he heard a bit of wheedle in the voice. If she thought women's wiles were going to change his mind she was dealing with the wrong man. I'm more than sure, I'm certain, says Tom, thinking, don't be wasting any more of my time. Especially as he could see, out of the corner of his eye, two regulars raise their empty glasses in search of a refill.

'Fair enough,' said Mags 'Sorry, order cancelled. Come on, Sisters.'

They were flying out the door before the old barman found his voice, leaving brandy, Bacardi, gin, Campari, all doused in mixers and a Babycham and Snowball already poured out. It was a great old wheeze and what Mags loved most about it, was not that the pub lost out on a few quid, but the rage it engendered in men used to being kings of their own castles. It felt like a smidgen of revenge for their *Late Late Show* humiliation.

They got into Mulligan's just before the lock-in, and were served creamy pints. Lettie said she was still incandescent. Others felt likewise. While Hilary and Mary favoured the conspiracy theory that Gaybo had FitzGerald waiting in the wings all the time, Mags and the rest disagreed, seeing it more as a perfect illustration of the point they had been trying to make: men thought they always knew best. Once Gaybo heard that articulate and highly intelligent Dr Garret FitzGerald had deigned to pop by to offer his pearls of wisdom, it never even occurred to him that, having announced that tonight's show was women only, it wasn't appropriate to put this politician on-air. And as for Dr Garret FitzGerald? 'Unbelievable!' 'The arrogance!' 'I wanted to throttle him.' 'Patting us on the head and telling us he's on our side.' 'Like Moses with his tablets of stone.' 'The ones who mean well are the worst.' Máirín inclined to the positive view that, even though the show had been hijacked by a pompous opinionated politician, something special had happened all the same tonight and they should capitalise on it. But how? The battle to get a word in edgeways began again. Ronnie the barman had little chance of being noticed or heard when he came to the group, so he tapped Mags on the shoulder and made the phone call sign with thumb and little finger. She followed him back to the counter.

'I checked with Gaybo if it was all right for me to barge in on a group of women drinking in Mulligan's and he said I'd be welcome if I was a male feminist.'

'That leaves you out then. What did you make of Garret's intervention?'

Mags could hear Michael's voice curdle.

'FitzGerald's a privileged wanker. Knows it all and wants everyone to hear about it. He'd have a position paper on how much butter you should put on your bread.'

As usual Michael didn't delay on the phone. He said he'd keep his chauvinist arse well away from Mulligan's, but he'd be happy to come and pick her up at a time of her choosing.

Sheila sang 'I wish I was in Carrickfergus' as the women tumbled out sometime after one o'clock, having drank and talked themselves into a more positive frame of mind and made big plans. They hugged and kissed and went their separate ways. Mags, feeling merry rather than outright drunk, spotted Michael's car outside Hawkins House and waved. Headlights flashed back.

'There's my lift. My chauffeur awaits.'

The inebriated Sisters were impressed.

'You have him well trained. Keep him that way.'

Four: May 22nd

Still undecided, Mags had gone to bed earlier than usual and had set the alarm for seven, the hope being that after eight hours of deep sleep she'd wake up with her mind clear about whether to go or not, and either hop enthusiastically out of bed, or roll over and enjoy a Saturday lie-in. But her brain refused to rest. She wanted to be part of the trip, no doubt about that. And she'd more or less promised that she would. What was the matter then? Too old? She was thirty-seven, not a doddering old lady. June, the head and tail of this caper, was older than Mags, but another of the older women, Nuala had refused to go. Did she think it was too vulgar? Maybe she was right, at least in the sense that this particular little protest was for the young radicals. Was it better to give them their day in the media spotlight? Nonsense. She would go. Then she thought of her mother's reaction. Oh for God's sake, was she actually worried about Brenda Perry seeing her face on the newspaper, or on the television news? For this stunt, yes, maybe. And what if, having made up her mind to join in and arrived all excited at the station, she found a huddle of only a half-dozen Sisters waiting? That would be too humiliating and sad to bear. She couldn't face that.

Some sleep punctuated this frustrating turn and turnabout of thoughts, but there was no need for the alarm clock. She woke at half six and, knowing there would be no more rest, thought, right, she'd go. And crawled from the bed.

On the way to their Gran's, Simon was contentedly silent, but Susan became annoyingly curious. 'What are you doing?' 'Just something with my women's group' wasn't quite enough of an answer for her. What and where soon followed. Even as Mags ventured, 'One of our outings, that's all', she knew that would only excite her daughter's interest further. Finally the inevitable question, 'Why can't I come?' followed more surprisingly by, 'If it's a women's group. I'm a woman.' Mags' instinctive, 'No you're not,' sounded all wrong, even when she quickly added, 'yet'.

By the time the taxi turned up St Attracta Road, Susan was announcing her determination to accompany her mother on this mysterious outing for women. Mags said no, no and no again. And meant it, right up to the time she opened the rear door to let the children out. Then, for no good reason thought, what the hell, she's thirteen, might as well be hung for a sheep as for a lamb. Mags kissed Simon goodbye, and sent him to knock on the door. When her mother appeared, she called from the open taxi window. The coward's option.

'Listen, can you take him for the day? Sorry, I'm in an awful rush. Susan's coming with me.'

'Where are you off to?'

'Haven't a second. I'll tell you later. Bye. Bye, Simon love. Behave yourself.'

Susan jigged with pleasure and delight.

'Where are we going?'

'We're going to the train station.'

'We're taking a train!'

'Yes.'

'Super. Where to?'

When she said Belfast, Mags could see that Susan was very surprised and didn't quite know what to make of that revelation. No doubt she was thinking of soldiers, riots and burning cars.

'Why are we going there?'

Mags hesitated longer this time.

'Shopping.'

'Ah Mum, tell me.'

'I told you.'

'Ah Mum, seriously.'

'Wait and see then.'

The long walk up the ramp to the platform at Connolly Station allowed time for uncertainty to return. This was a brash, radical and, yes, vulgar adventure and only the hardest of the hard core would turn up. There were hundreds of women on the platform and queuing for tickets, but Mags knew by their shopping bags and head-scarves, by the way they moved and chatted to each other, that none of them were part of her group. It was nearly ten to eight. If there was no one here by now then the whole scheme was a disaster.

Then she saw Mary Kenny. How could she not, in an enormous floppy mauve hat and a Victorian mantle cape in Paisley wool that collided gloriously with a leather miniskirt and high boots. Then she saw four other ordinary Marys in quick succession. And there was Nell, jigging impatiently from foot to foot. And June, busy already of course, distributing a leaflet. As if Mags had put special glasses on, the Sisterhood all came into sudden focus: Maureen, Hilary, Margaret, Marie, Joan, Lettie and a bunch of young women on the platform posing under a banner for some press photographers. IRISH WOMEN'S LIBERATION ORGANISATION: Helen, Brenda, Collette, Iris, Nora, Rosita, Moira, Rebecca, Caroline, Ann without an 'e', Anne with an 'e', and two Noreens. There were plenty more who Mags didn't know by name. She was relieved to spot three other children about Susan's age, including one boy, Maureen's young lad.

'Glad I'm not the only one.'

'It's a birthday treat. He wants to see the soldiers. It was this or the zoo.'

It was so much better than Mags feared. Fifty or so?

'Isn't it just pathetic? Barely fifty of us.'

Mags didn't argue the toss with Nell. Her saucer eyes lent themselves so easily to hurt and accusation. It was only natural that she'd dreamed of returning to her old university town at the head of a powerful force. She'd probably expected five hundred, not fifty.

With so many other women crossing the border for cheap

shopping it was too late to commandeer a carriage of their own. June managed to organise everyone in two adjoining carriages. Mags felt a little sorry for the misfortunate man in a donkey jacket suddenly surrounded by her, Susan, and a younger woman who introduced herself as Trish. As the train pulled out he fixed his attention on the apparently fascinating rooftops and backyards of North Strand passing below them. Trish's accent was West of Ireland: Clare or Galway. Mags' intuition that she was naively overexcited was confirmed by her suggestion that they should go around the train and try to drum up more recruits from amongst the shoppers. Mags looked along the carriage at the women clutching large empty shopping bags and guessed that their noisy happy chatter was unlikely to centre around the liberating effects of tasting menstrual blood or sipping breast milk. To forestall this enthusiastic Sister, Mags said it was a very inventive suggestion, but better check with June or Mary first. Trish, the hard thin beauty of her face softened by the grinning pleasure of the escapade, was sure they'd easily get a few more converts.

'Sure I'd heard nothing about any of this stuff until a pal of mine dragged me along – and I mean dragged, I had no more notion of going – to the meeting in the Mansion House last month and look, here I am now. All 'cause of that night. Were you there? Wasn't it just something else? *Thousands* of us. It was a bit freaky finding out that so many other women were having the same lunatic thoughts as meself. Afterwards I was kinda raging I didn't speak. I'd love to have told them what happened five years ago last March when Mammy collapsed on the floor in front of me. She was six months gone at the time, number nine it would've been, poor little thing. I was only fifteen and I tell you I'll never forget it, the screams and –'

Mags was relieved that Trish suddenly remembered Susan.

'Well anyway, I'll tell you one thing: that day I decided it was never going to happen to me.'

She dropped her voice, almost to a whisper.

'Not if I had to keep these legs crossed for the rest of my life would I put up with what Mammy put up with.'

Mags couldn't help hoping that poor Donkey Jacket next to Trish really was as lost in the beauty of the Laytown coastline as he appeared to be.

'Of course, the laugh of it all is, I'm brave now, but if there's cameras waiting for us when we get back I'll be hiding my face for fear Mammy'd see me. Isn't that pure stupid now? But sure she'd just die with the mortification of it.'

'Not at all.' Mags was entirely sincere. She admired the brash courage of Trish and all the other young ones in the group. Some of them were probably still living at home. She thought of respectable little mouse Margaret Perry at twenty-one, thrilled and excited to have met the man of her dreams and perfectly content to be told by him what her future would hold. She looked down at Susan and silently promised it wouldn't be like that for her.

'Mum won't tell me why we're going to Belfast. Will you?'

For some reason, Susan's accent sounded much more English and alien.

'I told her we're going shopping, but she won't believe me.'

'That's right, honey. We're going shopping.'

'Are you serious?'

'Cross my heart.'

Mags was delighted that seemed to silence Susan. But not for long.

'Shopping for what?'

'Ahh… well…' Trish's look to Mags said, sorry, don't think I can help you here.

'Isn't it more fun if it's a mystery?'

'You're just saying that so I'll stop asking. It must be something really horrid if you're ashamed to tell me.'

The English tinge to her dismissiveness somehow made Mags feel that much smaller and more pathetic.

'I'm not ashamed. Don't be silly.'

'Well, tell me then.'

Mags was flummoxed. She glanced down at the leaflet June had distributed, hoping for inspiration from that.

1. Declare nothing and risk being searched.
2. Declare contraceptives and refuse to be searched.
3. Declare contraceptives and refuse to hand over.
4. Declare contraceptives and hand over with protest at infringement of your constitutional rights.
5. Declare contraceptives and throw over the barrier to sisters waiting beyond.
6. Declare contraceptives and sit down in anticipation of customs action.
7. Declare internal contraceptive. Allow search from female officer only and shout 'April fool' on entry.

Nothing there that might illuminate matters for an inquiring thirteen-year-old. Susan's face had that terrifying combination of innocence and serious determination. It would not be denied. Dropping her voice so as not to distract Donkey Jacket from his intent scrutiny of more shoppers getting on at Dundalk station, Mags attempted to explain what the trip was all about.

'Well, you know how babies start.'

'When a man and a woman are in love they –'

Exactly. Just like we talked about, okay? But sometimes a man and a woman can be in love and never have a baby at all. Remember in Marlborough, Mr and Mrs Hopcraft, down the road? They had no children. And then sometimes a mother has so many babies that the doctor says she'll be ill if she has any more.

'That happened to my mammy.'

'Yes, like Trish's mammy. And sometimes a family is very poor and can't afford another baby. So, there is ah…'

And now, language failed Mags. She was grateful to hear Trish's voice.

'There's medicine you can take.'

'Yes, exactly, a special medicine you can take so that the

woman doesn't get pregnant. It's called a contraceptive. And this medicine… well, you know Ireland, where we live now, is one country and England, where we used to live, is another country and Northern Ireland, where we're going today, is part of England okay? … Well, we can't buy contraceptives in Dublin but we can in Northern Ireland. So we're all travelling to Belfast to buy them and bring them back.'

Susan considered this very carefully. She looked at Trish for confirmation. Then spoke a bit too loudly.

'Because you all want to stop having babies?'

Donkey Jacket suddenly rose, muttered 'Excuse me', pushed past Trish and more or less ran out of the carriage. Trish muffled a snigger.

'Ah no, no. We're only buying the contraceptives as a protest against our government, because they won't allow contraceptives to be sold in Dublin.'

'Why not?'

'Exactly. Very good question.'

Susan was clearly lining up more questions. Mags looked wearily at Trish who smirked back.

'A fair few miles to go yet.'

Nell arrived. Mags hoped she would provide some much-needed distraction.

'Look out there. Crossing the border. Heads down now or you'll all be shot.'

From the way she kept tapping a foot as she talked and her slightly manic smirk it was obvious that Nell had overcome her initial disappointment at the turnout. It would surely be her day, her triumph if the protest worked. The concept was brazen and cheeky and funny and aimed unerringly at the hypocritical heart of things, and that was pure Nell. But Mags recognised something else in the very depths of her, something innocent and idealistic and vulnerable that reminded her of Susan, even though, on the surface, no two females could be more unalike. Nell's short-cropped curls, aggressive dress sense and the weary cynicism coursing through every jaundiced observation might seem like a full frontal challenge to her daughter's fairy princess persona, but that wasn't how they related to each other: Nell would greet Susan with a sly wink and she always grinned back with instinctive understanding. Now, seeing her daughter accept a Rolo and laugh at some laconic Nellism, Mags was suddenly and definitively pleased that Susan was with her today.

At Central Station, the women gathered together on the platform and another leaflet was passed out detailing what products to ask for. Now Nell came into her own. She knew the territory. Waving a hand like Tonto she took off and everyone followed. No, not Tonto, Mags thought, more like the Pied Piper.

'You still haven't told me why you can't buy... what are they called again?'

'Contraceptives.'

'Yes. Why can't you buy them in Dublin?'

Mags knew this question wasn't going to go away. There was a complicated answer and there was an easy answer.

'Remember when you came to Ireland first and you found out that you couldn't buy Opal Fruits like you could in England?'

'Yes'

And remember the first time you tasted Taytos in Dublin and you couldn't understand why you couldn't buy them in Marlborough?'

'Yes.'

'It's like that.'

Mags felt guilty, but told herself there would be plenty of time in the future for the longer answer that involved Irish history, Catholic mysogyny, male politics and so much more. They followed the gang into the chemist's on Great Victoria Street. Mags could see that the mournful-looking man behind the counter didn't really know what to make of this sudden invasion and unusual level of chatter as dozens of women grabbed packets and read instructions aloud and discussed which products to buy. Some of the younger ones now seemed rather less brash. There was a lot of nervous giggling and face-making. Poor June and Marie, clearly identified as older and wiser in these matters, were being pestered with questions. Mags realised that she might be viewed in a similar light by those who knew that she'd been married and used to live in England, whereas the truth was contraception had never featured in her sex life at all. At least not until very recently. It briefly crossed her mind how differently things might have turned out if it had. Mags retreated, pulling Susan by the hand.

'It's too crowded. We'll find another chemist.'

Great Victoria Street felt oddly empty and silent for a Saturday. Mags didn't even know if she was walking in the right direction. Instinctively she turned left. Both she and Susan stared silently as some kind of armoured vehicle rolled past them. A few moments later they stopped at a corner and, as Mags looked around for a pharmacy sign, she heard a shriek and felt Susan back into her. She turned and saw a soldier lurking only a couple of feet away in a doorway. He carried a very long rifle or was it a machine gun?

'Pardon, ma'am. I think I gave her a scare.'

He smiled shyly at Susan. He had the face of a boy. Was he even seventeen? Mags nodded and walked on.

'Oh Mum! Simon is going to be so jealous when I tell him I was right next to a soldier with a gun pointing –'

Mags realised she didn't like the notion of Susan spouting all the details of the trip to her brother. And perhaps others? She thought quickly.

'No, he won't be jealous. Do you know why? Because today, you're one of the Sisters. Don't you know what that means, Susan? Whatever happens when you're one of the Sisters is only between us. Do you understand?'

Mags was gratified at how instantly this worked. Susan nodded very gravely and Mags felt her hand gripped more firmly as they walked down Bedford Street. Finally they spotted a sign: Rud-dock's Pharmacy. There were no other customers inside. It was tiny and, too late, Mags saw that the condoms were behind the counter. She would have to ask for them. The chemist's expectant smile and the silent emptiness of the shop were discomfiting. Once again language was failing her. She was afraid to hear the sound of her own voice. It would be either booming and hectoring or such a cracked whisper she'd be required to repeat herself. Mags had never bought condoms before. She'd always known them as 'French letters' and was familiar with the old fifties euphemism, 'something for the weekend.' She only knew the term 'rubber johnny' because of Michael. He had laughed out loud when he heard about the scheme. A great stroke, he called it. His view was that the government was mad not to make contraceptives freely available, especially rubber Johnnies, because the tax take would be huge, the business would create jobs.

'Think about it, unlike any other product, demand would always exceed actual usage, because fellahs'd buy far more than they'd ever need, just to show off to their pals. Imagine, three boyos go into a chemist shop. One buys a pack of twelve, say. What're the other fellahs going to do? Buy a pack of three? Not on your nelly!'

As so often with Michael, Mags wondered should she be pleased or appalled that they had come to the same conclusion from such different perspectives.

'Ten packs of Durex, please.'

It sounded just awful. The cheerful expression on the woman's face did not change.

'Gossamer, featherlite –?'

'Just any ten packs'

'Sixes? Twelves?'

Was the woman trying to torture her?

'Twelve. Ten packs – ten packs of twelve. And, ah, ten tubes of… of… spermicidal jelly.'

The words hung horribly in the air, but at least it was done now and the woman was gathering the goods. Susan was staring intently at the items on the shelves behind the counter.

'Is that all, pet?'

Mags felt strongly that the Pill should feature significantly when it came to the hoped-for confrontation with customs on the way home. The protest definitely shouldn't be all about French letters. But a prescription was needed for the Pill.

'Ah… I need some white pills. Something like Aspro, but not Aspro as it might be too easily recognisable, you know, for what it is… I don't know, really.'

The woman spoke quietly.

'Have I got you right, pet? You want a white pill that doesn't look like Aspro?

'Yes, you know, if I were to show it to someone… ah… they might think… it's the Pill.'

'The Pill? Oh the Pill…. Oh I have you now. I know just the thing.'

Mags was so surprised at how matter-of-fact the woman's reaction was. She returned with a jar, opened it and shook some pills onto Mags' hand.

'How's that? Sugar pills. Placebos.'

'Perfect.'

'There's a fair dose in that jar there. Is that enough for you?'

'Plenty.'

Mags paid up. The woman bagged everything. Mags looked down at Susan and whispered.

'You see, she's a Sister too.'

And put a finger to her lips.

The journey home was more tense and silent. There was a lot more walking about by some of the women, as if the group needed constant tending and comforting. Máirín expressed her worry that, as their intended protest at Connolly Station was known, customs might try to deny them their public confrontation by hauling them off the train at Dundalk or Drogheda. Mags didn't really believe that would happen. Nevertheless she sensed everyone around her relax when, after what seemed like a suspiciously long delay, the train left Dundalk station without incident. A few of the young ones showed their relief by blowing up condoms and letting them whizz around the carriage. Mags noticed pursed lips and disapproving whispers amongst the shopping tourists and guessed they might be worried that this loudly volatile bunch of women's libbers would only draw unwelcome attention to their ordinary decent smuggling.

Mags had never noticed before just how achingly long it took for a train to stop. The slowdown began as it entered the station. Everyone stood. The ordinary shoppers were now busy burying their goods at the bottom of bags. Some were even wearing new blouses and coats, ripping off labels. Slower and slower. The Sisterhood took out their goods and checked their leaflet to remind themselves of their options. Mags favoured number 5. 'Declare contraceptives and throw over the barrier to Sisters waiting beyond.' If there were any.

'Mum, you're hurting my hand.'

It was like a moment from four years ago: the terrified runaway mother waiting as the boat train pulled into Holyhead. This time Susan wasn't sleepily oblivious of the drama.

'Are we going to be arrested?'

'No, they won't dare.'

Slower and slower. Would it ever stop? She looked around and saw Trish, who waved her bag of goodies. Mags did likewise.

A lurch. Forward. Back. Finally the Belfast train stopped. The regular shoppers raced ahead along the platform, determined not to be implicated in whatever debacle was about to unfold. The carriage exits strained and buckled at the pressure of the impatient departures. June and Máirín corralled everyone behind the banner. Now was the moment. Patience was needed. They had to act together for maximum impact. It seemed quite a distance to the gates, where Mags could see something that had not been in Connolly Station for a considerable time: a genuine customs presence. A proper long table had been set up and a battery of customs officials, all in full uniform, stood behind it. Susan was now squeezing Mags' hand too hard, but that was all right.

The women set off behind their banner, each holding their ammunition ready. Forty-seven now seemed like a very small troop, particularly when compared with the hundreds of women ahead of them, scuttling unimpeded through customs.

The chanting was suddenly close and very loud. Mags wondered why she hadn't heard it until now.

'Let them through! Let them through!'

Now she saw the crowd held back by police barriers. There were hundreds. Women and men. Cameras flashed.

'Let them through! Let them through!'

Mags felt tears spring, but had no time to think of doing anything about that. The boss customs man tried to keep a certain dignity while making himself heard.

'Have you anything to declare?'

Máirin, waving a tube of spermicidal jelly, led the shouting.

'I've got contraceptives. I've got jelly.'

'I've got condoms!'

'I have the Pill.'

'I have a coil. I'm wearing it!'

Mags, over her own shouts, heard a little girl's voice beside her screaming 'I've got condoms! I've got condoms!' and didn't dare to look down at Susan for fear she'd laugh and spoil the moment. The crowd beyond was singing 'We shall not conceive' to the tune of 'We shall overcome'. From somewhere close to the customs table Mags heard a shout, 'Loose your contraceptives.'

Hundreds of condoms arced in the air. Tubes of jelly flew past the heads of officials who made no serious attempt to prevent them reaching eager hands behind the barriers. Mags pushed her way to the front and opened her jar. She spilled out little white pills in front of a nervous-looking young customs man.

'Look, I have the Pill. The dreaded Pill. Look I'm taking the Pill.' and she popped two in her mouth. 'I'm breaking the law, arrest me.'

Then she tossed a handful in the air and, utterly drenched, soused in the mad joy of the moment, Mags poured out handful after handful and flung them towards the chanting crowd. By the time she threw her last one the officials had given way and the women were sweeping past to join their wonderful, beautiful friends behind the barricades.

Someone called a halt, then Collette stepped forward and turned back towards the customs table. She read a short statement.

'This law discriminates against women. Today we have shown that this law is hypocritical and obsolete. We have brought contraceptives into this State and you have not been able to prevent us. We say again: either arrest us or CHANGE THE LAW!!'

The cry was taken up

'Change the law! Change the law!'

And even the camera pointing straight in Mags' face, and the thought of Brenda Perry's mortification when she saw her daughter screaming on the nine o'clock news did not make her lower her voice or look away.

1972

Five: January 17th

The door set into the sliding partition between the two classrooms was irritatingly resistant. The semi-circular metal ring that had to be pulled out in order to turn the lock was quite pernickety. Brother Carew realised it required leaner, more elegant fingers than his own. When he did manage to tickle it out and twist it, the old door rattled and jammed, precisely because in his anxiety he'd tried to get it open too quickly. The frustration was greater because he could see, through the frosted glass, the movement of bodies and clearly hear the noise, but the delay in getting the damned door open would inevitably afford the boys of 1A too much warning.

When it finally gave way and Brother Carew stepped through into 1A, it was indeed too late. The entire class was now seated and silent. There was not even one boy he could legitimately single out for punishment. This was disappointing, but Brother Carew had no intention of letting it go at that. Seeing the paper pellets strewn about the floor of the classroom, he quelled his immediate instinct to instruct one of the boys to gather them up. They might prove more useful left where they were.

Francis hadn't fired any pellets during the battle, but only because he didn't have any ready when Dave Flannery and Ian Barry launched their surprise attack. His rubber band was in his schoolbag so he'd ducked under the desk to get at it. By the time he'd raised his head there were pellets flying everywhere. Then the boys had heard the rattle of the door and saw the dark twisted shape of Brother Carew in the frosted glass.

Like the rest of 1A, Francis now sat very still, hoping not to draw attention to himself as the thick black glasses swept round the silent room like a special camera that could see into the mind of every boy.

A pregnant pause, he thought.

How hellish it would be if he was still in primary school and had Brother Carew all day, every day, instead of just for English and Religion. But to be fair to the fearsome Brother, Francis, who had thought he already knew loads about English, had learned so much more, since starting secondary school last September, thanks to Brother Carew. He'd told them about the four different kinds of nouns, transitive and intransitive verbs, irregular verbs, complex sentences and clauses; relative clauses and adjectival clauses and adverbial clauses and conjunctive clauses. And moods. Brother Carew had explained the Indicative, the Interrogative, the Imperative, the Conditional, the Subjunctive. And, best of all, in the last couple of weeks Brother Carew had taught them all about figures of speech.

The thick black glasses stopped at fat Cónal Collopy, who was sitting nearest the partition door.

'Mr Collopy, look at me.'

The Imperative Mood. The deep dark voice. Francis often wondered why Carew was the only brother in the school who didn't have a country mucker accent. He was standing quite still, but the leather strap hanging from his belt swayed slowly. As Cónal Collopy looked up, Francis noticed some of the other boys smirking. Cónal didn't have many friends because he'd come from a different primary school and sometimes acted a bit weird.

'Would you care to tell me who was causing all the disturbance?'

The Interrogative Mood.

Cónal hadn't been part of the rubber band battle. Francis had noticed him with his head down all the time, using his hand to protect his face from pellets. He'd kept scribbling in his copybook with the other hand. Probably drawing cartoons as usual.

Cónal didn't sound nervous, but surely he must have been. 'I don't know, Brother.'

'No, I didn't think you would.' The Indicative Mood. 'But,

should any further disturbance bring me in here again' – the Conditional Mood – 'I'll expect you to be much more forthcoming with information. If not, Mr Collopy, you will be punished on behalf of the whole class.'

Brother Carew knew that this particular approach to discipline had rarely resulted in a boy informing on his pals, but as this odd overweight creature wasn't very popular, he might be willing. Not that it mattered if he wasn't. Brother Carew would punish him, *pour encourager les autres*, and there would be no more trouble from anyone.

What Francis found so hard to understand was how the man who was being so mean and unfair to Cónal Collopy, who had done nothing wrong, could also be such a brilliant English teacher. On a freezing January morning a couple of weeks ago, so gloomy that Brother Carew had to switch on the lights in the big old grey classroom, he had also switched on something in Francis' brain. FIGURES OF SPEECH he wrote on the blackboard in thick, neat, orderly capitals. Then underneath, a list of words. Francis had never seen any of them before.

Simile, Metaphor, Personification, Alliteration, Assonance, Onomatopoeia, Hyerbole, Synecdoche.

Thus far, Brother Carew had said, he had been teaching them how the English language had rules to help people communicate correctly. Now they would begin to learn that it was so much more than just a way of conveying meaning clearly. The English language had fathomless riches in it, mysterious qualities beyond grammar, important though that was. Qualities of colour and tone. Poetry. There were layers and layers of mood and degrees of feeling and these figures of speech – he pointed to the list – were the passwords, the 'open sesame' to a treasure trove. Francis had never heard Brother Carew talk like this. Then abruptly, he changed back to his usual self, barking out questions:

'We will begin with a simple example. Hands up if you are feeling cold this morning.'

A few boys put up their hands. Brother Carew ignored them

and turned to one of those who hadn't: Andrew Liddy, sitting next to Francis.

'So, you're not feeling cold, Mr Liddy? Does this mean you are feeling warm?'

Francis knew Andrew had kept his hand down to avoid being asked questions. Now he was caught.

'I'm not sure, Brother.'

'Just choose one, Mr Liddy. Are you cold or warm?'

Poor Andrew didn't know what answer Carew wanted.

'Compare how cold you feel with something else that is also cold. Can you think of a comparison?'

Francis knew that Andrew would easily think of one if Carew wasn't standing over him like that. If he didn't say something soon Carew's tone of voice would change, his cheeks would get redder, his mouth would turn down, and suddenly there'd be some kind of punishment. Lines, or a whack on the back of the head, or the leather if he was in a really bad mood. Amazingly, none of this happened. Carew just gave up waiting for an answer and looked around the class.

'Mr Collopy, can you compare how cold you are, to something else?'

Cónal's answer came without any hesitation.

'I'm as cold as a Nazi soldier in Stalingrad, Brother.'

Carew looked completely surprised. Of course he didn't know that Cónal was always drawing cartoons of soldiers, especially Nazis, and he could do Captain Hurricane and Maggot Malone exactly like they were in the *Victor*. Carew stared at him for a couple of seconds. Then he went to the blackboard and wrote down exactly what Cónal had said.

'An unusual choice, but not incorrect. "As cold as a Nazi soldier in Stalingrad". This, boys, is an example of' – he pointed to the first word on his list – 'a sim-il-ay.'

He said it like three words. So that was how to pronounce it. Francis would have said it sounding like 'smile' and made a fool of himself.

'A simile is a comparison, ideally an imaginative, enlightening, and, as in Mr Collopy's example, a surprising comparison. A simile always uses the words "like" or "as". Here you see Mr Collopy has used "as cold as". And here is an example of a simile using "like".' He wrote down, "He was so cold his fingers were like icicles".'

'All right. I want everyone to think of your own example of a simile using cold. Write it in your copybook. Remember you must use 'like' or 'as'.

Francis tried to think of a simile even more clever and unusual than Cónal Collopy's. Anything to do with snow and ice and winter were too ordinary, but it was hard to get them out of his head. Brother Carew walked around the room looking at what the boys were writing.

'Yes… yes… fine… yes… I don't think the world is familiar with your dog's nose, Mr Leddin… Like or as, Mr Kelly. It has to be like or as… yes… good, yes… Hurry up Mr Strong…'

He tapped the back of Francis' head and passed on. Too late he scribbled down a really good one. 'As cold as a killer's smile.' Brother Carew was already back at the blackboard, writing a list of similes that he said were from poems they would soon be learning.

'I wandered lonely as a cloud that floats on high'

'Where the wind's like a whetted knife'

'Blue were her eyes as the fairy flax, her cheeks like the dawn of day.'

'I think on thee, and then my state, like to the lark at break of day arising'

Francis was raging that Brother Carew hadn't seen his simile and jealous that fat Cónal Collopy's was written on the board, especially when he hadn't even bothered to put his hand up.

Every day Brother Carew explained another figure of speech and each one added to a magical, mesmerising menagerie of language, squealing and screeching and howling and hissing in Francis' head. English class was a million, billion, trillion times better than any other class. It wasn't just educational, it was exceptional, sensational, inspirational. Francis began to hear figures of speech everywhere. His Auntie Mona said a man on her street was 'A lazy lout, wouldn't work to warm himself. And sneaky? Oh slithery as a snake, that fellah.' When Martin was playing his Deep Purple LP really loud his mam shouted at him, 'My head is lifting off me, my blood pressure will go through the roof listening to that noise.' Marian had little Eugene in her arms and she got a bad smell: 'Mam, I think Eugene has left a little present.' He heard his godmother, Auntie Mary, explaining why she couldn't stop smoking, 'Sure every time I go into Curtin's, the packets of fags are there staring at me, tempting me.'

Finally, this morning, Brother Carew had explained the meaning of the last and strangest-sounding figure of speech. Never in a zillion years would Francis have guessed the proper pronunciation of synecdoche. It was a very hard word for a very simple thing. After English class, while 1A had been waiting for 'Jake' Mahony the geography teacher to arrive, he'd been trying to think if anyone in his family had ever used synecdoche, and it was just as he heard a 'thang' behind him and Billy Shinnors yelped and the rubber band battle started, that Francis had remembered his mam giving out about the miniskirt Marian wore for a date with Stephen. 'You can't go out in that,' she'd said 'The whole street will be staring at you.'

A paper pellet pinged past Francis' ear. He looked round to see who was firing. Ian Barry and Dave Flannery, who sat together near the back, both had rubber bands wound round their fingers like slings and a big pile of pellets on the seat between them. A pyramid of pellets. They were both laughing like lunatics because they'd caught everyone by surprise. Ping! A pellet popped off Patch Dollard's cheek and he yowled like a cat whose tail had been stood on. 'Zing! Boing! Thang! The class went crazy. Hands plunged into pockets, like frantic ferrets foraging for forgotten pellets. Other boys ripped strips from their copybooks, making more missiles while dodging the white killer wasps whizzing round the room. It was a miracle that they had heard Carew rattling the partition door. Boys had barely got back to their seats, hiding their rubber bands just in time. Only the pellets, scattered like snowflakes – no, snowflakes wasn't right… confetti?… no – like tiny twisted torpedoes strewn about the classroom floor, were a clue to the battle that had raged.

It was strange that when Carew came in he hadn't seemed to notice them. Usually those thick, black-rimmed glasses missed nothing.

'Mr Mahony has been unavoidably detained. Take out your geography textbook. You may decide to use this time usefully or not, but you will certainly use it quietly. I will not have my class disturbed again. Is that clear?' Once he'd heard the muttered chorus, 'Yes Brother', he turned and walked back to 1B, confident that those pellets on the floor would prove too tantalising a lure for some foolish boy.

The partition door had barely closed behind Carew when Francis had an inspired idea. The whole class was petrified, no one would dare move a muscle or make a sound for the next minute or two. There were lots of pellets on the ground close to where he sat. If he dared be the first to move, it would take only seconds for him to gather up loads of ammunition and return to his desk, armed and ready for the next battle.

Francis counted the pellets. There were twenty or so he could grab easily. He glanced left and right. The class was silent, every boy still as a headstone in a graveyard. Francis slid from his desk to the ground, delighted at his own daring, and reached out to gather his booty.

Brother Carew had taken no more than three steps away from the partition door and stopped. 1B regarded him, silent, complicit in the ruthless way of young boys, content to see a rival class in trouble – especially the 'A' class. The moment Brother Carew heard the tell-tale sound he strode back to the door which he had not been so foolish as to lock fully, so this time it opened silently. And quickly.

Francis, on his knees with two hands full of pellets, heard the lion growl.

'Mr Strong, stand up.' When he looked around, Carew was already detaching the leather strap from his belt as he swished to the front of the classroom. Francis didn't know what to do with his handful of twisted paper. It would make things worse if he dropped them on the ground again. Carew tapped the leather on his desk and Francis spilled the missiles onto it. He held out his right hand. Carew's mouth was downturned and sour as he raised the leather high. He cracked it down three times, then pointed to Francis' left hand. The leather cracked three more times. Each sting was an instant electric shock. His palms blushed red. When it was over, Francis prayed Carew would leave the room quickly so he could lick them.

'Come and see me in the monastery at four o'clock, Mr Strong.'

Brother Carew didn't even glance at the rest of the class as he went back to 1B. This time he shut the partition door decisively, confident he wouldn't need to open it again.

*

By now every boy in first year and some older boys too would be talking about what happened in 1A today. From the parlour window Brother Carew could see the swamp of students ooze their way to the school gates. How were they telling the tale? What legend would emerge and be passed on? If Brother Carew understood anything about the minds of young boys he was sure that none of them would relate the events without emphasising that Carew – he knew how they referred to him, that he had no nickname – had been so smart and sly, returning to 1B, pretending to shut the partition door, but then turning back like lightning and hah! – Brother Carew could imagine the melodrama some boys would create around the moment – Strong had been snared. Caught in the act.

Now he observed a tall thin frame wave a sad goodbye to some classmates and limply approach the monastery door. It was interesting. Brother Carew had not expected him to be the one, yet he had not been unduly shocked either. There was something about the boy. It wasn't very obvious, perhaps because it hadn't yet taken proper shape – was he even thirteen? – but Brother Carew perceived the outline of something. A little too pushy and persistent, was that it? He was beginning to manifest himself in a way that was not for his own good. Now was definitely the time to rein him in.

Brother Carew waited in the deepening gloom of the parlour until the yard was more or less clear before going to the front door. There seemed to be no defiance in the boy's demeanour. Good. He didn't invite him inside. This wouldn't take long.

'Now Mr Strong, enlighten me. Why are you always what I would call, the ringleader? Whenever there is any difficulty or disturbance in 1A you seem to be at the centre of it. Do you enjoy making trouble? Do you get some perverse pleasure from inciting other boys to get themselves into trouble? You are in the "A" class, but it's difficult to be certain how intelligent you are because your work is often slovenly and grubby, as though you want to make it quite clear to me that you couldn't care less. Perhaps you think that you don't need to make as much of an effort as other boys, that your own genius will carry you through. You want more free time to cause disruption and mayhem. If that is what you have been thinking, Mr Strong, then I hope you now realise that you are very very wrong.'

It was working even better than he had hoped. The boy's face was a spontaneous pantomime. dissolving from surprise to pained disbelief and now – relatively quickly, all things considered – tears were beginning to well up. He had broken easily. If any part of his tirade had been remotely true, Brother Carew was confident it would not be so in the future. Having no desire to listen to blubbing, he ended abruptly with, 'I'll be watching carefully for signs of improvement. And I'll be asking your other teachers to do likewise. Now go home.'

Francis didn't know what Brother Carew was taking about. He didn't recognise himself in these words. They weren't true, they just weren't. Troublemaker? What had he done apart from today?

And he hadn't been the ringleader, he hadn't fired even one pellet. Francis couldn't understand why Brother Carew thought these things. One day, ages ago he'd whispered something to Andrew Liddy that made him laugh really loud and Andrew had got lines. Was that 'inciting'? Brother Carew's words muddled him. What other awful things was he being blamed for? When he wrote his first essay he'd forgotten to draw a margin and Brother Carew had refused to mark it. Was that what made him think that he couldn't care less? He cared, he really cared – why didn't Brother Carew see that? What else had he done wrong? He couldn't think. The pain from the slaps hadn't made him cry, but these words, spoken in a voice as cold as a corpse, stung somewhere else inside him. As soon as Brother Carew closed the monastery door, Francis hurried towards the gates, keeping his head down. The yard was empty now and it was nearly dark, so at least no one would see him sobbing.

*

Ann Teresa stepped inside Elizabeth's basement nightclub, looked around quickly and relaxed. Her informant hadn't misled her. The people she was hoping to see, the cheerful fundraisers from the Central Remedial Clinic, were sitting in a discreet corner, tucking into Elizabeth's famous rough and ready roast beef and champagne. It would be the simplest thing now to step nearer and catch Tania's eye.

There we go. Now give her a Terry wave. 'Tania, darling!' Just a short walk to the table and Ann Teresa turned on full Terry for everyone's benefit.

'What an intriguing gathering! Des O', Lady Val, Geraldine… and you again! Well, they do say good things come in pairs – or is that troubles?'

They all laughed when Terry explained, with full elaboration, how she had met CJ for the first time only days before at an Iveagh house do, and now it seemed they were destined to meet each other *everywhere*. Lady Val was astonished that they hadn't encountered each other previously, Dublin being so small that way, but Terry said, 'Oh enough about me and CJ, I'm *far* more interested in hearing how the fundraiser went.'

While Terry filled the air with chat, her bright flitting eyes engaging everyone at the table, Ann Teresa's attention remained resolutely focused on CJ and recalled how, the other night, his gaze had astonished her with its openly carnivorous glint. Initially she had worried about what Sam, who had just introduced them, would think, but quickly realised that he was quite used to such shamelessness from his married friend.

Ann Teresa allowed Terry – under protest of course! – to be cajoled into joining the table for just one *tiny* glass.

'For years Dublin has been *begging* for an Elizabeth's. At last, somewhere sophisticated and almost comfortable for the lucky few who don't have to be tucked up by ten o clock.'

Lady Val had been completely unaware of the club until tonight and was astonished to hear it stayed open until 4 am. Terry wickedly suggested that Lady Val might become a denizen of this basement lair from now on: a regular on the dancefloor, boogieing on down to the theme from *Shaft*. Such merriment. Terry was *so* bold.

Ann Teresa felt his unrelenting blues fixed on her, penetrating. Did CJ believe in coincidence? Did he care either way? She didn't know yet how matters would be negotiated between them, but knew that somehow they would be.

A couple of hours of sparkling, fabulously meandering Terry-orchestrated table talk slipped by. Fuelled by acceptable champagne, the chatter ping-ponged effortlessly from uproarious laughter at Terry's account of a catastrophically *horrific* velvet collection in Simon Richards – *ça va de soi* that word 'horrific' never appeared in her column – to general enthusisasm for next weekend's long-awaited accession to the EEC. Europeans at last! Des O' joined Terry in brazenly teasing CJ. Wasn't he *thrilled* for an Taoiseach and the Foreign Minister? What a proud moment for Jack and Dr Paddy.

It was time for Ann Teresa to have CJ all to herself. Could he dance? It scarcely mattered, especially on a dance floor the size of a pub pool table. She felt confident that CJ would share Shaw's view of dancing as merely a vertical expression of a horizontal intention. At that very moment a song intro offered Ann Teresa the perfect cue to spring up in full Terry mode. 'Oh! I *love* Marc Bolan. Such a beautiful boy. Gay, surely, and much too *young* for my taste, but still, so very beautiful.' A hand stretched toward CJ. Terry *needed* him to dance with her. Get it on, bang a gong.

On the microscopic dance floor one of his hands clasped hers and she felt the other land confidently on her bottom. As they shimmied and gazed at each other very directly, Ann Teresa decided Terry could take a back seat now. She could reveal a little more of herself. Not the discontented young wife, of course, no one ever got to see *her*, but glimpses of the sweet dirty girl she sensed CJ was keen to pursue. Likewise she hoped he had an inkling what was drawing her to him and it wasn't his callow notion of charm and sophistication, nor even the much talked-about whiff of sulphur. Ann Teresa had detected something else, oozing from way down, deep deep down; a restless Dublin bowsie lurking in his darkest place. A flick knife in a Dior giftbox. Unwrapping that would be, as Terry might say, heartstoppingly thrilling.

It couldn't be 4 am, but it was. The music had stopped and the ugly lights had already replaced the pretty pulsing ones. Where were Tania and Des O' and Geraldine and Lady Val? And almost everyone else?

Normally, Terry herself would have choreographed an extravagantly teasing exit long ago, but Ann Teresa had not been able to tear herself from CJ. That must mean something. His hand almost wrenched a chunk of buttock away as he croaked, 'Come to London with me.'

Six: January 26th

It was an education to watch CJ operate far from his natural habitat: The way the head leaned in to pint-swollen faces, as if determined, despite the band and the buzz, to draw as close as possible to whatever pudden hand had gripped his arm and receive wisdom and spittle in his ear. His smiling, regal salute to Country Flame, when the singer dedicated 'King of the Road' to him. The enthusiastic noises he made and the roguish kiss he planted on the cheek of the quivering, giggling biddy who presented him with an overflowing plate of sandwiches and sausages. Michael, keeping well back, leaning against the bar counter, swallowing warm pints with whiskey chasers, was thoroughly entertained. But it was the speech that revealed what a showstopper CJ could be when required.

His listeners, eager as new-born chicks with beaks open to their mother, were assured that he was one of them: UP for local business, UP for the Republic, UP for the party. There wasn't a syllable any local hack hungry for controversy could quote against him, but the crowd got the message all right. Michael could feel them lap up the nuances, the secret signals. CJ was embracing their Fianna Fáil, red-blooded and rural. Not the Fianna Fáil of fumbling, sell-out Lynchites who were leading them to disaster at the next election, EEC or no EEC.

Michael had hoped for respectful enthusiasm tonight. It went way beyond that. CJ's presence seemed to induce the giddy intoxication of a load of lads touring Soho strip clubs. Markeen, heir-apparent to the seat next time round when Daddy Mark stepped aside, stood grinning in the pelting rain outside Gullane's, a pudgy paw rammed in the passenger window like a horny boyfriend grabbing a last feel.

'Smashin', absolutely smashin', CJ. A memorable night. Lovely hurlin'.'

As Michael pulled away he could see Markeen in the rain-splashed rear view, soaked but still waving. CJ snarled.

'What the fuck was in those sandwiches?'

'Ham.'

'Not the ham, the other ones. Jesus!'

'Calvita, I think. Oh, and sandwich spread.'

'What's sandwich spread?'

CJ stared at the wiper swishing and licked the roof of his mouth. If he hadn't had London to look forward to his mood might have been more dangerous. Keeping Terry to the forefront of his mind had made tonight's menagerie some way bearable, otherwise he'd be telling Liston to remove himself and his lunatic scheme from his sight. He swallowed and grimaced.

'And Guiney is happy enough? That's organised?'

'Don't worry, he's delighted you thought of him. So he should be.'

CJ found it hard to imagine colourless, wordless Gabriel Guiney ever showing delight about anything, other than, perhaps, a big rezoning decision going his way.

'That Kerry hoor knows he wouldn't be wiping his arse with tenners now if it wasn't for you. Guiney Developments would still be knocking up Mickey Mouse kitchen extensions.'

It was pleasing to hear that Guiney was conscious of his debt to CJ. It confirmed the wisdom of his change of plan. Using Guiney's Knightsbridge apartment was a much better idea than the Churchill Hotel. A woman like Terry would appreciate the greater discretion and privacy. It would also be no harm to let her see what favours he could command, what influence he still possessed. CJ still remembered his astonishment when he visited the opulent Wellington Court penthouse, overlooking the Serpentine. He would never ever have suspected the Kerry hoor of such audacious discernment. Liston was of the opinion it was shag-all to do with discernment. He probably hadn't even looked at it before buying.

So Wellington had trumped Churchill and his gilla had sorted it very quickly.

'I told you, people want to help.'

CJ lit up. Swish... swish... swish... He blew smoke at the windscreen wipers and contemplated his weekend in London. Maybe not too much London? Such was the extravagant ambition of the interior design, the space, luxury, atmosphere and grandeur of the views, he and Terry might not want to leave Guiney's penthouse at all. And, from what he recalled, the bed looked like it would take a lot of punishment. Harrods could deliver.

Seven: January 31st

'Can you believe it? When you left yesterday, it was a normal peaceful Sunday. Then a couple of hours later…'

Mags' hug was fierce. Michael realised he should have known that today there would be only one topic of conversation: the thirteen people murdered by paratroopers in Belfast. He could forget about venting his rage at that Jesuit bollocks McCormack and the way he talked down to him, about Matthew, boasting about his 'breakthrough' with him over the last year.

'The days of long silences and dark looks seem to have passed. All things considered this is quite an achievement.'

Especially with such an inadequate father, had been the implication. Somehow Michael had managed to keep a civil tongue in his head, but drove away from the school vowing that the next time he crossed its threshold it would be to take Matthew the hell out of it for good. The question was, what to do with the boy? Did he want a surly teenager around the house? As a man who never took anyone's counsel but his own, Michael had surprised himself when the notion of asking Mags for her opinion took hold. This morning he'd decided to do it. Bad timing.

'Coffee? I called last night but you were engaged for ages, so I gave up.'

Michael just nodded. He'd been engaged all right. As soon as he'd heard news of the killings he'd phoned Wellington Court over and over again. Eventually there was a growl at the other end.

'Yes.'

'It's Michael Liston.'

'What the fuck do you want?'

'Have you seen the news on the telly?'

'We're not here to watch the telly.'

Michael told him what had happened in Derry. A long silence. The suggestion that he book a late flight to Dublin was followed by a longer silence. When CJ eventually spoke, his voice was quiet, but it invited no further discussion.

'I'll be back on the first flight tomorrow.'

Michael hoped he could safely presume that CJ and the woman would travel separately.

'I'll pick you up. And listen, there might be journalists hanging around Heathrow or Dublin, so answer no questions about Derry. Don't get pulled into this, do you hear me? Say it's a matter for the Taoiseach and the Minister for... CJ?'

'I'm listening.'

'This is going to get very bad. I can feel it already. Thirteen dead and it's looking like it was unprovoked. People are already comparing it to Sharpeville. Now we're in agreement, yeah? The North is off-limits. Now more than ever.'

Michael could tell CJ was listening. Really listening. Which was a relief.

He was distracted from his thoughts by Mags holding up the *Irish Times*. What was she saying?

'The front page. Nell's report is astonishing. Have you read it yet?'

Michael shook his head.

'She was there of course, in the thick of it. Listen to this: "Among the thirty arrested was a woman whom I watched protesting to the soldiers. A paratrooper struck her across the face with the butt of his rifle."'

Michael tried to look as shocked as Mags would wish him to be.

'And this: "A young female wearing a white coat with the red cross clearly marked ran into the courtyard waving her arms at the soldiers. I watched her duck and run for cover as a soldier fired on her." I mean, did they just go mad? Could they have been ordered to do this?'

Michael wished he could say, it's the fucking North, Mags, we should be running a mile from the whole quagmire. Let them at it. But he knew that attitude wouldn't go down well right now, not with her pal, Nell, risking life and limb up in the Bogside. Best follow his own advice and say as little as possible. He had enough on his plate making sure this mess didn't jeopardise CJ's long road back. Silence had its dangers, but it was a whole lot better than words in this situation. Words would only come back and bite them in the arse.

Michael realised Mags was waiting for an answer to her question. Except that he couldn't remember what she'd asked.

'Good question. Hard to know.'

Her nod told him he'd got away with it. It wasn't that Michael had no sympathy for the victims. He had plenty, like he had sympathy for the victims in Bangladesh. He just wasn't that interested. Anyway, wading in on this thing was like hopping one-legged down a spiral staircase carrying gelignite.

Mags could see that Michael was so numbed and distressed by the events he was finding it hard to put his feelings into words. She set about making coffee and left him alone to read Nell's front-page story. What an extraordinary writer. An inspiration. How would Mags have reacted had she been trapped in such a dangerous situation? Could she have met a deadline, filed her story, borne witness so coherently? Unlikely. She hadn't even been able to concentrate on her own work this morning.

Mags noticed Michael's surprised look when he heard the kids coming downstairs.

'Oh yeah, I decided to keep them out of school. I thought… well, with their accents, especially Simon. Just today, in case there's any kind of anti-English atmosphere, you know what children can be like –'

'No, spot-on, absolutely the right thing to do.'

It was obvious to Michael that, like himself, the kids weren't that upset about the goings-on in Derry, but were wary of looking too cheerful in front of their mother. He wondered if Mags herself really cared as much as she thought. Wasn't it a fact that her kids being bullied in school mattered more than thirteen dead? That's just the way it was with people only they didn't like admitting it. For the first time he was struck by just how English the kids did sound. Today everything carried meaning and danger, even an accent. In Harry Byrne's last night the place went silent during the news until some para colonel popped up to defend his men's action. As soon as the crowd heard the plummy accent, everything he said was buried under boos and heckles. Michael could well imagine Susan or Simon getting a puck in the schoolyard today. What were those fucking Jesuits saying to Matthew and his pals? No doubt lots of pious praying for forebearance and olog\óning for the innocent victims.

Mags was holding out sheets of paper.

'Would you mind doing me a favour? This piece for *Hibernia*, I was going to spend the morning cleaning it up, but I just haven't been able to focus. See the first sentence. I wrote that Saturday evening.'

"Just at a time when the northern part of the island seems to be sinking further into sectarian turmoil –" I see what you mean.'

'Should I change it?'

'Let me read the whole thing.'

Michael settled himself in the corner armchair.

"– in the north of Dublin a quiet revolution is taking place, proposing how the next generation of Irish children might be educated to take best advantage of the complex interplay between sincere religious belief and secular ethical opinion now emerging in the Republic. A small Protestant fee-paying boys' school and a Protestant all-girls' school are merging to become Ireland's first multi-denominational, co-educational State-funded school. Mount Temple Comprehensive will open its gates next September to children of all religions and none.

"When I met the headmaster last week I could see that, mildly spoken though this late middle-aged educator was, he was the philosophical driving force behind this radical initiative –"

Michael looked up, intending to ask something, but he was surprised into silence at the scene before him. There was nothing strange or special happening: Mags and her kids sitting at the table, slurping and munching and talking quietly about this and that. But somehow he had never before felt just how casually, messily, satisfying it was. Family life. Mags caught his eye.

'Well?'

'Oh, sorry. Not finished yet. This school –'

'It's actually only about ten minutes' walk from your house.'

'And no priests or nuns?'

'Not a cassock or wimple in sight.'

'So, it'll be just sex and drugs and failing their exams.'

'Oh, inevitable. Goes without saying.'

Michael smiled and quickly read the rest of the article… openly liberal, more secularised model of education… opening next September… daring experiment.'

Strange. It was as if the question Michael had come to ask had been answered, even though he hadn't had a chance to ask it.

'Well?' Mags looked anxious.

'Hm? It's great. Nothing wrong with that all. I wouldn't change a thing.'

'Really?'

Sometime in the next few days he would find the right moment to ask Mags if she thought this Mount Temple place would suit Matthew.

Eight: June 12th

After her terrible date on Saturday night it was a relief for Marian to go into work on Monday. She loved her job anyway. Mr Harrington's suits never fitted him properly and the few stray hairs he combed across his bald dome looked silly, but he had a hearty laugh and he was always polite. It felt especially calming this morning to hear his low, slightly halting voice dictate the day's letters. Marian knew his style so well now, with the something inst, or the something ult and the recurring legal phrases – 'motion for discovery', 'without prejudice', 'ex parte proceeding' – that she had developed her own shorter shorthand, signs she'd usually finished writing by the time Mr Harrington had spoken the first syllable of the familiar phrase.

'That should ke-keep you going for the ah, the ah, the rest of the morning Mars, even at the terrifying speed you–you–you type.'

It was nice to feel appreciated. She even liked him calling her 'Mars', though no one else ever called her that.

Two men came in. The one who was smoking looked familiar and, as soon as he opened his mouth, Marian knew she'd heard the voice before, but still couldn't remember who he was. Long harsh nasal vowel sounds made him sound swanky, but the local accent was still strong. Marian definitely didn't know the other man at all, a bulky fellow in a heavy overcoat who sat on a chair near the door and didn't say a word. Mr Harrington stuck his head out his office door.

'Well Go-Go-God between us and and and and all harm. We're privileged, Minister.'

Marian could have kicked herself for being so slow. It was the

Minister for Justice. She knew him from the telly and the papers. His face had been on posters everywhere during the by-election he won after his uncle, who'd been Minister for Education, dropped dead suddenly from a heart attack. Marian had been too young to vote that time but everyone said the nephew wasn't a patch on the uncle, who'd brought in free education. He shook hands with Mr Harrington and called him Dan. It was obvious how thrilled he was to see him as he ushered him into his office, saying they were not to be disturbed, no matter what. Marian could take her lunch break as soon as the batch of letters was ready for signing.

The bulky man hadn't even been introduced. It felt odd typing with him sitting in the corner, staring ahead and smoking. He didn't glance at a paper or a magazine. Marian was relieved to finish the last letter and get her coat, sandwich and flask of tea. Should she ask if he wanted her to bring anything back? In the end she just smiled and said bye. He barely nodded.

It was only when Marian got out onto the street and saw another large man in an overcoat leaning against a black Mercedes in front of the office that she understood. How stupid of her! Special Branch. The Minister's bodyguards. On account of the North and these new laws he was bringing in against the IRA. Were the men armed? Was that why they looked so bulky? Now she wanted to go back and get a closer look at the other one. The man leaning against the car was definitely friendlier. He winked and said how're ya doin', in a Dublin accent. She'd never been face to face with an armed policeman before. Marian muttered 'grand' and hurried on along Davis Street. Wait till Stephen heard about this – except she wouldn't be telling Stephen. After Saturday night she had no intention of talking to him again.

It still made her mad thinking about it. They'd often gone to a picture that one of them didn't like as much as the other, but they'd never had a stupid row about it before. If *The Last Picture Show* wasn't his kind of thing that was fine, but he hadn't even given it a chance and went out of his way to spoil it for Marian, behaving like a big child, shifting in his seat and, at one stage, getting up and going out to the toilet or somewhere and not coming back for ages. Also not putting his arm around her.

Marian was crossing the road to the People's Park when she saw a postman cycling towards her. He waved. Marian knew Stephen's delivery round was in Rathbane and Janesboro. What was he doing here in the middle of town? And in a big hurry by the look of it.

'Hi.'

All smiles now. Not like Saturday night when they'd come out of the pictures. Surly silence as they'd walked towards his precious motorbike. Marian had said she didn't need a lift, the bus would be fine and he'd just said yeah, grand.

So what now? It was obvious that he'd cycled up this way deliberately, hoping to catch her coming out of the office on her lunch break.

'You going to the park?'

They were standing at the entrance, where did he think she was going? He got off his bike and walked alongside her.

'What kind of sandwich have you?'

Of all the stupid things to ask. Marian nearly didn't bother to answer, but she said 'salad' and then nothing more. They kept walking until she picked a bench and sat down. He stood, holding on to his bike, looking gawky. She poured some tea from the flask, wishing he'd either say something proper or go away. She avoided his eyes, knowing he'd have that lost sheep look and she didn't want to start feeling sorry for him.

'Can I sit down?'

'You can do what you like.'

He leant his bike carefully against the end of the bench and sat. Marian reluctantly started eating her salad sandwich.

'So.'

Was that it? Nothing more to say? She could feel his eyes on her. How was she supposed to enjoy her lunch like this?

'You see, it was in my head that we were... I thought... I was really looking forward to seeing *Dirty Harry*. Like, everyone was going to it.'

'That's why we couldn't get in.'

'There was a few seats left.'

'We'd have been stuck at the front.'

'I wouldn't have minded.'

'Well I did.'

'I know.'

Well.'

'I know. I'm just saying I wouldn't have minded.'

'Well you could have gone in on your own if you wanted and I could have gone to *The Last Picture Show* on my own.'

'Ah no, Jesus, Marian, We were out on a date.'

'So, you preferred to stay and spoil the picture on me.'

'I didn't mean to –'

'Yes you did.'

'I didn't, I swear.'

'Well you spoiled it whether you meant to or not.'

'It's just… it was in black and white and I kept thinking about *Dirty Harry*.'

This was hopeless. Marian finished the sandwich she hadn't enjoyed and didn't feel like more tea. Then she heard a catch in Stephen's voice.

'I didn't mean to, I swear I didn't fuckin' mean to. Don't call it off with me, please Marian. Please don't.'

Was he going to burst out crying? That was the last thing she wanted. Here in the park? As soon as her hand touched his shoulder he fell against her, kissing her neck.

'We can go see *The Last Picture Show* again if you like. I'll never do anything like that again. I promise I won't.'

'Okay, it's all right Stephen.'

Although surprised at the effect of her disapproval, even unsettled a little, Marian liked the way he was holding onto her so needily. He calmed down in her arms, smiled and drank some of her tea. She told him about the Special Branch men and he was goggle-eyed, all up for going round to the office for a gawk, but by the time they got there the Mercedes was gone.

*

Through the passenger window, Mags tried to read the body language as Michael and his son drifted further away along the beach. So far there had been nothing that signalled anything seismic between them. It wouldn't surprise her if Michael's nerve failed even now, given that he'd let months go by since confiding his big secret to Mags: his wife had died giving birth to Matthew in June 1959 and he had never told the boy this fact. On the face of it not a hugely significant dilemma apart from the embarrassment of not having dealt with it years ago. But, after an uneasy silence, Michael had revealed a complicating factor. Mags guessed that he had never spoken these words to anyone before. Back in 1959 he'd had enough of his wife, he hated her and was arranging and to get the hell out, escape to Dublin, but this pregnancy out of the blue had put the kibosh on the plan. Mags wondered about the way he said out of the blue. Was there some suspicion that Matthew might not be his? The dark momentum of his narrative had stopped her from enquiring. He'd said that, in all honesty, her unexpected death would have been a release to him, if it hadn't been for the sting in the tail. A new-born child. She'd snared him, as if with some devious malignant bequest. Did Mags understand at all how the twisted history with the mother, had complicated his attitude to the boy?

She understood it too clearly, and afterwards felt guilty of a certain hypocrisy in having heard this uneasy outpouring of a long-suppressed stone in the heart without sharing the parallel in her own history. The tragic tale of a death in childbirth was not Michael's true secret. It was this other most private revelation: the silent hate coursing through him, unsated by the death of the object of that hate. It had surged on, spilling over onto the head of an innocent child. It had remained unspoken for thirteen years. His confession stirred something in Mags: her own secret was also unspoken, even in the affirming, sharing environment of her consciousness-raising group. So many times she had gone over the history of her marriage and the circumstances of her flight, as candidly and self-critically as anyone could expect – except for the one important detail she left out.

She was always absolutely clear – humorously so – about how delighted twenty-one-year-old Margaret Perry had been to marry this confident well-spoken young dentist. What a catch! She was always unequivocal in describing the joy of their first years together and the rapture of Susan's birth. And when in November 1958 Marcus announced that he had the opportunity to buy a dental practice in Marlborough in Wiltshire and they would be leaving Ireland very soon, she never pretended that she'd baulked or thought it remotely strange that he hadn't bothered to discuss it with her.

Oh the sighs and nods of recognition from the group at the way it was in the fifties. That's how it still is for some, one of the women had muttered.

Marcus had just informed her, there's no future here, and that was that. Off they went. And she'd never deny that she really loved Marlborough at first. It was like a never-ending honeymoon in this perfect little English town with its broad welcoming high street, thatched houses and elegant town hall. And the boys from the college of course, polite little angels in grey blazers and caps. Their house was the stuff of fantasy, a listed detached cottage with an idyllic walled garden. Then in 1961, Simon was born.

Simon. It was only through the consciousness-raising sessions that Mags had slowly begun to understand the true significance of the naming of her son. Mags had wanted to call him Seamus, after her dad, but Marcus wouldn't have it. He said Seamus Breslin sounded like someone who worked on a building site. He insisted on Simon. It hadn't occurred to Mags at the time that, even though she liked the name Susan, that had been Marcus' suggestion too.

Controlling, her feminist friends pounced, the man wanted to control you.

Not really. The truth, as Mags had eventually begun to understand it, was simpler, more innocent perhaps and more pathetic too: Marcus loved England and needed to feel English. He preferred the sound of Simon or Susan to Seamus or Shelagh. He never altered his own accent, he was much too intelligent and self-aware to do that, but he acquired Englishisms. From quite early on he'd say 'darling' in public, just a little too often. The sitting-room was the drawing-room. Lots of things were 'charming'. His love of cricket was genuine, but his overuse of cricketing terms in casual conversation: 'state of play', 'hit for six', 'sticky wicket', 'back foot', began to sound embarrassing to Mags' ears. Most infuriating however was his obsession with sending Simon to Marlborough College.

That breakfast conversation. He had wanted to discuss the state of play. In particular, significant household economies they would need to consider in order to ensure that they wouldn't be caught on the back foot when the time came to pay Simon's fees at Marlborough. He spoke as if there had been some prior discussion about this. Susan's educational future didn't rate a mention. Mags subsequently recognised that this incident marked the beginning of a very slow, reluctant journey towards an uncomfortable truth: she didn't like her husband. It didn't help to remind herself over and over of his qualities: he could be affectionate, he rarely showed anger, he was a decent father (although definitely better with Simon) and a fine dentist. It proved impossible to disown her hardening, albeit shameful opinion that her husband was a dull, occasionally rather petty little snob. She had married the wrong man, but was stuck with it. Back then, divorce had never entered her head. Even if it had, she would have presumed that disliking your husband hardly constituted a valid ground, even in Godless England. The crazy truth, as she subsequently protested to her friends, was that Marcus' betrayal had been a lucky break.

No! Don't even think of blaming yourself. The bastard. To be at it downstairs while you were in your sick bed!

But Mags wasn't blaming herself. At least not for that.

How practiced she'd become at telling her story without mentioning the vital detail. The casual question Dr Turner had asked on the sleety ugly November day when – because of Marcus' solicitous insistence – he had made a house call to diagnose Mags' symptoms of fever and exhaustion. Dr Turner had decided it was a touch of flu. 'Oh and was Mrs Breslin aware that she was pregnant?'

However many times she'd thought about the moment, Mags still could not believe how *happily* surprised she'd managed to sound in reply, how somehow she'd made her smile bashful as she asked the good doctor would he mind allowing her the pleasure of revealing the news to her husband? Oh, how grateful she'd been at that moment for bourgeois village delicacy. Dr Turner's smiling nod had assured her he wouldn't dream of spoiling such a happily intimate moment for a couple, although when he called Marcus in and explained that Mrs Breslin could do with a week of absolute rest and sleep, he couldn't resist a little sly reference: 'But perhaps this little cloud will have a very special silver lining, Mr Breslin.'

Mags had wanted to scream like a fishwife at him, Shut up, you stupid bastard! Get out! How seriously Marcus had taken her need for absolute rest. His secretary's daughter had just finished university and was at a loose end, so he arranged for her to hold the fort, do the shopping, look after the children, even bring her meals and medicine. The reality was that Mags had no desire to get better. The secret she was keeping was in danger of overwhelming her. She had no idea that the sweet-voiced graduate with perfect teeth would, in her way, be an angel of rescue.

Five years on, the details of what she now thought of as the night of her awakening were as clear and immediate as images in a photo album: The Angel of Rescue handing her the pills, picking up the tray, 'Goodnight Mrs Breslin'. Then, waking to find the pills still clutched in her hands, the room pitch black. The muggy, distracted feeling. Then the sound. The little sound that changed her world.

Now, staring out the passenger window, Mags shivered at the memory. Far down the beach, Father and son had become two tiny black tufts. It was impossible to tell anymore if they were moving away or standing still, or returning. What was it about the female cry she'd heard that night that had told her instantly, even in the disorientating darkness, that it wasn't a scream of pain, nor a shriek of fright, but a cry of pleasure? A moment of climax. A curious and absolute silence had followed. She'd turned on the bedside lamp to see the clock. It was precisely twelve minutes after nine. November 24th 1967. The moment everything changed. Almost literally it had been like learning to walk again, understanding the world all over again: crawling from the bed and dragging herself to the top of the stairs; the closed door of Marcus' beloved drawing room; feeling like her childhood self, in Dublin, eavesdropping on a grown-ups' party, wondering what amazing adult secrets she might overhear; the softest murmuring, so intimate; the door opening and Marcus emerging; a lady's' shoe visible on a corner of rug; imagining the smiling, toothsome Angel of Rescue curled up on the sofa; Marcus returning with a bottle of wine and two glasses; the whispered 'Casa San Georgio' in a jokey Italian accent; the drawing-room door quietly nudged shut.

In Mags' memory the fever began to leave her from that moment. Certainly she was up and about in days, planning her escape. On the first morning of the children's Christmas holidays, as soon as Marcus left for work, she'd packed quickly, ordered a taxi and told the children about the great surprise. A visit to Ireland to wish Granny Perry Happy Christmas. By lunchtime they were in London, with her old school pal, Noreen Flannery, who had offered to put them up in her tiny flat overnight. She did that and much, much more. Five years on Mags' greatest guilt was that she still had not found the courage to tell others about Noreen's extraordinary, unquestioning support. The following morning she'd taken the children to Hamley's as a Christmas treat, so that Mags could keep her appointment at the clinic.

The tiny black tufts on the beach were growing larger and assuming human form again. Mags hadn't noticed before that father and son were about the same height, although Michael's lean purposeful stride emphasised the delicacy of Matthew's movements and gestures: the uncertainty of adolescence. Well, at least no punches had been thrown: no faces slapped: no one had stalked off. And they were talking. Heads turned and mouths moved, but absolutely nothing in either expression told her what the mood might be. Mags suddenly recognised a revealing similarity. They both kept their treasure buried deep.

It was embarrassing to Mags how hard she found it to speak about her abortion, especially when her feelings were so clear, then and since. But that was precisely her difficulty, because such clarity of feeling seemed neither allowable nor acceptable, even for many of those who supported the right to choose. It was considered too selfish somehow, too cold. Even a supportive and reassuring listener required talk of trauma, pain of loss, and at least *something* about guilt. Mags knew there had to be women who felt just as she did, if only they could recognise each other and find the courage to share.

So it wasn't hard for her to empathise with Michael's dark internal struggle. His revelation was far less shocking to her than he thought. She'd been happy to say yes when he'd asked her to be with him when he finally got around to telling Matthew. It was another example of the odd way she and Michael seemed to be drifting closer. Could this be how actual love happened, by minute increments, happy accidents, apparently insignificant choices? All nudging something along. Whereas, with she and Marcus, the momentum of their relationship had continually been the other way, petulant salty waves, scouring away at their limestone marriage.

Smiling, Mags got out of the car to welcome them back and offer Matthew the option of sitting in the front seat with his dad.

No thanks. No, really, he liked it in the back. Yes, absolutely sure.

The Lady was killing herself trying to be nice. Matthew knew she'd be dying to know how the Big Chat went, but couldn't ask directly of course. If she only knew what he'd really thought when the pair of them turned up at the school to collect him. Oh shit, why was she here? And his father all jumpy and then, out of nowhere, this idea of a sandwich at Jack White's and a walk on the strand because it was such a lovely day, which it wasn't really.

'Well, he's delighted about changing schools, aren't you?'

Seeing his father with a big wide grin was the freakiest thing, but the Lady's smile really fitted her. She was beautiful like an actress. It was obvious that the two adults were really anxious for this to be all happy, which felt strange because he'd got used to no one caring much about him. Now Matthew had this pair – strangers basically – going out of their way to please him. Grinning at him.

'Yes, I'm looking forward to it.'

And he was. That had been the first surprise. Walking along the strand listening to his dad trying desperately to bring the conversation that wasn't a conversation round to something, Matthew had thought, Just say it, I know what it is. Say you're going to marry her, just say that. Don't go all American: 'You're getting a new mom and a new brother and sister.' Don't pretend it's the *Brady Bunch*. So it was discombobulating when, instead, his father started talking about some school. Near home he said. Home? A day school, a comprehensive, mixed religion, boys and girls together. Was there such a place? Would he prefer to go to a school like that instead, his father inquired. Live back home in Dublin? Who was this man asking him these things? Matthew thought of Oliver Twist meeting Mr Brownlow. But even as he answered, saying yes he'd like that, Matthew smelled a rat. Of course! This was the lead up to the *Brady Bunch* bit. Her kids would be going to the same school, he'd bet.

'Did your dad tell you that it's only become a comprehensive this year?

'Oh. No, I forgot.'

'Susan and Simon are really jealous actually, but it's much too far to travel every day from Ranelagh to Clontarf, so they'll just have to put up with where they are.'

Such an intelligent lady. It was as if she understood that he needed to be reassured that nothing else was changing. He'd never wanted her hugs before, but now he wouldn't mind being held close to her. She really was beautiful. How had his father bagged her? Was she Nancy? But then wouldn't that make him Fagin or Bill Sykes, not Mr Brownlow. Maybe he was all three.

'Ah slow down now. It's not sorted yet by any manner of means. You have to meet the headmaster. Don't go assuming it's all sorted.'

Yeah, yeah, yeah, Matthew thought. However confused his feelings were about his father, he knew one thing for sure: he could fix things. If he wanted Matthew to go to Mount Temple Comprehensive then it would happen, simple.

Even though he'd guessed wrong about them getting married, he'd been right that the little walk on the strand wasn't really about the brilliant new school. That was the cover for the something else his father was nervous about, like the joke on *Rowan and Martin's Laugh-In* that always started, I have some good news and some bad news. But then Matthew got it all wrong again during that mad few minutes when his father had started muttering about being thirteen soon and there was something he should know about his mother. Matthew had immediately thought that there was going to be a big revelation that his mother was alive and it was the Lady, which was off the wall of course because he'd seen photos of his mother and she looked nothing like her.

Her. She. The Lady. Mags. Mags.

Why was it so hard? The very first time they met she'd said, I'm Mags. When he was told Susan Breslin and Simon Breslin he thought of her as Mrs Breslin, but then he found out that she was Perry because she left her husband, so then he wasn't sure how to think of her because Mrs Perry was wrong and Miss Perry didn't sound right either, but it was still hard to call someone old he hardly knew by her first name.

Matthew looked at his father, now sitting back with one relaxed hand on the wheel, and wondered, just as he had half an hour ago, why it had been so hard for him to say what at last he had said. His mother had died while giving birth to Matthew. It was sad, tragic even, like in a book. Matthew had read that things like that happened a lot in the past didn't they? His father had said yes to that, really eagerly. Yes, yes, exactly yes, especially back in the fifties, he'd said. The fifties. People always said *the fifties* like it was something scary from Dickens' time, but Matthew had been born in 1959, which meant he'd been alive in three decades even though he was barely thirteen. Weird. So, that was it. The big bad news. Matthew used to imagine how his mother died, but hadn't done so in a long while. Now at least he knew. Had she seen him alive at all, even for a few seconds? Not much point in asking his father that. He probably didn't know, and anyway, he'd just make up something that sounded nice.

After dinner in Ranelagh, when Mags' kids took the boy upstairs to play records, Michael finally got to give the blow-by-blow on how surprisingly well it had gone. The boy had taken it in his stride. Asked a few questions all right, like, didn't that happen a lot in the old days and did he miss her a lot? To which Michael had said – wisely enough he thought, considering it was spur of the moment – that it was a long time ago and he felt a lot different now to the way he'd felt back then. All in all the boy had dealt with it in a very grown-up way, which Michael took to mean he'd been correct to wait until this time to tell him. However, later, on the journey home – silent, apart from Matthew turning the tuning knob on the radio from station to station –there was a little sting. It must have been in the boy's head for a while.

'Were you ever… did you ever… blame me?'

'Blame you for what?'

'Well, even though it happened a lot back then, did you ever think… you know because someone you loved had died that way. Didn't you ever think it was my fault?'

Michael stopped himself from laughing out loud, and had to

concentrate hard to keep a suitably grave expression on his face as he reassured his son that no, no, no, no matter what his feelings were for Matthew's mother, there was no question of him blaming Matthew. It never ever occurred to him because there was nothing to blame him for. He was to put that out of his head. Seriously now.

Michael was relieved that the boy appeared to be satisfied with the sincerity of the answer.

Nine: September 5th

After his shower, Matthew dried his hair and tried it with a centre parting the way Timothy Agnew had it. It didn't look as good, but maybe that was because his hair wasn't long enough yet. Now that he had seen what boys got away with in Mount·Temple, he'd let it grow much longer and try the centre parting then. Being in class with girls, mingling with them in the yard, was so strange at first. He wondered why they seemed to find it much easier to talk to him then he to them? During break on the first day, a girl who said her name was Gillian had smiled at Matthew and said if he wanted to hang around with her and her friends over by the tennis courts he wasn't to feel shy. The girls told him that it was also strange for them to have boys around because they used to be at the girls school, Bertrand and Rutland, that had become part of this new comprehensive.

'We're not used to exotic creatures like you,' a girl called Trudie said, and she wasn't making fun of him. Exotic? The way she sat on the grass made her miniskirt seem even skimpier and her legs stretched golden and smooth. He felt her eyes on him a couple of times after that, but he hadn't the nerve to return her look.

By the end of the second day Matthew pronounced Mount Temple *perfecto*. No patrolling priests; girls and boys roaming together as if someone had forgotten to round them up, separate them, fix their hair and encase them in uniform. The place itself was a kind of construction site with the new school building across the tarmac yard still unfinished. But one thing was becoming very clear to him: he needed to buy more interesting clothes. It was only when he overheard some of the girls gushing about how gorgeous Toby Rennicks looked in his velvet waist-jacket and Wranglers

112 • GERARD STEMBRIDGE

that he realised how important these things were. Sure enough it didn't take him long to spot Toby. He stood out like the baby-faced one in a hairy rock group. Matthew began to notice that lots of the boys had pretty neat gear. He wondered how much Wranglers cost.

At assembly, the headmaster, Mr Brooks, said that yesterday's tragic events in Munich were a grim reminder of the awful consequences of sectarian hatred. After a special prayer in memory of the dead athletes, he said today should be a day for quiet reflection, so after roll call and the first period, they could, calmly, perhaps even thoughtfully, go home. Alternatively, the Christian Union was hosting a special all-morning meeting for prayers and reflection, and all students were welcome to attend.

Matthew headed for home after the first period, although he felt the tiniest bit guilty because yesterday he had joked about the siege. How was he to know then that it would end so violently? He'd said it was a pity the terrorists hadn't taken *all* the athletes hostage, because then they'd have to cancel the Olympics and there might be something worth watching on TV again. Trudie Marsh and Robert Drew both thought it was funny and Robert, who was crazy about comedy, started talking to Matthew about Spike Milligan and couldn't believe that he had never read any of his books. He said they were all hilarious, but *Puckoon* was the funniest ever and Matthew would have to read it.

Now Matthew heard a voice behind shouting his name. Robert Drew was running towards him waving a book. He had brought *Puckoon* in for him. Was he not going to the Christian Union meeting? Robert looked a bit sad when Matthew said no, but then he kept walking with him down Malahide road, talking about *Puckoon*. Matthew had to stop him giving away the best bits, so then Robert told him about other Spike Milligan books, walking with him all the way along the seafront saying things like, 'oh this is brilliant' and 'yeah, and then there was a fantastic bit' and 'wait 'til you hear this, this is epic', laughing to himself all the time and driving Matthew crazy. As he crossed the road near his house, Robert was still tagging along. Did he intend hanging around all day telling him hilarious things?

This might have been why, when he saw his dad's car pulling out, instinctively he waved. His dad rolled down the window looking surprised. Matthew explained about the day off. His dad said, oh, then asked if he wanted to come to Castlebar with him.

The last thing Michael expected was that the boy would say good luck to his pal and jump in. He'd lobbed out the invitation purely because he was caught on the hop when he saw him. What now? What was he going to do with him in Castlebar? Well, he'd just have to amuse himself. Michael would have enough on his plate keeping CJ focused. From what he knew of this school-master fellah who had his eye on the Mayo seat, he'd demand a serious amount of arse-licking before he'd pledge himself to CJ's cause.

Michael was relieved to see the boy pull some book from his pocket shortly after they took off. Grand. Keep him occupied. Less than a minute later he heard a little laugh. Then another. And another. Funny book, obviously. Every half minute or so there seemed to be another fit of giggles. It was peculiar listening to his son laugh. An unfamiliar sound.

'I'm glad you're enjoying yourself anyway.'

The dark head didn't lift from the book. Michael spoke louder.

'Is it some class of a comic thing?'

'Yeah. It's hilarious.'

'I kinda got a clue from the odd little chuckle I heard out of you.'

Had he ever read a book that made him laugh? Not intentionally. The rest of the long journey to the west passed in silence apart from regular fits of the giggles from the boy.

Matthew didn't notice the car had stopped until he heard his father say they'd arrived. He looked up from page 120, where it was night and a bunch of characters were creeping about Puckoon graveyard. In Castlebar, it was getting darker and they were in a huge crowded car park at the back of a building, from which jutted an enormous single-storey concrete extension. Matthew said he'd stay reading for a while if that was all right. His father said grand and clicked on the light. He'd be in the new function room.

Matthew, almost sick from laughing, finally forced himself to close the book when the Milligan character and his pals and the two ragged-arsed IRA men had each dug up the wrong coffin and brought them to the wrong side of the border. He was so near the end it was tempting to go on, but he was determined to have the special pleasure of finishing the book at home in his bed. He left the car and went into the huge, ugly function room.

It was packed and to Matthew, feeling a bit high on Spike, everyone seemed like a mad comic character. Men had squeezed ballooning bodies into shiny undersized suits, but he imagined that beneath the glam surface clung the same old scarred and tattered underwear. Long tables sagged dangerously under the weight of pints, as did the bellies of most of the men. The bar that ran the length of the function room seemed a living, breathing, heaving creature with hundreds of tentacles twitching and shivering in the air, as pound notes were waved and pints were pinballed. All drink was held aloft either in some kind of sacramental devotion or just to keep the precious liquid safe from the bumping of belly on belly below. Every blowfish head that Matthew saw seemed to have a tilted pint soldered to its lips. If the livers of these men could talk they would lodge formal complaints with the authorities, alleging cruel and unusual punishment.

A banner behind the band proclaimed

JOHN JOE FAHY'S
RAMBLIN' MEN

One of the band told the crowd, 'Now a quickstep: John Joe will sing "The Race is On".' But, far from stepping quick, the man-dancers scarcely moved at all – apart from the involuntary wobbles of their protruding bellies. Only their hands seemed lithe and athletic, swooping and swirling, jerking the girl-dancers towards them, then nudging them away again, fluttering high above their heads and twirling them round and round and round. The girl-dancers responded instantly to every flick of a finger, leaping out and sliding in, wriggling and spinning, madly grinning throughout. Most of them had dresses cut so low and raised so high they resembled party jellies with bright ribbons wrapped round, their chests bouncing above and their thighs quivering below.

Matthew figured that in the shiver and shake of this delirious knees-up no one would notice him. He was a dark, willowy sprite, moving invisibly among them. If only he had the power, like Spike's narrator Milligan, to make these jiving muckers do even madder things… Although he suspected that, if he did have such a power, his comic imagination mightn't be as inventive as Spike's.

In a corner near the stage, his father's boss looked tiny next to an impossibly tall man. Next to them Matthew saw his father lurk, a still dark presence, the shadow of a statue. His virtual invisibility contrasted with the ostentatious presence of the impossibly tall man. Matthew tried to think of the kind of comedy name Spike would give this creature if he had created him; Theophilius Pole, something like that. He would probably be married to an abject wife who was the butt of his neverending sarcasms. Spike would have great fun with the fellow's extraordinary smile. It was not, as smiles should be, either welcoming, warm, or affectionate, but neither was it a villainous smile. It was more a peculiar arrangement of facial muscles creating a portrait of concentrated self-delight, as if he had a hand thrust down his trousers and was secretly pleasuring himself. Undoubtedly Spike would have climbed inside his head and gleefully revealed the contented contents.

'Look at me, the fine mane of hair on me swept across me head like a great Atlantic wave, the charming eyes of me, the twinkling teeth of me, the majestic Croagh Patrick height of me, towering over the lot of you. Where would you find the like of me? Look at me, the fine mane of hair on me...'

But for all the huge height of him and the smile of him and the daring creamy-white casual suit of him, Matthew knew the man he was calling Theophilius Pole wasn't much more than a passing figure of fun, a mucker like the rest of the crowd, only taller. The little man next to him however was something else again. His father's boss was like a different species. It had nothing to do with how tiny he was, nor that his shirt and tie were elegant and his suit fitted perfectly, although these were strikingly unusual features in that function room. The real difference was in his eyes. Matthew had noticed all kinds of eyes as he meandered round: wild eyes, eager eyes, bulging eyes, bloodshot eyes, roguish eyes, misty eyes and, in the case of Theophilius Pole, squinting self-regarding eyes. But the eyes of his father's boss showed none of the simple laughable human frailty that was so obvious in others. These eyes swept the room unblinking. An eagle surveying prey. Even Spike would have struggled to find anything funny to write about them. The puzzle for Matthew was why his father's boss would want to be in such an alien place at all.

When the quickstep ended, Theophilius Pole escorted his father's boss to the stage and breathed close to the microphone.

'Friends, party colleagues, the moment you've all been waiting for –'

His tongue appeared and hovered, as if in search of something gorgeous to lick. Himself, presumably, top of the list.

'– A returning hero, a man with Mayo blood coursing through his veins –'

Whoops and cheers and yaroos. Matthew was sure he heard shouts of 'Good man, P!' Wouldn't it be funny if the impossibly tall man really was called Pole?

'As Yeats once said, a great man undone. A man we all want to see back where he belongs, back on the top of the political tree, dining at the top table!'

His father's boss responded to the wolf-like howling of his name and stepped up to the microphone.

'It's good to be home.'

With his first calmly-spoken line he raised the roof. Behind him, Matthew could see P applauding dementedly, his smile now stretched so far it looked like he was achieving ecstatic climax. His father's boss raised a hand like a Roman Emperor quelling the rabble.

'It is my privilege to speak to you tonight, because you are part of a great National movement. Proud Mayomen, Proud Irishmen and, above all, proud partymen!

A pimply lump of a lad in a stained white shirt passed in front of Matthew carrying a tray with whiskey and a bottle of Mirinda. He offered it humbly to his father who took the whiskey and flicked a finger towards Matthew. Only now did the pimply lump look in his direction and hold the tray towards him with a pudgy smirk of contempt. Rumbled, Matthew picked up his Mirinda, no longer a dark willowy sprite, no longer the all-seeing narrator of an outlandish comic interlude, just a poncy city boy out in the sticks, out of his depth. Why was it his father's boss could bamboozle a whole function room full of locals, and he couldn't fool this creature who'd never appreciate Spike Milligan's humour.

The hooley in Castlebar no longer seemed as funny as *Puckoon*.

Much later, in the silence and the darkness of the journey home, Matthew kept thinking about the last part of the night, when he'd finished his nancy-boy's drink and just wanted to get back to the car and speed home, but had to stay watching his father's boss being rattled about in a throng of hand-squeezers and cheek-kissers and back-thumpers. The man was so tiny, he was actually swallowed up inside them until finally his father had reached in, found him and managed to prise him free.

Matthew had, on and off over his young life, wondered what it was his father actually did. Now that he had seen him at work, it only made the mystery greater.

1973

Ten: January 12th

The gap between 200 and 210 metres on his transistor was very small, so Francis turned the dial really slowly. Crackle… crackle… crackle… Then suddenly music, very clear. Andrew Liddy had told him that Radio Luxembourg was 208 on the medium wave band and the needle was nearly at 210 so this must be it. The DJ started talking over the last part of the song.

'Yeah, yeah, yeah! The Wizzard himself, Roy Wood, and this is your royal ruler, Tony Prince, here in the palace of peachy platters where nothing else matters. Luxembourg rocks Britain!'

He'd found it. Then he heard a chorus sing.

'Fabulous 208! Powerplay!'

'I'm no twit, I know a hit, and this is it. Our Powerplay this week, ELO, The Electric Light Orchestra… Oh! You hear that, Beethoven? Roll over baby, roll over!'

Andrew Liddy had told him that Radio Luxemburg played pop music all the time and it didn't close down until three in the morning. Francis couldn't understand why he'd never heard about it before. After the Christmas holidays loads of his classmates were suddenly talking about pop music and all the records they'd got as presents. It hadn't even occurred to Francis to ask for any. Some of the boys had started going to a disco on Sunday afternoon in the Royal George. They said there were loads of girls from Laurel Hill and the Salesians and even Villiers, the Protestant school. Francis decided he'd better buy some records. A single would cost nearly all his fifty pence pocket money, but if he found Radio Luxemburg and listened to it while he did his eker in the front room, then surely he'd hear at least one record that he'd really like to buy.

$2x^2+5x+3=0$... The music didn't distract him from his quadratic equations, but Tony Prince's stupid rhymes and tinny voice did.

'Your royal ruler, I wouldn't fool ya, nothing could be cooler, stay in, stay on!'

The next DJ, Dave Christian, didn't sound so annoying. Francis found it easier to work and listen. While he was memorising the four main consequences of the Diet of Worms, he noticed that his head had started nodding with the beat of whatever was playing. Next thing he was up and rocking round the room. He couldn't make out the words properly but it didn't matter, the song just made him want to dance.

'It's high in the charts and it might go even higher. Status Quo! Riding on their "Paper Plane".'

Francis wrote down the name of the song and the band. Dave Christian played more songs that he really liked. 'Block Buster' by The Sweet was great and so was 'Solid Gold Easy Action' by T Rex and 'Gudbye to Jane' by Slade. His list was getting long. 'Block Buster' started again. At least, the intro sounded just like it, but then the singer began and it was a completely different song: a much weirder one. His voice had a kind of a sneer in it, more like chanting than singing. His dad would say he wasn't a proper singer at all. The beat of the music was angry and every so often the guitar or something made a sound like a rattle snake. Francis couldn't concentrate on the Irish poem he had to learn because he kept trying to figure out the freaky lyrics.

Tránóinín beag déanach... Strung out on what? Ate what? Was it razors?... *I lúib na coille craobhaí is*... Poor little greenie? or was it greedy? What did that mean?... *Bhí an chuach is an lon is an chéirseach*... Smiles like a reptile was a brilliant simile... *Is i mbun is i mbarr gach béarsa*... Making underwear out of dead hair, yeugh!...*Go mBeidh Éire fós ag Cáit Ní Dhuibhir.*

The song sounded creepy and dirty in a way Francis didn't understand, but he knew he had to hear it again to figure it out better. Dave Christian said 'The Jean Genie' was the first single from David Bowie's new album. Francis wrote it down. That was the record he was going to buy, definitely. His mam stuck her head in the door and asked how could he learn anything with that noise blaring, but when he said it was easy, did she want to test him on his Irish poetry, she said, 'Oh go on, I believe you, but turn it down a bit at least, the whole house can hear it.' Synecdoche.

Bob Stewart was the next presenter. His voice was deep and calm. Francis finished his Latin translation. All he had left now was to learn his English poetry.

There is sweet music here that softer falls
Than petals from blown roses on the grass.

In class today, Mr Cronin had said 'yes, very good' when Francis put his hand up and asked if 'from blown roses on' was assonance. And, Mr Cronin added, did the class notice how Tennyson used 's' sounds to create a soft, sleepy atmosphere?

Music that brings sweet sleep down from summer skies

Francis sat back in the armchair, closed his eyes and recited it in a whisper, very relaxed now. 'Fabulous 208!'

A low thump of some kind of drum, then piano. Really dramatic. A girl singer. Her voice was very clear. Francis heard every word. She was telling this guy he was full of himself, the way he looked at himself in the mirror and thought all the girls were dying to dance with him.

Just as the singer was telling the guy he was so vain, Francis felt his mickey swelling up and pushing against his pants. He touched it and felt the lovely tingle that he'd felt in bed a couple of times, but always stopped because he was a bit afraid. Now he couldn't stop, it felt even nicer rubbing against his underpants and the rhythm of the song seemed part of it. The singer was telling the guy she had dreams about him. Francis pressed harder even though he was a bit worried that he'd hurt himself. As the singer sang about a total eclipse of the sun, the shivers went all the way up into his head and he felt woozy and wobbly and the guitar played really high. He scrunched up his eyes and knew that, he didn't know what, but he was sure something else was going happen soon and he was really scared and wanted to stop, but it was too late.

He squirted.

It was like a rattlesnake's tongue darting out and back and out and back.

It was like pouring a whole sherbet fountain into his mouth.

Every bit of him shivered and jerked. Francis thought his head was going to fall off, but he kept rubbing to feel the bliss again, again, again, again.

It stopped. When he opened his eyes he had slid off the armchair.

Now he felt really afraid and the girl was singing don'tyoudon'tyoudon'tyou like an accusation. What time was it? His mam or his dad would come in any second to tell him go to bed. He had to get upstairs before that.

'Is it about Warren Beatty? Is it about Mick Jagger? Is it about… you? Who cares, it's a classic. Big stateside, Big in Britain. Carly Simon –'

Francis switched off the transistor. He dumped his books into his schoolbag and held it in front of his trousers as he opened the door very slowly. The hall was empty and the back room door was closed. He could just about hear the telly. His mam and dad and Marian and Martin were in there. He ran for the stairs and up. In the dark he tore off his clothes except for his underpants and ran to the bathroom. He locked the door and pulled his underpants open. The sticky mess looked like he'd blown his nose in it.

'Francis! Are you upstairs?'

He urgently needed to pee, but he'd better answer first. What if his mam came up? He opened the bathroom door a couple of inches.

'I'm going to bed.'

'Well, you left the electric fire on in the sitting room. Do you think we're made of money?'

'Sorry.'

His mam started saying something else, but he locked the bathroom door and ran to the toilet, pulling his underpants down. Just in time. No sound now from downstairs. He turned on the hot tap and scrubbed his underpants. To his relief the sticky stuff washed away easily. He squeezed as much of the wet out as possible. Then he listened at the bathroom door, opened it really slowly and tiptoed naked to the bedroom. Once he pulled the sheet and blanket over him, he spread out the damp underpants under his pillow. Hopefully they'd be dry in the morning.

At last the mad fear faded and the memory of pleasure returned. Francis' heart beat slower and slower, drowsy now, blood flowing warmly. A haze of bliss.

Eleven: March 1st

For over a week the announcers on RTE had been telling everyone that transmission would begin earlier than usual on Friday, for the special general election results programme, which would be in colour for the first time. Francis asked if that meant people like them, who still had a black and white set, would get different results? No one seemed to realise he was being funny. His Mam looked at him as if he was thick and said no, it would be exactly the same.

When he got home from school the telly was turned on even though there was no one in the room except little Eugene. His Mam was hoovering upstairs. Francis sat at the table and took out his copybook and pen. Mr Cronin had told them to write a composition about Proportional Representation. Even though it was a complicated voting system Francis thought he understood it, but it wasn't so easy to think of an interesting idea for a composition about it. His Mam came in and stood staring at the telly. 'What's Brian Farrell done to his hair?' Francis knew that wasn't really a question. Then she said, 'Don't ask me why they start the programme this early.' Why was she standing there looking at it then? 'Oh there's Professor Basil Chubb. He's absolutely brilliant now. What's he saying?' Francis didn't know why his mam was asking him, when she could hear the programme the same as he could, if only she'd shut up. Professor Basil Chubb said was it was going to be a very long night and vote transfers would be vital in determining the final outcome. His mam said, 'I love the way he talks. He really knows the ins and outs of the whole thing.' Then she went back upstairs to make the beds.

When there was an ad break, the telly showed the whole set

from way up high and Francis suddenly remembered that he'd been in the same studio the day of the last election and had looked down on the set from that exact spot. Gavin, the brilliant guy who'd brought him and Ian Barry and Mr Barry on the tour, had taken them up the narrow metal stairs in Studio One and they looked down on the set for that election. 1969. Francis was only a child then. Gavin was really funny. He was going to work in American television. How was he was getting on there? Francis remembered him saying, 'The world is my oyster.'

He thought of a really good metaphor for his composition on Proportional Representation. He wrote down 'THE ELECTION RESTAURANT' and started thinking it out.

On the telly, Professor Basil Chubb was getting very excited. A first count result had come in from Roscommon/Leitrim, which had three seats and amazingly there was now a possibility that Brian Lenihan, one of the government's best known faces and a minister for over ten years might – just might – be about to lose his seat. It all depended on transfers. Brian Farrell asked, was this a sign that after sixteen years there could be a change of government?

Francis started his composition with Mr V. He knew Mr Cronin would be smart enough to spot that V was for Voter. Mr V went for a meal in the Election Restaurant. The waiter gave him the menu which had six choices. Francis hoped Mr Cronin would like the idea of a menu as a metaphor for the ballot paper. Mr V read the menu very carefully, even though he knew straight away what his first preference would be. He chose the cheeseburger. The waiter went to the kitchen, but came back and said he was very sorry, they were out of cheeseburgers. He would have to eliminate it from the menu. Was there anything else he fancied? Mr V made fish and chips his second choice. The waiter said excellent, and went to the kitchen.

Marian and Martin came in from work. Marian had voted for the first time, but she wouldn't tell Francis who for. 'It's a secret ballot.' Francis tried to make her give something away by jeering her. 'I know who you voted for. You voted for the Minister for Justice because he's your boss's pal and you want to lick up to him.' But he couldn't catch her out.

'Who I voted for is my business and no one else's.'

'Mam told us who she voted for.'

'No, she said she didn't vote Fianna Fáil, that's all.'

'Well tell us who you didn't vote for then.'

'It's a secret ballot.'

Francis stayed quiet for a minute. Dr Garret FitzGerald had arrived into the studio and Brian Farrell was congratulating him on his tremendous result in Dublin South-East, elected on the first count, way over the quota. Dr Garret FitzGerald was very modest and said that his personal success would be of little importance if the government wasn't defeated this time. Francis asked Marian was she delighted that Dr Garret FitzGerald got elected? Marian said he was wasting his time, her lips were sealed.

He went back to his composition. The waiter came back all apologies saying, believe it or not, the fish and chips were gone. Was there anything else on the menu Mr V would be willing to choose? He'd be happy enough with the steak and kidney pie as a third choice.

When his mam came in and saw Dr Garret FitzGerald talking, she got all excited. He was such a clever speaker, she said. He wiped the floor with that Fianna Fáil crowd every time, and he was an absolute gentleman. How was he able to talk so fast and not trip over his words?

When Mr V discovered that steak and kidney pie had been eliminated from the menu as well, he was a bit annoyed. 'I hope you're not making a fool of me,' he said. 'Is there any food in this restaurant at all?' 'Oh definitely, sir, there's still pizza, chicken curry and bacon and cabbage.' Mr V thought pizza was okay and he was just about to order one, when another waiter went by with two pizzas balanced on either arm. Mr V's waiter looked at him and said, Wait just a moment, sir. He scurried into the kitchen and came back looking very pale and sad. I'm so sorry, sir, he said, pizza has just been eliminated. Mr V was very very fed up. What kind of a choice was left? Chicken curry or bacon and cabbage.

Brian Farrell said they were going to one of the most interesting constituencies, Dublin North-East, where two highly controversial figures, CJ Haughey and Conor Cruise O'Brien were hoping to keep their seats. Francis thought it was funny that, because the returning officers knew they were on live TV, they spoke really slowly, like they were in an elocution class. When CJ's vote was announced, 12,901 first preferences, there were whoops and shouts and the camera showed him being lifted up onto men's shoulders and bounced up and down. The returning officer had to shout quiet please three times. Conor Cruise O'Brien's first preference vote was 7,854, and no one hoisted him on their shoulders. Brian Farrell asked him if he was confident that he would keep his seat and he said yes, he was only eight hundred votes short and he expected to be elected on the third or fourth count. Brian Farrell had a smirk on his face when he asked Cruise O'Brien if he wanted to congratulate CJ on his enormous vote of nearly thirteen thousand. Francis could tell from his reply that he didn't like CJ. He never mentioned his name and said that anyone the people, in their wisdom, voted for, was worthy of congratulation. From the tone of his voice, Francis wondered if, secretly, Cruise O Brien thought the voters weren't that wise at all.

Mr V, after thinking about it for a long time, decided he didn't like chicken curry much, but he really hated bacon and cabbage, so he said he'd prefer the curry. The waiter got it for him and it didn't taste too bad and it was definitely better to eat something than go hungry.

Francis finished the composition by saying that was the good thing about Proportional Representation: even if your first choice didn't get elected you still had a chance to vote for someone else and stop the person you really hated getting in. He was worried that the composition was still a bit short, so he added in a last bit about Romeo and Juliet which 2A had started studying. He said if Juliet had known about Proportional Representation she wouldn't have killed herself when she woke up and found her first choice, Romeo, dead. Maybe Paris wasn't such a bad second preference after all. Better than killing herself anyway.

Francis hoped that Mr Cronin would think that was funny.

Now Fianna Fáil had sixty-seven seats and the coalition had sixty-nine. Whoever got seventy-two would win. The result of the election depended on the last five constituencies. Professor Basil Chubb said it was fairly certain now that Brian Lenihan would lose his seat in Roscommon, which meant meant things looked bad for Fianna Fáil. Based on the figures in front of him, Professor Basil Chubb now called the election for the Coalition. It was almost one in the morning.

Francis heard murmuring in the hall. Marian had arrived home. She was saying goodnight to Stephen. Kissing probably. The front door closed and she came in, yawning.

'Isn't it over yet?'

'Nearly. Professor Basil Chubb says the Coalition are going to get in.'

Francis searched for some reaction on Marian's face, but she just nodded and went to the door. Pulling it behind her, she suddenly stuck her head back in.

'Good.'

She grinned and closed the door. Francis wished he could understand exactly why he felt the same as his sister. Just for a change maybe? Was that it? Something different at last.

Twelve: March 14th

When Fonsie Strong opened his eyes he wondered why the wallpaper was different. Why was the bed pushed up against the wall? Was he awake at all? The throb at the back of his head told him he was. Then he remembered the party. Then he remembered everything else. He'd slept in the boys' bedroom. Ann was with Marian. His brother Peter and Alice, back from Croydon, were in their room. Fonsie lay on his back, glad of the gloomy light. That was a late one, well after three, but a great get-together, the best in years, his mother's house jammed with family, old friends, and neighbours. Ninety was a remarkable age by any standard. And her mind sharp as ever, still determined to outlive de Valera. Marg had baked a mighty cake, and she'd managed to stop her husband Peadar singing IRA songs, which would have driven his mother mad. It wouldn't be right anyway these days, with the goings-on up north.

There had been an awful lot of drink. In fairness to Gussie he'd done a great job organising the bar, but he gave out very big measures, especially the whiskey. There were a few falling around the place before the sing-song even got going. By the time someone made a noble call for Paddy Dundon to sing '*Catari*', he'd already dozed off in his chair. 'We're spared that at least,' Ann had whispered. First time ever Paddy hadn't done a turn. Gussie must have been giving himself big measures too, because he got a bit messy later on. Fonsie didn't like to see his sons drunk at all, but at least Ritchie and Martin just got more high-spirited, whereas Gussie could be very cranky in drink. But sure, by the end of the night everyone had a few too many taken. Even Peter, who never in his life opened his mouth to sing, was joining in all the choruses. What was that thing Francis sang? Something about being part of a trade union. Fonsie didn't know where he got it from, but Peter told him it was top of the pops in England on account of all the strikes. 'On the radio day in and day out,' he said. 'Sure Heath's making a bags of it.'

Francis was no great shakes as a singer, but Fonsie had to admit he was well able to get everyone to join in on the chorus. He even stopped and gave out when people weren't loud enough and made them sing it again, until they were lifting the roof. Everyone thought his carry-on was funny, but he was a bit too cheeky all the same. He needed to watch his manners. That business with Peter and the book yesterday – Fonsie was definitely going to talk to him about that. It was thoughtful of Peter and Alice to bring little tokens for everyone and Fonsie was mortified at Francis' reaction when Peter said he'd heard he was a great reader and gave him a very nice-looking book, *Nicholas Nickleby*. The way he took it and flicked it open and just said, 'It's very thick.' Not a word of thanks. Peter only laughed of course and said, 'There's a lot of reading in it all right, but you might take to it.' Fonsie was raging. He didn't want to be giving out and Peter and Alice only in the door, but he was determined to remind the little pup of his manners as soon as he got a chance. Too full of himself altogether.

The house was completely silent, everyone still conked out after last night. Now that there was evening mass, they didn't have to rush out on a Sunday morning, although Fonsie didn't like going in the evening. It didn't feel proper somehow. He might get up now anyway. A nice quiet cup of tea on his own would sort out the headache. He threw back the blankets and sat on the side of the bed. In the gloom he could make out the shape of Martin in the lower bunk. A bit too big for it now, but it was only for a couple of nights. Eugene would be moving from the cot to the bunk soon. He was growing so fast. Time flying.

Rather than fumble around searching for clothes Fonsie decided to chance letting some light in. He stood up and pulled the curtains a little. When he turned around he got an awful shock.

On the top bunk, Francis had kicked the blankets off. He was lying on his stomach, his face to the wall and there, for anyone to see, was his naked bottom. Fonsie immediately turned away. What was he at, sleeping with no clothes on? Maybe with the party and so on he just couldn't find his pyjamas last night, was that it? So why hadn't he left his underpants on at least? Ann could walk in any minute. Peter might have stuck his head in. Fonsie realised if someone opened the door right now, he'd be caught standing there right next to his naked son. Oh flip! Directing his eyes elsewhere, Fonsie very very cautiously untangled the blankets and placed them as gently as possible over Francis' back. He pulled on his trousers, grabbed the rest of his clothes and left the room.

Grateful to have time to himself in the kitchen, Fonsie boiled the kettle, made toast and had a nice calming cuppa. Apart from having a word with Francis about his manners, he'd have to talk to him about growing up and so on. The last time with Martin had been easy because he'd cut across Fonsie straight away to tell him they'd learned all about it in school, which was a great relief. He wasn't sure he believed Martin, but it was obvious he'd learned it somewhere all right, the way he went through girlfriends like a dose of salts. Talking with Francis would be more awkward. And how the heck was he going to bring up the subject of wearing pyjamas – or something anyway – in bed?

He heard soft steps on the stairs and was glad that it was only Peter.

'I looked in and saw that you were up.'

There now, Fonsie thought, he might well have seen Francis naked, even though Peter would probably have just laughed. He didn't want to think about it.

'Her Ladyship wants a cup of cha and bread and butter.'

'There's plenty in the pot.'

'Mammy enjoyed herself last night, I think. Isn't she a wonder?'

'Oh, tough as old boots.'

'Is she still giving out orders?'

'Does her best to. Ah sure you know. Water off a duck's back.'

'Oh well. It won't be long now.'

Even though he knew that his mother wasn't going to live forever, this wasn't something Fonsie wanted to talk about. His brother had always been more straightforward.

'We're all moving up the line. Every time I come back I see the changes. Someone gone bald or a bit grey, the young ones all grown up. Ritchie with a baby, I couldn't believe it. Grandad.'

Peter carefully laid out a tray. Alice had him well trained.

'Marian's lad, Stephen, seems like a nice youngfellah. We had a grand chat before I had too much taken.'

Fonsie was about to joke that of course they'd have lots to talk about as he was a postman too, when Peter picked up the tray and winked.

'From the way he talked about Marian... well... I hope you've a few quid put by to pay for the big day out. Pour me a cuppa, will you? I'll be back down as soon as I've served her Ladyship.'

His Marian getting married? Such a thing hadn't occurred to Fonsie at all. Surely Peter couldn't be right. He was only giving him the raz. Maybe Stephen Stokes had notions in that direction, but Marian would soon put him right. Sure they'd only been going out for... Fonsie realised it was more than two years. A serious line all right. But no. Not his Marian. Fonsie didn't want to believe it. Nothing to do with Stephen, he was a grand lad. It was just... ah no.

Thirteen: April 1st

It was the maddest fast set of the afternoon. Mike Rave played 'Hello, Hello, I'm Back Again' and then 'See My Baby Jive' and then, best of all "Cum On, Feel the Noize!' The dance floor was completely jammers with everyone bumping and banging off each other. Goodness gracious! Hundreds of fingers wagged in the air for the chorus of 'Hello! Hello!' Wuh-oh! wuh-oh! The boys especially went wild, wild, wild, during 'Cum On, Feel the Noize!' and despite how crowded it was, Francis made enough space to fall back on one hand and bounce up again three times in a row. He'd gone a bit too mad, but didn't care. It was only after the fast set finished, when he was sweating so much his hair was wet and he had to go douse his burning face to cool down, that he realised this wasn't the best way to get off with a girl. In the mirror he could see the dark sweat stains on his new wine shirt. Under his arms stank. He wet his hands and slid them inside to get rid of the smell, which stained his shirt even more. But that was only water, it would dry soon in the heat of the dancefloor. He combed his hair, parting it in the middle. It wasn't as long as he wanted it to be yet, but it was getting better. His mam had mentioned a haircut, but hadn't made a big deal about it. Yet.

A slow set was just finishing when Francis went back out. Andrew Liddy and Patch Dollard were both up dancing. Francis didn't think much of the girl dancing with Patch and he couldn't see who Andrew was dancing with because she had her face buried in his chest and looked like she was squeezing the life out of him.

Another fast set started. 'Superstition.' Francis felt his body jig again. He really wanted to dance to this, but he stopped himself.

This was his fifth week at the Sunday afternoon disco and he hadn't got off with a girl yet. Maybe it would never happen, even though there were hundreds of teenagers here from all over the city. Every week he'd seen so many boys kissing girls and walking them home, including Andrew and Patch and others from his class. It was nearly half five. He had a little plan. Girls often said no if they were asked up for a slow set – probably because they knew what boys were after – but they usually said yes for a fast set. Mike Rave almost always played three fast songs then three slow ones. Francis' plan was to wait until the last song of the fast set, then ask a girl to dance. It would be a bit too rude to sit down after only one song, so more than likely she'd stay for the slow set. And that would be his chance to get off with her.

Francis didn't bother looking for the most beautiful girl because he knew that if someone really sexy wasn't up dancing, then she was probably a bit snotty and there was no point in asking her. During 'No More Mr Nice Guy' he prowled slowly around the oval curve of the hall, scanning ahead. Through a small gap he saw pretty curls. The girl they belonged to was sitting down, and her face was in shadow. Without getting so close that she'd notice, Francis shifted to a better place to look at her. Finally he saw her face, small in a horseshoe of curls. Petite, he thought. 'Now, our very own chart-toppers, Thin Lizzy' said Mike Rave. Francis checked that the stains on his shirt had dried out. The girl saw him just before he smiled and held his hand out. She looked surprised to be asked, which surprised Francis because, closer up, her face was definitely very pretty. He touched her shoulder as they went out on the dance floor.

Francis reminded himself not to go ape. Luckily 'Whiskey in the Jar' wasn't one of the songs that really sent him wild, so he danced the way Andrew danced a fast set, just shifting from foot to foot and moving his shoulders around, real cool. The girl with curls was a very awkward dancer. Maybe that's why she was surprised to be asked up? Her friend, a few feet away, waved over. The girl smiled back. Luckily the friend's wave seemed to encourage her. When 'Whiskey in the Jar' ended Francis started talking straight away. What's your name? Jenny. Mine's Fran. He never called himself Fran. It just came out. Where do you go to school? Laurel Hill. She didn't ask him about his school so he didn't mention the Christian Brothers. He nearly asked where she lived, but stopped himself because that would sound a bit too pushy. He said he was surprised he had never seen her here before, as if he'd been coming here for years instead of a month. She said this was only her second time.

'Now let's slow it down, boys and girls...' Yes! She'd stayed for the slow set. 'Killing Me Softly.' Francis stepped closer and remembering that his underarms might still smell a bit, he kept his elbows down as he put his hands on her shoulders which were very bony. Her hands were on his waist, but so lightly he could barely feel them. The way her head bent down he could only see her beautiful hair. It smelt nice. They turned and turned and turned. All Francis could think about was what should he do next to find out how much she liked him. He could caress her shoulders, or neck, or touch her hair, or try to nudge her closer. 'Killing Me Softly' ended before he did anything. As Jenny looked up he was afraid she'd say thanks, so straight away he said the first thing that came into his head. Had she heard that 'Killing Me Softly' was supposed to be about Don McLean? She said yes. Francis put his arm around her waist. She didn't pull away, but she didn't put her arm around him. He wondered what this meant.

'Who's this? It's the man from The Who, that's who. Roger Daltrey... 'Giving It All Away.' Francis kept his arms on her waist this time. He could feel her hip bone. She really was very thin. And tall. Her chest wasn't very big, just two little bumps. It occurred to Francis that her hair was very like Roger Daltrey's. They turned and turned and turned. He slid his hands along her back until they joined together. Jenny let herself be pulled closer, but still kept her hands on the front of his shoulders. It was very hard to figure out what she was thinking. This time, when the song ended, Francis forced himself not to speak and just smiled in what he hoped was a dreamy Donny Osmond kind of way. She smiled back! Hers was shy and she dropped her eyes, but this time, as they waited for the next song, Jenny put her arm around his waist too. For the first time since he'd started going to the afternoon disco, Francis thought he was in with a real chance.

Over the intro, Mike Rave said, 'Time to get kinda cozy, guys 'n' gals. This is a beautiful hit, from Harold Melvin and the Bluenotes. It's called…' He timed it perfectly to the opening line. Francis loved 'If You Don't Know Me By Now.' He couldn't have picked a better getting-off-with-someone song. He closed his eyes and rested his head on her shoulder, pressing fingers against her spine. Slowly, together, they turned and turned and turned. When the chorus began the second time he lifted his head to look into her eyes. Her hands were still just resting on the front of his shoulders. She hadn't really given him any clear signals, except now she smiled shyly again. This might be his last chance, because it was the last song of the last slow set. So he leaned in and Jenny didn't pull her face away. She closed her eyes. She was going to let him.

He kissed her. Then he kissed her again. But it didn't feel as he thought it would. He realised after the third kiss, that it was because Jenny wasn't really kissing him back. Her lips stayed still and just let his press against them. He stopped kissing and fondled her hair. She moved her hands a little along his shoulders. Was she encouraging him. What now? He really wanted to kiss her again, but he also wanted it to be better. What about a French kiss? Would he dare? Maybe that's what Jenny was expecting. Maybe she was waiting for him to put his tongue in her mouth before she kissed him back? He was nervous thinking about it. French kissing had sounded a bit disgusting when he first heard about it, but the more he thought about it he wondered was it a metaphor for actually having sex? Even Andrew had only French-kissed one girl. He said it was amazing.

It was very near the end of 'If You Don't Know Me By Now.' There was no time to waste. Francis swallowed to get rid of any saliva. He leaned in again. This time Jenny seemed to make more of an effort to kiss him back, Francis was encouraged, but still nervous. He opened his mouth more and pushed his tongue out. As soon as it touched her lips he felt them shut tight, like a lift door. Nothing else changed, her hands stayed on his shoulders, she didn't pull her face away, but his tongue was rammed against an unyielding barrier. Was he doing it right? He tried one more time, a little harder, but her lips pressed even more tightly. He gave up and kissed her normally again. Then the song was over and Mike Rave was talking.

Francis was utterly confused. He'd dared to try a French kiss and Jenny hadn't let him, but she hadn't slapped his face or run off the dance floor. The slow set was over and she didn't say thanks and walk away. It was quarter to six. There would be one more fast set before the end, but Francis wasn't interested in dancing now. There was only one thing he wanted to know.

'Where do you live?'

When she said the South Circular Road, he knew that her family must be well off. He wondered what would she think if he told her he lived on Rowan Avenue?

'Can I walk you home?'

She said 'Okay.' Just like that. He'd been sure she'd say no, defo. Yes! He'd done it! He had really got off with a girl.

Because the clocks had gone forward, it wasn't dark anymore when the Sunday afternoon disco ended. Not so atmospheric. Still, he held her hand as they went up O'Connell Street, then, crossing the road at the Crescent he put his arm around her waist. Francis could hear himself talking too much, but when he did shut up to let her speak, there was only silence and he was terrified of that. Was Jenny too shy, or was it that she couldn't think of anything to say, or did she just prefer to listen? Francis wished he knew. While he talked he was also looking at her more closely. The evening sun made her hair flame and her face look even prettier. The rest of her was very skinny and flat. Or did she just seem skinny because she was so tall? After they passed the Redemptorist Church, Jenny took her arm from his waist, although she didn't push his away. Now they were on the South Circular Road. When she began to slow down he knew they must be near her house. Then she stopped walking and stepped away. He took her hand and held it. She pointed two gates up and said that was her house. So this was it. No sheltering under a huge old tree in the moonlight with their bodies pressed together passionately, just a tall skinny girl standing two feet away who wanted him to let go of her hand.

'Will I see you next week?'

'I suppose.'

Francis knew there was no point in even trying to kiss her again. She kept looking nervously towards her gate, although the garden was long and the front door wasn't even visible.

He tried to let go of her hand slowly, in a meaningful way, but he didn't know if it was successful. Jenny didn't look back.

He had got off with a girl, but it hadn't been as amazing as he'd imagined. The kiss on the dance floor had been weird and walking her home had been a bit boring. He definitely hadn't fallen in love, so he still didn't know what that felt like. Yet, with each step, his mood got giddier and wilder, and he didn't know why.

Fourteen: May 11th

Marian was grateful that the thumping rhythm from the front room, where Francis was supposed to be studying, drowned out the chatter of her mam and dad and Stephen in the back room. She needed this time on her own in the scullery, away from them, and took her own sweet time with everything; cutting the Galtee, and the tomatoes – thick slices of one, dangerously thin slices of the other; buttering the bread so slowly that the kettle had boiled before the sandwiches were made. It wasn't that Marian minded how well Stephen got on with her mam and dad. Not at all. But sitting in all night with her parents was not a date as far as she was concerned. She cut the four rounds of sandwiches in half. A few minutes' banter when Stephen called to collect her was fine, but settling himself in and then saying, that'd be lovely Mrs Strong, he was starving actually, when her mam suggested tea and a few sandwiches, really annoyed Marian. More then that, if she was honest, it was a bit unsettling. She definitely needed these few minutes on her own. The same song began again in the front room. What was it? She'd heard it before, but couldn't put a name on it. Imagine that. Not so long ago she'd have known not only the song and the group, but the chart position, and if it was going up or down. She and her pal Pauline Cosgrave used never to miss the Radio Luxemburg top thirty and they'd even get depressed if their favourite song went down. When had that all stopped?

Marian arranged the sandwiches on one of the good dinner plates, telling herself there was nothing to be nervous about, that Stephen's easy way with her parents was just part of his personality. Friendly, straight-up, proper and decent. Maybe a bit too proper. In all their time doing a line Marian never had to worry about him going too far. He always seemed to know when he was about to and never did. Then he'd apologise with a lovely compliment, like she was looking so beautiful tonight he'd nearly lost control of himself. Marian sometimes wished he'd let her decide when to say no. There had been a few times when she hadn't wanted him to stop. Could she have trusted herself? Recently, Stephen had said he was looking forward to going out for a drink with her dad: he thought he'd be lovely company over a pint. And last week Stephen had asked if she'd heard this thing on the news about the law changing to allow married women to stay on in their jobs. Marian knew all about this, but it would never have occurred to her that it would remotely interest Stephen. He asked if she thought the new law was a good idea.

'Of course. About time.'

'Yeah, I think so too. One of the lads in the sorting office was saying no 'cause he said they'd only be getting up the pole and taking months off, and then coming back again and no one else would get a look in, but I mean like, if we got married I wouldn't expect you to give up your job.'

'Honoured, I'm sure.'

'No, but you know what I mean.'

Marian had shifted quickly from that subject, although part of her realised that, after two and a half years doing a steady line, it wasn't surprising that someone like Stephen might want to get more serious. Some people would think it strange that Marian wasn't the one dropping the hints… She was taking way too long with the sandwiches. Mam would be out any second now asking was it a five-course dinner she was getting ready or what? In the front room the infectious handclapping began a third time. Marian remembered when she used to play her latest fave incessantly. She couldn't even name this one.

It was no surprise that her brother didn't notice when she stepped into the front room. He was sitting on the floor with his back against the armchair, his face hidden behind *Exploring English: Book One*. Her old copy handed down. How could he concentrate on the short story he was reading and at the same time listen to –? She remembered that was exactly what her mam used to ask her and Pauline when they were sprawled out, books open on the floor in front of them, Gary Puckett and the Union Gap blaring out 'Young Girl.' Happy days. The happiest days. Marian had hardly seen Pauline since she went nursing in Dublin.

'What?'

Her brother made that one word sound like, Get out and leave me alone, can't you see I'm busy? Marian wanted to tell him he obviously had no sense of irony. How often had he barged in on her and hung around asking question after question, and how nice had she been to him, explaining all kinds of things? *And* it was her old *Exploring English* he was reading.

'That song. I've heard it before, but I can't remember the –'

'"Stuck in the Middle", Stealer's Wheel. Now, do you mind?'

She'd never heard of them. Surely she wasn't that out of touch? No, she could still name lots of the groups going at the moment and she and Stephen had tickets for Horslips at the Savoy next month. She smiled at the straggle of hair peeping over the top of *Exploring English*. There were so many great stories from that collection. Her first grown-up stories. It had started Marian reading proper books.

'What one are you reading?'

An impatient sigh.

'Janey Mary.'

Marian had studied it for her Inter Cert. Such a sad, sentimental story. How impossible life was for that poor little girl. No hope. The song ended and Francis jumped up to catch the arm before it lifted and replaced it at the beginning. Better let him be. Marian gently closed the door, feeling a bit envious. She needed to start reading seriously again. Proper stuff.

'Lovely!'

'At last.'

'Were you churning your own butter?'

Marian put down the tray of sandwiches and tea. She decided

to allow Stephen ten minutes to feed himself. Then they were going out, whether he wanted to or not.

Fifteen: June 18th

'So, are we sneaking out or not?'

'Patch, was Dermo sure everyone else was going?'

'How was he supposed to know for sure who'd go? He just said a load of the lads were sneaking out and meeting at *an halla* at two o'clock.'

'Rendez vous, *an halla,* 2 am. Synchronise your watches.'

'Shut up Cónal! Spa.'

'And some of the girls said they'd go too.'

'Really? Is that true Andrew?'

'So Dermo said.'

The whispering in the dark got more frenzied at the possibility of girls. After an céilí mór, Francis had noticed the two lads from Drimnagh Castle CBS, Dermo and Marcus, going around whispering to various fellahs and girls as they collected their bikes outside *an halla,* organising mayhem for the last night. Everyone was high after the céilí.

'So, what time is it?'

'Five past one.'

Francis didn't tell anyone it was now officially his birthday. If they did sneak out it would be like his secret party.

'Well we'd better make our minds up if we have to get there by two.'

'What are we waiting for?'

'I'm up for going. Defo.'

'We have to, last night 'n' all.'

'It'll be savage.'

'Shh! Cula bula. Keep it down.'

Everyone went silent for a sec. After Brother Daly had turned the lights out and said '*Oíche mhaith.*' the whispering had been quiet at first, but bit by bit, had got louder and louder as they started interrupting each other. There wasn't a chance in the wide world, *sa domhain go léir,* that any of the boys could think of falling asleep tonight, even though all day had been non-stop, with the last Irish class in the morning, then climbing Mount Brandon in the afternoon, then an céilí mór, going on until midnight because it was the last one.

'Tonntracha Toraí.' Francis loved the name of that dance. *Tonntracha* made the sound much better than the English word – waves – and the dance itself was brilliantly complicated:

In and out, in and out. One, two, three, one, two, three.

Take a partner, up and down. One, two, three, four, five, six, seven.

Round the back, and meet your partner, hands together, make an arch.

All the couples passing under, one, two, three, four, five, six, seven.

Hands up. Hands down. Up and down, up and down, as the couples pass each other.

Over, under, in and out. Making motion like the waves. Tonntracha.

It was brilliant fun and hard to believe now that before coming to Irish college, Francis, like all his pals, had sneered at the idea of a céilí compared to a disco.

Boys held hands for 'Tonntracha Toraí', five in a row facing five girls. Some were embarrassed and would only place their hand near the other hand, almost tipping fingers yet without actually touching. Did the other boys notice the different ways everyone held hands? Francis never asked. Some grabbed him and squeezed hard, trying to show how manly they were. Some hands were damp and he didn't like the feel of them at all. Some just put their hand out and let him take it, but it was like holding a dead fish. One night, Marcus from Drimnagh Castle CBS was next to him in the line and, when 'Tonntracha Toraí' ended, he forgot to let go of Francis' hand, so they were holding hands and talking for a few seconds. Francis thought it was funny, but then Marcus jerked it away suddenly and looked puce, probably afraid that others would notice and start slagging them about being queers.

'Francis! Francis! Are you asleep?'

'Hm? No. What?'

'Are you up for going?'

'Yeah sure.'

To his secret birthday party? Of course. Tonight, when everyone was lining up for 'Tonntracha Toraí', Francis saw the boy from CBC in Cork, with apple cheeks and hair turned in at his shoulders, looking around because his line needed one more boy. He was about to join up with him when Patch and Andrew and Cónal and Tom called Francis to their line. Would the boy be out tonight for the last hooley? He wasn't in his group and he didn't live in the same *teach* but for some reason Francis noticed him a lot during the last three weeks. He had a very confident walk and was always hanging around with two girls from St Angela's, but he never held hands with either of them. They seemed to talk and laugh like they were pals, which was a bit strange. Maybe they were sisters or cousins.

'What's going to happen?'

'What do you mean what's going to happen? Anything we like.'

'Like what?'

Francis thought that Cónal was asking a fair question. What *would* happen out there tonight?

'Ah shut up.'

'Patch, are we going or not?'

Looking at the shape of Patch in the sagging mattress above him, Francis wondered would the shape stay or would the mattress spring up as he leapt from the bunk. In the end, it would be Patch who'd decide if they all snuck out or not. This was something he'd discovered, sharing a little bedroom with five school pals. Someone became the leader. No election, it just happened.

Francis didn't know why Patch became the one, because he never tried to be the boss of it all, yet everyone in the room wanted to be his pal. He was so easy to be around. He never got too excited about anything, and there was always this tiny grin on his face as if he wasn't bothered much about stuff, everything was grand. Yet everyone ended up waiting to see what Patch thought, what Patch wanted. Why was that? Cónal, for example, could say the smartest thing – and he often did say really clever things, even if they sounded completely off the wall – but no one ever paid him any attention. And some of the boys could be really mean to Andrew, which was only jealousy because he was so good-looking. What about himself? If he suddenly jumped out the window now and went off into the night, would anyone follow him? No. Andrew maybe. But if Patch said, Yeah, sure we might as well go, in that lazy way of his, as if he didn't really care much one way or the other, then the whole gang would be hopping out of their bunks in a flash.

Who did Patch like best? He was nice to everyone but did he have a real best pal? Maybe he liked different things about different people, the way Francis did. He liked Cónal Collopy for being freaky and funny. His cartoons were really brilliant, and since coming to the Gaeltacht they were even funnier, because now he made his Nazi characters speak in Irish. Instead of '*Donner und Blitzen!*' now they said '*Toirneach agus Tintreach! Maraigí, Madraí Sassanach!*' In Cónal's cartoons the Nazis were always the smart ones and Captain Hurricane always got it in the chops. Cónal's head really was away off in some mad place, but Francis loved talking with him on his own. In a group he could be a bit embarrassing, though. The nicest person to be with was Andrew. He was generous and Francis could make him laugh. He wished he was as good-looking. Girls flocked around him, even in the Gaeltacht. It was like he had magic dust that he just tossed in the air and any girl it landed on, fell under his spell. Was Andrew his best friend? *Mo chara cléibh.*

'Right, are we all going so?'

'Not me.'

'Ah come on, Cónal.'

'Your mission is doomed, gentlemen.'

'Ah Cónal!'

'Shh, if he doesn't want to go, he doesn't want to go.'

Francis admired Cónal for having his own mind, spacer though he was. What if it was all just talk and no one else turned up? Even if there was a big gang, what would they do anyway? Go down to the stony beach in the dark? Gather sticks and light a bonfire? Would just being out there for these last few hours be excitement enough, with the chance of something unforgettable happening, whatever it might be? Hadn't Francis had his own adventure earlier this evening?

He'd snuck out when *Bean a' tí* wasn't around and didn't ask anyone to come with him. He was in a mood to be on his own, meandering about the quiet little roads. There was no sign of the boy with the apple cheeks and hair turned in at his shoulders when Francis whizzed by his *teach*. He was probably inside, getting dressed up for an céilí mór. The cycle ended at the pier in Baile na nGall. He leant his bike against the dirty white wall of Begley's Pub that was strictly out of bounds. *Toirmiscthe,* the Irish word sounded much more forbidding, much better. He walked along the pier sucking in the seaweed air and cocking an ear to the fishermen in the boats below getting ready to go out for the night. It didn't matter that he couldn't understand much of their talk, it was part of the sound of the place, like the gulls screeching and the water slapping against the pier wall.

Then he heard something different, something he hadn't heard in weeks. An electric guitar. From a crackly radio somewhere near. Long crying high notes. Radios and cassette recorders and pop music were also *toirmiscthe* for the Irish scholars. The music of the last three weeks had been all jigs and reels at the céilís and *Cóilín Cóilín, tar abhaile liom* and *Beidh aonach amárach i gContae an Chláir* in singing class. He followed the sound, recognising the song now. It wasn't a guitar, it was George Harrison playing the sitar and singing about Love and Peace, and Hope and Birth and Freedom and coping and touching and reaching. Francis looked over the pier wall to a bit of grassy headland that soon fell away to the sea. A small blue tent was pitched there with a couple squatting over a little stove and listening to their transistor. Germans probably. As George Harrison cried out to his Lord, Francis thought of the first Sunday the Brothers herded them to the little church for *aifreann* and how funny it was to see the local men bunched in the doorway, smoking and staring at pictures of topless girls in the *Sunday World*. He'd presumed the Gaeltacht would be even more holy and Catholic than other parts of Ireland, but it wasn't at all and, whatever it was, Francis knew he liked it better for it. His feeling for this place, this holiday, his friends, were all tangled up like seaweed, and came from somewhere deeper below the surface than he had ever known.

'Now listen, everyone take it easy.'

Leader Patch was issuing instructions. They were going after all.

'Get out of bed one by one. No noise. You know what Daly is like. He hears the slightest thing.'

'Sin ceart, cloisim gach aon rud.'

Brother Daly's casual voice, saying, yes, he did hear everything, utterly silenced the room. If Dracula had tapped at the window whispering, *Let me in*, it couldn't have been more of a blood-freezing shock. What awful punishment would now be pronounced on the mad, bad rebels who hadn't even managed to get out of their bunks, let alone rampage in the dark of night?

'Codhlath sámh anois, a bhuachaillí.'

Having smirkingly wished them a peaceful sleep, Brother Daly said no more. Everyone waited, tense and utterly silent. Was he still standing outside the window, or had he floated away to his own bed without as much as a rustle or scrape? Francis wondered, but didn't dare speak. No one else dared either. Clever. Fiendishly clever and brilliant. Daly had completely outmanouvered them. Francis smiled at the genius of it. The next sound he heard was the soft rise and fall of someone's sleeping breath. Then another. Then another. Then a snore or two.

*

Buying a deserted island – what next? Michael Liston was convinced that the lady friend was the driving force behind this lunacy. Throwing away more money CJ didn't have. But if the idea had taken root in his head it'd be hard to dislodge. Well, he'd know more shortly. Mags was saying something from under the covers. He heard 'Matthew's birthday.'

'What?'

'I said we have to do something for Matthew's birthday. When are you back from your rendezvous with CJ and the lady friend?'

Mags enjoyed saying 'lady friend'. It amused her that Michael loyally concealed the name, unaware that, for some months now, she'd known it was Terry – Terry herself having told her. It was astonishing that it hadn't occurred to a mind as instinctively conspiratorial as Michael Liston's that most female journalists in Dublin not only knew each other, but enjoyed a much more eclectic range of social interactions than getting legless in three city-centre pubs like their male colleagues. Mags, though only a casual acquaintance, actually liked Terry. In fact she liked both Terrys, the brash legend of fashion launches and opening nights, and the more kindhearted, quietly candid edition. Terry could no more have resisted talking about this affair among her friends than she could have stopped breathing. What would be the point of a secret if it couldn't be shared with *someone*? That very merry night at June's place, Terry's references to the great secret, initially coy, had become gradually more suggestive, and at last, hilariously outrageous.

But this morning it was Matthew's birthday, not CJ and Terry, that Mags thought should be centre stage. They were on holiday together. If today had been Susan's or Simon's birthday she'd be making a big occasion of it. Surely Michael had something in mind?

'It's grand. Don't worry about it. I did what I always do.'

'And what's that?'

'I left him a card with a few bob in it. A good few bob, obviously, now he's buying things for himself. He likes that.'

'And that's it?'

'Why, what do you want?'

'What will Susan and Simon and I do for his birthday?'

'Ah no, don't worry about that. He won't even mention it.'

'So I've noticed. Not a whisper from him. I'd begun to wonder if he even remembered himself.'

'Well yeah… It wasn't a thing he ever made a big fuss about.'

'Why not?'

'In case people thought it was a bit off, you know.'

'Why?'

'Ah Jesus, Mags! On account of his mother.'

'But I thought he didn't know anything about that.'

'Yeah, sure, but *I* did. He understood from me it was better not to be making a big thing about his birthday, that's all. He's grand. It doesn't bother him.'

It was obvious that Michael wanted her to shut up, mind her own business and let him be off. His Master awaited, lady friend in tow. This only made Mags more determined. CJ and Terry could wait until this – frankly more important matter – had been sorted out.

'We're here together on holidays. We should all be celebrating his birthday.'

'Well, I'm gone for most of the day and honestly, Matthew won't be expecting anything. The moolah I gave him will be more than enough. He's like me, Mags. Sure I couldn't care less if no one remembered my birthday '

'Ah Michael you're forty-nine, he's fourteen!'

With sudden energy, Mags jumped from the bed.

'Give me a minute to get ready. I'll drive you into Dingle. That way I can keep the car and you don't have to rush back here to collect us.' Mags ignored Michael's protests. 'We'll meet back in Dingle for a birthday celebration later. Where, do you think, the Benner?'

'Ah… I suppose.'

He looked so uncomfortable Mags nearly felt sorry for him.

'Michael, it's not the fiifties anymore. Surely your son's birthday is a day to celebrate.'

'Okay, yeah. Sure. I know, yeah.'

'When you book the Benner, make sure to tell them it's a birthday do.'

'What for?'

Mags wanted to say, just so you can hear yourself saying out loud, I'm celebrating my son's birthday! But instead she said, 'They might do something special for him. A cake or whatever.'

After dropping him outside the Benner Hotel, Mags went to the bookshop, She had a little gift in mind for Matthew that she thought he'd like.

Earlier, Matthew had been awake, but kept his eyes closed, when his father tiptoed in and placed the envelope on the bedside locker. Once the bedroom door clicked shut, he opened the envelope, careful not to wake Simon next to him, and slipped out the card. Twenty-five pounds was the biggest ever present. Nice. The card showed a boy in football gear scoring a goal. His father hadn't a clue about cards, or more likely had just picked up the first one he saw with '14' on it. The greeting was the same as always.

Have a smashing day, Daddy.

Matthew hid the card under the pillow and, later, when Simon woke and stumbled out to the toilet, he transferred it to the safety of his rucksack.

He was having breakfast when Mags arrived back and flashed him one of her special smiles. He ached to embrace her, but Susan and Simon were there too, munching Weetabix.

'Isn't it a gorgeous morning? I think we might do something special today.'

And he got another special look.

'Are you taking us out in the car, Mummy?'

'I thought we might.'

'Well, a car crash would definitely make it a special day.'

'I see the Dingle air is making us all very sharp.'

'Even the dullest amongst us.'

'Susan! Your brother isn't dull. He just looks at the world differently.'

'The only thing he looks at is himself in the mirror.'

Ouch! Matthew thought Susan had nailed it, absolutely. Sharing a room with Simon he'd seen just how narcissistic he was. And solipsistic? Matthew liked the word but wasn't sure if he got the meaning right. Susan would know. She was really smart. And pretty. Why didn't he fancy her? Was he scared of her intelligence? He didn't think so, but it was definite that he didn't want to have sex with her, because a couple of days ago it had been sunny enough to go swimming on Wine Strand, and afterwards, lying on their tummies really close to each other, the drops of seawater trickling along her stretched body and her wet bikini top showing the outline of her nipples, should have given him the horn. But it didn't. This was a relief in a way. Was Susan becoming like a real sister? Like a twin, though a bit older? She definitely didn't treat him as scornfully as she treated Simon.

Mags leaned over. Her hand rested on his shoulder. She smelled of flowers.

'Matthew, I want to check something about the car. I forgot to ask Michael –'

'No use asking Matt about cars. Mummy. I'll be able to –'

'Excuse me, was I talking to you? Matthew, will you come and take a look? Stay exactly where you are, Simon.'

Outside she opened the passenger door for Matthew and pointed to something gift-wrapped on the seat. He picked it up and sat in. It felt like a book. Had his father told her it was his birthday? Mags sat into the driver's seat.

'Aren't you going to open it?'

It was a book. The cartoon on the cover showed an old farmer trying to beat a gigantic pig out the tiny door of a thatched cottage.

The Poor Mouth (An Béal Bocht) A bad story about the hard life by Myles na Gopaleen

It looked like it might be a comic story, but he'd never heard of Myles na Gopaleen. He opened it. Inside was written:

14! I think you might be ready for Myles now.
Happy Birthday and much love
Mags
(and Susan and Simon of course).

Much love. Her arms opened, inviting him to her. They were alone and the car was parked at the side of the cottage, not visible from the kitchen. Matthew dared to wonder if Mags had done that deliberately? He reached for her neck and felt her arms slide around his waist. His nose at the crook of her neck and shoulder breathed in the magical garden scent. He wanted to lie in it but felt her release his waist, so he knew he also had to let go.

'Two things. First, do you mind me telling Susan and Simon that it's your birthday? I'd like to because it means we can celebrate it properly, but it's up to you.'

He nodded. How thoughtful she was.

'And secondly… About your mother. Now tell me to mind my own business if you want.'

'No, it's okay.'

'Why don't you do something this morning to remember her, something symbolic maybe, or even spiritual. I don't mean religious, although of course if you want to, that's fine too. Anything you choose as a commemoration. Once that's done it might allow you to feel more free to celebrate the other significant and very happy thing about this day: the fact that Matthew Liston was born.'

Mags had this lovely old hippy vibe about her, but what was she on about? He hadn't thought about his mother at all until she mentioned her. What was this spiritual, symbolic thing? Light a bonfire on a hill? Dance around magic stones? Matthew knew it would be very rude of him not to take her seriously. The last thing he wanted to do was offend Mags.

'What do you think I should do?'

'Well… these things are very personal. You may not even want to have others around. Tell you what. I'll go and tell Susan and Simon that it's your birthday. Take your time, come in whenever you want. And remember, the day is yours, we are your slaves to command, all right?'

The glow of her smile, lingering after she left, made him want to please her by thinking up some amazing ritual to commemorate his mother. He loved her present already. What did she mean when she wrote 'you might be ready for Myles now'? The cover looked like a funny book, but inside it said 'translated from the Irish' so how could it be funny?

He started reading, just to see what it was like, and laughed three times in the first two pages. He turned back to the translator's preface to check that it really had been written in Irish first, and was even more surprised to find that it had been published in 1941. If the 1950s were dark and bitter and ugly, the 1940s must have been worse, but this writer had managed to find comedy in misery and poverty. Matthew read on. The book was set in the Gaeltacht. At first he wondered if Corkadoragha was anywhere near where they were now, but when he read that the hero, Bonaparte O'Coonasa, lived in a tiny cottage in the corner of a glen and could see Gweedore in Donegal out one window and Connemara out the front door and the Blasket Islands out the other window, even though these different Gaeltacht areas were hundreds of miles from each other, he clicked that Corkadoragha was just a made-up place, a benighted hell-hole of rain and muck and smells and potatoes and drunkenness and squalor and unbelievable poverty, where the misfortunate inhabitants spent all their time sitting on henhouses or lying on rushes among the pigs, forever discussing the misery and hardship of life, their only consolation being, as the writer kept reminding the reader, that at least they spoke about these horrors in the sweet Gaelic tongue. The book pretended to be the life story of a man from Corkadoragha; a story of the poorest poverty, the hardest hardship, the filthiest filth, the unluckiest ill-luck. Page after page, the narrator's hunger and misery and deprivation grew, and the more grotesque his degradation, the more Matthew cackled and couldn't stop reading.

Susan and Simon were both delighted to hear about the birthday, knowing it would mean treats. Where was he? Mags told them to wait, Matthew needed time on his own. Simon asked what for?

'Do I ask you what you need time on your own for?'

Simon went red and shut up. However, after nearly an hour passed, Mags became a little concerned and decided to check discreetly. At the corner of the cottage, the sound of choking laughter took her by surprise. It was out of control, like he might throw up if he wasn't careful. Through the rear window of the car Mags could see the back of Matthew's head rocking back and forth. She came closer and, though she stood silently at the driver's window for a full minute, Matthew was so lost in *The Poor Mouth* and laughing so much, he didn't notice her.

Mags tiptoed away feeling hugely, giddily proud at the effect of her gift.

*

Terry flung out her arms and tilted her face towards the whipping wind.

'Isn't it delicious! Intoxicating!'

And for once, the effulgent Terry words were Ann Teresa's too. She grabbed CJ's hand and they climbed, stumbling and laughing to a better vantage point. They stopped and kissed as if their lips were magnetised. Through the layers of cotton and wool and oilskin she could feel his clattering heart. At least the Loathsome Accountant seemed to have sufficient *nous* not to trail after them. Ann Teresa spotted him skulking off along the rocky western perimeter, probably compiling the dullest list of reasons why buying Inishvickillane would be foolhardy. Forget about him, They had little enough time together.

Arm in arm, they were blissfully silent now. The black rocks and dull dirty greens of the grasses and the innumerable dots of extravagant colour made for a fabulously complex fabric that nothing man-made could imitate. It was shaped by the relentless chiseling of that restless, malcontented sculptor, the sea. Below where she and CJ stood, the mess of stones that had once been a dwelling warned that humans stopping in this place had better be resilient. Like me, Ann Teresa thought. What a perfect hideaway, as far west as anyone could go, with only the Atlantic between here and America and, even though on the other side the mainland seemed alarmingly close, in between, the Great Blasket was a crouching guard dog and the strip of choppy sea made a sparking, glittering electric fence.

She noticed that CJ was also staring towards the mainland as if calculating the distance between here and there. Was he thinking the same as she? Escape. How untouchable they'd be here. Young tearaways on the run from the authorities. Playing a gangster's moll would suit Terry. Virginia Mayo? Faye Dunaway? No. Gloria Grahame in *The Big Heat*. Incomparable.

'It's so desolate. And isolated. It would be just us. We could put a roof on that pile of rocks. The simplest cottage. A *tigín* for two.'

She knew that Terry line would make him laugh and added, 'The bare necessities.'

'So, no champagne then?'

'I never said that. I said the bare necessities.'

He laughed again and she dared believe the tearaway rapscallion in him was convinced already.

Her enthusiasm was catching, although chasing her up that rough terrain, CJ had felt some strain in the groin and it was hard not to seem out of breath when they kissed. *Tigín* for two. She could be funny all right, but it was hard to place her in a wilderness like this. Terry, for him, was Paris and London, Walewska and Langtry, the squeal of delight when, in candlelight at La Tour d'Argent or Parkes, with champagne on ice nearby, he flourished another extravagant bauble for his favoured mistress. It made him wary that she was so keen about the island. What was she at? What was she trying to get out of him? The look in her eye was ferocious, her grip feral. Did she have some notion of the pair of them galloping wild in their pelts? What goblins and demons and sprites might be let loose out here? Tempting but Terry-fying. He liked that, he'd never thought of that one before. He'd suspected for a while now that Terry might want to expose a part of him that he didn't want her – anyone – to get near. And yet the danger was horn-making.

But other possibilities for the island were crowding and exciting CJ. What was that line, something about a king of rocks and stones? That could be him. This could be his kingdom in exile. Here he could wait and plan. Liston had assured him everything was on track. A few of Lynch's old guard had lost their seats in the general election and the country and western acolytes were gearing up for next time round, which surely would be sooner rather than later. CJ couldn't see this coalition of Lefties and Blueshirts lasting any time, especially with arrogant fuckpigs like Cruise O'Brien at the cabinet table. The king of rocks and stones would need a little more than a *tigín* of course: something comfortable, with a certain rustic grandeur: the sort of place to which people could be summoned. It might even become an official summer residence. In which case, a helipad would be necessary. It wasn't always possible to get here by boat. Of course Liston would try to corrupt his vision with talk of budgets. Always money. CJ didn't want to be bothered about money. What needed to be done would have to be done.

Ann Teresa saw the watchful eyes instinctively flick round and knew that the other more controlled, more calculating CJ had emerged, the one made paranoid by enemies and events. He was seeking out the Loathsome Accountant, who was probably spying on them behind some hunk of black rock. Ann Teresa understood precisely the effect of her persona on the Loathsome Accountant and those like him: what thing she was, as far as they were concerned. Such creatures hadn't the imagination to see beyond Terry. He thought there *was* nothing else but Terry and wouldn't understand, could never even begin to fathom the way in which Ann Teresa loved CJ. Whether or not such feelings were fully returned she had no idea. Wasn't that part of the excitement?

*

'My teeny weeny fellow, will you be after diving off the pier in Baile na nGall?'

'I'm not answering if you keep talking like that.'

'Because if you so intend, little son, then 'tis the mighty fine pair of goggles you shall need to be after attaching to yourself.'

'I'm not listening. It's not funny anymore.'

'I would argue that matter, my sweet boy, until the end of time.'

'Mummy, please tell him shut up!'

'Matthew, I know it's your birthday, and I'm delighted you found Myles so amusing, but please, give it a rest.'

'Woman, I by no means will not... All right, all right I'll stop.'

As they drove round Smerwick harbour, almost everything he saw, whether it was the sea spitting over black rocks and mounds of seaweed, or smoke from a cottage tucked away off the road, or some auld fellah in a cap waving his stick as they passed, reminded him of something funny in *The Poor Mouth*. In Muireach village there were buses parked outside the ramshackle hall, the destination signs in Gaelic: *Corcaigh, Baile Átha Cliath, Luimneach. Dúrlas*, and hundreds of boys about his own age swarmed all over them. When Mags said they were Christian Brothers students going home from Gaeltacht summer college, Matthew thought of Myles na Gopaleen's description of the first sign of spring in Corkadoragha, when strange but harmless gentlefolk came rambling round, writing Gaelic words in notebooks, proud to be proper Gaelic Gaels who spoke only Gaelic and never talked about anything in Gaelic apart from the importance of speaking in Gaelic and being a Gael and Gaelicism.

'Are you laughing at those poor students?'

'Woman, that I was not doing by any means. My laughter was not cruel English mockery but only sweet Gaelic merriment.'

'Please make him stop!'

Matthew was glad that, even though he had probably carried the joke on too long and was now driving everyone mad, at least they definitely knew he *was* joking, because, recently, he'd become conscious that his outer self often gave the impression of someone who existed only on the dark side of the moon. Was he a modern-day Bonaparte O'Coonasa, forever brooding on the hardships of life and the misfortunes of the world? His friends in Mount Temple, especially the girls and, most especially, lissome Trudie Marsh, often asked, 'What's up?' even when he was feeling perfectly content, kissing her by the trees near the tennis courts. 'Ah melancholic Matthew, how is't the clouds still hang on you?' Mr Bennett, the English and French teacher would intone as they passed in the corridor, although he never waited for an answer. Melancholic Matthew sounded cool and, on balance, he preferred to project an enigmatic brooding aspect, rather than to be a grinning fool. But today he wanted Mags and Susan and Simon to know that he was having a whale of a birthday, so he risked looking like a grinning fool and offered up a big smile.

'Okay, I promise. I'll stop right now.'

He was rewarded with a wink from fragrant Mags.

Sixteen: July 3rd

It was right in the middle of town. Why had he never noticed the place before now? Hassett's Hotel looked a bit grubby on the outside but Francis thought, why not give it a go? Inside, the front area had tables and comfy old chairs but no customers and no one at reception. He stood listening. Not a sound apart from the traffic outside. Francis leaned over the reception desk as if he expected to find someone crouched, hiding on the other side, or stretched out, dead. There was no bell to ring. He could see a narrow, arched entrance leading to what looked like a bar area, but it was closed off by a wrought iron grille gate. It was obvious that this place was a waste of time, but the emptiness and silence was weirdy-weird. There must be someone here. Upstairs? The wide old staircase turned back on itself halfway up so he couldn't see the first floor landing. He was tempted to creep up for a look.

'What do you want?'

If the voice out of nowhere was a jolt, the sight of the woman standing on the other side of the wrought iron gate was scary in a Hammer Horror picture kind of way. It was the lips Francis noticed first, so thickly red they looked like some strange separate object glued to her face. The bright blue make-up around the eyes and the long hair combed so straight it looked mock, completed the effect of a mask. Her stare made him feel like he'd been caught doing something awful.

'I was wondering… I'm looking for a summer job.'

'We didn't advertise any jobs. Who told you there were jobs going here?'

'No one. I was just passing. And hotels are busier in the summer, so I came in to –'

'Without making an appointment?'

'Sorry. I thought maybe I could just inquire.'

The squeaking floor had given Gretta Nagle a terrible fright; and at first sight the boy, tall and scruffy, had seemed quite menacing. But he was well-spoken and his politeness of tone made her less nervous of him. Gretta guessed he hadn't been spying on her doing her face. It was probably safe to open the gate and come through. A summer job?

'What sort of work were you looking for anyway?'

'Anything at all. Cleaning, or in the bar, or anything.'

Polite. Quite humble actually. And younger than she first thought. Fifteen maybe?

'What age are you?'

'Sixteen.'

A lie, an absolute lie! The boy's face even went red as he said it. Mind you, with his height he might pass for sixteen with the customers. They might well be fooled, but not Gretta, and she was going to make sure he knew that straight off.

'You most certainly are not sixteen. You won't get any job from me by telling lies. You're only fifteen, isn't that so?'

Francis had been about to admit that he was only fourteen, but he thought it was better not to contradict this oddball so he just nodded. He couldn't make her out. First there are no jobs, then she's asking questions and saying she won't give him a job if he tells lies. The woman poked at the corner of her lipstick mouth with her baby finger, the two blue saucers fixed on him.

'I'm the manageress here, you know. I could consider you for a position.'

Francis didn't know why she took the long way round him to go behind the reception desk. She examined sheets of paper, rubbing the ends of her hair between finger and thumb.

'I have no vacancies as such. But casual summer work? Well, let me see now.'

It had been easy to make the boy admit that he'd lied about his age. His manner was courteous. Gretta was beginning to fancy the idea of having him around. A lounge boy would add some style to the place. He'd also be useful doing those fecky jobs she hated: changing beer barrels, emptying smelly skips and so on. But would Councillor Hassett be willing to pay for the swank of having someone in a white shirt and dickie bow – no, not a dickie bow, black tie, much better – serving at tables?

'I might have some use for you in the bar. As lounge boy on busier nights.'

Francis was surprised at the turnaround. Was the woman going to offer him work after all? She looked a bit mad, but if there was any kind of a job he'd take it. Her tongue flicked at the corner of her mouth as she stared at him. What was she thinking? With all that make-up it was hard to figure out what the expression on her face meant.

Gretta wondered how much would Councillor Hassett be willing to fork out? A couple of pounds a week? Surely 50p a night would be enough for the boy.

'If – and I say if – I needed you three or four nights a week, could you do that?'

'Yes.'

'From eight o'clock until midnight?'

'That's okay.'

It was a lot better than nothing. Francis liked the idea of working at night. He hoped his mam would let him. Was the woman going to say for how much? If she didn't, was it all right to ask?

'You'll be operating directly to my instructions. And it won't be just serving at tables, you'll have other tasks, is that clear?'

'That's fine. I'm happy to do that. I'll look forward to it.'

The eager politeness in the boy's voice attracted Greta even more. He wasn't ugly as such, just poorly turned-out and not menacing at all. It might be quite pleasant having him around.

'Now, don't presume I've made my mind up about this. It all depends on how satisfied I am with how you present yourself. Have you a white shirt?'

'Yes.'

'A nice plain tie, black or charcoal?'

Francis wasn't going to let the lack of a tie stop him getting this job. His dad would have something.

'Yes.'

'All right. Come back the day after tomorrow, properly turned out, white shirt, dark tie and dark trousers. Do something with your hair. If I'm satisfied then, I may *consider* starting you before the end of the week. Fifty pence a night. Plus your tips of course.'

If Councillor Hassett refused to consider her idea, Gretta could just tell the boy his presentation wasn't up to the mark. When he left she closed the wrought iron gate again and glided back to the empty bar. Something in the way the boy had looked at her had raised the tiniest uncomfortable suspicion that her lipstick might be off-kilter on the right. She sat on her little corner stool and took out her compact. No, perfectly even. She tested a smile. Lovely.

As she closed her compact her eye was drawn to a mixer bottle on the shelf that didn't have its label facing out. Looking more closely she realised there were *dozens* in the same state. Aidan's fault! She constantly had to cover for that fellah's carelessness and laziness. The new boy could be useful for all these little jobs. It would be nice to be in charge of someone.

Seventeen: August 9th

A quiet night: four customers at the bar and, at tables, a young couple, three women done up to the nines, drinking Kiskadees and coke and, in a corner of the outside lounge, the priest from the Augustinians with a woman, drinking whiskey. There wasn't much for Francis to do and Gretta wasn't finding him little jobs because she was too busy leaning at the bar, smoking and flashing her teeth at Mr Grey, which was puzzling because on Francis' first night working she wouldn't even acknowledge the man's presence.

The place had been completely empty that night. After she'd walked round Francis twice to make sure he looked neat enough and made a little speech about what was expected of him, Gretta had sent him to the stock room for crates of mixers, Smithwicks, and Carlsberg Specials. Then she'd pointed to a damp cloth and told him to wipe every bottle before putting it on the shelf, and to make sure that every label was facing out. While he was on his knees, Gretta just stared out the window, smoking. Not a word. Francis worked on quietly and was nearly finished when he felt a pinch on his shoulder and heard an urgent whisper.

'Francis! Get up! There's a man coming in now and I want you to serve him. He'll ask for a Gordon's and Schweppes. That's a gin and tonic, do you understand? Gordon's gin and Schweppes tonic.'

She trotted to her little stool in the corner and waved Francis down, hissing.

'Keep stacking. Wait until I call you.'

Francis heard footsteps as he put the last few bottles of Smithwicks on the shelf. Someone pulled up a barstool. Gretta's voice sounded too loud and really false.

'Francis! I'm on my break. Would you look after the customers, please!'

The man was about the same age as his dad, with shiny grey hair combed back, stiff with Brylcreem.

'Gordon's and Schweppes.'

Francis knew about measuring shorts from seeing his brother Gussie at work, but as he picked up the little metal cup he glanced sideways towards Gretta. Just to be sure. She took a puff and nodded carefully as she blew out the smoke, like she thought she was in a spy film. His hand shook as he poured the Gordon's and it spilled over into the glass. Then he took one of his freshly wiped bottles of tonic from the shelf.

'Is that Schweppes?'

Francis showed Mr Grey the yellow label. In the deadly silence the *skksssss*! as the bottle opened was like a geyser erupting.

'A slice of lemon. No ice.'

Francis realised he didn't know how much to charge. He dropped the slice of lemon into the gin, and glanced towards Gretta, but she had taken out her compact and was puckering her lips at the little mirror. Mr Grey smirked. He had a mean down-turned mouth, but his voice was friendly enough as he told Francis the price.

'It's 22p for the Gordon's and 9p for the tonic. 31p.'

He counted out the exact amount onto the counter. As Francis picked up the coins, Mr Grey looked at Gretta, looked back at Francis and threw his eyes to heaven. Now another problem: Gretta had said that he was not to go near the till under any circumstances. Never. He was a lounge boy – that till was none of his business. What was he supposed to do now? He spotted Gretta making some gesture with her cigarette hand, but had no idea what it meant. He stayed frozen with the coins in his hands and heard a little contemptuous snort from Mr Grey. Gretta jerked her head, glared, and finally spoke: 'Just leave the money *beside* the till! I'll deal with it when my break is concluded. And return those crates to the stock room, please! Don't have them cluttering the work area.'

When Francis returned, Gretta and Mr Grey were as before. He at the counter, she below it curled on her little stool, silent. What was going on? Then, as soon as another customer came in, Gretta sprang up and offered him her Rocky Horror smile.

But it was the opposite tonight. She sighed resentfully whenever she was called away from Mr Grey. Francis wandered to the outside lounge to see if the priest and the woman were ready to order again, but they were taking their time sipping their Black Bush and Gold Label. The same as last week, sitting in the same corner. They'd stayed all night and only had two rounds. No tip.

Back in the main bar, Francis tried to eavesdrop on the story Des was telling his pals, Malachy and Mr Reidy. He stood back from the bar counter as usual, so he could do actions, but kept his voice low, which meant the story must be even more over-18s-only than normal. Judging by his stories, it seemed that Des had sex, or nearly had sex, every night. Something funny always seemed to happen and his pals always laughed and said things like 'The hammer man strikes again' or 'Did you give her plenty of rod?' Des never stayed long. He'd buy his round, tell the boys about his latest escapade, and then say something like, 'The cock is crowing. I must be up and at it.' 'Ah, not off chasing tail again?' Mr Reidy would say in pretend surprise and Malachy would sing the same line every time, 'It wasn't the grass that tickled her ass, 'twas my little finger.' And they'd all laugh. But Francis thought there was something fake about it. Were the pals envious of Des and his adventures?

'Francis! Empty that skip before it gets busy.'

He was glad Gretta had given him something to do. Better to sit alone, sorting out empties in the chilly stock room, than wandering around the quiet bar pretending to look busy. And it meant he could listen to Radio Luxembourg. He got his transistor from his coat, put in the ear piece and arranged various crates around the skip. There was one kind of crate for mixer bottles and another for pint bottles. Coca-Cola had its own crate and the big spirit bottles went into a special pile. Francis enjoyed seeing how quickly he could take random bottles from the skip and pop them in the right crate, but Barry White, murmuring, *Oh baby,* made him pause. It sounded like he was having sex, as if the girl was there with him. Francis transferred the bottles more slowly, quietly now, lost in the moans and whispers. Barry White's hands couldn't keep still and he kept saying *I love ya, love ya, love ya, love ya, love ya.* Francis knew all about the pleasurable shocks he got when he pulled himself off, but this song told him he had no idea how much better it felt to do it with a girl. How long would it be before he had sex? Would he ever? And would it feel as good as that?

The stories Des told made sex sound more like some sort of funny game: his bottom pressed against the cold passenger window when he did it in a car; banging the girl's head accidently against a headstone when he did it standing up in a graveyard; doing it in the hall of some young one's house and, suddenly, her father is at the top of the stairs, steam coming out of his ears. Des had to hop it out the door like lightning and drive off with his trousers still round his ankles.

Were Gretta and Mr Grey having sex? Francis tried to imagine such a thing. What would happen to all that make-up when they kissed? And his brylcreem when she grabbed his hair? No, they couldn't be having sex. But if not, then what was going on between them? And what about the priest and the woman? Imagine if they were doing it? Why were they meeting here, sitting in a quiet corner all night, drinking whiskey and whispering?

There was something freaky about Hassett's Hotel. The place hadn't been done up in years, no one worked in the hotel part, so what was Gretta supposed to be manageress of? The only other person on the staff was a fellah called Aidan, who Francis hadn't even met yet. And there was something odd about the customers too, like they weren't here just to drink and chat. There was something more going on in Hassett's and it was to do with sex, but not the kind of amazing sexy sex – with low lights throbbing and silk sheets twisted and beautiful bodies beautifully entwined

– that made Barry White moan in ecstasy. The sex that Francis thought he had smelt in Hassett's Hotel seemed to be a different kind of sex altogether.

'Francis! Change the Smithwicks barrel, number two, and get back up here, there's a crowd after coming in.' Luckily, Gretta was barking so hysterically, Francis had heard her over Barry White coming to his climax. 'And wash your hands!'

She banged the stock room door shut. Francis, relieved she hadn't spotted the ear-piece, changed the beer barrel quickly and rinsed his hands.

The 'crowd' Gretta had got so excited about was two middle-aged couples who already had their drinks, and two young girls in spray-on jeans and low tops who ordered Carlsberg Specials by the neck. When Francis put the bottles on the table one of the girls leaned forward to pick up hers and he could see right down her top. She asked was Aidan working tonight and seemed very put out that he wasn't. Francis could tell she wanted to have sex with Aidan.

In the outside lounge the priest ordered another Gold Label for the woman, but nothing for himself. Francis wondered if he was trying to get her drunk so he could have sex with her. Back in the bar Des had left his pals to go off and have sex somewhere. Then he saw Gretta giggling like a little girl at something Mr Grey was saying and, though he couldn't hear her reply, the way her glistening scarlet lips were moving seemed to whisper, *I want sex, I want sex, I want sex.*

Eighteen: September 12th

Tháinig long ó Valparaiso,
Scaoileadh téad a seol sa chuan.

On his way to work, Francis pedalled with the rhythm of the poem he had to learn off by heart for Irish class. Trochee tetrameter. Macker hadn't told them that. Unlike Brother Carew, he never bothered much with iambic or trochee or dactyl or anapest,

Chuir a hainm dom i gcuimhne
Ríocht na Gréine, Tír na mBua.

He tried to fix it in his brain before he got to Hassett's. 'Thainig long ó Valparaiso.' The poet saw a ship arrive from Valparaiso. It anchored in the bay and the very name put him in mind of enchanting kingdoms in the sun. Macker had said Valparaiso was a real place in Chile in South America, but in the poem, the name, its sound, also represented a feeling, a notion of something wonderful far away that he had never seen or experienced. Francis understood. Valparaiso. It sounded exotic. Macker used the Irish word, *coimhthíoch*. Francis preferred exotic.

Aidan was on duty tonight. Francis had only worked with him a couple of times and wasn't sure if he liked him or not. He was a friendly guy, but jittery, always pacing around and glancing this way and that, especially at himself in the mirror. Tonight he checked even more than usual because he'd got his hair trimmed and blow-dried so it was like David Cassidy's, and he'd bought new flares. They were kind of purple and so tight at the waist he could barely tuck his shirt in.

Mr Grey came in, looked around and asked Aidan was he on his own tonight? Then he left. Francis wondered had he been hoping to see Gretta, but then he realised it was the exact opposite, because a minute later he returned with a lady. He didn't bring her to the bar: they went to an alcove. When Francis took the order for a Gordon's and Schweppes and a Hennessey and ginger he noticed Mr Grey didn't have his wedding ring on.

The two girls who drank Carlsberg Specials and fancied the pants off Aidan arrived in.

'Hi, Aidan.'

'How's it going, Aidan?'

It was all Aidan, oh Aidan! Francis could see he just loved having both girls falling at his feet, especially when they complimented his new flares. Mouseyhead made him turn around and went oooh! in a dirty voice, but Redhead just stared. As he served them their Carlsberg Specials Aidan said something too quietly for Francis to overhear. The girls went to the outside lounge, and for the rest of the night competed with each other to see who could drink more Carlsberg Specials. By the time they'd had five each, Mouseyhead was falling off her chair, but Redhead looked like she'd been drinking nothing but lemonade. They kept saying, tell Aidan to come out to us. Finally he asked Francis to keep an eye on the bar and came back, looking so pleased with himself. He couldn't help showing off, an eye on the mirror as he whispered, 'Jesus, your one with the red hair squeezed my arse and she'd a' squeezed something else too if I'd let her, you know what I'm saying? Lovely little titties on her.'

Just before closing time, Des arrived back. Francis was surprised because usually once he took off on one of his adventures, he wouldn't be seen again until the next night. Even more strange, he'd returned with a girl. Francis had never actually seen Des with a girl before. They joined Mr Reidy and Malachy at the bar, Des sniggering all the time and pawing at her. A few minutes later Francis saw him, arm around Aidan's shoulder, whispering. Then, a minute after that, Aidan called Francis over and asked would he mind staying on late and helping out as there was going to be a lock-in?

'Just a few regulars, but I might need you to keep an eye on things, you know what I'm saying?'

Francis didn't. What was a lock-in? He thought about those sexy Carlsberg Special girls in the outside lounge and Des bringing a girl back for the first time and Mr Grey, still here with his new lady, and wondered was it some kind of orgy? He'd read about wife-swapping parties in *Titbits*. He suddenly thought of Gretta and what she'd think about Mr Grey with a lady having a lock-in. Her make-up would crack with the shock of it.

He said yes, sure. He'd stay on no problem.

'Good right yeah, well listen get yourself a pint of coke if you want, while I clear everyone out.'

Francis was well pleased. Aidan grabbed two bottles and opened them on the sly before going to the outside lounge. Francis checked the shelf he'd taken the bottles from, although he'd sort of guessed already: Carlsberg Specials.

'Thank you for your time! Ladies and gentlemen, please!'

Aidan came back, ricocheting around the bar, gathering glasses like mad and encouraging people to drink up and go. Francis washed the glasses as they were dumped on the counter. He noticed Mr Reidy whispering to Mr Grey. Malachy and Des and his girl stood up as if getting ready to leave, but still hung on to their drinks. Francis was a bit surprised when Aidan said,

'Check everyone's gone from th'outside lounge, would you?'

Surely the Carlsberg Special girls were still there? No, the place was deserted. Francis was amazed, but as he was collecting glasses he noticed something. There were ten empty bottles of Carlsberg Special on the table. The girls hadn't let Francis clear them up because they were keeping count. He'd served five each. So where were the two extra bottles he'd seen Aidan sneak out? Francis was sure the Carlsberg Special girls were still here somewhere! Hiding in the toilet? Would they appear as soon as the lock-in started? Were they strippers?

When Francis came back and said the outside lounge was empty, Aidan became brisk. 'Right lads, shift. We'll bring you another round. What's it? Smithwicks, Smithwicks, Gordon's and

Schweppes, Hennessey and ginger, vodka and white, and still a Powers for you, Des?'

Aidan turned out the lights in the bar and closed the wrought-iron gate while Francis carried the brimming tray. In the outside lounge the six were sitting in a circle around one of the tables. In the centre was a deck of cards. Was it going to be some kind of strip game? Was that what happened at a lock-in? But surely not with four men and only two women. And Aidan. And what about himself? What did they expect him to do? Where were the Carlsberg Special girls? Mr Reidy picked up the cards and started to shuffle.

'Okay, Rubber of three, a quid each. 50p presents for a jink. Everyone happy about that?'

A rubber of three? Francis had heard of rubber Johnnies and knew they had something to do with sex. Was that what he was talking about? And what was a jink?

'Sorry you can't join in, Aidan.'

'You're grand. I've stuff to do.'

What was Aidan talking about? What had he to do? The game began. They all put a pound in. It seemed like ordinary '45' played with partners. Des and his girl, Mr Grey and his lady, and Mr Reidy with Malachy. Aidan drank his Harp quickly, foot tapping, looking around. Francis figured the card game was the last thing on his mind. He was thinking about the Carlsberg Special girls.

After three rounds, Mr Grey and his lady, who they called Tilly, reached 45.

'We're away. One, zero, zero' said Mr Grey.

Aidan nudged Francis and whispered.

'Will you mind the house for a few minutes? Don't let any of them into the bar, but serve them whatever they want. Keep a tab. I'll sort it all out later.'

'Sure.'

'Good man. I'll see you right, you know what I'm saying?'

He went behind the reception desk, but Francis could see out of the corner of his eye that he was only pretending to be working.

Then, as soon as he thought no one was paying attention anymore, he slipped out and nipped upstairs, three steps at a time.

So that's where the Carlsberg Special girls were!

Francis worked it out. When Aidan sneaked those bottles to them earlier on, he'd sent them to wait in one of the bedrooms. Was he going to have sex with both of them?

Francis was dying to find out for sure.

'And the knave! That's 45.'

'Okey-doke. One for Malachy and me, one for the Grey fox and Tilly, zero Des and Mary. Slow train running, Des.'

They ordered another round. Francis got it lightning fast and hardly even noticed the big tip Mr Reidy gave him. All he was thinking about was Aidan upstairs with two exotic girls. He tried to imagine what they were doing. Was he lying back with the girls on top of him? Or were they on either side and he was going one way first, then the other? Maybe the girls took turns and the other watched?

'And 45 again. That's two, one, and still a big zero on my left!'

Malachy and Mr Reidy were delighted with themselves. Francis had copped on that a rubber of three meant that the first team to win three games took the pot. It had nothing to do with sex at all. Partly because they were so drunk now, everyone was very nice to Francis. Mr Reidy kept showing him his hand and explaining little tricks of the game. The lady called Tilly asked what age he was and was he still in school and did his mother mind him working so late, which was a bit annoying. Malachy just kept winking at him and saying stupid things: 'Make my day, punk. Gonna make you offer you can't refuse. I like your style, kid.' Des's girl asked him his name and said her name was Mary, not to be confused with the Virgin Mary. She kept saying out loud, 'We haven't a hope of winning, you know. Not a hope,' and screeching laughing. It was nice that they were so friendly but all the attention made it harder to slip upstairs unnoticed.

The next game became really serious. At the end of the first round they all had ten points each. During the second round Francis took a chance and slowly backed away. He leaned casually against the wall at the bottom of the stairs.

'Sorry, my friend, the five of trumps!'

'In the short corner, you bollocks. I knew you had something.'

'35, 15, 10. This is it, folks. Hit the high man.'

Now they were all concentrating on what might be the final round. Francis crept up the stairs. When he got to the first landing he looked one way, then the other. There were five doors. A light came from under the crack of one! If he crept nearer what would he hear? If he looked through the keyhole what would he see? Did he dare go that close? He cocked an ear, but huge laughs and shouts from downstairs drowned out any other sounds.

'Francis! Frankie!'

He nearly fell down the stairs in his hurry to get back.

'Same again, kiddo.'

'Hey, where the fuck is Aidan?'

'In the jacks, pulling his wire.'

When Francis came back with the drinks everyone grabbed and gulped. Malachy was very excited.

'Two, two and zero. Des and Mary still not out of the traps.'

Des started laughing. 'I don't need to win at cards, do I, Mary?'

Francis couldn't believe what happened now. Des opened his Farah slacks, put his hand in and whipped out his mickey and his balls.

'See this, this is the only winner I need and it wins every time.'

He was giggling like a little child. Francis couldn't help staring at it, fat and curled like a huge snail under moss. Astonishingly, no one paid much attention. Mary was the first to speak. Very, very casually.

'Ah for heaven's sake, Des, will you put it away?'

Mr Grey didn't even stop dealing the cards. The others picked up their hands and checked them.

'Are you playing or not, Des?'

'Come on. Pick up your cards.'

'Ah really now, not in front of the child.'

Francis wanted to say he wasn't a child and he didn't mind. Still giggling, Des bundled his meat back into his slacks and zipped up. Mr Grey turned the five of hearts. Everyone went 'Ooooh!' Mary reached in, and stole it.

'Jesus, she has the ace an' all!'

'She's on a jink, lads.'

The whisper in his ear gave him a shock.

'Everything all right? No problems?'

Francis thought Aidan's grin was more self-satisfied than usual.

'Listen, thanks a million. You can head home now. It's nearly one o'clock.'

Aidan's hair looked a bit tangled.

'Ah it's fine. I don't mind staying.'

'No, go on. Gretta'd go apeshit if she heard I'd kept you here till this time.'

Aidan's shirt definitely wasn't tucked in as neatly as it had been earlier.

'I won't tell her.'

'Look. Go home. This lot'll be out the door in a few minutes anyway, you know what I'm saying?'

Yeah, and he'd go back and have more sex with the Carlsberg Special girls.

As Francis cycled home he felt contradictory moods of giddiness and frustration. A lock-in wasn't exotic at all. It was only drinking after-hours and playing cards. He never got to see or hear what Aidan was doing with the Carlsberg Special girls. He didn't even know who won the rubber of 45. But he had witnessed one extraordinary sight.

Nineteen: October 28th

If Francis was with his pals he'd be making them laugh, playing a mock violin and singing the chorus of 'Won't Somebody Dance With Me?' in a funny whiny voice. But he wasn't with his pals. He was up in the balcony looking down at them – and everyone else in the Royal George, it seemed like – getting off with each other. Francis felt left out of it. He knew something about himself deep down. Of course he would die rather than even whisper it to anyone, but he knew that Lynsey de Paul was singing about him, even though the song was about a girl, and even though a wallflower was a pathetic thing to be.

The balcony was supposed to be closed for the Sunday afternoon disco, but there were only a couple of chairs blocking the way at the top of the stairs and as long as you weren't a messer no one took any notice. It was a great perch for spotting the talent below. Francis sometimes liked standing back from the crowd, not taking part. Who was with who? So many partners. But today he'd crept up here because he was feeling sad and undesired. 'Won't Somebody Dance With Me?' only made him feel worse. He decided to get his coat and go. It was his first time ever leaving the Sunday afternoon disco early.

He felt so silly in his platform shoes that he was relieved it was nearly dark and people on the street wouldn't notice them. He'd bought them with his work money and loved the way the wine stripe across the front matched his good wine shirt. But he was tall already, what was the point of being taller? And platforms were harder to dance in.

It was too late to go through the park so he walked round it, thinking of girls he fancied and wondering why none of them would choose him, even the ones who liked him. Hilary Flannery, who was so beautiful that Francis shivered involuntarily every time he saw her, was really friendly and laughed at funny things he said, but she wouldn't slow dance with him. What was the matter with her? What was the matter with him?

At the corner of Edward Street, just as he was about to cross the road, a hand was waved in his face. 'It's not that dark, is it?'

His cousin Eva Durack was standing right next to him. He had been so lost in sweet unrest he hadn't noticed her approaching.

'We were waving like mad. You were away with the fairies.'

Eva wasn't wearing her glasses. She had her arm around a fellah.

'This is Mickey, my boyfriend.'

So Eva had a boyfriend. Francis noticed that she couldn't help giving the word a tiny proud emphasis. Despite his own melancholy he was happy for her. About time. She looked so pleased as well. Mickey squeezed her waist and Eva doubled up, giggling.

'She's mine, all mine. How's it going, Franny? Listen, we'd better get moving, Gorgeous.'

'Okay. Listen Francis, don't say you saw me, sure you won't? I know it's stupid, but I'm still sneaking out.'

'You know her ma, yeah?'

'Well… she's my aunt.'

'I told you, Francis is my cousin –'

'I know what you told me. I'm not fuckin' thick.'

His eyes seemed to dare Francis, challenge him to disagree.

'Anyway, so you know what kind of a mad bitch she is.'

Francis didn't know what to say to that. Would Eva say something? Mickey didn't give her a chance.

'I keep telling Eva, fuck that for a game of cowboys, just tell her where you're going and who you're with and tell her there's nothing she can do about it. I'm right, right? You're seventeen, for fuck's sake.'

Now Eva was getting the cold eyes.

'Yeah. Well, next birthday.'

'Anyway come on, we'd better be going.'

'Right, sorry Francis, listen we must meet up for a chat. How are you anyway?'

'Come on! Shift! See you when I see you, Frannie.'

Gripping her hand, Mickey marched her off, leaving Francis wondering had he ever taken a dislike to someone so quickly. The guy was like one of those little snarling dogs. It was quite funny the way he threw shapes with his muscle-y arms, but his voice was whinier than his dad's Philishave. The creep was wired, those eyes were only a blink away from a fight. It had been really obvious that he had no interest in meeting Francis. And why had he kept calling him Frannie when Eva had said Francis? But worst of all was the way he spoke about Auntie Mona, although the mad thing was, he was sort of right. It *was* lousy that poor Eva was still having to sneak out like that. Hadn't she the right to choose who she fancied?

It was a bit mad that only a few minutes after being delighted to discover that his favourite cousin had a boyfriend at last, Francis now hoped Eva would cop on and drop him. It would mean she'd be alone again. But maybe she'd do better? Maybe alone was better?

Twenty: December 12th

It was such an important victory. Mags knew she should be thrilled. Outside the Four Courts, Susan was jigging with delight and even her mother was exultant. So why was Mags not feeling the same elation about this Supreme Court ruling, that the 1935 law banning the sale of contraceptives in Ireland was unconstitutional if it prevented a married couple, like the plaintiffs Mr and Mrs McGee, from importing contraceptives for their own use? She told herself that Susan's reaction was largely teenage sentimentality, and despite Brenda Perry saying 'proper order', Mags was pretty sure her mother's support for contraception was limited to women in Mary McGee's specific situation: married women who had been advised by a doctor that pregnancy was a health risk.

Nonetheless, along with Susan and Brenda, she joined the crush of women to congratulate and hug Mary McGee and shake hands with Mary Robinson – somehow hugging a senior counsel didn't seem quite proper. But Mags still couldn't wish away the spasms, deep in her gut, of frustration, dissatisfaction, even anger. She told herself to cop on and consider how enormous and unlikely a victory this was, how much admiration this ordinary couple deserved, having fought all the way to the Supreme Court to establish their right to conduct their relationship without State interference. She appreciated absolutely how important their vindication was for all married couples, and so on and so on. But, a nagging voice persisted: why married couples only?

A tap on the shoulder. Trish! It had been ages. They hugged.

'Well? What do you think?'

'Sure it is what it is. Half a loaf. Better than another slap in the puss.'

Sound attitude, but was half a loaf good enough? If Mags believed contraceptives should be available to all adults, and that women should have total control over their own bodies, then why celebrate, as a great landmark, a legal opinion that referred to married couples only? Listening to the Chief Justice, Mags had felt such raw resentment that all the power in this matter was entirely in the hands of five elderly gentlemen. Maybe she just reacted badly to courtrooms. Even though today was a much more positive occasion – there was even a female barrister leading the case – that didn't ease her frustration, just as meeting Michael for the first time on her previous visit hadn't made the Arms Trial any less loathsome.

Susan and her gran strolled ahead, along Ormonde Quay, arms linked, laughing and whispering. How quickly and easily they had moved on to other things. Mags heard Gran Perry on about Christmas in the old days: live turkeys on Moore Street and Jimmy O'Dea at the Gaiety. She was in her element, and Susan lapping it up. Mags steered them along Grafton Street to a favourite spot, the Coffee Inn. They all had the bolognese and argued about miniskirts and school uniforms, glam rock and boys wearing make-up, nudity on television and 'dirty talk' as the Widow Perry called it. Susan seemed to find her gran's attitude merely amusing, which made Mags wonder why couldn't she deal with it like that, instead of working herself into a rage over stupid things? It also suddenly occurred to her how special this was: all three generations out on the town together. They should do it regularly.

The Widow Perry wanted to take her granddaughter swanning down Grafton Street under the Christmas lights, and Mags was more than happy to let them off. When she called Michael from a phone box across the road, she noticed herself speaking about the Supreme Court ruling far more enthusiastically. The Coffee Inn effect?

'Isn't it fantastic news? It's such a breakthrough.'

'Ah sure the whole situation was an embarrassment, couples

from abroad coming over on holidays, being told they couldn't bring contraceptives, having their gear impounded, made to feel like criminals. Fuckin' medieval.'

Although Michael meant what he said, he didn't bother to share with Mags the real cause of his exultation at the Supreme Court judgement. This thing might create trouble for the government, who would now have to introduce a new act legalising contraception. Michael smirked. Like an Irish version of the butterfly effect: a woman, for health reasons, decides to go on the Pill and as a result a government falls. Loony Blueshirts like Oliver J. and Dick Burke would chop a woman's hand off to stop her getting hold of such sinful objects, while their Leftie colleagues would want to flog rubber Johnnies on every street corner. If the Coalition split over contraception… Well, the voters would just reef them out of it.

As soon as Mags got off the line Michael rang CJ to tell him that, if the cards fell a certain way, he might find himself contesting an election before next Christmas.

*

After being stuck in school doing exams all day, the centre of town looked brilliant with the Christmas lights and the huge moving crib in Todd's window. As soon as holidays started Francis would spend all day in town, choosing presents. Between his Christmas club money and his wages from Hassett's, he was loaded. He'd be able to have fish and chips sitting down in the Golden Grill.

At home, his mam handed him a packet in a red wrapper. 'This came in the post for you. From England.'

Had his mam opened it? She'd better not have. That'd be really annoying.

'How do you know it's from England?'

'Look at the stamps.'

Francis saw Princess Anne and Captain Mark Phillips. Of course his mam would notice that. She was interested in all those people and what they wore and the way their hair was done and how kind and charitable they were. She and Aunt Mona could drone on for hours as if they knew them. He stared at his name. He'd never got a packet addressed just to himself before.

MASTER Francis (Frankie) Strong.

From the jokey big 'MASTER' and then 'Frankie' in brackets he guessed it must be Uncle Peter, and from the shape of the packet, it was probably a book.

'Well, aren't you going to open it?'

Francis wanted to enjoy opening the packet all on his own without his mam staring and commenting. 'Sorry, I have to go to the toilet.'

And he hopped up the stairs as if it was really urgent. He locked the bathroom door, sat on the side of the bath and opened one end of the packet. Inside was a paperback. He slid it out. The cover was a drawing of a long skinny girl in the kind of dress girls wore dancing at high speed in old silent films. For some reason there was a halo over her head.

Vile Bodies by Evelyn Waugh.

The cover was definitely intriguing and the name of the book sounded quite sexy. He had never heard of the writer so he wasn't sure how to pronounce 'Waugh', but it looked onomatopoeic. Like the sound someone would make throwing up. When he saw what his uncle had written inside, he laughed.

> Happy Christmas Frankie!
> This one not so thick… I think you'll like it.
> Your Uncle P.

He was right, it wasn't anywhere near as thick as *Nicholas Nickleby*. His dad had given out stink to him over what he'd said to Uncle Peter that time.

'Pure rudeness, that's all it was. What kind of way is that to speak to someone who's been thoughtful enough to give you a gift?'

He'd gone on and on about it, even though Francis had said sorry right from the start.

'Are they teaching you anything in school these days? Not manners anyway, that's for sure.'

His dad had been in such a weird mood that day. One minute he was ranting on about rudeness and *Nicholas Nickleby* and education: 'If you think getting good marks in your exams is the be-all and the end-all, it's not, you know.' The next he seemed to be talking about something else, but in such a roundabout way that at first Francis couldn't figure out what he was on about: 'There's other things you should be learning. Things that prepare you for life. Don't they teach you things that aren't in exams? You know… things a boy your age should know.'

Thinking back, Francis felt like such a dope for not copping on what his poor embarrassed dad had been getting at.

'Well… we do Civics. We learned about the voting system and local government –'

'Right, yes, yes, all that, I suppose, but other things too. You know. About life and… About ah… Well, you're fourteen now, so I thought that in school they might have explained…'

Then, at the exact moment his dad had used some phrase in a particular way – 'boys growing up' or something – he had hunkered down, picked up the poker and – the image would stay forever fixed in Francis' mind – started poking the fire. Which was the exact moment it had begun to dawn on him what this meandering chat might be about. The notion that his dad, who never uttered a swear word stronger than 'heck!' and who got really upset about bad manners, might be about to start talking about sex, made a nervous spider tickle inside him. The quiet crunch of the poker against the red-hot coals seemed a rumbling premonition of an eruption which, once it occurred, could no longer be ignored or sidestepped. He was uncomfortable enough at the thought of having to listen to his dad talking about sex, but the notion that he might have to offer some reply was petrifying.

But the crisis passed in seconds, in a few halting sentences.

'I mean… if there's things you're… you're… wondering about

and if they haven't… ah… haven't… you know… told you about them in school –'

'No! No. They explained everything…. in biology class.'

Even with his back to him, Francis saw his father's body relax. He picked up the coal bucket and rattled a relieved load into the fire.

'Oh yes, good. Biology, yes. I thought they might have done that all right.'

Then, muttering 'Good, grand, right', he jumped up and disappeared with the bucket as if there was some big queue for coal he urgently needed to join.

To keep his dad happy, but also because of genuine guilt that he still hadn't read beyond the second page of *Nicholas Nickleby*, Francis had written a thank you letter to Uncle Peter saying how grateful he was for such a thoughtful gift. Now, he would definitely have to make a more serious effort to read this new book, but that was okay, especially as it was very thin and had such an enticing title.·Sitting on the side of the bath he turned to chapter one. Just to see.

Three hours later he walked with his bike in to work so he could keep reading. Even though he had exams in Geography and Science the following day, once he tumbled into Evelyn Waugh's drowning-in-drink world of never-ending London parties and gossip and sex, a world of characters with crazy names like Throbbing and Circumference and Malpractice, he couldn't drag himself away. The story skipped about between prime ministers, mad old aristocrats, gossip writers, a sinister Jesuit, a creepy evangelist with a troupe of dancing girls, a hotel porter who wore expensive perfume and a crowd called Bright Young Things, whose chatter and behaviour was – as they would say – too, too silly. It was an upside down world where young viscounts had to make a living writing gossip columns and the main character had no money, but put a thousand pounds on a horse. A thousand pounds! His dad barely earned a thousand pounds in a whole year. What Francis loved most was how *adult* the book was, even though all the characters seemed like spoilt children who didn't know what to do with themselves apart from have parties and try to sound frightfully clever. Just as he got to Hassett's the novel took a darker turn. One of the viscounts, a gossip columnist, put his head in the oven and gassed himself. All because he had been thrown out of an exclusive party.

Aidan and Gretta were both on duty tonight because it was Christmas party time. Francis knew they simply couldn't bear working together and thought it was *too, too funny* observing them behind the bar like a pair of caged creatures, a peacock and a turkey vulture, pretending, in the *friendliest* way, that the other didn't exist. Even though there was a horrid crush at the bar it was *so* like Gretta to serve even more slowly than usual, sometimes ignoring customers, sometimes scowling at them and even openly insulting them when the mood took her. Francis observed a particularly intemperate example when a semi-regular called Billy joined Malachy at the bar.

'Season's greetings, Malachy. You'll have one on me.'

'No, I'm grand, sure I just started this pint.'

'Ah go on, I mightn't see you for another year.'

'No, honestly, I'm fine.'

'Ah Jasus, it's Christmas. I'm not buying myself a drink and not getting you something.'

'Don't mind me, work away.'

'I won't hear of it. Gretta! A Remy Martin for me and a pint for Malachy.'

'Honestly now, Billy, I couldn't take on another pint.'

'Please yourself. Have a small one then.'

'Well…'

'Ah go on. Gretta! Cancel the pint. Make it two Remy Martins.'

Gretta banged down the pint glass and turned to pour another brandy. Her remark, to no one in particular, was perfectly audible. 'Malachy loves the cognac when someone else is paying.'

Too, too awful! Francis made a mental note to keep well clear of Gretta tonight.

Aidan seemed even more jittery than usual, trying to look as if he was doing all the work, performing several tasks at the same time; pulling a pint with one hand, while reaching back to grab a bottle from the shelves with another, while demanding to hear Francis' order. 'What, what, yeah, go on.' When he asked for two Carlsberg Specials, Aidan's face went from its customary pale to a sickly white. His eyes darted nervily around the packed bar.

'Where are they?'

Francis knew who 'they' were. The Carlsberg Special girls.

'In the outside lounge.'

'Jesus Christ! Do they know I'm on tonight?'

'Well, one of them said to say hello.'

'Fuck. Which one?'

'Redhead.'

'Fuck. Jesus. Fuck! Did she really? What exactly did she say?'

'She said, tell Aidan we said hello.'

'Was that it? Nothing else?'

It was awfully puzzle-making why Aidan seemed *so* nervous about the Carlsberg Special girls, considering he had taken both of them upstairs one night, not so *very* long ago. More recently, when Francis had carried Mouseyhead – gay and legless after seven Carlsberg Specials – to a taxi, who had not accompanied her friend? Who had lingered behind as Aidan locked up? None other than Redhead!

The Carlsberg Special girls snatched the bottles and guzzled them like baby milk. Redhead stretched her neck back lubriciously. Glug, glug, glug! Underneath her fashionable skintight t-shirt, she was fashionably bra-less. Too, too titillating.

'Same again, straight away.'

Mr Reidy stopped Francis to order drinks for himself and his wife. Francis had never met the buxom lady before and, standing directly over her, he couldn't help noticing how much her plunging neckline revealed. She screeched. 'Look at this youngfellah, Tim, gawking at my knockers.'

How red-making!

'Can you blame the kid? Aren't they a lovely pair?'

'Ah God help us, he's gone pure scarlet. I'm only slagging you, honeybunch.'

'No harm in smelling a man's steak, Frankie, but don't steal it off his plate.'

As if the situation wasn't already quite too shaming, Des arrived at that moment and Mr Reidy summoned him loudly.

'Des! The very man. Would you advise young Frankie about tit-watching on the sly?'

'Getting a little bird's eye view, were you, Fran? Thanks for the mammaries.'

Still flushed, Francis gave Mrs Reidy a wide berth when he returned, setting the drinks on the other side of the table. The Carlsberg Special girls were impatient for their second round.

'What kept you?'

'Sorry, we're really busy tonight.'

'Tell you what so, honey. Bring us four more straight away, then we won't bother you for ages.'

'Not for ten minutes anyway.'

They cackled and guzzled.

'Did you say hello to Aidan for us?'

'I did.'

'And he said?'

'He said… say hello back?'

'Yeah but like, did he mention one of us more than the other?'

'Well… when he heard you were here, he got all excited.'

'Did he, yeah? Serious, like?'

'Oh yes, you should have seen his face. His eyes nearly popped.'

Lying to the girls was divinely seductive, but Francis was summoned by two couples he'd never seen in Hassett's before. As he approached he heard one of the woman muttering viciously.

'It's him. It's that bastard.'

'Shh.'

'I won't shush. Look at him, the dirty scumbag bastard.'

'Ah Ber, can't we just enjoy the night?'

'With that fucker sitting over there? After what he did?'

'Now youngfellah, a Guinness, a Smithwicks –'

'You wanted to come here. Can't you just ignore him?'

'And two vodkas 'n' orange, please.'

'Look at him, smirking away.'

How very curious-making. Who was Mrs Furious staring at? Francis discreetly followed her glare and realised it could only be grinning Des!

'Ah, look, will you let it be –'

'After what that bastard did to my sister? No way, no, no way. And if you were any kind of a man you'd go and claim him –'

'Will you give it a rest!'

'Hey you – scumbag! Don't ignore me, ya bastard ya.'

Francis was sure that Des had definitely heard Mrs Furious and knew she was hissing at him, but he ignored her. Too, too tense-making.

When Aidan heard the order for four Carlsberg Specials, his voice lifted into the squeaky zone.

'Four? Slow them down. Can't you slow them down?'

'How can I slow them down? Why do you care how much they drink?'

Aidan looked around quickly, his eyes so fearsomely guilty.

'I'll tell you later. Just try and slow them down, you know what I'm saying?'

Mr Grey arrived. Gretta ignored him, with nobs on. Francis saw her pretend to be busy polishing glasses, then glide straight past him to her little corner stool and take out her lipstick and compact. Bonkerama! Mr Grey didn't even bother calling to her. He waited wearily until Aidan was free.

Francis brought four more bottles to the Carlsberg Special girls. They had already polished off their drinks.

'What's he wearing tonight?'

'Is he wearing his new mauvy flares? His arse looks great in them.'

'You think his arse looks great in anything.'

'It looks even better when he's not wearing them.'

'But what about his chest, only four measly hairs?'

'I love those four little hairs. C'mere, is he wearing the chain I gave him? It's a little Celtic cross.'

'Ah Jesus, Fran's not one of them queers, looking at other fellahs' jewellery.'

Francis had noticed the cross, but he decided not to tell the girls that. They glug-glug-glugged their third Carlsberg Special, their lips sucking, their throats rippling. Too tumescent-making.

The Christmas revelry became noisier and sweatier and more delirious. Even Mrs Furious seemed finally to have been persuaded to relax and enjoy herself. All friends here. The four of them bawled out, over and over, the only line they knew of 'Oh I Wish it Could be Christmas Every Day.'

Francis couldn't overhear conversations any more and had to roar out his orders. He hadn't time to draw breath, but he was delighted with the clinking bulge in his right pocket. He'd definitely make more than his wages in tips tonight. Maybe twice as much. Between now and Christmas he would earn three pounds in wages and more than a fiver in tips and two pounds fifty Christmas Club money. More than ten pounds! He'd never been so rich. Rapture!

He saw Mouseyhead lurch towards the toilet. She slipped and slid, but somehow stayed upright and stumbled on. Redhead never seemed quite so horribly drunk, even though she matched Mouseyhead bottle for bottle. She pulled Francis' ear close to her mouth. Too, too Special Brew-smelling.

'Tell Aidan something for me, will you? Tell him I meant what I said the other night. Tell him I really did.'

Francis waited until Gretta was too busy to notice and ducked in under the counter. He pretended to rearrange spirit bottles as he spoke to Aidan.

'Redhead asked me to tell you something.'

'What? Oh fuck, what?'

'I'm to tell you that she meant what she said the other night.'

'Oh fuck. Fuck, fuck, fuck. Oh Jesus. Oh fuck!'

How provokingly perplexing! Francis simply *had to* ferret it out. 'What was it she said?'

There was real fear in Aidan's sideways glance, as he muttered.

'She said she wants to have my baby. Doesn't care that I'm married, doesn't mind that at all, she just wants a baby off me. She's gone pure simple, you know what I'm saying? I was hoping it was just the drink talking. Fuck, I should never a gone near her.'

A screaming voice erupted from the babble.

'Bastard! Whoremaster! Where are you sneaking off to now? Off whoring I suppose are you?'

Mrs Furious must have had a vodka and orange too many. Horridly shriek-making.

'Off to get some other poor young one up the pole, are you? Just like you did to my sister, you fuckin' whorin' bastard!'

Francis saw Des moving towards the exit, for once not pleased to be the centre of attention.

'My poor little sister is ruined on account of you. You're no better than dirt, you rotten fuckin'… whoremaster!'

'Ah shut up, y'aul bitch!'

Too, too far Des! Mr Furious, who had been holding out a despairing hand to persuade his wife to calm down, now had no choice but to spring forward and defend her honour. His pal had to support him. A shocking scene ensued as they both barrelled towards Des. The crowd went 'oooh!' and pulled back out of harm's way. Blows rained down on Des, who fell on a table and then to the floor. Francis saw a spurt of blood. Now they kicked him. He tried to fight back when curling up and begging for mercy was probably the better strategy. It was all too horror-making.

Then something happened that astonished Francis. Mrs Furious burst into tears and wailed.

'Ah Jesus, stop fighting! Stop it, John love. He's not worth it. Stop fighting, will ye!'

Her friend joined her in a keening peace women's chorus. Quite too bogus, Francis thought. Gretta and some of the customers stared at Aidan, as if he should be doing something. He vaulted extravagantly over the bar.

'Come on, lads, come on now, break it up!'

Francis admired how Aidan managed to drag the two men from the almost unconscious Des without getting blood on his silk shirt. Gretta now turned her discomfiting mascara'd gaze on Francis and gestured for him to help Aidan. He took the long slow route under the counter-flap and nudged politely through the crowd, praying that by the time he got anywhere near the battlefield, the danger would have passed. He was lucky. The men had retreated, grabbed their jackets and were pulling the wailing women toward the exit.

'What're ya after doing to him? Didn't you hear me saying stop?'

'Ah Jaysus, come on!'

After they fled, others began to leave too. Gretta dialled 999 and spoke in her most managerial tone.

'There's been an incident of an extremely violent nature and we require an ambulance at once.'

'No point in waiting, Gretta. I'll drive him down,' said Aidan, and Francis helped hoist the groaning, spurting Des out to Augustinian Lane and lay him in the back of Aidan's car.

'Listen, you know what Accident and Emergency can be like. I doubt if I'll get back tonight, you know what I'm saying? But don't tell her.'

He winked. Francis wasn't sure if he was referring to Gretta or to Redhead. Either way, Aidan had engineered a cunning withdrawal.

There was hardly anyone left in the bar. Gretta, slumped in

her corner with a cigarette and a small Gold Label, instructed Francis to clean up the broken glass and get J cloths and Ajax from reception to wash the bloodstains before they dried in. He returned in time to see Mr Grey leaning over the counter and hear him quietly hiss.

'What I said the other night had to be said, all right? That's that. Now, I'm a customer here and you're the bargirl. So do your job, bargirl, and serve me a drink.'

The frozen horror mask that was Gretta's face rose. She picked up a glass and poured a large Gordon's gin. Then she opened a bottle of Schweppes. Skkkkssss! The expression on her face did not change. Apart from the tiniest shimmer of the scarlet lower lip it really did look as if the make-up had at last solidified. She approached Mr Grey, gin in one hand, tonic in the other. Only at the very very last moment did Gretta Nagle raise both hands high and pour the liquids over Mr Grey's head.

Francis thought, sometimes women could be too, too scare-making!

Twenty-one: January 15th

'Submissively' really annoyed Marian. The word made her stop reading, but, actually, it wasn't just that word out of the blue. A vague resentment had been building over the last couple of nights, and it would probably have developed more forcibly if she'd been getting through the book faster. But because Marian had been seduced by how beautiful the hardback edition of *The First Circle* was, it hadn't occurred to her that it would be too bulky for reading on the bus into work, and that having such a fat tome on her desk in the office might seem like showing off. So she'd left it at home, which meant her only opportunity to read it was in bed, which was a pity because, having raced through *One day in the Life of Ivan Denisovitch*, Marian was really looking forward to getting stuck into this huge book. For her, reading was always about exploring the unknown, and the setting of *The First Circle* was certainly that: a special kind of prison called a *Sharashka* ,whose inmates were all dissident intellectuals. She admired the precision with which Solzhenitsyn detailed how the massive technical and intellectual resources of a paranoid dictatorship were deployed obsessively to control not just what people did, but what they thought. That this fiction was based very closely on historical reality made it more chilling to Marian than the horrific imagined societies of *Brave New World* or *1984*. This was not a vision of a possible future, but a revelation of the recent past and, she presumed, the reality of the present in the Soviet state. Solzhenitsyn's own history was now world-renowned because he'd been refused permission to leave Russia to collect his Nobel Prize for literature. Marian had been so thrilled to spot this beautiful edition in O'Mahoney's and had told Stephen, very specifically, that was what she wanted for Christmas, knowing that otherwise he'd waste his money on something ridiculous and expensive that didn't interest her.

But by the third night of reading she had begun to notice something that, very gradually and very reluctantly – given how much she admired such a brave writer – irked her more and more: Solzhenitsyn's portrayal of an important female character. All the dissident males in the Sharashka were highly intelligent, complex and flawed. They thought deeply about political philosophy, and freedom of thought and the very nature of living. The discussions and arguments between them were stimulating. This just made it more disappointing that the only significant female character so far, Simochka, seemed dull and needy: a character swept along by her emotions, without the capacity for the kind of sardonic observation, ironic reflection and lofty scepticism the profoundly intellectual male characters possessed. Tonight, Marian's disappointment swelled to impatient anger when Simochka seemed to become that infuriating thing, the 'love interest'. Surely, Marian thought, that shouldn't happen in a book as thoughtfully written as this.

It was that word. *Submissively.* Simochka responded to an instruction from her new love, the dissident, Gleb Nerzhin 'submissively'. Maybe it was the translator's fault, maybe the original Russian didn't have that connotation. Marian hoped this was so, but that didn't answer a bigger question now troubling her: why did men of intelligence and understanding still make degrading assumptions about women? Her boss Mr Harrington loved talking about politics, but never, in over three years, had he begun a political discussion with Marian. He might occasionally offer his opinion on some item of news or controversy and invite her to agree with him, but clever and decent though he was it would never have occurred to him that she might have a view of her own worth hearing. A year ago, during the election campaign, Marian had realised quite early on, that he had simply assumed she too was a fervent supporter of his pal O'Malley. At the time

Marian, not wishing to create tension with her boss, hadn't expressed her real opinion. Tonight she found herself wishing she'd had a good row with him on the matter.

Submissively. It was astonishing the effect of one word. Especially when, in the actual experience of her only serious relationship, 'submissively' was very far from the reality. Stephen was definitely more of a Simochka, and Marian could reasonably claim to be more like Gleb Nerzhin. It was she who had had the mental strength to turn down his marriage proposal, even though she felt some obligation, after doing a line for three years, to 'get serious'. When she'd shouted in his ear at the Horslips gig in the Savoy that he was the dead spit of Barry Devlin, the bass player – without the droopy moustache obviously – Stephen had laughed and kissed her and then went very quiet. A few minutes later, during 'Cú Chulainn's Lament,' he'd drawn her close and whispered, 'I love you, Marian, will you marry me?' She'd got a terrible shock. Had he been planning this, or had her comment and the emotional buzz of the gig swept him along? Her fatal pause and hesitant 'Let's talk about it after' not only spoiled their enjoyment of the rest of the gig, but made it very hard to persuade him that her eventual 'no' didn't mean she wanted to dump him, that she did love him, but right now didn't feel the need to change the way they were.

This was partly a lie of course, and she was annoyed with herself for being afraid to grab his hand and pull them both towards that no-man's land between doing a line and getting married. What would happen in that mapless place? It was a dilemma. The old idea of finding your one true love and entering the marriage state as a blissful virgin was still deeply attractive in a fairy-tale way, but Marian was feeling the force of some stronger instinct. Relationships needed a lot more sorting out, a lot more exploration, before permanence could be considered. Yet she was still reluctant to take the lead. Instead, when it had come to it that night, she'd been prepared to let Stephen go, and even enjoyed the short period of freedom that followed when he sulked, before he'd returned and pronounced himself willing to wait and see if there might be some chance of a future together.

Marian told herself it was unfair to criticise how a writer depicted a relationship just because her personal experience was different, but what genuinely deflated her was the discovery that intellectual understanding did not necessarily produce a deeper and richer appreciation of how men and women should relate to each other. It was curious that the only adult male who unashamedly admired her intelligence and was truly interested in her opinions on all sorts of questions was Stephen. She had taken that for granted. Now she had to consider that perhaps this was something rare in relationships, even when Russian intellectuals were involved.

*

Mags knew she was ranting but didn't care. She would not accept it. Marcus was trying to take her son away from her. Dorothy ordered two coffees and listened calmly.

'And what about Susan? Nothing about her. He couldn't give a damn about her education.'

'Mags, Mags, Mags.' Finally Dorothy got her to shut up. 'We can't argue both ways. We can't object to this proposal on the basis that Simon would be better off staying with you in Dublin and at the same time claim that Marcus is discriminating against his daughter by agreeing to let her stay on with you in Dublin, and accepting very stringent access terms.'

'But it's wrong to separate the children. You see what he's at. He's trying to set Simon against me.'

'That may well be his intention, Mags, but let's, just for a moment, take his proposal at face value –'

'Not proposal. Demand.'

'Hear me out, please. All right. How Susan is educated will be your choice and Simon's education will be under his control. Marcus will pay the cost of both. Is that, in itself, an objectionable –'

'Yes, because he wants to send him to Marlborough College.

'But it could be said that he's offering Simon a great

opportun–'

'Is that what you think?'

'I only want to know what you think. Is it your view that it's a bad thing for Simon to finish his education at Marlborough College?'

'Yes, obviously.'

'Mags, I understand that you don't like the idea, which is fine, but do you want me to make the argument that attending this very highly regarded school is, in itself, bad or wrong or –?'

'Yes. I'm not keen on single-sex schools and I think boarding school is a cruel, outdated concept. I don't want my child going to a school like that.'

'I understand.'

The coffees arrived. Mags tried to stop being annoyed with Dorothy who was, after all, doing her best for her. Trish had nothing but good to say about her, and on the flight to London this morning they'd got on like a house on fire. Mags sipped and told herself to listen.

'Why do you think there's no divorce in Ireland, Mags? I've grown to believe a lot of it is about male pride. I've seen it. They simply don't want to be called 'a divorced man'. It makes them feel less of a man. Couldn't you see how unhappy and uncomfortable Marcus was this morning? He's thinking this could never have happened to him if you'd both stayed in Ireland –'

'He's the Anglophile.'

'What I'm saying is, his unhappiness has nothing to do with the specific arrangements. I think he hates the very idea of being divorced.'

This was observant of Dorothy, given that she'd never met Marcus before. This morning, Mags had got herself into a positive mood, but it had been immediately obvious that Marcus was not of the same mind at all. Not that the self-pity act had any effect. He was no more to her now than some guy she'd accidently spilled drink over on a bad date, someone she'd prefer, on balance, not to encounter. A source of mild discomfort, no more.

'My concern would be that, in his mind, this proposal, demand, whatever, is the only thing that makes the idea of accepting a divorce arrangement even remotely palatable. Do you see what I'm saying, Mags? It might be the only thing that restores his dignity. Or his sense that, while he has sacrificed a great deal, at least he has salvaged something from the wreckage, something important to him. This dream of sending his son to Marlborough College. If that's his state of mind then he might be happier to walk away.'

'Refuse to divorce me? Can he do that?'

'He can delay it, drag it through the courts, make everything very unpleasant. Mags, you need to tell me: do I collapse the whole arrangement if Marcus won't back down on this point?'

Mags didn't know what to say apart from screaming, 'Are you on my side or not?' which was hardly helpful. Had Dorothy always had that deep, calm voice, or was it something she had acquired over the years as an asset in the legal world? It was a little cold in its clarity.

'May I ask a question that might help us come to a view?'

'Of course.'

'What would Simon think about going to Marlborough and being closer to his father?'

The child was thirteen. How could he know what was best? Mags knew that reaction wasn't good enough. Her hesitation had probably given away the answer.

'Well… He likes visiting his father, much more than Susan. I admit that. What he really hates is that we broke up. And… I suppose I sometimes sense that, in his head, I took him away from his father. He used to devour Billy Bunter and *Tom Browne's Schooldays* – is that relevant?'

'I used to love *Malory Towers*, but it never made me yearn to go to boarding school. As I've said – and it's just a feeling – this may be the one issue that Marcus is clinging onto. There was something even in the way his solicitor brought it up. I heard it in his voice. He didn't say 'deal-breaker' obviously, we never do until there is nothing else left to say – but it was in the air.'

Mags sipped. The coffee was tepid now. These snug Soho cafés should be for easeful encounters, gossiping with friends or lazy mornings-after, not ugly manoeuvres around horrible choices. The truth was she already knew the answer. It only remained to discover if she was willing to admit it. She bitterly resented Marcus for exposing her in this way.

'We should be going back. We agreed a fifteen-minute break. May I make a suggestion?'

'Please.'

'Rather than argue against the proposal, let us say we accept it, on condition that Simon is consulted and that it cannot happen without his assent. It he wants to stay with you, Marcus will have to accept that.'

'And if not?

'Won't it be some consolation that he's where he wants to be?'

Mags didn't think so. Which was worse, sending him away simply because his father demanded it, or finding out that her son was choosing to leave her? But at least Marcus would have to relinquish control and leave the choice to Simon.

'Yes, yes. All right. Let's get it over with.'

*

As soon as she saw the boy waving at her, Gretta Nagle couldn't help wondering if he'd seen her leave the dole office. He said, Hi Gretta. He was going into the Royal to see *The Exorcist.* Enjoy that now, was all she said and gave him a big smile so he'd see she was in flying form. Definitely, she was far enough away from the dole office. He'd come from Catherine Street and probably hadn't seen her until he was crossing the road. What did he know? What were they all saying in Hassett's? What stories were being spread? Councillor Hasset would never be talking directly to the likes of him so he wouldn't have heard anything from that quarter, but what lies had Aidan been telling him? And that horrible man whose name she'd never again let cross her lips as long as she lived? Had he been having a good sneer at her expense? Why was the boy asking how she was? She was fine, thanks for asking. Yes, it was desperate cold. Why wouldn't he just go, he'd miss the trailers? There was no question of her ever mentioning Hassett's, but if he brought it up, fair enough, she'd let him say whatever he had to say and not show any great interest, but the name Hassett's wasn't going to cross her lips, no more than the name of that horrible man.

What? What did the boy mean he got the sack as well? *As well?* What was he insinuating? She couldn't let that go. As well as who? She spoke very tartly. Who else got the sack? That flustered him all right – he didn't seem to know what to say. Gretta didn't feel a bit sorry for his embarrassment, nearly falling over himself trying to talk around it. He said what he meant was that this new woman had taken charge and the same night had sacked him *as well.* No notice or anything, no explanation. Gretta didn't want to hear about what some cow who'd robbed her job had said or done, so she just let him know that giving in her notice before Christmas was the best thing ever on account of the great new offer she'd got. A much better position, with much better conditions. Of course she knew to have an answer ready for when he'd ask where this new job was: Horan's Hotel in Thurles. Perfect. But the boy didn't ask where. He just said oh right and Gretta didn't like the look he gave her at all, so she told him anyway all about taking over as manageress of Horan's, a lovely well-run hotel and how delighted they were to be getting her and how they absolutely insisted that she take her time organising everything before starting, which was why she wasn't actually in Thurles yet. The boy said he was delighted for her. He was always polite, to be fair to him – certainly not the worst of them. It was sly Aidan she blamed. She was sure he had gone to Councillor Hassett, telling tales. Well, she'd managed to tell a few tales herself about Aidan and his whores, those dirty whores he thought she knew nothing about. She said it straight up to Councillor Hassett about Aidan pulling the wool over his eyes, making a right fool of him, and warned him to check the till extra carefully whenever Aidan was on duty alone. When she told him a few home truths about that other horrible man as well, with his filthy dirty ways pretending to be so respectable, Councillor Hassett had suddenly shouted 'Quiet, woman!' at her, and said that terrible hurtful thing about getting herself seen to. How dare he! What about that man? What about that horrible horrible horrible horrible man, who thought he could do what he liked with her, thought he could use her, treat her like dirt, thought she'd lie down and be walked on? He was the one who needed to get himself seen to. Horrible man. Horrible man! Never talking to her afterwards, just zipping himself up and closing the door behind him so quiet and sneaky. 'See you above,' was as much as he ever said. See you in hell! With his notions and his Gordon's gin. What about the night she put Cork Dry Gin in the Gordon's bottle and he drank it and didn't know the difference? She should have shown him up in front of the whole bar, only she was stupid enough then to believe the promises that came out of his mouth.

Why wouldn't the boy just go in to see his horror picture and let her get home, instead of talking and asking her things? Of course she was well able to make her voice sound very carefree and relaxed as if she hadn't a care in the world, but she wished he'd take that look off his face. Was something the matter? Her hair? Her lipstick? What? What? What? He was going on again about getting the sack. She wished he wouldn't use those words. He was saying he'd miss the few bob. She said yes, of course it was a pity he hadn't been lucky like her, walking out of one job straight into another and Horan's paying her from day one, even though she wasn't settled in Thurles yet, because she had arrangements to make.

Finally the boy said, nice to see you again, Gretta, and she said, yes, you too, and there in the nick of time, the name came. Francis. Yes of course, Francis. Yes, he was a well-behaved boy, a bit untidy, but a good worker. She laughed brightly and said if only Francis lived in Thurles she'd be happy to give him a job in Horan's. And Francis said that's very kind of you.

She had to walk away fast, she couldn't bear the way his eyes went watery. Feeling sorry for himself probably. Before turning up Catherine Street she gave a quick look back and there he was still. He hadn't gone into the pictures at all, the little liar. He was just standing there, staring. He'd better not follow her. She gripped her handbag close on account of the dole money inside and trotted down Catherine Street fast so that he wouldn't catch up with her if he came after. She looked back again at Roches Street corner but there was no sign of him. After watching a few more seconds to make sure he didn't appear, she wandered into Flannery's off-licence.

Twenty-two: July 18th

It was past midnight but Dr Garret FitzGerald could not sleep. There was no question of him sleeping. How could he sleep after such an astonishingly wretched turn of events! The Contraceptive Bill defeated in such a humiliating manner! After the vote he had of course expressed his utter embarrassment to Conor and Justin and Barry. Not wishing to be disloyal to his own party he had quietly apologised to these Labour Party ministers on a personal basis for the debacle while assuring them that he had had no advance warning, whatsoever. It had been a bombshell for everyone on the Fine Gael side of the coalition also – well, almost everyone! The Labour Party ministers were, naturally, shell-shocked and who could blame them? One by one they had stepped forward and argued passionately for this bill, pledging to support it even though many of them had serious reservations about its conservatism and indeed said so, honestly and clearly, in the chamber. Similarly, Dr Garret FitzGerald had his own criticisms of elements of the bill, and had expressed them last week – quite trenchantly! – round the cabinet table. But, recognising the urgent need to respond to the Supreme Court judgement in the McGee case, as well as the broader societal responsibility to legislate in a sensible way for married couples to access contraception, this bill was, in his view, steering a very delicate course between the Scylla of recalcitrant Catholic conservatism and the Charybdis of the radical liberal agenda. Both sides of the Coalition would have to compromise a little to ensure its passage.

Filling a kettle in the kitchen, his restless brain rummaging through the debris of the night's disaster, Dr Garret FitzGerald felt he could, in all modesty, claim that his own contribution –

taken quite late in what had been an exhausting and frequently turbulent parliamentary debate! – ought to have ensured – had rational thought prevailed! – the passage of the bill. Had it been a competitive university debate, he would in all probability have emerged as gold medallist. In preparing the speech, he had felt the weight of expectation on his shoulders more keenly than usual, given that the government had – accepting that any issue related to sexual morality should be regarded as a matter of conscience – had – quite sensibly in Dr Garret FitzGerald's considered view – decided to allow a free vote on this bill. Surely there were more than enough responsible deputies on the opposition benches to counteract the few grimly – albeit sincerely and legitimately – conservative Catholic members on the government back benches? As it transpired, it was not backbenchers who caused the trouble. Dr Garret FitzGerald's sudden laugh was uncharacteristically sardonic and hollow, more akin to Byron's, 'And if I laugh at any mortal thing, 'Tis that I may not weep!'

Was anyone on the opposition benches prepared to listen to reasoned argument? His extensive quotations from the Supreme Court ruling were partly designed to remind responsible opposition deputies of their constitutional duty to legislate in this matter, and partly to establish that the basis of Justice Walsh's ruling was respect for the privacy of family life, in particular his key sentence.

'It is outside the authority of the State to intrude into the privacy of the husband and wife relationship for the sake of imposing a code of private morality upon that husband and wife which they do not desire.'

Dr Garret FitzGerald was convinced that, at a pinch, many decent citizens might be willing to accept that, for married couples in difficult circumstances, contraception could be considered an acceptable remedy. Indeed in his own constituency of Dublin South-East there were many venerable ladies who had, in their younger, sexually active days, availed of the contraceptive services always discreetly available to private patients who knew which doctors to choose. But such people would also recoil in horror from the kind of moral free-for-all advocated by radical feminists. Therefore it was important that Dr Garret Fitzgerald should plant his flag in the popular centre-ground and assure like-minded opposition deputies that this bill would not threaten public morality in the State. After all, in Northern Ireland, where contraceptives had, under British law, been legally available for many years, Catholic morality had not disintegrated or even suffered. Indeed Catholicism was thriving in the Province, despite the sinister presence of contraceptives in the local chemist shops! This led him seamlessly on to the argument aimed most pointedly at Fianna Fáil. The United Ireland question. How, he asked, could they hope to convince Northern Unionists to consider any link with the Republic when rights they considered basic were denied in this jurisdiction?

He had done all he could. If cogency of analysis and clarity of thought, if compassion allied to pragmatism could have won the day, Dr Garret FitzGerald would be sleeping peacefully in his bed now, instead of morosely pouring a cup of Lyons in a cold kitchen. But the Fianna Fáil opposition cared little about constitutional responsibilities. Its strategy was cynically to manipulate the political situation in the hope of embarrassing – perhaps even dividing – the government. Dr Garret FitzGerald had, in the chamber, accused them quite fearlessly and directly of playing games with a matter of serious public policy involving human rights and public morality: 'It would not be an honourable act by the opposition to play politics so far as this bill is concerned.' Not to mention that for some of them – CJ inevitably sprang to mind – voting against a bill allowing the availability of contraceptives constituted the rankest hypocrisy!

Yet, that was how every Fianna Fáil deputy had voted. But they had not been alone.

Dr Garret FitzGerald would never forget the look on the Chief Whip's face. They had both voted and were observing others going through the 'Tá' and 'Níl' lobbies. He had turned to his colleague, about to offer the hope, however improbable, that the conservative backbenchers might choose to abstain rather than embarrass their own government. Noticing the Chief Whip's sudden expression of horror and confusion, he had looked round to see what was causing such visible shock and upset.

Dr Garret FitzGerald would have to concede that it was the most devastating moment of his political career to date!

His party leader, An Taoiseach, Liam Cosgrave, the head of the government, was going through the 'Níl' lobby, voting against his own government's bill! The titters on the opposition benches were audible. They couldn't believe their luck! Dr Garret FitzGerald was, quite singularly, left speechless! He had never been a confidant of his party leader: indeed there were many who, convinced he was the natural choice as Minister for Finance, believed that Cosgrave had appointed him to Foreign Affairs just to keep him away from the centre of things. As he paced the floor wearily now, his tea almost cold, pondering all these matters, Dr Garret FitzGerald still could not understand how the leader of the government could sit in cabinet, as Cosgrave had done, while his ministers spiritedly debated this bill and never apprise his colleagues of his intention to vote against it. Had he never considered that it would make the party and government a laughing stock? Even though technically, it might be argued that, because it was a free vote, it wasn't therefore a 'government' bill as such... Nonetheless, it was a devastating turn of events. Given the turbulence of his own feelings at this late hour, Dr Garret FitzGerald could well imagine the rage and frustration of the Labour party partners. In the face of such an egregious insult from such an elevated source, could the Coalition hold together?

*

Being Paris, being the Hotel de Crillon, Ann Teresa was allowing Terry free rein to luxuriate in quite the most exquisitely presented late breakfast in bed, when CJ swanned in from his early morning flight, looking disgracefully, puggishly, pleased with himself. He tossed several newspapers on the bed before treating her to a long, hungry, succulent kiss, his breath perfumed with cheap Aer Lingus champagne. Then, his face brimming with the most gloriously scruffy schoolboy grin, he said, 'Take a look' before twirling round to tip the boy. Look at what? Ann Teresa was beyond mystified. Surely not the Irish morning papers? That would be the very last thing after the last thing on her 'things to do in Paris' list. Apart from the essential dullness of it, what could have happened since she'd flown out yesterday afternoon that was so –? Then she saw a headline.

'TAOISEACH VOTES AGAINST GOVERNMENT BILL.'

She started to laugh and laugh.

'COSGRAVE IN DÁIL SENSATION.'

Ann Teresa had long thought of him as a ridiculous man. But this?

'TAOISEACH MARKS HIMSELF APART FROM LIBERALS.'

Hardly news, darlings - Ann Teresa leapt into Terry mode –That face alone! Straight out of Dickens: Gradgrind or Wackforth Squeers. Griping, cantankerous, puritanical, it would sit comfortably alongside those Notre Dame gargoyles. The fellow who did him on TV as the Minister for Hardship? Hilarious. Inspired. Minister for Morality now as well, it seemed. Brackets gaga close brackets. Only in Holy Ireland. A risible, preposterous leader, for a risible preposterous nation.

CJ whipped away the tray and hopped onto the bed on all fours, brimming with bowsie euphoria, growling for her. Terry swept the morning papers aside and pulled him closer.

Hours later, CJ still slept so silently that Ann Teresa put a hand close to his mouth to check his gentle breath. Later they would walk along the Quai de Tuileries in the evening sunshine before dinner at Laperouse. She retrieved the papers and amused herself with some choice quotes from the debate. Young Des O'Malley – 35 going on 75, apparently – thought the Dáil had a duty 'to deter fornication and promiscuity, to promote public morality.' Clearly not carrying on the spirit of his lovely uncle.

Knowing it had been CJ's intention not to speak in the debate,

Ann Teresa was surprised to see that one of the Labour party speakers had nonetheless singled him out as someone 'sophisticated' who should 'appreciate' the need to make contraception available.

'Let nobody suggest that that sophisticated politician, Deputy Haughey, does not appreciate the dilemma of the government. Who are we trying to cod? I do not want to name any more names.'

It was a curious remark. What other names? Could it be that, oh so indirectly, opaquely, insinuatingly, this was the first public reference to their affair? Could this be the beginning? Might the veil be lifted further? How brave would the press be? Not very, in her experience. Ann Teresa found herself smiling at the prospect of the affair being mentioned in print. As Terry would say, deliciously funny, darling. As long as it was done with discretion and taste, of course, strictly for insiders to enjoy. Ann Teresa guessed that CJ might not feel quite the same way, not if his little dream of clawing his way back was ever to be realised. Sliding under the sheets and easing closer, she curled a hand along his soft hairy tummy, feeling the satisfied fall and rise, and gently spooned him.

*

Gráinne Kiely hated the way her shoulders sloped. You hunch forward, that's the problem, her mam never tired of telling her, your posture is all wrong. *Here's me head me arse is coming.* Her mam hadn't said that, some uncle had said it, referring to someone else, but it stuck in her mind. That's me, she often thought, *here's me head me arse is coming*. Her mam kept saying deportment, deportment, as if the word was a wand to wave over her. Head up, keep the base of the spine straight. She tried it, Jesus she tried, but in the long run, couldn't be arsed, which, now that she thought about it, wasn't a bad pun. Anyway, her hair was pretty, that was a fact, everyone liked her hair, and it was full and long enough to rest on her shoulders, so the slopiness was less noticeable. But, in a bathing suit, with her best feature tucked up into a bathing cap, the shoulders were exposed in all their depressing, dreary droopiness. So much for good deeds. One of her dad's many hundreds of thousands of boring wise old sayings was 'a good deed never goes unrewarded.' Well, here she was about to do a good deed, help her best pal Emer get off with a fellah. And her reward? Public embarrassment.

'Do I look all right?'

There were times when Gráinne Kiely had to work really hard to ignore how maddeningly needy and reedy her best pal's voice sounded. She had the perfect figure for a bikini. Little Miss Slim and Gorgeous. Even the bathing cap was an advantage as it hid one of her less attractive features, lifeless hair, and instead showed off her pretty swan's neck. Gráinne knew that Emer Bennis knew exactly how good she looked. Why wouldn't she, having worn out her mirror at home, testing different bikinis and bathing caps to find the perfect combination that would finally catch the eye of the divine Andrew Liddy?

'You look fantabulous.'

If she answered, 'Do I really?' in her usual 'pity me, I'm a poor little orphan girl' voice, Gráinne decided she would just say, 'Ah fuck off Emer!'

'Do I really?'

'He's going to fall at your feet.'

'Ah go way! God, Gráinne, imagine if he's not here today!'

'You said he would be.'

'Well, I was told they were talking about it.'

Was she serious? They had cycled all the way out to the Two Mile Inn, Gráinne had forked out the price of a pack of fags to get in to a swimming pool she didn't want to go to, and all because Emer, in one of her regular Andrew Liddy updates yesterday, had said she'd been told that he and his pals would be there this afternoon. This fact seemed to be so amazingly mind-blowing it merited several repetitions, until Gráinne had finally taken the bait and suggested that Emer go to the pool and get talking to Andrew Liddy, knowing that as official best friend and martyr to the cause, she was walking herself into an afternoon of humiliation. Well, okay, humiliation was an exaggeration, but definitely, Gráinne would prefer to be somewhere else. Was Emer now seriously suggesting that gorgeous Andrew mightn't be here at all?

'Well, if he's not, then we'll have a nice swim and go home.'

Emer looked shocked for a second and then giggled.

'You're gas! Would you go first? See if you can see him.'

'No, come on.'

Stepping from the pokey ladies' changing room into the wide-open pool area, Gráinne did feel a twinge of sympathy for her pal, imagining what it must feel like to be suddenly exposed in the huge, harsh, cold light, knowing that dream-boy might be near, judging her already. But Gráinne also told herself that there was no way José *she'd* ever go to a public swimming pool and prance around in a bikini to get any boy's attention. Not even Bryan Ferry, who was an absolute ride!

'He's here! He's here!'

The squeeze on her arm was in danger of drawing blood. Gráinne saw a gang of four lads hanging around at the deep end too far away to recognise faces, but obviously Emer could pick up the scent of Andrew Liddy from very far away.

'What'll we do? What'll we do now?'

Gráinne instructed herself to suppress her cynicism and try to share some of her pal's excitement.

'Well, why don't we just do the normal thing, hop in at the shallow end' – how appropriate, she thought, but didn't say – 'and swim a length. We'll end up where they are.'

'Would it be a better idea just to walk round the pool, you know, and go past them?'

Because she thinks she'll look sexier dry and showing off the bod, rather than splashing about. Gráinne was going to have to work harder at suppressing cynical thoughts.

'Well, I'm swimming.'

'Okay, right. Me too.'

The water was warmer than Gráinne expected and, swimming

freestyle, she enjoyed feeling the stretch of her body. No such thing as sloping shoulders now. She'd forgotten what a decent swimmer she was. When they popped up at the far end, lo and behold, Andrew Liddy was barely three feet away. The sunlight bouncing off the water caught the melancholy brown eyes gazing upwards, and gave his face a saint-like glow. He was pretty perfect all right. Gráinne followed his gaze to the boy on the diving board. She recognised him. Patch Dollard. An odd name, but Emer, who not only knew everything about Andrew Liddy, but an alarming amount about his pals, had once told her that his first name was actually Pachelli. Rather than die of embarrassment, he insisted on being called Patch. According to Emer he was Andrew's best friend. He bounced at the edge of the diving board, messing. Would he jump or not, lads? Andrew and the other two boys were encouraging him. Gráinne didn't know who the chubby one was, but she recognised Francis Strong. His brother was married to her oldest sister, Áine. The christening of their first child three years ago was the last time she'd met him, although she had spotted him sometimes at the Sunday afternoon disco, but never said hi. He seemed like a bit of a clown, going mad dancing to make his pals laugh, full of himself. Gráinne had also noticed him hanging around the balcony on his own, surveying everyone, standing apart, looking down on all the mediocre creatures below.

Clutching his knees to his chest Patch Dollard created a big splash. Gráinne figured this was a perfect moment for Emer to do a little girly scream so that the boys would say something, but she didn't. Instead Gráinne felt an underwater nudge. What? Did Emer expect her to do everything? She started swimming back towards the shallow end, not really caring whether her pal followed or not. Emer came splashing behind, out of breath and annoyed.

'Why did you swim off like that?'

'I felt like swimming.'

'But when we got splashed, that was a great chance to start talking to them.'

'Well why didn't you?'

'I thought you'd do it.'

Emer was her pal, Gráinne reminded herself. She was in the grip of forces stronger than herself, or something. Give her a break.

'Come on so, let's go back.'

'No, we'll walk round.'

'You walk round if you like. I'll swim back.'

Moving smoothly through the water, Gráinne decided she would help the cause. Just brazenly start a conversation with Andrew Liddy and find some way to bring Emer into it... Two pairs of boys' feet dangled underwater in front of her, so she popped up near them. Francis Strong and the chubby fellah were almost directly above. No sign of Andrew Liddy at all. Or Patch Dollard. Then she spotted them at the shallow end. Ah Jesus! Poor Emer was dancing a jig, not knowing which end to choose. The two boys would surely swim back soon, so Gráinne decided to fill in time talking to the other two. It was an easy conversation to start.

'Are you Francis Strong?'

The way he looked down reminded her of his arrogance at the Sunday disco, scrutinising from on high. No recognition at all.

'My sister is married to your brother.'

It took about two seconds, then his face changed completely.

'Oh – Gráinne Kiely?'

Then he was all apologies, his mind had been somewhere else... her swimming hat... How long had it been, three years? But it was the change in his expression that Gráinne noticed most of all. The know-it-all smirk on his face had changed to an eager bulging-eyed fish. He dropped down into the water next to her, full of questions. Of course there was plenty to talk about because of the family connection, but Gráinne was still surprised when she realised that Andrew Liddy and Patch Dollard had arrived back without her noticing, and she hadn't felt, as often happened, that if she didn't keep chattering there would be an embarrassing silence. Francis Strong wasn't what she expected at all.

In the middle of a sentence he seemed to lose track of what he was saying. Gráinne could see he was distracted by something going on behind her. Because they were treading water she was able to adjust her position casually and saw what he saw. Emer and Andrew Liddy were getting playful. She, looking pink and lovely with one foot dangling prettily in the water, was splashing him playfully. Playfully, he grabbed her ankle. Gráinne thought her pal's playful wriggles and shrieks before being pulled in were perfectly performed. Emer disappeared underwater and, a moment later, Andrew Liddy laughed as his legs were grabbed from below. He struggled free and chased after her. All sorted then, without Gráinne's help. No clever chat-up required. Panicked by the silence between herself and Francis, she said the first stupid thing that came into her head.

'Race you.'

Halfway, Gráinne slowed a little to make it a closer contest, but, as she reached for the wall at the shallow end, she felt an arm curl round her waist and try to yank her back. She wriggled and still managed to touch the wall first. He laughed and said, 'Sorry, I know you won.'

But Francis Strong's hand was still touching her waist.

Then, suddenly, he let go and pulled away a few feet, as if he'd done something he shouldn't. It felt a bit weird, as if they were cousins or relatives, which they weren't. Were they even in-laws? Gráinne wasn't so sure again what she thought about Francis Strong.

Patch Dollard backstroked lazily towards them.

'Patch never looks like he's in a hurry.'

It sounded a bit jealous. Patch glided in and stayed floating on his back at first. When he did stand up it was like one of those special effects shots in nature films of a plant or flower opening. He seemed to stretch out in slow motion. Gráinne noticed the tiny smile that was like part of his mouth, as if he was always remembering something pleasant. Before long the three of them were leaning on the side of the pool, letting their legs float behind, not saying much, certainly not having a conversation. Just enjoying the sun on their faces through the big glass panels and staring at the car park outside as if it was some fab golden Saint-Tropez vista. Gráinne didn't exactly know how Patch had done it, but this laid-back atmosphere had definitely been his doing.

In the changing room, Emer showered in seconds and dressed at lightning speed, then spent the rest of the time fixing herself at the mirror, nagging Gráinne to hurry up. Andrew had arranged to meet her outside. So what was the hurry? Let him wait.

'Please, Grá!'

Gráinne badly needed a fag anyway, so she flung on her clothes. The chubby fellah was the only one there, squatting on the tarmac, reading a book. The cover had a big swastika and a soldier twisted in agony. *Comrades of War* by Sven Hassel. Either he didn't notice them or just ignored them. Gráinne lit up and sucked hungrily. Oh life-enhancing nicotine! Emer wouldn't take a drag, not wanting to risk cooling Andrew's passion with tobacco breath.

'So, where'll you go?'

'I don't know. You'll come too, won't you?'

'Playing gooseberry? No thanks.'

'You won't be. What about Patch?'

'What about him?'

'Don't you think he's good-looking? I mean definitely compared to' – she flicked sneering eyes towards the chubby fellah – 'and that other guy.'

'What are you after getting me into, Emer?'

'Nothing. It was just that Andrew and me' – Andrew and me already, Jesus! – 'we thought you and Patch seemed to be getting on very well.'

When the other three appeared, the chubby fellah heaved himself up and came over. Gráinne thought Emer might die of smiling when Andrew wandered over next to her. When Patch said he was gasping for a fag, Gráinne took what she assumed was a hint and offered one of hers. No thanks, he rolled his own, and took out a little bag. He crouched down and got to work: very expert, very coolabula. When he asked if anyone else wanted one, Gráinne thought, why not and said, yeah sure. They all stared at Patch like he was Dr Christian Bernard. Gráinne couldn't bear the silence and asked Francis did he not smoke? He said he'd tried it but it didn't do anything for him. Then she thought that in fairness she should ask the chubby fellah. The shock of being spoken to made his fat face look scared, but his voice was withering.

'Why would I want to do that? Nicotine is a poison.'

Then, abruptly, he said he was heading and just walked away towards his bike. Jesus! Was he always that odd, or just when girls were around?

As soon as Cónal said he was leaving, Francis knew he had to go too or else end up a real spare tool. He watched Patch handing Gráinne a rollie and lighting up, dead casual, as if there was nothing going on between them, and Andrew and the other girl standing close together not saying a word, but dying to start holding hands and getting off with each other. Of course, as soon as he shouted after Cónal to wait, Patch did a big 'Ah hold on, don't split yet, I thought we were all going to hang around town,' like he hated the party breaking up.

Francis knew that, once they cycled away, Cónal would be all talk. In company he was either silent or freaky, but on his own he was smart and entertaining, although still a bit freaky. He loved reading several things at the same time. Right now it was the Sven Hassel rubbish, this month's Spiderman comic and *Zen and the Art of Motorcycle Maintenance*. Yet he wouldn't even look at Evelyn Waugh. Poncy imperialist shithead, he called him. Francis tried to convince him that he'd really get into the eccentrically passive heroes that so fascinated Francis: men who seemed always to stand outside the action, either observing the world turn, or letting themselves be carried along by events. No chance. Not even the short humorous novels like *Scoop* or *Black*

Mischief, let alone *Brideshead Revisited.* But, to be fair, Francis had no intention of reading *Zen* and the rest of it, or *Lord of the Rings* or, most definitely, any Sven Hassel so-called novel.

Cónal was rabbiting on about the bombings in Dublin and Monaghan. He had a conspiracy theory naturally. Francis wanted to ask him about Gráinne Kiely, but there was no point because he never talked about girls, or sex, unless it was animals in the wild. He'd only been to the Sunday afternoon disco once. Someone once told Francis that his dad was a religious maniac and had punished him for going that one time. He didn't know whether to believe that or not, but definitely, Cónal was the last person to ask about girls.

Why, having discovered today that talking to Gráinne Kiely was good fun, had he messed things up straight away by grabbing her waist? No, it wasn't that he grabbed in the first place, that was okay, it was that he held on too long, so it wasn't like messing anymore, more like… more like he was getting a feel. Maybe he was too, for those couple of seconds. And he knew Gráinne knew. The really mad thing was Francis hadn't been thinking of getting off with her at all. He'd been enjoying just talking.

Would it be okay? It seemed okay afterwards. Definitely not anywhere near as bad as what had happened with Joanne. Francis cringed, remembering how in the Carlton, at *Jonathan Livingstone Seagull,* he'd pawed at Joanne. If he could do it again he'd behave better, wouldn't he? Would he, though? Would he? That's what Francis didn't know, because he didn't know anymore if he could control himself. That's what felt so bad. That's what made him really afraid.

The date with Joanne had started off fine. She was a really good kisser. He'd known that already after getting off with her a couple of nights before, but curled up together in a jumbo seat in the Carlton was a lot better than kissing in the cold at her front gate. If he'd been satisfied with just good kissing, then maybe he'd be on another date with her today. But she wanted more than kissing too, he was sure of that. When he put his hand inside her t-shirt, she curled in closer and fondled his hair. Francis wanted to cry now, thinking about it, because he knew that was the moment his brain exploded and went crazy and started demanding, what next? Her bra. What next? Her nipple. What next? What next? His hand obeyed and down it went, down, down, sliding inside her jeans. Down, down. What next? His hand reached the rim of her panties and felt a tiny tangle of hair. His hand stopped, the screaming in his head got even louder. WHAT NEXT?

And when he looked up at Joanne's face, there was no sign of the smiling, chatty, perky girl he'd danced with at the end of Inter Cert exams mega-disco, who said yeah, sure, let's meet up and gave him her number, cool as you like. That girl wasn't there and the one staring at him now wasn't really kissing him back anymore, and her fingers were limp on his shoulders, and her whole body was still. Oh Jesus, what had he done? Had he scared her?

His hand retreated, trying to make like it was all still lovely. He pecked her cheek and neck, he eased the t-shirt down to meet her jeans. He took her hand and playfully interlocked fingers, but it was all too late, and he felt like such a lying pig. Even turning to the screen only made him feel more guilty knowing that he'd chosen *Jonathan Livingston Seagull* for the date because it was a film he had no interest in seeing.

She'd let him hold her hand as they left, but hadn't held his. Goodbye.

'What's up with you? Why are you going so slow?' Cónal had stopped at Sarsfield Bridge to let him catch up.

Francis didn't know how to begin explaining what was up with him, because he didn't know. And anyway, Cónal wouldn't be interested in that stuff. And his other friends would only laugh. He went too far and got dumped, they'd say. Big Deal. As if there was nothing more to it.

*

It was odd for Auntie Mona to leave so quickly and abruptly. Usually if she was there when Marian came home, she'd be asking for the latest office gossip and would probably mention yet again that Mr Harrington had asked her out to the pictures years ago and she'd turned him down. But today she was silent and looked red around the eyes. Had she been crying? It couldn't be a death or an illness because her mam would have told her that straight out. Instead, after seeing Auntie Mona off at the door, she'd just bustled into the scullery saying was that the time already, she'd better get on with the tea. It was what she hadn't said that Marian really noticed. There was no, 'You wouldn't believe how long she kept me there talking.' or 'Of course time means nothing to Mona Durack, she has the whole day to do what she likes.' There was no pretend impatience, no light-hearted irritation, no comment about Auntie Mona at all.

About half an hour later, when they were laying the table, her mam asked, 'Do you know the Quinlans over on Hogan Road?'

'Don't think so.'

'One of their sons would be about your age. Mickey. A little muscly fellah.'

'I'm not sure. If I saw him I might. Why?'

'Just wondered.'

Marian guessed this had something to do with Auntie Mona. Now she was even more curious. Someone her own age? Had there been an incident, a row? Had he shouted abuse at her? No, far from making her aunt cry, that would have been a great excuse for a rant about manners and young people today. Now that Marian thought of it, she couldn't remember ever seeing Auntie Mona cry.

It wasn't until they were alone together again in the scullery doing the washing up after tea, that her mam asked something which made things a lot clearer to Marian.

'Have you seen Eva lately?'

Marian had to think for a moment because definitely she hadn't talked to her cousin in ages, but she had – yes – she had seen her a couple of weeks back. She and Stephen were taking off on the bike. Now Marian remembered noticing that Eva was with someone. A little muscly fellah.

'Only in the distance. I was coming out of the pictures with Stephen and I waved at her.' Marian deliberately left the important bit to the end so she could observe her mam's reaction. 'She was with her boyfriend. I didn't recognise him.'

'Oh Jesus, that must have been him.' Then her voice dropped very, very low and it all poured out. 'That must have been Mickey Quinlan, the fellah I was asking you about. Mona's after finding out that Eva's been going out with him for nearly a year. Behind her back.'

Ah, for crying out loud, Marian thought, poor Eva. That was all Auntie Mona's fault – she practically had her in a straitjacket.

'She's in an awful way about it. We both know Mrs Quinlan. Her family were Powers from Gerald Griffin Street, and she's a very nice woman, but Mona says that this Mickey fellah is a right scut.'

'But Mam, Eva's no fool.'

'I know, I know, sure she's a great girl and I've always said Mona mollycoddles her too much.'

More than that, Marian thought, she's suffocated her. No one would ever be good enough for Eva as far as Auntie Mona was concerned.

'But the poor thing was bawling her eyes out. She even said it wouldn't be so bad if Eva had met someone like your Stephen instead of a lowlife like Mickey Quinlan.'

'If Eva was going out with Stephen behind her back she'd be saying he was a scut too.'

'Ah no. Now, in fairness, she'd never say that.'

Stephen could do no wrong. Her mam trusted him completely. When Marian had cautiously broached the idea of an overnight trip to Ballybunion at the end of the month for the Thin Lizzy gig, she'd been amazed that there was no hysteria about it at all. Her mam just took it for granted that Stephen would behave impeccably. And she was probably right. If only she knew what *Marian* had decided was going to happen in Ballybunion, she'd have a seizure. Or lock Marian up.

Which thought made her realise that cousin Eva wasn't the only one who felt the need to keep a secret from her mother.

*

'Well?' said Michael.

'I don't even want to talk about it.' Mags at this point, genuinely did not care if she never heard the word 'contraceptive' again.

'I'm with you there. But sure the Blueshirts were bound to make a hash of it. There they were, trying to pass a bill legalising yokes they wouldn't even know how to use in the first place.'

'It's just so depressing. And insulting.'

'You're right, and if Labour has any balls their ministers'll walk off the pitch. Show Cosgrave you can't do the like of that without consequences.'

'Anyway, let's forget about it. I've a dripping tap, will you have a look?'

Mags had obsessively followed the gruesome spectacle that was the Dáil debate and had heard just one speaker, Barry Desmond, get beyond self-important male breast-beating. 'It is ironic that we have had only one woman member contributing to the debate. I find that situation very, very sad. We have a male-dominated assembly deciding whether or not 41,000 women currently "on the Pill" are acting criminally or otherwise. There are all the elements of a rather sick debate.'

At which point he should have said, 'So, let's wrap it up, gentlemen.' Most of the others shouldn't have opened their mouths at all. The Taoiseach's shock vote at the end was only the last vicious kick after the abused women of Ireland had been well and truly slapped and battered and left unconscious.

Michael's amused diagnosis on the leaky tap was that a half decent plumber would fix it in no time. Always leave it to the professionals. Mags noticed that her reply, to the effect that she'd never have thought of that all on her own, had more edge on it than intended. Then during dinner, as she watched Michael round up the black olives in the pasta sauce and corral them at the side of his plate, she found herself counting silently to ten. Try them, they were part of the sauce after all. He asked if anyone wanted his olives and Simon said, yes please. When he passed them from plate to plate by playfully flicking them with a fork and making Simon laugh, Mags began to feel something like rage.

After dinner Michael suggested a few rounds of poker, but she insisted on rummy instead. A hundred points, 50p stake. Throughout the game she found herself watching him like a hawk, doing nothing that might help him win while frequently laying off cards that would benefit Susan next to her. What had he done to trigger this reaction? Was it just because he had misjudged her mood earlier? He had seemed to agree with her about the contraception debate, but she could tell from his smirking tone that it hadn't really dawned on him just how repellent, how insulting and demeaning, she had found the whole spectacle. In fact she had begun to wonder if the fiasco pleased Michael for some reason. And what about his boss? CJ had sat listening to the nonsense, still and silent as a salamander, then slithered along and voted against. What did Michael have to say about the hypocrisy of that?

Susan won the big £2 pot, thanks to Mags deliberately laying off the queen she'd been waiting for. The kids went happily to bed. Any warmth in the atmosphere seemed to go with them.

It was clear in Mags' mind that it would be better if Michael went home tonight, but she didn't want a row about it. Surely he was sensing the mood? He wasn't saying much. Waiting. Probably wondering what the hell was up.

Silence.

Finally, there was no choice but to put words on it.

'Michael, would you mind if' – stronger – 'I think I'd prefer if you went home tonight.'

For a moment, Mags feared he was going to ask that infuriating male question 'What did I do?' knowing he hadn't *done* anything. He'd score the point. He'd feel vindicated. The tension would remain. But he hadn't said anything. She wasn't sure why. The effect of her words? His own pride? He simply let his dark gaze linger, then he shrugged, and left. Definitely not happy. After the initial relief of his departure, Mags realised that being alone was not what she wanted either. Alone meant thinking about Simon upstairs, how soon she'd be packing him off to England, how hurt she was that he had chosen boarding school and his father, how guilty she felt that she'd allowed such a situation to arise at all. Was Simon the cause of this mood of hers rather than Michael? Why had she felt such a surge of anger when she'd seen them laughing together and messing with the olives?

Trish's basement flat was only ten minutes away. Would she mind company? Was it okay to phone at this late hour? Of course not, come on round. The voice at the other end of the line left her in no doubt that she'd be welcome. Trish even promised a little something that was much more fun as a shared experience. Mags offered a couple of half-hearted are you sures, before saying see you in ten. She slipped upstairs to Susan, who was glued to her latest Jean Plaidy nonsense.

'You're going out *now*?'

'Shh. Yes. Please don't ask.'

'And where's Michael?'

'*Please* don't ask.'

A sigh and mature shake of the head from the sixteen year-old. Mags scribbled Trish's number just in case and promised not to be *too* late She thought for a moment about looking in on Simon, then decided not.

It was impossible not to feel a certain adolescent giddiness sneaking out of her own house into the cool night. In the Belgrave Square flat, a bottle of Barolo was breathing in front of the real fire and, as they talked, Trish put on *Blue* and rolled a fine fat joint. The cozy flat filled with Joni's clear soaring angel-woman's voice and, after the first toke, Mags felt the mesh in her head begin to untangle. Because Trish assured her that she wasn't being boring in a dark café, and could tell her anything she liked, finally the words came and they weren't about Simon or Michael after all. Though in a different way, perhaps they were. Mags spilled out everything, absolutely everything she could remember about her visit to the abortion clinic that morning nearly seven years ago.

*

Matthew Liston, wearing nothing but a t-shirt, pushed open his father's bedroom door. Durex, Durex, Durex! You'd better be where you were. He rummaged in the bottom of the bedside locker. Yes! Daddy's stash. He opened a pack. Two would do. He hopped quickly downstairs, his erection beginning to droop. It shrivelled and died altogether when he heard, even over the shrieking falsetto of *Kimono My House* pumping from the living room, the unmistakable slam of a car door outside. Matthew froze. No. It couldn't be. His father had said he wouldn't be home tonight. Then he heard the key in the front door

Michael had stoked his dark anger on the journey home. So Mags had copped on that he wasn't all cut up about the failure of the Rubber Johnny bill. So fucking what? It was the Coalition's balls-up – be annoyed with them. No need to get in a snot with him because he was pleased that it might bring an election that much closer. He didn't like being spoken to like that. Sent home like a bold child. He opened the door. What in the name of the sweet living Jesus was the youngfellah listening to? Ah fuck! Why wasn't he in bed or out chasing young ones? Michael could have done with a drink, but he wasn't in any mood for talk. Leave him to it. He turned upstairs.

At the living room door Matthew's stomach swirled when he heard the thump on the stairs. Could he possibly be that lucky? He spun to Toby Rennicks, squatting on the floor, also naked apart from his unbuttoned shirt. He barely got the whisper out. 'He's gone upstairs. Hurry.' They scrambled for clothes. Even in the drunken heart-drumming panic of it all, Matthew saw the farcical element. This was like being in one of those excruciating British sex comedies. *Carry on up the Window Cleaner's Ladder*. Toby, flat on his back, pulling on his boxer's, couldn't stop giggling. Surely Matthew didn't look as wasted as him? How quickly they had gone from careful sips of vodka – vile – to alternating mouthfuls of gin and slugs of tonic, to filling ice-crammed glasses with everything they could find: Tia Maria, Bacardi, Crème de Menthe, Glenmorangie, Hennessey's. And the more they drank the wilder Toby's new Sparks album sounded and, as they bopped around laughing, Matthew, like he was just messing, had started pulling down Toby's jeans. It was so obvious that Toby only pretended to fight him off and, once the jeans came down, he'd waved his prick, saying 'mine's bigger'. So Matthew had unbuttoned his fly and took his out and wiggled it close to Toby's. He'd stared deep into his eyes and, just like he wanted him to, Toby had reached out and grabbed hold. Matthew had been surprised at how suddenly it swelled. Toby's was getting hard too, before he'd even touched it. Then he had and the giggling stopped. Matthew had wanted to kiss Toby, but he wasn't sure that'd be the cool thing to do. He didn't want to scare him off. Then he'd heard himself breathe.

'Have you ever… ever put a French letter on it?'

Toby had shaken his head.

'The old man has some, will I get them?'

And Toby had whispered.

'Yeah, cool.'

Their clothes back on, Matthew now started to shove the bottles back in the cabinet. Toby was so unsteady he scratched the record as he lifted the needle. He crammed *Kimono My House* back in its sleeve. They looked at each other and Matthew was pretty sure they were both trying not to laugh, which was good.

'I'd better split.'

'Yeah, I suppose.'

Matthew opened the door a few inches and listened and then they tiptoed to the front door. Outside they stood, swaying, but going nowhere.

'Jesus, you said he was staying with his girlfriend tonight.'

'I know, sorry.'

The cold air was making him feel more muddled and drunk now. It had felt so fucking great a few minutes ago. He wanted to touch Toby, to find out if it was all right, if they were still cool. Maybe even…

'Okay. See you.'

'Okay.'

But still, Toby didn't turn away. He stood very close, swaying a bit as if he was waiting for something else to happen. Then he grinned.

'Fuck. Were we lucky or what?'

'I know. Are you around tomorrow?'

'Yeah, sure yeah.'

'We could go down to Dollymount or something.'

'Okay.'

'Okay.'

Finally Matthew reached out and tipped Toby playfully. Toby leaned his body in and grinned.

Back in the living room, Matthew flopped into an armchair. No sound from upstairs. Was his father asleep already? He felt pretty heavy himself now. Like the nephew in *At Swim-Two-Birds*, he was conscious of several addled and contradictory emotions.

Describe contradictory nature of feeling: on the one hand, elation; having been the beneficiary of a quite remarkable stroke of luck. The odds against a man entering his own home at a late hour and, upon hearing the insistent beat of music emanating from the largest, most comfortable room in the house, deciding not to, at the very least, 'stick his head in' and greet the occupant, but instead, disappear upstairs without any interaction, verbal or mechanical, were surely very long indeed.

And on the other hand? A contrary and equally powerful feeling of deflation or detumescence. Having embarked on a significant experiment of a sexual nature, it could not be other than frustrating to be forced to abort the test on the very brink, thus extending an already trying period of uncertainty,

Any other emotions? Yes. A restless undercurrent of anticipation occasioned by the intimation of a resumption of said experimentation, possibly within a twenty-four hour period, in the dunes behind Dollymount strand.

'Jesus Christ!' Matthew jolted forward in the armchair and his eyes scoured the carpet. Where were the condoms? He had completely forgotten about them. He walked slowly about the room, eyes down, trying to recall. They'd been gripped in his left hand as he'd hurled himself from the hall to the living room, to avoid his father. But after that? Had he dropped them in the scramble for clothes? Matthew got on his hands and knees and repeated the action of his frantic dressing. They might have been kicked. He grovelled under the coffee table, he tipped back armchairs and the sofa. How could it be so hard to find two distinctively-wrapped condoms? But they were nowhere. Had drink affected his sight? He inched up and down the room. They had disappeared. It was eerie, disturbing. The condoms were no more. Ex-condoms, as Monty Python might say. Reluctantly, with some foreboding, Matthew lurched upstairs, his head throbbing now. There would be no sleep tonight. In his bedroom the action of unbuttoning his jeans reminded him of earlier. He peeled them off, and flung them disconsolately towards a chair. As the jeans landed two small square glinting objects fell from the back pocket. Matthew dropped to his knees, his heart soaring. He snatched them up and read the word Durex. Twice.

1975

Twenty-three: February 5th

CJ had to hand it to Liston for timing. Because his return to the front bench had been announced yesterday, the banking gentlemen were in retreat even as they greeted him.

'Congratulations. You must be delighted.'

Out of intensive care after nearly five years. Wounds not fatal after all. CJ knew his handwave, modest and dismissive, would seem to imply that his resurrection was a matter of little importance, but he knew they knew he knew they had to be more simpering now. With inflation running at twenty per cent, Cosgrave a laughing-stock after the contraception vote, Cruise O'Brien despised the length and breadth of the land and bombings in the State, the Coalition was becoming a rabble. CJ could easily be a government minister again before the year was out.

The banking gentlemen had a peace wall of paperwork in front of them. Much good would it do them. He let them talk. Figures. Tiresome figures. £180,000 overdrawn. He'd spent £18,000 last month apparently. CJ listened, his gaze unblinking. And? Did they really think he was going to argue detail? Scarcely a minute had passed since the banking gentlemen had introduced themselves and he had already forgotten their names. One of them was a little more fixated than the other two: younger, close-shaven, good tie. He seemed to think that CJ needed to be reminded that his salary as a backbencher was only £7,000 p.a.

And?

CJ let his eyes do the work. This banking brat, cosseted, accustomed to gorging on low-hanging fruit, terrorising misfortunates with accusations of profligacy, bullying them into confessing the error of their ways and begging for leniency, thought he could squeeze CJ's balls. With Liston beside him? He would make the *banbh* shrink and shrivel and whine.

'In the light of the present situation we feel it's in everyone's interest that your chequebook facility on these accounts be withdrawn.'

CJ did not respond by word or nod; just listened with interest.

And?

The oldest of the triumvirate was desperate for everyone to be friends.

'We – we – we were also wondering if ah… if you had any proposals yourself? Are there likely to be other ah… income streams – other than your Dáil salary that is, – which… which might allow you to… ah… initiate a schedule of repayments?'

CJ's gesture towards Liston suggested that, being a very busy man, this kind of detail was always delegated to his advisor.

'Well, first, let's remind ourselves that the combined value of the family home, the island, and the bloodstock is estimated at over a million, so there is ample security for the various loans –'

Though the gentlemen were now looking in Liston's direction, CJ knew they were never unaware of his eyes on them, never unafraid that it might please him to tear chunks of flesh as large as the head of a month-old child from any one of them. This skirmish would be over soon and he was getting hungry. Where for lunch? He felt like rewarding his gilla, who was serving him particularly well of late. Even the forays into the midland wilderness were becoming surprisingly addictive. The yowls and frenzied backslaps and bone-crunching handshakes had a clammy honesty. The beetroot faces and moon-surface faces and Ordnance Survey faces glowed with more drooling energy than the pallid milk-fed trio across the desk. Being bull chief of tribes could be intoxicating.

'– and if it helps, you could also freeze the overdrawn accounts until repayments recommence.'

It was amusing to see realisation dawn on the banking gentlemen that Liston had done little more than drop an elegantly-shaped warm turd onto their desk, whose effluvium they now had to inhale, murmuring 'Mmm, lovely!' The only alternative was to bully the newly revived Lazarus, party spokesman on Health, of all things, and government minister in waiting.

Michael enjoyed watching the fuckers fold. They actually held all the best cards, but were too shit-scared to use them, especially that little prick Sheehy, a spoiled la-la if ever there was one. CJ had been the business, coolly inviting them to call his bluff. Michael loved his stillness and patience in these situations. The Stare-Master. In the lead up to this, these alickadoos had probably been sniggering amongst themselves about gun-running, sneering about the abject has-been politician who dared to be too *flaithúlach* with their money. They'd carve him up. Oh yes, these lords of the financial universe would put the squireen to the sword. Instead they sat there like empty suits, making careful notes, nodding agreeably, desperate to convince themselves that it was all jimdandy, when in fact they were at the wrong end of a drubbing, a rout.

In the lift on the way out, CJ's only words were to suggest the Mirabeau for lunch.

Kinsella came galloping from the kitchen to welcome his valued patron. CJ knew how impatient Liston was with this ritual. Gilla wanted his grub and no messing. And it was true that Kinsella had never quite acquired the skill of not lingering too long, but, it being his own restaurant, there was no one to whisper wise words in his ear. He could learn a thing or two from the midlands boys, the convulsion of well-wishers in the Longford Arms last week had been ruthlessly marshalled. Everyone had been poked and herded along very briskly. 'Come on there now, give the man a bit of space.'

'What will you tempt us with today?' CJ hoped to redirect Kinsella's attention towards the kitchen.

'Oh, the rack, CJ, unquestionably.'

'Then let it be the rack. Feed us, astonish us. Honeydew, Maestro! The milk of paradise!'

Pink and oozing, the rack eventually arrived. CJ let Liston talk with his mouth full while he silently sliced and ate, sliced and ate, chewing, chewing, chewing, the better to relish the youthful sweetness of lamb's blood. Once he'd stripped the swollen eye of flesh from each cutlet, he snatched up the little pink-flecked bone and sucked and gnawed.

Liston was elaborating on the limitations of offshore accounts, the most obvious being the investor's inability to access his own money for a period of time. Did CJ agree that if a way could be found for the wealthiest investors to place considerable funds beyond the grasp of the taxman, while at the same time being able to withdraw any amount they pleased, from the comfort of their own homes more or less, such a unique facility would be very popular? Nodding, CJ agreed, guessing that the wise gilla's plan would be an imaginative one, otherwise he probably wouldn't have bothered opening his mouth at all.

'I think we both know there'd be a rolling maul to sign up for an offer like that, and, more to the point, everyone'd be more than happy to support the kind of political thinking that showed such balls and vision. Exactly what the country's been crying out for, they'd say. Wealth tax my hole. Now, fair enough, we gave those alickadoos a kicking this morning, but it won't be forever. They'll come slithering back. You need committed long-term backers, CJ, but not that many of them actually, as long as we can persuade the most important players. I'm confident we can.'

Normally CJ savoured the ceremony of the cheeseboard; the naming, sniffing, tasting and appreciative murmuring. Just now its arrival was a tiresome interruption and, of course, Kinsella had to come swanking back, truffling for compliments.

Eventually, they were left alone and Liston could explain his scheme. Trust funds, naturally, most likely in the Cayman's… yes, an innocuous private commercial bank in Ireland – Liston was already a director of one – a snakes and ladders game of parallel transactions across several countries guaranteed to bewilder and disguise the final result: the client could access his offshore funds right here in Dublin, more or less at will, via nothing more complicated than a phone-call to Liston himself.

While CJ had little interest in the fine detail of how the scheme operated, he was fascinated by how much it revolved around Liston personally. For the thing to work at all, everyone would have to trust him. He was Cú Chulainn, keeping the gap of the North, defending his clients, single-handed, against the predatory taxman, using this unique facility as his magic spear, his *Gae Bolg*. The wealthiest in the land would sign over huge sums of money, trusting that whenever they needed funds, Liston would arrange for an envelope to find its way to the client, quickly and discreetly.

He had created a complex, high-value loyalty test. Was that what he got out of it? Trust *me*. Trust *me*.

As he gazed deep into the dark caves of his gilla's eyes, CJ wondered what it took to trust someone in that way. Yet he anticipated that many would. An opportunity like this: the gall, the daring, the conjury of it? Irresistible. And it was a reasonable assumption that these grateful clients would respond generously when the wise councillor came calling on CJ's behalf. It was hard to resist an impulse to hug him close, nibble his ear and whisper words he remembered from God knows where: *Fill my purse with money.*

*

Bryan Ferry, by a pool in white evening jacket, dickie bow, and a maroon cummerbund around his waist, one hand casually in his pocket and a cigarette in the other – an elegant and nonchalant extension of his fingers – stared directly at Francis Strong. *Can you believe how cool I am?*

It was certainly more restful to sit gazing at the cover of *Another Time Another Place* than to make another attempt at *Ulysses*, whose flat black cover with plain white lettering, not even in capitals, made no effort to lure him.

james
joyce
ulysses

Inside, the thickness of the book and smallness of the type was daunting, taunting. Francis didn't yet regret his resolution to finish the novel by Bloomsday, just two days before his sixteenth birthday, but he knew now he would have to be sedulous.

You think I care if you read me or not? You're probably not up to it anyway.

Their new English teacher had mentioned Joyce in class one day, but with a pointed absence of avidity; Mr Nolan didn't encourage them to read anything not on the Leaving Cert course. 5α1 might appreciate a couple of stories in *Dubliners*, he opined, but they weren't really ready for *A Portrait of the Artist as a Young Man* yet, and as for *Ulysses* – a sardonically dismissive chuckle – brilliant writing, literary fireworks, no question about that, but far too much fuss about it. Not really worth the bother.

A red rag to a bull. Francis had vowed to read Joyce and start with *Ulysses*.

The last track on side one began. 'You Are My Sunshine.' He would let it play out, before opening *Ulysses* again. Three weeks in and only as far as page 47. Stream of consciousness? An attempt to put on paper the never-ending buzz in every person's brain. But why had Joyce written a character with such a relentlessly intellectual never-ending buzz in his brain? 'Agenbite of inwit': 'ineluctable modality of the visible': thinking in French at the drop of his Latin Quarter hat. And where was Leopold Bloom, who Francis had understood was the main character and who they named Bloomsday after? He hadn't been even mentioned yet. What kind of novel didn't introduce the most important character right from the start? Last night he had peeked ahead and discovered that the first words of the next chapter were: 'Mr Bloom ate'. Page 57. He was determined that today he would read that far at least.

Wrestling with the complexity of Stephen Dedalus' stream of consciousness had coaxed Francis into listening to his own, but it was difficult. Each time he isolated a thought, the rest of his consciousness flowed on around it. It was like trying to capture running water. And yet sometimes a moment held long enough to be lingered over; a bundle of photos snapping a single event.

Joe Malone's. Smiling at Gráinne who's sitting on Patch's knee because it's so packed. She winks and lifts her pint.

'You have a fan.'

'Me?'

'Yes, you, who else am I looking at, Francis Strong? *You*' – waving the pint – 'have a fan. And she's lovely.'

Gráinne is pissed. but not so pissed that she's talking shite. She winks. Holds up a forefinger.

'Oh yes. I think ye'd suit each other.'

Gráinne's wink. That was the night in Joe Malone's when he first heard about Collette. But why was that image so pellucid in his consciousness? As far as he could tell, four weeks on, he had no regrets about calling it off with Collette, even though it meant he didn't have a girlfriend now.

He scooped another brimming handful from the stream.

Laughs. Applause. Francis sits down, his face a mask. But within, a pumping pleasure fountain. Patch's face, Andrew's face, alive with astonished approbation. Even Cónal's face from the stage. Raucous cheers. All for him. This moment is a restless camera shot, panning, sweeping round the crowded school hall.

Francis didn't know Collette then, but she was somewhere in the crowd that night. After seeing and hearing him at the schools debate final, she'd told Gráinne she fancied him. Because of, not in spite of him being a smart-alec and a bit of a showoff, Gráinne said. Imagine that?

He and Patch and Andrew had gone to the debate because their pal Cónal was on the CBS team, it cost nothing and it was against Laurel Hill convent, so there would be girls. After the teams had spoken and the judges had withdrawn to choose the winner, the chairman had asked for speakers from the floor. Francis, on impulse, not knowing why, shot his hand up.

Although, deep down, he did know why.

Cónal's speech against the motion, 'That the Watergate investigation showed that democracy is alive and well' was so brilliant it had made Francis a little bit jealous and want to show off. The other boys on the CBS team were dull and the Laurel Hill girls had just parrotted trite literary references probably given to them by some nun. 'George Orwell's *Nineteen-Eighty Four* showed us all a frightening vision of a world without democracy' and 'in Aldous Huxley's brilliant *Brave New World* we see how society can be controlled when there is no free press to ask questions.' Cónal's speech was different. He spoke without notes but with real vehemence. All Watergate proved was that if two journalists hadn't been so persistent and courageous, then nobody would have realised how democracy had been undermined. Was it being undermined today, maybe here in Ireland, without anyone knowing? Could the gullible Laurel Hill team prove it wasn't? Cónal said that forcing Nixon finally to resign didn't help the million dead in Vietnam – and what had changed in Chile? Nixon was gone, but Pinochet's death squads were still rampaging with American support. Watergate hadn't saved democracy there. Of course, as usual, Cónal had to bring Northern Ireland into it. He said look how Paisley used sectarian fear to frustrate attempts at peace and keep the Catholic population in its place.

Francis wished he hadn't dragged that in because the judges might find it a bit too controversial, but now, getting up to speak, he felt the urge to be a bit of a provocateur himself, although he also wanted to make the audience laugh, He started in a tone of mock politeness, calling each Laurel Hill girl 'Miss' instead of her first name.

'Miss Harrington's speech was a veritable cornucopia of ostentatious verbosity –'

He got an amused 'oooh!' from the crowd for that.

'And impressive-sounding quotations from books she obviously hasn't read.'

Another 'oooh!' Laurel Hill was where the snobs went, so Francis knew that everyone else in the hall would enjoy hearing them slagged off.

'The next speaker, Miss Wallace seemed obsessed with some strange link between democracy and biscuit-making. Now I like the odd fig roll myself, but her tortuous extended metaphor really did take the biscuit.'

A groan, but a friendly one. Francis could tell the crowd was on his side.

'And I'm sure she doesn't need me to tell her that the word biscuit comes from the Italian word biscotti which means, baked twice. I regret to say that, in tonight's debate, Miss Wallace's arguments didn't seem to have been baked even once.'

Cónal and the chairman were the first to laugh loudly at that witticism. Francis was delighted.

'Finally, little Miss Downey who is, I imagine, fifteen – are you?'

The poor girl was taken by surprise to be asked directly. She blushed.

'Am… ah… no, sixteen.'

'Sixteen already? Even more surprising then, because Miss Downey seems so innocent. Remember she proclaimed her absolute faith in our elected politicians? But she forgot to mention that she knows the tooth fairy personally, she lives on a street called Sesame, and has absolute proof that Mrs Slocombe's pussy is a pet cat and nothing more.'

That brought the house down; gasps of laughter and huge cheers. Francis was delighted to see the nun in charge of the Laurel Hill team direct a basilisk stare toward him, but, pleased with himself though he was, it never occurred to him that his performance would attract a girl.

The gift box is small, square, hard. Prettily wrapped. Open it, Collette's smile says. Why is he afraid to? Small, square, hard. He tears the paper revealing a corner. Black. A lid. No, please. A little black box. He knows already it's not anything he wants, but he has to open it now. FRANCIS.

His name, carved on silver, sitting in a crumpled bed of satiny blue. Oh Jesus, no! FRANCIS.

'Do you like it?'

'Wow!'

He has to take it out, hold it up. He has to jangle it on. He has to smile.

'It's not too loose?'

'No. It's… perfect.'

'Happy Christmas.'

Kissing her is easy. He likes kissing her. Hugging is better. No eyes meeting.

'Thanks so much, Coll. Thanks. Happy Christmas.'

Francis shivered. If only he could wipe that moment from the buzz of his brain, from the white-water stream of his consciousness. It wasn't that he'd expected some amazing present; but an identity bracelet? They'd been together twice or three times a week for five weeks. They'd drank in Malone's, and hung around Todd's. They'd both loved *Chinatown* and *Sleeper* and were bored at *The Odessa File* and they'd kissed a lot. She'd seemed to really like him as he was.

So how come she hadn't noticed that he never wore jewellery? Never ever. Patch had a Claddagh ring, Andrew wore neck chains and crosses and coloured wristbands, but Francis hated all that. To be fair to Collette, it had never come up in conversation.

Still, an identity bracelet? As if he needed to be reminded of his own name. The worst part was having to wear it every time they went out together. Did she know him at all?

Gráinne Kiely understood. As soon as she saw the thing she'd said.

'Well now, the things we do for love.'

'How do you mean?'

'You, wearing jewellery.'

If Gráinne understood it was the wrong present to give him, why didn't Collette? She mightn't be as cynical as Gráinne, but she was just as intelligent. Definitely not a silly cow like Emer Bennis with her 'me and Andrew, Andrew and me', wriggling all over him all the time. How did Andrew put up with it? Francis had been really looking forward to having a girlfriend at Christmas for the first time. He'd thought it was going to be the best ever.

But the identity bracelet ruined it.

Now it was in its little black box in a drawer in his bedroom under a pile of stuff, where it would stay hidden. He hadn't worn it since the second last time he was with Collette. Did he feel no guilt? Not even about the way he had called it off so soon after New Year's Eve? He definitely didn't miss her.

So why was it all still buzzing in his brain?

Silence. When had Bryan Ferry's plangent vocal faded away? Francis placed the album cover out of sight and opened *Ulysses*. He flicked to page 47, wondering what hope had he of understanding Stephen Dedalus' stream of consciousness when he couldn't figure out his own?

Twenty-four: March 29th

At the end of part one of *The Non-Stop Connolly Show*, Mags was delighted and more than a little relieved that the teenagers both seemed quite high on the performance. Matthew was really taken with the style of it, how the play never stopped even though the scenes kept changing. He said it was exceptional the way moving a bit of furniture or introducing a new prop could create a different place and time. Susan was amazed that such young actors could play so many different parts.

But after part two, when they stepped out of Liberty Hall for a breath of fresh air, Mags detected a different mood. She could hear scepticism in Matthew's question.

'Did they really talk like that?'

'Who, what?'

'You know, people from that time.'

'Well, not all the characters are meant to be actual people, they're more like emblems. Grabitall, for example, represents greedy grasping capitalism.'

'Yeah, got that. But James Connolly was a real person, right? And Lillie?'

'Oh sure.'

'So if they fell in love and got married and had children, they wouldn't have spent all their time discussing the exploitation of the workers, would they?'

Mags could think of a few couples, some of whom she had spotted in the audience, who probably did, but she nodded.

'That's fair enough, but remember, they were political agitators all their lives. Connolly died for his beliefs. And in a play there's only so much time to focus on particular things –'

'Mum, this play is going to go on all night. Surely there's time to show us – you know like Matthew says – not politics all the time… Other more personal things about them.'

'Say… Okay, say, the first time James and Lillie… you know… ah… did it. Well, what was it like for them, what did they say to each other? I bet it wasn't, "Hey Lillie, are the banners organised for tomorrow's march?"'

Mags looked at the black tangle of Matthew's hair, its careless look carefully achieved, his slim frame from fashion not hunger. Poverty was unknown to him. Feelings were everything.

'Have you any insights into what they might have have said?

The merest flush chased across his taut cheekbones. Interesting.

'Ha, ha, very funny.'

'Okay, seriously, I understand what you're getting at, Matthew, but you know, plenty of people really do like talking politics and ideas, and maybe the authors think we don't do enough of it. Anyway, look on the bright side, there's only another twenty hours to go.'

Mags enjoyed seeing them try not to show their horror. She had no intention of forcing them to watch more. They had sat like lambs through the first five hours. Entertained though they were by all the high-energy action and singing, the colourful backdrops and inventive masks, it hadn't tempted these teenagers to swallow great globs of political argument and revolutionary theory.

'Have you better things to be doing?

'Would you mind, Mum?'

'Of course not. Going to the theatre isn't meant to be a duty.'

'We enjoyed loads of it. Really.'

'One of Matthew's friends is having a party. He says I can come too.'

'But if the party's a dud we might come back here for the last part.'

'It's fine, Matthew, you don't have to.'

'No, really, I wouldn't mind seeing how they do the whole

execution bit. Connolly was tied to a chair wasn't he, because he was too ill to stand? That'd be interesting.'

'Mum, the buses will have stopped by the time the party's over.'

They looked at her doe-eyed. Mags opened her purse.

'James Connolly wouldn't have expected his mammy to give him taxi fare.'

Her pleasure at watching the pair chatter along Eden Quay, was interrupted by the usual guilty confusion about Simon. Why did it upset her that he seemed so at home at Marlborough, seemingly besotted by this new world of his 'house' and their games and rituals and friendships and rivalries? Shouldn't it be a relief to know she had made the sensible choice? Was it so hard to accept that her son might not need her around? Was that why she felt closer, warmer towards Matthew? As soon as he'd asked about James and Lillie talking the first time they made love it had crossed Mags' mind that he was no longer a virgin and she was only slightly startled to find herself wondering had he been with a girl or a boy? Just something about him, a hint of a notion, nothing more, but it was enough to make her worry how Michael would cope with a bombshell like that. Smart and funny and attractive and well-provided for though Matthew was, he might need her protection.

She stared up at Liberty Hall, burning orange in the setting sun, stridently ugly, lowering over every other building along the quay. The rest of the show wouldn't be much fun without the teenagers. Extraordinary though the event was, *The Non-stop Connolly Show* was probably not something to enjoy alone.

By the end of part three, Mags admitted to herself she was wilting. Even though there was some sort of food available out of a huge pot in the bar area, she had a sinful craving to slip up Grafton Street to Captain America's and sit, surrounded by garish murals and loudmouth rock music, ravishing a big fat capitalist burger with bacon and cheese and fries. Had Susan and Matthew's teenage solipsism infected her? All through part three the Lillie

Connolly character had increasingly jagged on Mags' nerves. What an upright ideological helpmate she was to her James. No doubt the various like-minded couples Mags had spotted in the audience – and waved at and mouthed 'hi!' to – had enjoyed a cozy feeling of kinship with the heroic couple at the centre of the drama, whereas Mags sat alone. Her own odd relationship, if relationship was the appropriate word, was hardly a meeting of political minds. A meeting of what then? Remarkably, when they made love, there was always a moment when Michael still gazed in silent wonder, as if her effect on him was some kind of miracle. These moments still excited her, but for Mags the greater wonder was that, five years on, genuinely neither tried to control the other person's life. Mags had no interest in being Lillie Connolly, encouraging and supporting her man.

But…

Respect for the other's independence of thought and freedom of action was one thing. Sleeping with a white collar criminal was another matter.

Her discovery yesterday morning had been more shocking for being so accidental. Waking early, needing to go to the toilet, the only thought in her head as she had returned to Michael's bedroom had been whether to get up straight away or try to grab another hour of sleep. It was entirely fortuitous that the shaft of dawn sunlight piercing a crack in the curtains had landed on Michael's open suitcase, spotlighting two ticket pouches. As far as Mags knew, he was flying to London, so why two tickets? If curiosity had caused her to kneel by the suitcase and pick them up, it was genuinely nothing more than the casual curiosity of a moment. Yet, as soon as she opened one pouch and read what was on the ticket she immediately thought: tax dodging, money-laundering.

British Airways, 1st class. Departing Heathrow, 13.20, arriving Owen Roberts Airport, Grand Cayman, 22.50.

What would bring someone like Michael to the Cayman Islands? His silence about his real destination suddenly acquired the stench of an unsavoury secret. Mags replaced the pouch and went downstairs. She had an hour alone to think before Michael appeared. Whatever dodgy business he was conducting in the Caymans – how quickly it had become fixed in her mind as 'dodgy' – was it on his own behalf, or someone else's? Michael wasn't Grabitall, more like Grabitall's little helper, Grabitall's bagman. Mags realised she wanted CJ to be at the bottom of this. It made much more sense and entirely fitted her notion of the man.

Only much later, long after she'd seen Michael off at the airport, did it dawn on Mags how quickly and easily she had drawn corrupt conclusions from nothing more than a destination on a ticket. Owen Roberts Airport, Grand Cayman. Such suspicion wouldn't go far in a court of law, but might it infect a relationship?

A summoning voice interrupted her thoughts. The committed ones were on their way back into the auditorium. The crier cried. Part four of *The Nonstop Connolly Show* was about to begin.

Twenty-five: April 1st

Michael smelled a big fat rat. There had been something in the air when Mags and the youngfellah collected him from the airport. She was polite, not her style at all. 'How was the trip? Did everything go well? Good journey?' Then why all that talk about the youngfellah? It'd begun back at the house and didn't stop when they went to Nico's for dinner. From the ravioli in brodo through to the espresso, she kept on about Matthew. How sensitive and thoughtful he was underneath all the comedy stuff. She said 'sensitive' a few times. It began to get on Michael's wick. There seemed to be some implication in it, though Christ knew what. Why were they spending the whole evening on this anyway? It wasn't normal for them. There was no slagging off the other diners. No laughs at all. The food didn't even rate a mention. Just the youngfellah, who as well as being sensitive and lovable was much more like Michael than Michael might think, according to Mags. He had the same dark edge, though it probably sprung from a different source, a secretive side. This was when Michael really smelled a rat. Was this shite about Matthew at all? Was she talking about the boy so as not to talk about something else? There was something going on all right, although it wasn't a big strop like the night she lammed him out of her place and he had to go on eggshells for weeks afterwards, nothing like that. But something was up. That became more obvious when, as they left Nico's, she suggested a bit of a walk before heading for Ranelagh. Whatever was going on, Michael wasn't in the mood for it. He'd arrived home in great form, with a very different notion of the night ahead: a nice bit of Italian, a few laughs and, hopefully, a much-needed ride at the end of all. Everything had gone well in the Caymans, more than well. The trust was up and running, Michael just had to make sure now that he had total control of the Dublin end of it. Minimise the footsteps, that was the key – no intermediaries, no interference from anyone else in the bank. Investors would get involved in this deal because they trusted Michael and had a direct line to him. That was essential. The thing couldn't operate otherwise. Too much money at stake. Too many important people involved.

Michael heard a word: 'Honesty.' What was she saying now? Did he agree that honesty was the most important thing in any relationship, especially the kind of relationship they had? He knew what the answer to that had to be. No ifs or buts or hesitation. Of course. Absolutely. Now Michael's brain was on red alert. Where was this heading? Nowhere he liked, that was sure, and it was a right pisser that he didn't have more information to work with. He was feeding off scraps. Her intense mood, sensitive Matthew, honesty… What was up?

He let her lead them onto Westmoreland Street even though they were drifting further away from where the car was parked on George's Street. It was turning into a long walk through the city centre wasteland, and, at last, Mags said there was something she felt she had to tell him. Michael thought, here we go, now it begins.

Something had happened years before they met and she ought to have been honest about it long ago. It was unfair that he didn't know. It was information he should have. Michael wondered why the big build-up, not wanting this conversation at all. Suddenly she had them back in 1967, doing a runner on her husband; all familiar until she got to the bit that wasn't; the thing Michael had never been told. At the time she ran away with her kids, she was also pregnant. As soon as he heard 'pregnant' Michael copped on where this was heading and, for the rest of her story, told in whispers now, with hesitations and pauses and occasional cracks in the voice, he was way ahead of her. The low-tide stink on gloomy Aston Quay was putrid. They should never have turned down this way. He was getting every detail about some schoolpal who minded the kids while she went to the clinic and how sweet the young Irish nurse was and how irritable and dismissive the first doctor who examined her had been and how cold and superior the second one, whose manner implied that such work was beneath him, while crisply demanding payment in cash.

So, she'd had an abortion. Nearly eight years ago. If that was all she had to tell him, Michael was relieved. He had no particular feeling about it, not even much surprise. She'd never told him. So what? Of course he knew not to say any of this, although he vaguely resented having to search for the right noises, the appropriate tone, particular words. He carefully squeezed out a few phrases about understanding her dilemma and her right to choose. He chanced a question about how hard had it been to get over the experience. The bit he really had to fake was when she asked if he agreed how important it was for her to be honest with him about it. He said yes of course, but couldn't help adding that if she hadn't wanted to reveal this, that would have been fine too. Entirely her choice.

Naturally he didn't say that her secret history didn't interest him very much.

By the time they finally wound their way back to the car and set off towards Ranelagh, it was no surprise that Mags asked would he mind if she didn't ask him to stay the night. Any desire was well gone off him at this stage so of course he said he understood completely.

On the face of it, whatever was troubling her had been aired at least, but Michael's initial relief was replaced by a persistent groan in his gut. Driving down Grafton Street, eerily quiet after the Easter weekend, his mistrustful brain posed questions. Why tonight? Something on her mind while he'd been away? Something about Matthew? Something about honesty? Why after eight years, had she decided to tell him her big abortion secret *tonight*? There was more to this, he was sure. Women's games. Then Michael realised how energetically he was burrowing into deeper gloom.

He took hold of himself. This was Mags, this was a woman who made him happy. Stall a ball there. Relax the head.

Still, her behaviour was a bit of a mystery and Michael Liston didn't care for mysteries.

Twenty-six: October 4th

After waiting twenty minutes for the bus, then haring through the pelting rain and still arriving late, only to have her suspicions confirmed that Patch hadn't bothered to turn up, Gráinne had every right to be hopping. Oh she knew him well enough after more than a year: up, down, in and out. Jesus! A year and three months to be precise. Too long doing a line. Too heavy.

Patch Dollard never said no, so it was the way he said yes. She knew that well, Of course, half-pissed last night in Joe Malone's, everyone was up for it. Going on the march seemed like a fab idea. Poor auld fellah kidnapped, done no harm to no one, his factory keeping half the city in work. Gráinne's sister's husband had two brothers in Ferenka. Everyone in Joe Malone's last night had a relative or a friend working there. The place might close down because of this. Of course there were a couple of shit-stirrers saying the kidnap was a cool operation all the same, you had to hand it to whoever did it, dressing up like cops and waving your man Herrema down. Being Dutch, he'd be very law-abiding of course. Then out of his car, into theirs and that was that. You had to admire the finesse of it, one of the shit-stirrers said, but no one was agreeing.

It wasn't that Gráinne thought marching around the city centre and listening to the stupid mayor make a stupid speech would be of any use, but if everyone was going, they'd have a laugh and it was a change from the usual hanging around Todd's, so of course she was up for it. There must have been ten or a dozen going yeah, yeah let's all go, brilliant, savage, yeah!

She arrived, soaked and late, to find nobody except Francis Strong sitting on the library steps. Two dopes. At least, because of the rain, Francis had to wear his grey duffel coat in the normal way, not draped over his shoulders like he usually did, trying to look – Gráinne wasn't sure what he wanted to look like – different, artistic – whatever it was, it didn't work. That fucker, Patch, not turning up. And yet she wasn't totally surprised. Thinking about it now, sober in the rain, 'Yeah why not?' from Patch actually meant 'Highly unlikely,' or even 'Nah, I'll be on the couch with a mug of tea.' She should have known, even though knowing didn't make him any less of a selfish fucker.

'Big crowd.'

Amazingly, there was. It looked like a few thousand.

'So, none of our gang turned up?'

'Who were you expecting?'

'Good question.'

'I could have told you there wasn't a hope of Patch coming. Saturday afternoon? In the rain? I only came 'cause I thought it'd be lousy if someone ended up here alone.'

'But you could have been the one alone.'

'Nah, I knew there'd be at least one other poor eejit.'

'Lucky for Herrema we're here.'

'Oh yeah, the kidnappers are quaking.'

Eventually the march shuffled off, trying not to look too organised. They turned at Tait's clock down past the Glentworth Hotel. Gráinne asked if she'd heard right that Herrema had a son around their age. Francis said he didn't know, then smirked.

'Imagine what it would feel like having your dad kidnapped. If it was mine, I wouldn't worry too much 'cause he'd just go along with everything, saying things like. "That's grand, no the blindfold is grand, sure aren't I only sitting here, there's nothing I need to be looking at."'

On O'Connell Street, Gráinne was surprised that people watching started clapping.

'My dad would drive them crazy, interfering all the time. "Now, even though I can't see with the blindfold, instinct tells me you took that last bend a little too fast for comfort." After a couple of hours it would be them or him. Or else he might escape after boring them to sleep with his little sayings. "Only your real friends will tell you when your face is dirty." "The future depends on what we do in the present." "Those who criticise our generation forget who raised them".'

'Jesus, are you making those up?'

'You think I could make up shite like that? I'm listening to it since I can't remember. One for every occasion. His latest is, "The trouble with retirement is that you never get a day off".'

'Has your dad retired?'

'A couple of months ago.'

'I didn't realise he was that old. What's that like?'

Gráinne wondered what exactly to say. That it was a real pain? That her dad didn't know she smoked, definitely didn't know she drank, and still treated her like she was ten. He was aware of the existence of some lad called Patch, but had met him only once by accident and Gráinne usually mentioned him along with two or three other names as if he was nothing special, just one of her gang of friends. It seemed the easiest way to deal with it, especially now that she was the only one at home. Alone with two parents in their sixties. Jesus, it sounded really pathetic.

Francis, noticing Gráinne had gone quiet, hoped he hadn't put his foot in it.

'He sings with the musical society, doesn't he? I saw him years ago in *Oklahoma*. Oh and *Oliver!*'

'Oh Jesus yeah, that'd be another way he'd drive kidnappers spare. After a few verses of "Reviewing the Situation" they'd be calling the cops, begging them to take him back.'

'Couldn't he get them all singing along to "You Sexy Thing"?'

That made Gráinne grin.

'He thinks Hot Chocolate is something you drink before going to bed.'

She was surprised, but delighted at how loudly Francis laughed. He came back with one straight away.

'Does he think Genesis is a book in the Bible?'

'Yes, and Nazareth is a town where Jesus lived.'

'And Boston is where the Kennedys came from.'

'And Chicago is… ah shite…'

'A song Sinatra sings.'

Silence for a few seconds.

'I've got one. 'He thinks Black Sabbath is a satanic ritual.'

'Thin Lizzy is a skinny friend of yours.'

Before they knew it the rain had stopped and they'd arrived at Arthur's Quay. The mayor got up on a platform to make a speech that was even more stupid than Gráinne expected. He called on the Pope to intervene and plead for mercy. The whole city was praying for the safe return of this poor man who brought them so many jobs in the middle of a recession. Gráinne had had enough. She made a face and Francis nodded. They went over to Café Capri for chips and coke.

Twenty-seven: October 11th

Poor Mona. Ann Strong felt so sorry for her sister. It was just shocking to see any mother look so miserable at her daughter's wedding. That day she'd called over and broke down in tears and Ann not knowing what to say. What was the matter? Who was sick? And then that awful wail. 'My heart is broke, Ann!'

Fr Duggan stepped onto the altar and welcomed everyone on this happiest of occasions, the joining together of a loving couple in holy matrimony. He was a big cheery priest with lovely flyaway sandy red hair. Why hadn't Mona asked him to have a little talk with Eva? But if she wouldn't listen to her own mother why would she pay any attention to the poor curate? Anyway, what could he say? The Quinlans lived in the parish too. Fr Duggan could hardly be making little of them.

'In the midst of such joy let us not forget that, for some, it's a time of desperate trial and worry, so, before beginning this celebratory mass, let us take a moment to pray that Dr Herrema will be found and returned safely to the bosom of his family.'

Now there was a woman with troubles, Ann thought. Imagine trying to look after two children and her husband taken off to God knows where. She was so brave on the telly the other night, spoke so well and so clearly, although the Dutch always had great English, better than some people born and bred here. Ann couldn't imagine having to go on telly like that, pleading to those IRA blackguards to let her husband go. She'd probably go mad and end up giving them a piece of her mind, telling them exactly what she thought of them, cowardly little scuts, hiding under those balaclava things. Mrs Herrema had been so calm, so dignified. And not afraid to wear her glasses, Ann could never have done that, she hated the way she looked in glasses. Luckily she only needed them for sewing.

Eva wasn't wearing her glasses today either which really did change her face. The only time Ann could remember her ever taking them off was swimming in Ballybunion. Without them she seemed to have a bit of a stare, but her smile was big and bright, so she must be feeling happy. And the dress suited her shape. He looked good in his uniform as well. Not as scutty as the first time she saw him; a bit taller or something? To be totally honest Ann didn't have much time for Mickey Quinlan but he couldn't be as bad as Mona made out. Evil? That was just ridiculous.

'He has no respect, Ann, no respect. Sure the first time he came inside the house he back-answered me. "Take your feet off that couch, please", says I to him "Oh excuse me, Mrs Durack, I didn't know it was an effin' antique," says he, only it wasn't effin' he said, and the look he gave me. If I'd only known sooner she'd been going out with him behind my back, I might have been able to put a stop to it before it went too far.'

Ann couldn't help thinking, wasn't that the way? Mona who heard every bit of gossip going, never knew a thing about her own daughter doing a strong line.

'Seán's afraid of him, you know. No, I'm telling you, Ann, he is. And do you know what? I don't blame him. There's something evil in his eyes and whatever hold he has over Eva I can't get through to her anymore. She won't listen to me. In fact, I daren't say anything at all now for fear she'll just go and do the exact opposite.'

And again, the tears took over. Ann felt so sad for her sister, but at the same time couldn't help thinking Mona had brought some of this on herself. Not that she'd ever say such a thing. Mona had always been too hard on Eva, since she was a little girl, forever correcting her: the way she spoke, the way she sat; pulling at her clothes; slapping her on the back of the leg. It was definitely something to do with being an only child and having her so late in life. Oh, Eva was given everything, much more than her Marian ever got. Elocution lessons, ballet lessons, Irish dancing lessons, flute lessons. The poor thing was weary of traipsing around from one to the other. The one thing she didn't get was a bit of freedom. The laugh of it was, Mona herself was the very one who was free as a bird, wandering around town every day: tea and buns in the Stella, plenty of time to gossip with whoever she met, and plenty of money, thanks to Seán's good job in the gas company. All she ever had to do was throw a steak or a couple of chops on the pan and boil a few spuds and he was happy. Sometimes the poor man even had to wait for that much, because he'd arrive home from work to find Mona still out gallivanting. But poor Eva was watched and guarded and corrected. Was it any wonder she broke out eventually? Maybe she'd even picked him deliberately, just to annoy her mother.

'I know the whole crowd of them, Ann. Mrs Quinlan is grand, Lily Power that was, but I'd have nothing to do with the rest of them and he's the worst. There's something about him. He's worse than sly. He's… he's… evil. That's the only word I can put on him.'

Ann could see that Mickey Quinlan was much too cheap and vulgar for a girl like Eva who had always wanted to be a primary school teacher. Was it going out with him put a stop to that idea? Still, 'evil' was a bit much. What was Mona suggesting, that he might be violent? Her arm touched Fonsie next to her. Was she just lucky to have married a man who wouldn't dream of raising a hand to her, or had she chosen well? Mona and Seán the same. There were other girls she'd hung around with when she was young who'd ended up in an awful way. But surely Eva was clever enough not to get herself into such a situation?

'You're not saying he's hit her?'

'I don't know if he has, she'll tell me nothing. But I know his kind, Ann. And I've learned to hold my tongue when he's around, because I'm afraid that if I say something he doesn't like, poor Eva will pay for it after. How do I stop her marrying him?'

But it was much too late for Mona to tug at Eva's skirt and tell her to how to behave.

Mickey was putting the ring on Eva's finger. Fr Duggan spoke solemnly.

'I unite you in wedlock in the name of the Father, the Son and the Holy Ghost.'

Then he relaxed and smiled, more like himself.

'Well done, the pair of you. Now, do you want to give your lovely bride a kiss?'

When Eva and Mickey went into the sacristy with the witnesses to sign the book and everyone sat waiting, Ann noticed there was no mixing between the Durack side and the Quinlan side. No one slipped over to congratulate the parents or have a bit of a laugh with the new in-laws the way you would. They weren't even smiling across at each other. Ann wasn't looking forward to the rest of the day one little bit.

The wedding march started as Eva and Mickey came back down the aisle. Both of them looked absolutely thrilled, but poor Mona behind them had huge bags under her eyes and she'd aged twenty years. Ann wanted to go to her, put an arm around her and say. 'It'll be all right, it'll be all right.'

Twenty-eight: October 21st

The failure of the dawn raid on 1410 St Evin's Park was unfortunate and quite exasperating! Dr Garret FitzGerald thought that, after such an embarrassingly long time searching for the kidnappers, it would have been quite a coup if the country had woken up to news that the matter had been settled and Dr Herrema was safe and well. Instead, they now had stalemate. As he listened to Paddy's report to the cabinet of a gun battle in the unlikely environs of a housing estate in the little town of Monasterevin, he couldn't help considering how, if he was head of government, he would deal with this dangerous new development. Special Branch had succeeded in storming the house, but the kidnappers had managed to retreat to an upstairs room with their captive. As they were still armed, there was no way to get at them without endangering Dr Herrema's life! This stand-off – a siege by any other name! – with police occupying downstairs and the kidnappers and Dr Herrema trapped above was extraordinary and quite unprecedented. Clearly a moment when the most delicate leadership skills were required. A man's life hung by a thread! Dr Garret FitzGerald was by no means confident that Cosgrave's dour, hard-line, unyielding approach was the correct one. After all these kidnappers were not traditional criminals looking for a cash ransom. They were ideologues: fanatics who, if antagonised, might well instigate some terrible orgy of misguided martyrdom, killing themselves *and* Dr Herrema!

This was not the time for Cosgrave to take his lead from cabinet members like Cruise O'Brien who would encourage an even more implacable approach. Dr Garret FitzGerald had actually seen him smirk, when Paddy mentioned in his report that the location of the hideout had been revealed following questioning of suspects by Special Branch. Dr Garret FitzGerald had an inkling what that smirk was about because, just before the cabinet meeting started, Cruise O'Brien had not been able to resist whispering to him that his Special Branch driver had told him *precisely* – his emphasis – *precisely* how his colleagues had extracted the information from their suspect. 'Perhaps better for you not to inquire further,' he'd added in his most infuriatingly supercilious tone and strolled off to the tea trolley. It was abundantly clear that he was hinting – without any great subtlety! – that strong-arm tactics of some kind had been employed. Left-wing and Republican journalists loved to accuse the Coalition of turning a blind eye to police brutality and it was typical of Cruise O'Brien to enjoying playing up to that image. No doubt he had encouraged his Special Branch driver to boast about how ruthless his colleagues interrogation methods were. Exaggerate the reality by all means! Though always a great admirer of Cruise O'Brien's intellect, the man's rather juvenile attachment to machismo increasingly repelled Dr Garret FitzGerald. His tone in their brief exchange had conveyed the insulting message that, though they might be intellectual equals, his appreciation of *realpolitik* was greater, accepting that sometimes deeply unpleasant things had to be done for the greater good, whereas Dr Garret FitzGerald was not of that mettle. Too nice, in the fullest meaning of that word, too fastidious – too squeamish even – to be told about certain harsher realities.

In other words, Dr Garret FitzGerald did not have the stomach for leadership. An assessment he would utterly refute! Not that he was proposing himself as leader of course, merely that, should circumstances ever require him to take on the role, he would hope to be equal to the task. A slave to machismo, Cruise O'Brien was making the schoolboy error of confusing strong belief in the power of persuasion through rational argument with weakness. Imagine if – Dr Garret FitzGerald found himself debating with Cruise O'Brien in his head – imagine if the suspect who had revealed the address of the hideout had, as was hinted, been roughly handled.

And imagine further that word of this reached the ears of the kidnappers. Would that not put Dr Herrema more in danger ? An eye for an eye perhaps?

The kind of leadership needed now should place the highest priority on the positive value of saving an innocent man's life. Unite popular opinion behind this crusade! Make the kidnappers understand that harming Dr Herrema in any way would merely destroy any lingering popular sympathy for the Republican cause.

If Dr Garret FitzGerald was Taoiseach he would already have dispatched a high profile emissary to the site of the siege with a powerful argument that it was in the kidnappers' own interest to free him immediately. Surely their passionate commitment to the cause they believed in included such traditional Republican principles as justice and mercy? By any definition their captive was an innocent civilian. Therefore he should not be victimised. The emissary would also be authorised to hint strongly that the speedy release of Dr Herrema would surely reflect very well on the kidnappers' basic humanity, both in the court of public opinion and in the eyes of the law itself. Surely such an appeal to the kidnappers' sense of honour, as well as the possibility of lighter sentences would yield a highly satisfactory result?

Sadly, the bellicose mutterings that occasionally broke through his reverie seemed rather to suggest that once again, at this cabinet table, he was something of a fish out of water. Thoughtful and subtle statecraft, complex analysis, was never likely to find favour under Cosgrave's leadership. The Taoiseach preferred tough talk and a show of force. He was convinced that would go down a treat with ordinary voters who felt great sympathy for Dr Herrema, and were palpably angry at how his kidnapping had shamed the nation.

Twenty-nine: November 7th

St Michael's Church was on the same street as Joe Malone's pub so Francis passed it all the time, but he couldn't remember the last time he'd been inside. The funeral mass had already started when he slipped into an empty pew at the back. Through the small huddle of mourners, he could see a bit of what looked like Cónal's head. Francis was the only one here from his class and that was only because his mam read every single birth, death and marriage in the *Leader*.

'One of your pals in school is Collopy, isn't he? Where does he live?'

Francis didn't know exactly where Cónal lived. He'd never been invited to the house, and had never even cycled past it. Cónal always arranged to meet somewhere in the centre of town.

'I'm not sure. It's near Pennywell.'

'That's it. There's a Collopy from Pennywell after dying. Only forty-eight, God help us. Would that be his father, I wonder?

Cónal hadn't been in school that day. No one had paid much attention.

'Sadly missed by his wife Teresa and children, Brigit, Catríona, Gubnait, Cónal, Marie –'

Definitely it must be Cónal's dad. Francis did know he only had sisters.

'Funeral mass Friday 7th November at 10 am in St Michael's Church, followed by –'

Francis had a feeling Cónal wouldn't want any of his school-friends to be there. It wouldn't even surprise him if he came back to school next week and didn't tell anyone his dad had died. Still, he decided to bunk off the next morning and go to the church.

'George Collopy was a hardworking and loyal employee of Matterson's Meats for over 29 years. He was also a loving husband to his wife Teresa and a devoted father to his seven children: his daughters Brigit, Catríona, Gubnait, Marie, Maeve and the youngest, little Teresa, and his only son, Cónal, on whom now falls a great responsibility, but it's some consolation to know he had the best of role models, for George Collopy wasn't just a great provider for his family, he was also an inspiring moral guide. He put Jesus at the centre of all their lives. He was a prefect in the Archconfraternity of the Holy Family and a member of the third order of Saint Francis, he worked indefatigably for St Vincent de Paul and I can attest to what a tireless volunteer he was. In addition to good works, prayer and worship were part of his daily routine. Though his job took him all over Munster, he never let a day pass without visiting a church somewhere on his route, and Teresa was telling me that, right up to the evening before his sudden recent attack, the rosary was still a nightly routine in their home. At a time when personal ambitions and individual appetites seem to be becoming more prized in our society, when secular greed is taking hold of our young people, George Collopy represented something different, something rarer. He was a man who understood the value of a life devoted to the glory of God. And his loved ones can be confident that he has now gone to reap his reward.'

Francis wasn't sure if it was just the creepy sonority of the priest's voice that made Mr Collopy sound creepy too. No wonder poor Cónal never let his friends anywhere near where he lived, nor ever came drinking to Joe Malone's, or went to discos. It was hard to imagine the Cónal Francis knew, or thought he knew, kneeling down to say rosary every night. This father the priest droned on about would never have approved of most of the books Cónal read, or his anti-authoritarian opinions, or those freaky, sometimes sick cartoons, like those drawings of the Herrema siege he'd shown Francis only last week. The house looked exactly like the one where the kidnappers were trapped. It had been on the news every night for more than two weeks with nothing happening, but Cónal had created a gun battle with Eddie Gallagher and Marian Coyle shooting out the top window at the police and the army, who were scattering and running for cover, holding on to their hats, scared and useless. The kidnappers looked determined and heroic. As usual Cónal thought it was funny to turn normal perceptions upside down. He said that Gallagher and Coyle were like Mattheus Baader and Ulrike Meinhoff, and Herrema wasn't innocent, he was a representative of International Capitalism. Didn't Francis know about the working conditions in his factory? Fellahs were forced to change shift every two days, first eight in the morning until four, then four in the afternoon to midnight, then midnight to eight in the morning. How could anyone have a normal life switching around like that? Workers had to ask permission to go to the toilet as if they were children, and if they were caught smoking in the toilet, they were docked pay. Francis wondered if this was true. He had heard his mam saying that some people didn't know how lucky they were to be working in Ferenka, that there were fellahs half his dad's age earning twice as much as he did in O'Neill's.

The priest walked round the coffin shaking incense. Francis finally saw Cónal when he and some older men stepped out to hoist it. Slow-marching towards him, his pal looked dire: his face pale and fat, his hair lank and greasy, his body lumpen. The biggest shock was that his dead expression made him look a bit thick. No one seeing him now would believe for a second he was one of the brainiest boys in their school. Francis tried to catch his eye but he marched slowly past, blank eyes focused straight ahead. Mrs Collopy and all the daughters followed behind the coffin. There was something odd about them. Their hair? Their clothes? Maybe it was just that they were all in black? Francis waited until everyone had passed, then followed. The day was bright and really cold. The family clung together near the hearse as the coffin was shoved in. The youngest was only seven or eight and the oldest was... well, she couldn't be more than twenty-two or -three, but she looked more like thirty-three or older even. Francis realised what was so odd. Grouped together, the Collopys with their hairbands and pudgy pale faces and shapeless clothes looked like some stern black and white family snap taken way back, before any of them had been born, long before this time.

His mother leaned on Cónal's shoulder for support as they walked behind the hearse. The sisters followed. A shiver across the back of his neck made Francis realise he had no desire to go to the graveyard. He was relieved to watch the weird cortége move slowly away. Five past eleven. Shift fast and he'd make it back to school in time for first class after little break. Nobody need know where he'd been.

*

Ann loved going to Ritchie and Áine's house in Kerry View. Áine kept it so lovely. Tonight, even though he was going to his own lads' night out, Ritchie still made time to collect her and Marian first, and drop them off. Áine, welcoming as ever, brought them straight to the kitchen/dining room. 'No one is getting even a peek into the living room until we start, so it'll be a brilliant surprise when we go in.' Because Áine was into her sixth month Ann asked her how was everything. 'Flying it, no problems.' The doorbell rang again so she left them to it. 'There's nibbles there on the table.' Nibbles! Áine had gone all-out as usual and the food looked gorgeous. Homemade mini vol-au-vents and cocktail sausages with a rasher wrapped round each one, and smoked salmon on homemade brown bread and two kinds of quiche. In the middle of the table there was a grapefruit and Áine had stuck loads of cocktail sticks into it with cubes of cheese and pinneaple on them. Where had she come up with that idea? It looked absolutely brilliant. There was never any danger of going hungry in Ritchie and Áine's house. Ann knew a few of the women already: Áine's best friend Carmel, who – imagine! – was due around the same time as Áine, and her next door neighbour, who she recognised, but for the life of her couldn't put a name on her. There was Áine's mother Louise, and two sisters, Collette and Catherine – oh and young Gráinne was giving out drinks. In jeans as usual. Ann thought she was a lovely looking girl if only she'd straighten up a bit and make something of herself.

'I didn't think you'd be interested in a party like this.'

'You're right, Mrs Strong, not the remotest interest but Áine was like a –' Gráinne nearly said 'a tearing bitch', but caught herself just in time – 'a... a... headless chicken flying around getting everything ready, so I said I'd help out.'

Gráinne wasn't revealing the gory details. When she got home from school Áine had been wailing down the phone to their mother who, without even checking, had said, 'Gráinne will come over and give you a hand.' Then Áine had the nerve to give out to her for not having dressed up. Gráinne hadn't had a notion of staying for the party. Strictly housewives. She was actually a bit surprised to see Marian Strong here, but maybe she was after getting engaged? Would she be like the rest of them in a couple of years' time? Cow and Gate and nappies and teething and afternoon naps and how fast they grew out of their baby clothes?

Gráinne was gasping for a fag, but couldn't smoke in front of her mother, which was really annoying especially when most of the women in the kitchen were puffing away. Once they'd all gone in to the front room she'd sly through the connecting door from the kitchen to the garage. It couldn't come soon enough. There were about twenty women here now. Surely the thing would start soon. Jesus, one, two three... at least six of them were pregnant. Áine was screaming laughing at something her pal Carmel was telling her, so Gráinne wasn't sure if she'd heard the doorbell or not. She went to answer, happy to escape even for a few seconds. She recognised the woman. Annette, was it?

'Sorry I'm late, it's ridiculous and I only across the road, but when the news about Dr Herrema came on, I had to stay and watch. Isn't it the best ever?'

Gráinne said she hadn't heard.

'Oh of course, sure you wouldn't have the telly on with all the gang here. The kidnappers surrendered. He's after being released, thank God. Imagine the embarrassment here in the town if he'd been killed?'

Annette swept through to the back room, thrilled to be the good news girl. Pleased though Gráinne was to hear that Herrema had been released and even half-interested in knowing exactly how it happened, what she really wanted more than anything was a fag, so hopefully this latest news wouldn't keep them standing around talking for even longer. Get on with it, get into the living room. It was a pain being stuck here on a Friday night instead of having a laugh in Joe Malone's, even though she hadn't intended going to Joe's tonight. Not because of any awkwardness with Patch, who'd taken the break-up very well. A bit too well in fact. Thinking about it afterwards Gráinne had wondered if it suited him for her to call it off. Knowing Patch, they could have been an item for a million years and he'd never have ended it. Too much effort. He was happier just drifting along, but suiting himself of course when he felt like it. Had he manoeuvred her into calling it off? Let her be the horrible bitch and Patch the poor hard-done-by guy. Anyway it was done and she'd decided to give Joe's a rest for a week or two, maybe even until Christmas. Gráinne heard squeals of delight from the back room as Annette's news flew round.

Ann was delighted, especially for poor Mrs Herrema. What she must have gone through these last few weeks, her husband trapped in a room with those two IRA blackguards and no toilet? What was that young girl doing getting involved with an animal like Gallagher? Two of them he had at his beck and call, and the other one after having his baby in prison! What was going on in these girls' heads? Had they no self-respect? Ann just couldn't fathom it. Were they brainwashed? Áine clinked a glass for attention.

'Quiet, ladies. Quiet! Well, first of all, isn't that news about Dr Herrema only brilliant?'

Ann wondered if anyone here had husbands working in Ferenka. They would have been worried sick that the factory would close down and they'd lose their good jobs.

'That puts us all in great form. So now Doreen, who you've all met at this stage, is going to lead us into the living room and we'll see what she's brought along. Bring your drinks with you of course.'

As the women in front of her crowded into the living room, Marian heard oohing and aahing and 'Oh my God!' and 'Doesn't it look *fabulous!*' Having never been to one of these parties before, Marian was surprised at just how much Tupperware was on display. It was everywhere, on the drinks cabinet, on the music centre, on the coffee table and on the floor.

Little mountain of bowls in different colours were piled high from the biggest to the smallest. There were cannisters of different heights and shapes: circular, rectangular, oval. There were square containers ideal for storing salads or leftovers, and round cake containers that kept a Victoria sponge springy to the touch for a month. There were jugs and tumblers and measuring cups and ice-pop makers and bread bins and butter dishes. Marian hadn't expected so many colours. As well as the usual white there was orange and avocado and creamy yellow.

Doreen had a strong voice and she needed it.

'Don't worry, there'll be plenty of time to look at everything later. Ladies! Ladies! Straight away, straight away I want to say a big thank you to Áine for hosting tonight's party. And as for the gorgeous food and wine! Above and beyond, it really was. Well, we certainly can't say we're not set up for a good night and I hope you'll all join in the fun and games, which is really the main reason we're all here, and if you happen to spot some item that will help make your life in the kitchen easier, then well and good. If not, don't worry.'

Gráinne topped up glasses and escaped as Doreen began what she called, 'a few little ice-breakers' adding 'although I can tell with you lot that the ice is well broken already. Now, everyone here knows someone, but you won't know everyone. So I'll go round in a circle and I want each of you to say your first name... and then make an animal noise.'

Jesus! Animal noises! Gráinne closed the door, but couldn't resist listening for a few seconds. She heard her sister say 'I'm Áine, mieaoww!' The next woman went baaa like a sheep, the next went mieaoww again, and then the next got very adventurous and made some kind of monkey sound and all the women shrieked. Gráinne scooted through the kitchen/dining room to the garage, grabbing a half-full bottle of wine on the way. She slugged it by the neck and lit a Carroll's. She inhaled and slowly released. Aaaah! If tonight did nothing else it reminded her how vital it was to get a good enough Leaving Cert to allow her escape to college. She'd been dossing too much lately. Only seven months to go. Definitely time she got her act together. Otherwise imagine, in a few years time, ending up at some do like this, aquiver at the sight of plastic containers. Hello, I'm Gráinne, woof woof! She took another long slug and another deep drag.

Ann thought Doreen was just great the way she got everyone to let their hair down and do silly things. And the story of Tupperware was very interesting. Doreen explained that the way it locked in freshness was unique. Just think, meals could be prepared in advance, ready to serve, leaving housewives with much more free time. Ann was especially impressed by Tupperware's guarantee. Not five years, Doreen said, not ten years, but for a LIFETIME. That was a real sign of a quality product. Ann loved the idea of buying something that would last forever, but she was still shocked at just how dear Tupperware was. Much, much dearer than she expected. But that didn't stop some of the younger wives. After Doreen finished speaking, they all crowded round her, ordering this, that and the other. Ann thought their husbands must have great jobs if they could afford to spend that kind of money on bowls and containers. For Áine's sake of course she'd buy something, she couldn't leave with one arm as long as the other.

Marian could see how useful a lot of the stuff would be, and even liked the unfussy utilitarian design of many of the products, but didn't think a kitchen full of Tupperware would look very attractive. The slogan Doreen kept repeating about locking in freshness was very clever too, but Marian was unable to get as giggly and enthusiastic about the products as most of the other women. Maybe if she spent a few years as a housewife, preparing food and cooking and cleaning, products like these really would become something to get excited about. Was it a bit like how thrilled she'd been when Mr Harrington bought an IBM Selectric for the office? At the time it seemed to make work so much simpler. How she'd gone on and on about it to Stephen, who did his best to show an interest of course, but it wasn't the same as being able to talk with someone who really understood. Most of the women here were Áine's friends and neighbours – all married, all with babies or about to have. Marian realised she felt strangely left out of that shared experience, the sort of thing her mam had with her pal Mary Storan for well over forty years. She decided to buy something and looked first for some item her mam might use, but ended up picking a selection of orange, avocado and yellow jelly moulds, just because she liked the look of them.

1976

Thirty: March 5th

'Good afternoon, gentlemen. So... 6α1. You're all fit and well, I trust? Exam time comes creeping softly, creeping ever closer. The reason I'm taking Brother Furlong's class today is because I wanted to have a little chat with you about your future. Now, I had a look through your university application forms before sending them off. Interesting choices, gentlemen. It seems there won't be any shortage of engineers in a few years' time.'

Francis realised that what he disliked about Knacker so much was his tone of voice, clotted with self-regard. The headmaster actually had the notion that he was an erudite and entertaining speaker.

'Clearly, as honours students, you are all thoroughly besotted with the idea of going to university, which is all well and good, but you know it may not be the be-all and the end-all, even if you get the required points and qualify for a grant, or if your parents can afford to send you. To put it bluntly, for many of you university may not be the best option. So now. Have I got your attention now?'

Was Knacker serious? Francis was determined to go to university and since reading *Ulysses* had decided that Dublin was the place to go. Nothing Knacker could say would change his mind. He remembered years ago in primary school, before he even knew what university was, gazing from the window of his high-up classroom, down at the railway station, knowing exactly what time the Dublin train would come chugging out and wishing he was on it. Now he had a real chance to be on that train, because, as long as he did well enough in his exams, his dad's pay was low enough to allow him qualify for a full college grant. Why was

Knacker sticking his fat baldy head in now, trying to put him off. Why would any headmaster do that?

'There are a number of fine options for boys of your ability and intelligence which don't involve another three or four years of study and examinations. Options which, instead of being a financial burden on your parents, will actually earn you a good wage from the minute you walk in the door. Options which also have excellent promotion prospects.

'First of all, there's the Civil Service. Every year An Stáit Sheirbhís employs an elite group of Leaving Cert students as Junior Executive Officers. Imagine, within a couple of months of getting your Leaving Cert results you could be working alongside the best and brightest in the land in the Department of Finance or Agriculture or Education and so on, each department a different challenge. You could find yourself, at 18 years of age, very decently paid, and in a job for life, safe as houses. And if you're talented and ambitious enough to rise to the highest levels, then you might end up in a very powerful position indeed, directly advising ministers, shaping the destiny of the nation. Let me tell you something, gentlemen: There are several former Christian Brothers boys holding those top positions *right now*. In fact, it would not be boastful to suggest that, thanks to our success in getting so many students into the Civil Service, this country has been shaped by our boys.

'The two other professions I want you to think about are both concerned with the world of finance. Money is the root of all evil, they say, but it's also what makes the world go round and you would be very foolish to ignore the opportunities on offer to bright candidates in the areas of insurance and banking. Now you're probably thinking that standing behind a cage in the local branch dealing with Old Mother Riley and her three-and-sixpenny account wouldn't be your idea of an exciting or even fulfilling job, but, gentlemen, think of the career potential. Think of managing that branch, being a decision-maker, a leader in your community. Or think beyond that again, of working in head office, deciding where to invest millions so as to yield the maximum return. Currency fluctuations, share dealing... Remember, banks and insurance companies are the veins and arteries of a country's economy. Money is an international language and those who speak it fluently reap tremendous rewards. Again I could reel off the names of my own ex-pupils who went straight after their Leaving Cert into that boring old job in the bank and are now among the most influential people in the country. Well, is that an eye-opener for you?'

Knacker was obviously under the delusion that he was holding 6α1 spellbound, but, glancing sideways, Francis could see that Patch's mind had wandered somewhere else entirely, and Andrew was keeping his head down so the headmaster wouldn't notice just how bored he looked. Francis imagined Cónal, directly behind him, one hand on his chin, the other slyly sketching Knacker as a bloated pompous British army officer being machine-gunned by gloating Nazis.

'Don't misunderstand me, university is a fine choice if a career in Law or Medicine or Engineering is truly where your future lies. But over the last few years it has also become a place where a certain kind of person goes just to hide away from the real world, or where those who have an axe to grind end up, or where those who want to poison minds and destroy cherished beliefs gather. You boys are the beneficiaries of free education which, let us not forget, was the brainchild of a government minister from this city, God rest his soul. But I wonder sometimes if he fully realised that in opening up so many more opportunities he also created greater potential for confusion. Our boys have always been aware of the great sacrifices their parents made to put food on the table while keeping them at school. The truly bright sparks understood that by choosing a secure and rewarding path, they would guarantee the future comfort and well-being of their own wives and families. It would be foolish for yourselves and unfair to your parents if these opportunities were squandered in favour of other more precarious alternatives... Yes?'

It was Ian Barry had his hand up. He wanted more information about the Civil Service exam. Francis was surprised, then surprised he was surprised. After all it had been a long time since they'd been best pals and he hardly knew Ian anymore. But years ago he had seemed exotic and charismatic, wearing the freakiest clothes that his mother – Mummy, he called her – made specially for him. He used to talk and even walk differently. It was Ian and his father – Daddy he always said – who brought him on that amazing trip to Dublin: one of Francis' best childhood memories. They drove all round the city and stayed in the Intercontinental Hotel and, most exciting of all, they were brought on a tour of the RTE studios by Ian's father's friend, Gavin, the floor manager. Francis remembered being dazzled by him all day and in the evening too when he turned up in the hotel and joined them for dinner. His memory was of the coolest guy who moved like he owned whatever space he occupied, with a voice that made everything he said sound amusing and clever. 'The world is my oyster.' Francis would never forget the way he said that.

A guy like Gavin wouldn't be caught dead working in a bank or the Civil Service.

Francis had been only ten when he went on that trip. Were his magical notions of Dublin just a child's fantasy? No. Memory couldn't be that faulty. Whatever about the details, he could never have conjured up this feeling out of nothing, and even though he didn't really understand what the feeling meant, it was enough to lure him on, on to Dublin and whatever would happen there.

Its call was certainly more melodious, more enticing, than Knacker's arid drone.

Thirty-one: August 28th–29th

'You're not going.'

Francis hadn't expected this. His mam kept hanging clothes on the line, her baleful eyes averted.

'What do you mean?'

'I mean you're not going.'

'Why not?'

'You're off to college in a few weeks. It's saving your money you should be, not spending it.'

'But it's only a few days' camping.'

'I don't care what it is, you're not going. You can forget about it.'

His mam had that face on her as she rammed pegs onto shirts and vests and underwear: implacable, no talking to her. Francis had chosen the wrong moment. The clothes hung between them, unruffled in the sun-steeped day and he didn't know what to say next, afraid to start a screaming match in the back garden. She hung the last shirt, bent to pick up the box of pegs and marched past him to the back door.

'Camping. You'd want to cop yourself on.'

He couldn't believe it. The unfairness of it. He'd got more honours in his Leaving Cert than he needed, he'd got a place in UCD, he'd got a grant. And he'd slaved in a hospital kitchen, washing pots, every scorching day of the most amazing summer ever, saving nearly every penny. When he'd seen her looking so cheerful in the sunshine and had wandered out to let her know about the camping trip, that he'd be away for a few days, it had never ever occurred to him that she'd react like this. If it was about the money, he'd explain that it wasn't a problem. The trip wouldn't cost much. No more than a few quid. They were hitchhiking to Kerry. They'd already borrowed a big tent. He'd worked it out.

His mam was in the back room, lifting the sewing machine on to the table.

'Mam, I've saved enough money –'

'You're not going and that's that. I don't want to hear any more about it.'

'But all the others are going to college too and they're allowed –'

'If their parents are earning enough to let them go off on holidays that's their business. We're not made of money. Everything you've earned in that job is for college –'

'I told you, I've saved enough –'

'Yeah, you think you know it all –'

'Mam, it's a few days in Kerry, a few days in –'

It took him all he could not to say, 'fucking Kerry!' but some instinct warned him to hold back from using a word never heard at home. Eugene appeared at the door, looking scared. His mam threaded the needle. She looked up.

'You shout all you like. You're not going, simple as that. You're not going.'

'Mam will you just let me –'

'You're not going to Kerry. That's the end of it. You should be saving every penny, t'would be more in your line.'

She pressed the pedal and the needle hammered, more-in-your-line, more-in-your-line. The sneer of cold command. He'd heard it before. Now and again she got in this mood. He'd seen her turn on Gussie. And Martin. Do as you're told. Don't raise my blood pressure. Now Eugene was seeing her do it to him. It wasn't about Kerry anymore. She was to be obeyed.

To his shame and horror he couldn't stop the tears.

'Why won't you listen? I'm trying to – I'm – I'm – I'm…'

It was embarrassing, screaming and blubbing now like he was Eugene's age.

'Why are you doing this? All over a – over a – few days in Kerry. I'm seventeen! Well I'm going. I'm going, do you hear me? I'm going!'

He raved and grew more fierce and wild, bawling on, like he was vomiting or having a fit. Mortified, demeaned, bewildered, but he couldn't stop, replete with too much rage, spewing bootless cries above the clack of the sewing machine which stopped suddenly and he saw his mam's face aghast at this spitting, purple-faced tantrum.

'Look at what you've done to me, look at me!'

His heart ached. He had nothing left except exhausted breathing and sniffing. Then another sobbing sound; Eugene, nervous and upset. His mam jumped from her chair and went to him.

'It's all right, love, it's all right. Shh. Shh! Now look what you've done!'

*

And now she couldn't get to sleep. How could she? Still not over the shock of it. The way his face went like a beetroot and the tears and his whole body stiffened like he was having a seizure. It reminded her of that time in Ballybunion years ago when he screamed like a devil and she'd nearly thrown him over the cliff, God forgive her. It was always a battle with him, much more than the rest of them. He always had to go his own way. Sure, collecting him after his first day at school he wouldn't even hold her hand. No matter how neatly she dressed him he'd manage to make himself look as scruffy as possible. That lovely boy, Andrew, who called to the house the morning the exam results came out – his hair was long but it was well groomed and shining clean and he was dressed lovely. That was all she wanted. Half the time he didn't even tie his shoelaces, for heaven's sake! What was he going to end up like in Dublin, with no one to tell him anything? Going round like a tramp, his head stuck in a book? And he was going to have to feed himself, what did he know about that? He'd never had to think about these things, there was always plenty of food handed up to him; Dublin was expensive, that was all she'd been trying to make him understand. But no of course he didn't want to hear any that, he knew everything as usual. No one else had a clue what they were talking about. He thought he could do without them all; off now and no need of his mother and father ever again. And he was delighted, that's what upset Ann more than anything, delighted to be away out of it. His last few weeks at home and he couldn't even be bothered staying around. No, he had to go off camping with his pals. Wouldn't he be away long enough? Screaming and roaring like he was being kept prisoner in the house. His home.

She poked Fonsie.

'You'll definitely talk to him in the morning, won't you?'

'I will, I will.'

Fonsie wasn't looking forward to it. How had this happened? Everyone was delighted last week when the results came out. That morning in the yard he'd just loaded a palette and, as he reversed, there was Francis smiling and waving a bit of paper in the air, so it had to be good news. It was an even better surprise that he'd come directly from the school to O'Neill's to tell him first; Fonsie would never have expected that. Of course he told him go straight home to his mother, because Ann would be fretting, waiting. That evening they both acted like it was no more than they expected, but Fonsie could see how made up Ann was. Bursting inside. The first child to go to college. Now, ten days later, holy war in the house. Maybe he should have seen it coming. Ann had started giving Francis bits of advice about Dublin, warning him not to let people make a fool of him. She kept on and on about getting himself organised, telling him what he should bring and what was no use to him. She even got a notion to travel up with him to check out his digs. Francis hadn't seemed annoyed and mostly he got round her with jokes, but maybe there had been something building up inside all along.

Now he had to have this chat with him before going to work. What was he supposed to say apart from his usual 'don't be upsetting your mother'? And if he dug his heels in, what then?

Fonsie eventually got some sleep but woke at dawn. It was so peaceful sitting in the scullery with a cuppa. Sunshine and silence. Might as well enjoy it while he could. He'd wait as long as possible before waking Francis. Not to be. A door opened upstairs. Footsteps sneaking down. When Fonsie saw the rucksack in Francis' hand he decided straight away to forget about any talk. Let him go. Lesser of two evils. Easier to put up with Ann giving out and in the long run he'd persuade her that a few bob spent camping in Kerry wasn't the end of the world.

'Are you having a bit of breakfast?'

'No, I'm fine.'

'Well, take an apple or something.'

Francis was amazed, confused. Did he wake or sleep? Despite his dad's words and tone he still couldn't quite believe there wasn't going to be another row. The plan had been to wake early and depart in lone splendour. Now he felt like a nervous wild animal drawn slowly towards what he feared might be a trap. His dad had picked up an apple and was holding it out. Francis put the rucksack down near the front door and crossed the vast and boundless deep to the little scullery. He reached across the table and took the apple.

'Thanks.'

'Looks like a nice day for hitching.'

'Hope so.'

'I'd walk out the road a bit before you start. Nobody'll stop for you in town.'

Francis didn't say that of course he knew that already. He just nodded. 'Thanks, good idea.'

*

There could be no doubt that, as the night went on, her gaze fell on him more and more. When she spoke, it seemed to be for his ears more than the others, he caught her glance across the table as if it was his reaction only that interested her. When he spoke, her smile and eyes encouraged him. Such silent signals from pretty girls were usually directed towards Andrew, or occasionally Patch. Francis had observed them often enough. He had no idea why paradise was opened in his face tonight, but, determined not to make a mess of things, he slowed his drinking to a crawl, thanking the Rain Gods that had brought them all together in Begley's bar.

His mood earlier this afternoon had been a little different. Ah not rain! Not fucking rain! Not after enduring day upon day in a sweltering exam hall, the sun taunting them from beyond the high windows, through parching hours of differential calculus and Rutherford's protons and neutrons, and organic nitrogen compounds and Hamlet's hamartia and the origins of the Second World War, and *Anthologie de Contes et Nouvelle Modernes* and Peig, Peig, always moaning miserable Peig. Then, with no respite, whipped from the exam hall to the Regional Hospital kitchen where, in adamantine chains and penal fire, he'd scrubbed pots and tureens and giant-sized utensils from seven every morning to five in the evening, seeing sunshine only through a little square of frosted glass set into the ceiling above the sink. Having finally escaped this bottomless perdition and his mam's efforts to burgle his bank of youth, day one of the longed-for holiday was spent standing in baking heat with a bag on his back and his thumb stuck out, hopefully, wistfully, longingly, desperately, at village ends and crossroads. Raheen and Rathkeale, Abbeyfeale and Castleisland, Tralee and Camp Cross... Until finally, landing in lovely Dingle, he said a relieved 'thanks a million' to the returned Yank in the hired car who'd squeezed his thigh playfully as he made jokes about lazy niggers.

At last, a brief lie in the sun licking an Iceberger allowed him leave the dreary intercourse of daily life behind. His holiday had begun at last. Nostalgia fuelled him on the winding evening trek out the peninsula through Muireach – an halla was closed and silent as he passed – to the pier at Baile na nGall, as beautifully grubby and seaweed-smelly as Francis remembered it, the whitewash on Begley's pub altered only by three more years of grime. The boys from *tigh* Bean ní Suileabháin were back, except for Cónal, who no one had seen since the last day of the exams. Word had gone round that he'd done fantastically well and was going to Galway to do electrical engineering. This holiday, there would no *bean a' ti*, no compulsory Irish speaking or morning classes or Christian Brothers, nowhere off limits, not even Begley's. They could run their heedless ways in scorching heat.

But this afternoon on the pier the waves were dancing fast and bright when, in the space of a minute, clouds, blackened grey as a mound of cinders, sucked all the light and heat from the air. Fortunately it was a short dash in their swimming togs, towels held over their heads – how ridiculous with hair already sea-soaked, Francis thought – up the pier and over the wall to the lump of headland where they'd rigged up the family-sized tent Patch had managed to wheedle on loan from Ailbhe De Courcy who fancied him. Ah! Woe betide. They stared out disbelievingly at the pearl-sized drops that pelted down. Coaxed gently by the others, Tom had got the guitar out and, with scrunchy eyes and hair hanging almost to the guitar strings, played his favourites: 'Needle and the Damage Done,' 'Freebird' and – without any sense of ironic allusion that Francis could detect – 'Before the Deluge.'

'Oh for a draught of vintage,' said Patch, who had answered the Keats question on the English Lit. paper. 'Let's go to Begley's.'

Allie was her name. Her face made simplicity a grace, the faintest flush heart-beating about her cheeks. Her lustrous eyes were direct and unafraid. She was playing pool with her friend, Becky, when the boys arrived. The girls had dropped in for a quick Club Orange to slake their thirst in the heat of the afternoon when the sudden rain trapped them. The gentle rain from heaven, Francis thought.

A tableful of glasses and the width of several bodies separated he and Allie all evening. Yet, when the time for leaving came and the shuffling for coats began and some swayed as they threw their heads back to swallow the dregs and some darted to the toilet, she and he edged closer to each other, secret agents approaching their contact.

The rain, which had stopped, had now restarted, but in a different mood. Like a concept album – after the electrifying downpour of side one, side two was a meditative mist. Crossing the gravel parking area Francis and Allie drifted to the rear of the group. Somewhere between there and the headland wall, while she was telling him that Kavanagh's 'Canal Bank Walk' was her favourite poem on the Leaving Cert course, her fingers curled around his and, genuinely, he did not know which of them had made that happen. Their shift of direction away from the tent towards the edge of the headland was unnoticed and, as they looked down all of twelve feet or so to the black water, they heard faintly from the tent, Tom wailing that it was four in the morning at the end of December.

Allie was tall so their lips met very directly and – an excuse to feel her skin – he brushed the wet from her flushed cheeks and made sweet moan. Then they were on the ground. Francis pulled her on top of him so she wouldn't have to lie in the soaking grass. He liked feeling the weight of her and curled his legs around her thighs and their tummies met and parted, met and parted and, loving her wild wild eyes, his hands rummaged through the silken tangle and gripped her crown, so their lips pressed even harder. They sucked on country pleasures, rolling and rolling, their groins desperately seeking each other through barriers of duffel coat and parka and jeans and underwear. Aching joys and dizzy raptures.

'Emily Brontë would be proud of us,' Francis whispered, and he lay in dreamful ease, soaking up her laughter. In comfortable hugging silence they staggered up. A piercing multi-keyed chorus of 'After the Goldrush' guided them on their stumbling kissing progress back to the tent.

Under the influence of Tom's repertoire, the mood there was drunken melancholy. Becky said she was whacked, so Francis walked them both back to their B & B where, once the best friend made herself scarce, there was more happy love, more happy happy love, and between the kisses now, a rush of information: he, uni, she, a job. He, in Dublin in a few weeks, she, back to Dublin with Becky in the morning. But could he… could they? Yes she wanted him to. Allie lived in Clonskeagh. Where was that? Not far from

UCD, as it happened. Francis liked the sound of Clonskeagh. Allie said take my number, but he had no pen and the only paper he could find was a crushed Dairy Milk wrapper in his pocket. Francis bent and dipped his little finger in oozy Kerry mud and, as delicately as he could, traced a mucky 982354 on the wrapper, a kiss celebrating the achievement of each number.

*

Her mood had been peculiar on the way to the party so CJ was pleased to hear Terry's voice above the throng, full throttle.

'Sam, darling, you know your parties are the only things that make Dublin even remotely bearable in summer.'

This was the Terry CJ liked to hear. She was born to dominate a room, gesturing magisterially with glass in hand, without ever spilling a drop. He'd laughed when she expressed an interest in going with him to what she called 'One of your rural hooleys'. He'd been tempted to take her to meet McEllistrom and his gang in Kerry last week. She'd have seen the party faithful red and raw there, but he had arranged to join the family on the island the following day, so it wasn't worth dragging her down for one night.

'What we city rats need, Sam, is occasional escape. You know, that whimsical, spontaneous urge to strike out, find a wilderness somewhere.'

CJ tried to imagine that voice ringing out as they sauntered into Austin Stack's clubhouse arm in arm. Cantering in on the back of a pink unicorn would probably cause fewer bloodshot eyes to pop or slack jaws to drop. Like stout Cortez' men the Kerry gang would have stared at each other with wild... what was it... surprise? More honest at least than Sam's urbane party crowd who betrayed no wild or even mild surprise. Observing he and Terry together was no big deal for these sophisticates. Old gossip. But CJ knew that, driving home later, their drunken talk would be all about them; the wives bitching, silently hysterical that some other Terry-type might tempt their man; the husbands satisfying themselves with innuendo-laden witticisms, while secretly envying CJ; what a swordsman he must be to arouse such an exotic bird. One thing was certain: they'd all be thrilled to have Been There, smug at being among Those Who Knew. On nights like this, as he lounged in the well of Sam's inspired open-plan mews, the fulchrum, the magnet, the sun of the event, CJ didn't feel fifty or any age. He felt immortal.

'I don't think you believe how much I yearn for the simplicity of nature, do you, Sam?'

'Of course I believe you, Terry.'

She was flying high tonight all right. It was hard to resist the urge to prowl behind her and press himself against that magnificent arse in full view of everyone. He sidled over and, without interrupting the flow of conversation, tweaked the soft rump playfully. CJ had no doubt that someone would notice the cheeky intimacy, and the whole room would have it in moments. The story told and retold, the legend amplified.

But why had Terry not even glanced his way?

'You know, I'm suddenly yearning for some fresh air.'

Before CJ could draw breath, she'd hightailed it through the crowd, a whirlwind thrashing towards the front door.

The night was so mild, Ann Teresa got to the end of the lane before realising she'd stormed out without jacket or handbag. But there was no going back after that exit. She looked down crowded Leeson Street. What now? Meander, half dressed, through mobs queuing at the burger van, pouring out of taxis and cruising between basement clubs. Imagine if she encountered people she knew.

'Terry! Terry!'

So, there he was, a little far-off silhouette holding up her jacket and handbag. Fair enough, he'd bothered to follow her out. Let him follow some more. Ann Teresa turned towards the canal.

'Terry!'

It was satisfying to hear how much he was struggling for breath when she allowed him to catch up with her at the bridge.

'Jesus… hhh… hhh… it was only a tap on the arse. If I'd…

hhh… hhh… if I'd known it was going to annoy you so much –'

'For Christ's sake, you know it wasn't that.'

If not, then CJ hadn't a notion what. It wasn't some woman's game, she was angry all right, expecting him to understand, waiting for an explanation. He didn't like any of this, not knowing what the story was, being forced to stand out here, exposed, out of breath. Terry had better be careful now. If she didn't watch herself he might lose his patience.

'I want to go to the island.'

'Oh? Well yes, of course. We're on for next week, aren't we?'

'I feel like going there now. Let's drive there tonight.'

'But you know we can't do that. The family is down there. We have to wait until…'

At last. Ann Teresa saw realisation dawn and trickle across his face. Had he really missed all her hints and signals until now? Had he been that oblivious? Didn't he, like her, also think of the island as their creation, their shrine, bolt-hole, hideaway, secret cave, the colour and texture, rocks and grass, mist and howling wind and force ten storm, the *juice* of their affair? If so, then how could he ever allow it to be used by… used for a *family* holiday. Why was it occupied all summer? Ann Teresa might hesitate to offer an opinion, but Terry shrieked in her head. *She* knows *exactly* what she is doing, darling. *She* is marking territory, taking possession, poisoning the well.

'What am I to do? Tell her she can't go there? She's my wife.'

Ann Teresa could not believe the lapse in taste. Spouses should never be mentioned; that was basic. Affairs were for pleasure and escape, not therapeutic whining. The night seemed impossibly chilly now. She took her jacket and bag from him.

'Oh come on, Terry! Look, why don't we go somewhere in the morning? An early flight to London. Lunch at Wilton's.'

She touched the handbag gently, sadly – Gucci, such a pity – before dropping it into the gushing canal lock.

CJ stared down at the squirming bag. The thought of her neck veins thumping in his grasp as he thrust her after it, headfirst, was tantalizing. When he looked up, Terry had already crossed the road at Fitzwilliam Street and was waving at a taxi. One 'Terry!' escaped his throat. It was rage, not entreaty.

Though it was something of a shock to Ann Teresa that she was going home after all, the grand gesture buoyed her up until, approaching the gates of the unlit house, she remembered that all her money was in the drowned bag. She had by then also begun to accept that the island was lost to her. At least the magic of it as their secret place – such a foolish notion – was lost. Like everything else about CJ, it would have to be shared or surrendered.

*

His sleep seemed so content, the snores little more than distant surf. Mags was envious. No chance of sleep for her, she had to make up her mind to do this thing or not. Was it not possible just to let things be, put it out of her mind? But, only minutes earlier, even as she had tried to abandon herself to him, the mesmerising intensity of Michael's black eyes had made her suddenly think, 'What is this man capable of?' Then, for brief delicious seconds, he could have been the Jackal or Scarface for all she cared.

Mags eased her feet out from under the blankets until she felt carpet and sat up very carefully. The argument had been circling in her head like an aircraft in a permanent holding pattern. Michael's business affairs were his own. Yes. Would she ever countenance any interference in, or even questioning of, her journalism or campaigning activities? No. Playing witness for the defence, she even came up with examples of things she had never mentioned to him, like the meeting last year of a new feminist group spearheaded by Nell. Had she just forgotten to tell Michael about it – no – or had she kept silent because Irishwomen United insisted on linking feminism to the nationalist struggle in Northern Ireland and this had made her uneasy? She had only gone to one meeting anyway, maybe she'd felt it wasn't worth talking about. Irrelevant. Was it her right not to tell him, yes or no? Yes.

So, didn't Michael's airline ticket to the Cayman Islands fall into that category too? Wasn't that his own business?

Mags had yearned to find a new way for two people to be together in equality. One of the vilest confidence tricks men played on women was to make them believe that they were the ones who craved marriage, and men, being utter gentlemen, merely gave in to please them. The reality was that marriage was designed by men to allow them acquire, at low cost, a breeder a domestic servant and a child-minder, three persons in the one *hausfrau*, while they roamed free. Michael's boss, for example, had a faithful wife to take care of his fine brood, while he conducted a secret affair, untroubled. Mags guessed that while most men were like CJ, unable to commit to anything except themselves, it would be hard for most men to match his hypocrisy. Certainly Michael couldn't be accused of that. She and he were already damaged goods when they met. Neither was interested in vows or contracts. They didn't need each other for respectability, or careers, or even children. What drew them together – the fragile skein of attraction, desire, passion, affection, fascination – would hold them together. That was the beauty of the arrangement. But if she left the bedroom and crossed the hall into his study, the relationship as it had been, this fragile thing that had for a while flourished between them, would be irrevocably altered. Did she accept that? No matter what she discovered there?

Mags urgently needed to pee. Well, that sorted out the first step, leaving the bedroom. She sat on the toilet in the dark, conscious of how loudly water splashed on water. Did she dare flush? What if it woke him? For Christ's sake, when had a flushing toilet ever woken either of them? And so what if it did?

Mags recognised what was starting to happen: nervous mistrust alone would destroy whatever she and Michael had. The thing had worked for so long mainly because such a virus had been entirely absent. Between them the relationship had been sort of made up as they went along, freeform, unencumbered. Astonishingly, in the oddest most unforeseen ways, the wary wounded animals had crept closer and grown more comfortable together; a couple for all the times and places they wanted to be, and independently apart for all the rest. Tentatively, Mags had begun to believe that she and Michael had stumbled across a miraculous formula. Had she really found a man who was nothing like her, yet in tune with her needs? A man who didn't need to own or control a relationship?

Tiptoeing from the bathroom towards the study door, Mags was reminded, to her horror, of creeping about at the top of the stairs in Marlborough all those years ago. Oh Christ! What was she doing? Wasn't this just acting like a wife again? No, this was wrong, all wrong. What she and Michael had, didn't deserve this kind of rummaging. Even their differences of opinion, their utterly divergent politics had always seemed further proof to Mags of the integrity of their peculiar relationship. At least their disagreements were loud and honest. And part of the fun. She wasn't anyone's wife and would never again behave like one. Mags was convinced now that to open his study door, to sneak in and pillage his files, would only demean her and them.

Back in the bedroom she sat on an armchair and stared at Michael, her brain unwinding slowly towards a conclusion.

Such a little thing, a little little thing, a stupid thing. An airline ticket. Did Mags wish she had never seen it? Useless to ask that now. This little thing, this grit, this gallstone.

Her inability to let go could only mean that she suspected the worst. And what was that, exactly? Could she name it? It was about money, obviously. Hiding money. Whose? CJ's? Mags was convinced this was all connected to him, and not just because of raw prejudice. For years people had puzzled over where CJ got his money. His salary as a politician couldn't finance even his public lifestyle, let alone the legendary profligacy – according to those in the know – of his affair with Terry and any other secret expenses he might have. Michael had always been straight-faced and loyal: CJ was a clever businessman, that was why the country needed someone like him in charge. If he could make the country even half as successful as himself, there would be no recession. Mags and he had agreed to disagree; it was little more than a joke between them. But Michael had gone to the Cayman Islands, at least once, maybe more often. It could only be for some dodgy deal, and her suspicion – no, her belief – was that it had to involve CJ. So, could she live with that, continue to share a bed with such a man, grip him close in the darkness, allow him inside her? Did it make their relationship experiment just a delusion?

Mags had considered asking Michael directly, but guessed that even if her suspicions were calmed, such a conversation would end the easy trust they had so fortuitously created. Up to a few minutes ago she had held onto the hope that a little secret investigation might solve her problem. Ascertain that Michael's activities were innocent and legal, then everything could continue as before; he would be none the wiser. If something was going on, well, she could act accordingly. But now she understood that proof was not the issue. It was a matter of faith. So, was she getting back into bed or not?

After a long time sitting still, hardly breathing, Mags removed the robe, quietly gathered up her clothes and, naked, left the room. It would be safer to dress downstairs.

*

It was such a gorgeous night that Marian, her helmetted head against Stephen's shoulder, her arms tight round him, came to a decision – and here, with the dark country road all to themselves, was as good a time as any to tell him. She bellowed through the visor.

'Stephen, you can ask me again if you want.'

'What?'

'I said, you can ask me again if you want.'

She laughed at his startled eyes as the helmet spun round to her, then back to the empty road again. He slowed down.

'Don't slow down, keep going. Don't slow down. Ask me now if you want.'

He said something but it was too muffled.

'What?'

A roar this time.

'I said. Are you serious?'

Marian hugged him tighter.

'Yes, really. Go on. But don't slow down. Faster even.'

'What are you at?'

'Nothing, honestly. You don't have to if you don't want to. But I'd like you to.'

For a few seconds there was no other sound but the chainsaw zing! of the Yamaha. Then, the helmet angled a little, as if Stephen was trying to look at her and keep an eye on the road at the same time.

'I love you. Will you marry me?'

Marian pressed her helmet against his. She didn't mind having to shout it out.

'I love you too. Yes.'

She clung for dear life and laughed when Stephen, the most careful of riders, started to weave over and back, over and back, taking both sides of the road like a delirious drunken snake.

Thirty-two: October 2nd

His dad helped Francis load his luggage onto the train. Two big cases and two plastic bags with the overflow. The last thing he said to him was, 'Write to your mother won't you?' Then, after saying goodbye, the awkward funny bit with Francis in his seat, smiling out the window at his dad on the platform, waiting to wave him off. Finally a merciful lurch and out, from the murk of the station into the green and golden morning. He had a few seconds to see, beyond the tracks and rolling stock and freight crates, a chunk of school building rising up beyond the high wall. He picked out his old classroom, but this morning there was no twelve-year-old face staring out longingly. If there had been, Francis would have waved. Look at me, on the Dublin train, all on my own. Free as the road, loose as the wind.

On the journey he read *Remembering How We Stood*, which featured so many alcohol-soaked anecdotes about famous writers in 1950s Dublin that Francis began to think of more appropriate titles for the book. *Remembering How We Staggered, Remembering How We Puked', Remembering Anything Was a Miracle.'*

That was one Dublin, and there was Joyce's Dublin, and his own magic memory from years ago. And now a new pleasure, the Dublin he was about to discover all on his own. He took the map from one of the plastic bags and checked one more time that Clonskeagh, was, as Allie had told him, very close to the UCD campus at Belfield, but not so close to his digs in Blackrock which was on the other side of the college. Pity.

The weight of the luggage wasn't a problem for the short walk from train to bus at Houston station, but once in the city centre it was a bit of a pain hauling it round in search of the number 8 bus stop. When he got off in Blackrock, he really felt the strain on the walk up Merrion Avenue, left along Sydney Avenue and right onto Green Road where his new home for the next year waited. 'Birchwood' was a detached bungalow, very neat, with border flowers and a rose bush in the centre of the front lawn.

The woman who answered the door said yes, she was Mrs Barrett, but no, she wasn't expecting anyone today. Yes, she kept students, but both rooms were taken already. Francis Strong? No, there must be a mistake. The permed hair looked like a hat on her long thin head. But he'd written to her weeks ago and she had replied saying there was a room available. Francis showed her the letter. Mrs Barrett, her mouth tight, impatient now, spoke as if to a half-wit. Yes, she got lots of enquiries but a booking was *never* confirmed until a deposit had been sent. He said the letter hadn't mentioned a deposit. Mrs Barrett pointed out a line in the letter: 'Please feel free to come and inspect the rooms.'

'I always like to meet the students before confirming. Freshers generally come with their parents and have a look around. Then if we're all happy, they pay a deposit and it's settled.'

It was obvious that Mrs Barrett, behind the pinched smile and the polite voice, was relieved that he, a shapeless lump like anarchy, hadn't sent a deposit.

'The accommodation office in college will help you find a place. I'd go there straight away.'

Her goary visage mimicked a smile as it disappeared behind the quickly closing door.

Now, chained and bowed, Francis struggled up Merrion Avenue to the dual carriageway. With suitcase handles digging into both palms and two plastic bags becoming more awkward to manage, he had to lie down like a tired child every few hundred yards. When he finally trudged across the motorway flyover to the campus entrance, the last hundred yards loomed remorselessly uphill. At first all he could see ahead was a solid low nuclear shelter kind of place, which turned out to be the college branch of Bank of Ireland. The main university buildings only emerged as he limped past. He dropped his baggage and licked his strangled palms. Here he was. A drowsy numbness pained his sense, but here he was. Homeless, etherised, but here he was.

Belfield looked vast and new, all concrete and glass, levels and pathways. A transparent tunnel on stilts connected the upper floor of two large buildings and a long sheltered walkway zigzagged to a third. Students need never get wet. Everywhere Francis looked there were steps, in groups of three, in groups of ten, sometimes going down only to come back up again. What genius had designed this gargantuan Legoland for Francis and his kind to play in? Then, at the corner of his vision, he noticed a dirty brown brick single-storey hovel with a cement block deformity jabbing out at one end. It was like the dive at the edge of the model town. Had the architect wept? Even as Francis tried to guess what it was, two students stepped out into the sun, holding pints. Ah.

Francis cursed his fate that he was not free to wander about, breathe it all in. Having to find somewhere to stay was a drag, especially when this felt like his real new home. What about phoning Allie? Yeah, sure, great idea. What would he say, that he was humping luggage around Belfield with nowhere to live?

He hauled everything towards the biggest building, down steps to a sign.

ÁRAS NEWMAN
THE NEWMAN BUILDING
ARTS, COMMERCE AND LAW

Then up steps to the entrance. At the porter's desk, as soon as Francis said 'accommodation' he was interrupted in the friendliest way and directed, in bewildering detail, to the Students Union Office. Was there any chance he could leave his bags at the desk? The friendly porter laughed.

'Ah now. This isn't left luggage, sunshine.'

Because it was empty of students today Francis really noticed the building itself. The concourse was gloomy and wide enough to drive a truck through. One side, all glass, invited him to a garden that was like a modern version of a quadrangle, but the entrance to it was locked. On the other side, strung along the grey brick walls, like icons to a kind of university long gone, were wood and glass notice-boards with gold lettering on top: The Rowing Society, The Choral Society, The Archeological Society, An Cumann Gaelach, The Orienteering Society. Francis imagined unsmiling young men and an occasional woman, in hats and high collars, the privileged few conversing with grave intensity about their passionate interests. But now this huge new campus belonged to him and lots more like him.

A bank of public phones jolted Francis back to his present difficulty. His mam had said she'd call his digs tonight, to see how he was getting on. Fuck! He'd better try to contact her first. His brother Ritchie had a home phone, but he'd be at work. Would Áine be there?

When she heard what had happened Áine said 'Oh janey no!' and 'I don't believe it!' and 'Your mam will be up the walls' and 'Gráinne is going up tomorrow. I hope she'll be okay.' Finally Francis had to remind her that the three minutes were nearly up and he had no more change. She said she'd ring Ritchie at work and he'd drive over to his mam with the news – 'God, Francis you're desperate, do you know that.' He'd ring again in an hour.

At the end of AD concourse, a sign, THEATRE L, tempted Francis to peek through the little round glass window set into the entrance door. He saw an enormous semi-circle of seats – was there a thousand? – sinking way down to a deep well from where lecturers would cast their spell in front of a long blackboard set into a vast brick wall. It was empty. He'd love to sneak in. Do I dare? Do I dare? He didn't.

Halfway along another perspex tunnel in the air, the Students Union area turned out to be just a few closed doors, and a mind-blowing collage of notices. The word CONDOMS drew Francis' attention. He read that they were available in the welfare office free of charge, but a small voluntary contribution was requested. Suddenly the door in front of him opened.

'You looking for condoms, yeah?'

The bearded smile was friendly. Francis didn't know what to say. It couldn't be that simple, could it? Did the Students Union really give out rubber Johnnies just like that?

'I'm closing up for an hour so make your mind up, man.'

Would it sound really stupid to ask how much was a small voluntary contribution?

'Oh yeah, no, well, actually ah… I was looking for information about ah… about accommodation.'

Now the Students Union guy noticed the luggage. He stared.

'Jesus, man, you've left it late. Are you a fresher?'

'Yes.'

'And you're looking for digs?'

Francis nodded, painfully aware he now stood confirmed in full stupidity.

'You'll get nothing anywhere near, that's for sure. And why're you dragging all your gear round? Only giving yourself more hassle.'

The Students Union guy got him an accommodation list and marked addresses that he thought might, *might,* still be available. The best bet at this stage would be to ring round to check first, no point dragging his shit all over the Southside. Did he know how to tap the phone?

'Come on. I'll show you.'

At the bank of phones, the Student Union guy warned Francis not to do this if there were porters around.

'You tap out each number fast, then leave a little gap before tapping out the next one. You can dial three, nine and nought, you'll be glad to hear. Watch. Call out one of those numbers.'

He tapped each number expertly, apart from a three and a nought, then he gave Francis the handset. It was ringing! A woman answered. Francis was about to press button A, but the Students Union guy stopped him and gestured at him to speak. Francis stuttered something about accommodation and the woman said sorry, she had nothing. He hung up.

'There you go. It'll save you a few bob anyway. Good luck.'

Free calls. This was like magic. A dozen inquiries later he had a sore index finger and still no digs. He'd decided to get back to his sister-in-law and tell her everything was sorted, his mam wasn't to worry, he'd found a place and was on his way to see it. That would give him time to think about what to do.

'Francis! Brilliant! Ritchie's just arrived with your mam.'

No! The last thing he wanted.

'Hello, hello? Francis?'

'Yeah, I can hear you, Mam.'

'Are you all right? What happened? What went wrong?'

'I don't know. She'd given the room to someone else.'

'What? But she wrote to you an' all? The cheek of her. I've a good mind to call her and –'

'No, no, Mam. What's the point? The room's gone.'

'You're right. I wouldn't waste my breath on the like of that. Anyway, listen, I've it all fixed up.'

'What?'

'You know Mrs Cosgrave across the green? Remember her eldest, Pauline? You do, she and Marian were great pals for years. Well, whatever made me think of her, only didn't I remember that she's been above in the Mater ever since she got her nursing qualifications. Anyway, myself and Ritchie went straight over and told Mrs Cosgrave what was after happening, and she was so good. "Come on, Ann," says she, "we'll go down to the phone box and ring her," and, as luck would have it, she got straight through to Pauline, and Pauline said there'd be no problem putting you up for a few days in her flat, as long as you didn't mind sleeping on the couch. "He'll sleep on the floor, Pauline," says I to her, "as long as he's safe –"'

'Are you serious? That's brilliant, Mam.'

'Wasn't it lucky I thought of her, and she away for years? Anyway, the thing is – are you listening now? – she's on duty today until four o'clock, so there's no point in going to the flat until about five, do you understand? She's in – where's this her flat is, Ritchie? – Fairview. Have you a pen?'

His mam called out the address slowly.

'Okay, I'll phone again when I get there. Thanks Mam.'

'Mind yourself now, love.'

What wondrous life was this? Francis was delighted with the latest twist, a nurse's flat in Fairview? Where was that? He was a bit disappointed to see on his map that it was miles away on the north side of the river. More lugging of bags, more bus journeys. Still, it was a whole lot better than wandering around the Southside begging fierce viragos with perms and pinched mouths to give him a room. Fresh woods and pastures new.

On the number 10 back into the city centre the conductor told him if he got off at Westmoreland Street, he could get a 20B from the same stop directly to Fairview. As soon as he was back on the street a warm spicy aroma floated past his nose. He'd heard of Bewley's café, of course. Was that how real coffee smelt? Francis moved closer and peered in. He was surprised to see it was self-service. He hauled his gear towards a huge old back room, where the competing smells of coffee and cigarettes and wood, the cacophony of mugs and voices, the look of the customers and the deep rich velvety benches they sat in, made the notion of having even one small cup irresistible. Could he ask someone to mind the wretched bags while he queued up? A group around his own age was sprawled at a table nearby. Chatting, laughing, ogling, all of that, they could have been his gang in Joe Malone's back home, except that this wasn't a grubby old pub and they were too good-looking and wearing much cooler gear. One face, framed in a gap of bodies, made Francis pause and stare. She had long ruffled ebony-black hair and deep hollow holes of eyes. She pulled on her cigarette and held the smoke for a long time before pursing her lips to blow: a languid exhalation, a radiance rare and fathomless. If only for the chance to see her close up, Francis decided to approach the group, but she suddenly stood, looking in his direction, and he saw the shape of the tall slim frame.

'She' was a guy, and walking towards him.

As the shock quickly dissolved to embarrassment, Francis

blushed the very deepest, hectic red. Fortunately the guy didn't notice as he ambled past only inches away. Francis felt like such a culchie, a mucker up in the big smoke for the day, laden down with bags, who couldn't tell fashionable city boys from girls

The guy was now hugging a woman. Smiling, she slid his hair back from his eyes. Francis now wondered how it had happened, how he could ever have mistaken him for a girl. What a dope. Was the woman his mother? With that mound of red hair falling generously about her shoulders and his dark eyes and hollow cheeks, they looked exotic; like actors playing Gertrude and Hamlet. They floated past him whispering and smiling. Francis, head down, pulled at his bags as if they were recalcitrant donkeys and got the hell out.

*

Matthew said, 'This is Mags,' quite casually, but was massively chuffed at the effect of her presence on his friends. He knew they were, with one mind, thinking, wow, his dad's girlfriend. Their mothers and fathers were all still together, so even trying to imagine the old man with a girlfriend seemed – apart from being kinda disgusting – impossibly way-out and American. It was really obvious that his male friends were actually a bit nervous, probably confused that they couldn't place her either as a bimbo or a typical old dear, and definitely not a spinster aunt. His girl friends, Debbie and Gillian, seemed shy, maybe even star-struck. The affectionate squeeze around his waist felt so cool as he said, Gotta go, guys.

Out on Westmoreland Street Mags said, 'Starting college is a very special occasion, so you can ask for anything. Where to?'

'Alias Tom.'

'Oooh, very trendy.'

Matthew told her trendy wasn't a word she should use anymore.

In Alias Tom's he tried on a belted leather jacket. 'Gorgeous.' The attendant was almost conspiratorial. Matthew looked at himself in the mirror, back, front and sides. 'Anything else you think I might like?' He saw the attendant appreciated the hint of double-entendre. Matthew guessed he was about twenty and looked like he spent a lot of his spare cash in Herman's Klipjoint. His vocabulary of compliments was limited – 'Gorgeous! Fabulous! Out of this world! Stunning!' – but Matthew relished the discreet dainty adjustments of a sleeve or lapel, along with certain glances, as he tried on numerous jackets. He wondered if Mags was giving the performance enough attention to appreciate what was going on. She was no fool, but older people very often missed what was under their noses.

Finally, he turned to her and casually said.

'No, nothing here.'

As they walked up Duke Lane, he glanced back through the glass front and was the tiniest bit disappointed not to see dismay or at least annoyance register on the attendant's face. He suggested the Dandelion Market. Mags laughed. 'From Alias Tom's to the Dandelion Market. You're eclectic, I'll say that.'

Then she asked what seemed to Matthew a peculiar question.

'Does Michael ever bring you on his trips?'

'I went with him to Castlebar once.'

'I mean when he goes abroad, to exotic places.'

'Like where?' Matthew wondered what her hesitation before answering meant.

'Hasn't he been to lots of great sunspots?'

'I don't know where he goes.'

'Really?'

'No, I never ask.'

'You have no idea where your father goes, ever?'

'We don't talk about it.'

'But that's… don't you think that's strange?'

'Not for us.'

Matthew had never given his father's trips abroad a second's thought. Was Mags worried he had another woman stashed away somewhere? That sounded like a mad idea, although nothing about his father would surprise him. If he turned out to be an international drugs boss Matthew would have no trouble believing it. Whatever was going on he hoped Mags hadn't been hurt in any way.

At the entrance to the Dandelion Market, they stopped to admire the serene, painstaking stillness of the Dandelion Clown. Matthew leaned in, watching closely for any hint of movement, then he dropped a 10p piece into the bowl and got his reward: the Dandelion Clown winked. Matthew liked that exchange. At No Romance he flicked a hand casually along the rack and pulled out a scratched fur-lined bomber jacket. It fitted perfectly.

'I'll take it.'

'Are you serious? It's only four quid. You could have stung me for fifty in Alias Tom's.'

'I know. I was a bit disappointed you didn't look more nervous while I was trying on the most expensive stuff.'

He loved making Mags laugh.

'You're sure this is what you want?'

'Don't you think it looks good?'

'You're a clothes hanger, Matthew. Throw a sack over your shoulders and you'd start a new fashion.'

She crushed him close and kissed his cheek.

'I hope you'll have the time of your life in this, and remember the day you got it.'

He wanted to hang about her neck, her warmth calmed him.

'We'll always be friends, won't we?'

That was the moment Matthew figured Mags was breaking up with his father.

*

Wrecked as he was, Francis understood why Pauline Cosgrave laughed when she arrived and saw him alone and palely loitering on her doorstep.

'Well, the happy wanderer. You haven't been dragging all those bags around since this morning, have you? Francis Strong. I wouldn't have recognised you in a million years, but sure what age were you the last time I saw you – ten, eleven?'

'About that.'

He had a little memory flash of his sister and Pauline, sprawling in their school uniforms, white legs in whiter ankle socks waving in the air to some record, the pair of them laughing at he never knew what. She showed him round the flat, which was the whole ground floor of the old house, telling him over and over again to make himself at home. The living room was high-ceilinged with a bay window, the bedroom was big enough for two double beds and a monster of an old wardrobe. The pokey kitchen was of Stygian murkiness. The bathroom had a shower and all Arabia breathed from the bottles lined along the bath. Pauline kept apologising that he'd have to sleep on the couch and he kept saying it's great, thanks a million. She told him to help himself to anything in the fridge while she had a quick shower. He made a sandwich, poured a glass of milk, brought them to the living room and sank into the cushions.

When Francis opened his eyes, he was puzzled at how far away the unfamiliar ceiling was. The only light was an orange beam breaking through a gap in drawn curtains. He was splayed on a couch. Lovely soft cushions. He heard far-off whispered speech. Female voices? On a coffee table near him, a half-eaten sandwich and a glass of milk. Now he remembered. He had faded far away, dissolved. What dreamful ease. He found the door and followed the voices to the little kitchen.

'Ah, you woke. You were fleadhed out. This is my flatmate, Elma. And this is Francis.'

Elma said it was awful the way he'd been let down, typical Dublin landlady, snotty bitches the lot of them. Pauline told him the immersion was still on if he wanted a shower, which he guessed was a kind hint. He probably stank after the day's odyssey. When he emerged, smelling like a pot pourri, having tried out every cream and oil, the girls were lounging in the big room watching *The Sweeney*. The lads were tracking down an army guy who'd deserted and gone psycho after serving in Northern Ireland. Elma said 'John Thaw or Denis Waterman?' Pauline said 'John Thaw every time, what a ride.' She asked how was Marian and said wasn't it an awful pity that she never got to go to university, like she wanted. She'd have made such a brilliant teacher. Francis had never thought about why Marian didn't go. It was a pity, he supposed, but it also occurred to him that, if she had, he wouldn't be the first from the family. He didn't like that idea so much.

The phone in the hall rang. Elma answered and shouted to Pauline.

'Gerry and Tony are round in Gaffney's. They want to know will they call here or do we want to go round?'

Pauline did a big, 'Ah for God's sake at this hour!' but Francis could tell she was delighted. Elma told them they'd be there in a few minutes.

'Are you coming, Francis?'

If they were meeting fellahs he didn't want to be a spare tool. Anyway, he fancied lounging on his own, green and carefree, watching telly.

'All right, don't wait up. We'll try not to wake you when we come back.'

'If we come back.'

'Elma!'

The girls had such an open, easy way about them, doing as they pleased. When they were gone Francis flicked from channel to channel and was surprised that, with four to choose from, there wasn't anything he particularly wanted to see. He pulled out the Cadbury's wrapper with Ally's phone number scrawled on it. The mud was now dry and smudged. He'd copied it properly into a notebook and, anyway, knew it off by heart, but he liked looking at this crumpled billet-doux, remembering. Tempting though it was he knew it was too late to call her. He imagined, what if this flat was his and he could invite her over right now? Bliss. But then he thought what if she said no, she'd changed her mind and didn't want to see him again? Now his heart was driven wild with doubt and though he told himself he was being stupid and there was no reason Allie wouldn't want to see him again, it was impossible to dislodge the fear. He stared at the TV without seeing or hearing anything, as his thought-tormented brain composed every possible variation on a phone conversation with Allie. Finally, after a hundred indecisions, his attention was drawn back to the TV by a vicious old lady who was calmly arranging for someone to be poisoned. The programme was set in the days of the Roman Empire. After the poisoning the old lady, whose name was Livia, arranged for someone else she didn't like to be falsely accused of rape. Then she ordered her grandson, a poor limping, stuttering character called Claudius to marry a monstrous hulk of a girl and laughed openly at how ridiculous they looked together. Livia was a mesmerising character: a vicious, controlling, power-mad monster. Francis thought of the tight-mouthed permed hag in Blackrock and what a lucky escape he'd had. But what if he found other digs and the landlady was just the same? What if all the landladies were like that? He could never invite Allie round, that was for sure. A notion that had been darting about in his brain for the last few hours settled and took definite shape. He wouldn't look for digs at all; no controlling, domineering landladies for him. He'd get himself a flat. Not an expensive one like this, obviously. A little bedsit. Cheap. He'd tell his mam that he didn't want to impose on Pauline's hospitality for too long and it was all he could get at such short notice. Yes. A room of his own.

Thirty-three: Oct 4th

After two nights on the couch Francis knew exactly where he was when he woke, but it wasn't until he'd tiptoed out and had a piss and tiptoed back that he remembered it was Monday and the girls had left for work long ago. He'd enjoyed his first lovely lazy Sunday in Dublin. The girls never even mentioned mass and brought him for a long walk on Dollymount strand. How they screeched when Francis asked if they swam there in the summer.

'Oeuch! Not a chance. You'd get more than a mouthful of seawater in there.'

Soon after, he noticed used rubber Johnnies along the water's edge and wondered if that was what they meant, but he didn't ask.

Today was flat-hunting day. At three o'clock he went to buy the evening paper. A small crowd was waiting outside the newsagent's and when the guy on the scooter arrived with a bale of *Heralds*, they swarmed in after him and snatched at copies. Francis guessed they must be flat-hunting too. Back at Pauline's, he spread the accommodation ads pages out on the table. He moved his finger slowly down the column looking for areas close to Belfield. Artane, no... Ballsbridge, yes. But Ballsbridge was all 'luxury accommodation' and 'suit two professionals' and rents were way beyond his budget. Cabra, no... Clonskeagh.... Clonskeagh? What about that? Just one ad, but it made him feel ridiculously excited.

CLONSKEAGH. Bedsits £5 pw and £7 pw. Suit students. 113 Clonskeagh Road. PH: 984572.

A bedsit for a fiver was a pound less than the digs in Blackrock. A pound more to spend every week. Surely it would be gone by the time he travelled all the way over there? Still, why not try? At the bus stop a passing car pulled in suddenly and he saw someone wave. It was Pauline on her way home. When he told her where he was going, she laughed.

'Come on, I'll run you over.'

113 Clonskeagh Road was a sweetshop in a small row along with a chipper, a chemist's, a bookie's and a hardware shop. Mrs Winter, the owner, could certainly talk.

'You're not the first, there's been a few before you and I may as well tell you the larger bedsit is gone half an hour since, so it's only the small one left. There's two said they're interested and they'll phone me later, but you know and I know what that means, they've gone to look at some other place before making their mind up so, as far as I'm concerned, if you definitely want it, it's yours. Will we go up? You are a student, aren't you? I prefer students, I've always found them very well-behaved, no matter what other people say. Mind you, I've only been doing this since my husband passed on three years ago. It's more a hobby than anything else really. There's the bathroom, shared, and here we are, in you go. As I say, it's not huge, but it's spotless and has everything you need.'

Twelve foot long and nine foot wide. Fold up table. Two chairs. A wardrobe set into one alcove, shelves in another, with pots, pans, cutlery and plates above a two ring-cooker and a sink. Wide window at the narrow end. Bunk beds.

'The bunks are handy because, you know, if you have anyone staying the night at least they'll have somewhere to sleep.'

Good thinking. Two-bar electric fire, ten pence meter. A two by four rug over the lino. One little room an everywhere.

'I'll take it.'

There was no reading lamp. He'd need one for studying. Mrs Winter said fair enough, she'd sort that out. In the car Pauline said quietly.

'Are you sure now? It's awful pokey.'

'But it's very close to college.'

And close to Allie.

'True. But honestly now, there's no problem staying on with us if you want to see a few more places.'

'Thanks, but lectures start Wednesday. Would I get anything better for a fiver?'

'Fair point. And you really don't mind sharing a bathroom?'

'Not at all. And I kinda like Mrs Winter.'

'Sure yeah, she seems decent all right. Nicer way about her than that Garda creeping Jesus who owns our place. But I don't want your mam coming up and giving out to me for letting you live in a shoebox.'

This bed thy centre is, these walls thy sphere.

'She won't, I promise. I really like it, Pauline. Honestly, I'm not just taking it to be out of your hair. It suits me.'

He meant it. It felt right. Delicious solitude. A place all to himself.

*

Click! The front door opened. Eva Durack wondered how would Garda Kojak shut it this evening – with a slam, a bash? Would he nearly rattle it off the hinges like he did the other night? The door closed with a normal dull thud. Did you hear that, Jean? We might be in luck this evening. Garda Kojak might be in a good mood for a change. Now she noticed how tight her grip on the infant had become. He appeared, unbuttoning his jacket, the muscly little chest stuck out. Of course as soon as he saw she was feeding, the eyes flicked away towards the scullery.

'How's tricks? What's for the dinner?'

The big nose, half the size of his head, sticking out, sniffing.

'Lamb stew.'

'Is it ready?'

'Yes.'

'Good. Put it up. I'm going for a rinse.'

The way he spoke and the way he trotted up the stairs relaxed Eva. He seemed okay tonight.

She managed to dish out the stew without disturbing Jean at her breast, although a sudden little bite nearly made her spill a ladleful. She wiped the side of the bowl carefully with a tea towel so it was spotless for Garda Kojak.

His face looked shiny from the wash and he'd put on a fresh clean tight white t-shirt; all hopeful signs. He still didn't look her in the eye though, nose down in the bowl instead.

'That smells fuckin' A-one. Nothing like a good stew.'

No point in wondering why the good mood, Jean, just be glad of it. Then Eva saw him pause before dipping his spoon into the stew. She guessed what was coming.

'Not while I'm eating.'

Well pity about you, the child has to feed herself too. But she stood up.

'Sorry. I'll finish her upstairs.'

We're just as pleased aren't we, she whispered to Jean, not to have to sit there looking at him pigging in? Upstairs was peaceful. Eva closed her eyes, the hungry nibbling so soothing. Then Jean's busy lips slowed and she began to doze. Gently, carefully, Eva eased her down into the cot. Shhhh, you don't want to wake up now and disturb Garda Kojak. She sat on the bed staring through the bars at the little bundle, making the silent promise yet again that she'd never pull at Jean's skirt, or correct the way she sat, or slap the back of her legs, or talk about her as if she wasn't in the room. The whine from below jabbed in her ear.

'Hey! Hey! Are you getting the tea?'

How could she have forgotten that Garda Kojak was too important to make his own tea? He couldn't be expected to get up out of his chair and drag himself all the way to the kettle. Eva came down. His bowl was licked clean. He actually looked at her and his smile was nearly friendly.

'That was tasty. You can't beat a good fuckin' stew.'

He slapped her backside playfully. She filled the electric kettle, watching him light up and stretch back in the chair. Weirdly, for just a second, she remembered clinging passionately to that tight body. Then Garda Kojak asked the usual casual, harmless-sounding first question.

'Were you out today?'

'I went into town.'

'For long?'

'No, I went out around three and I was back before five.'

'Doing what?'

'Getting a few bits in Quinnsworth's, mostly.'

Even as she said 'mostly', Eva knew that wouldn't be good enough for Garda Kojak. He'd want to pin that down, get more detail.

'Meet anyone?'

'No.'

'Sure?'

Who did he think she'd met?

'I said hello to the girl at the checkout.'

'Okay. Get the tin, will you.'

No chance he'd reach for it himself of course. Might strain his arm muscles to stretch across to the sideboard two feet away.

'You put today's receipts in?'

No, Kojak, I burned them and scattered the ashes. I flushed them down the toilet.

'They're there on top.'

He unscrewed the lid and took out the two loose receipts. Eva heard the kettle hiss and bubble. She was fairly sure there was only one danger item, the Toffypops, and she had that covered. When he asked what the twenty-four pence was for, she'd tell him, baby powder. He hadn't a clue how much baby stuff cost, or how often it had to be replaced. He was wary of all that. The amount of Johnson's she'd told him she'd bought over the last month would have kept poor Jean's little bottom rash-free for a year. Eva poured tea for both of them, waiting.

'Seven pounds fifty-six pence. So, what's the running total for the week so far?'

'Twelve pounds eighty-four pence.'

'That leaves seven pounds and fourteen pence for the rest of the week. Is that enough?'

'I think so.'

'You're sure? I don't want shite served up to me at the end of the week because you've overspent. It's happened before.'

Could she ever forget? Would he ever let her forget? Cow's liver one Friday and he stomped out of the house. Oh he wasn't having that! A puss on him for days after.

'It's enough. Just tell me what you want.'

'What do you mean, tell you what I want? You should know what I like at this stage.'

Wrong move. She'd allowed some tone to creep into her voice. Garda Kojak was very sensitive that way. 'Don't take that tone with me' was always a sign of real trouble. This wasn't that bad – yet – but bad enough to start him looking more closely at each item.

'One pound thirty-five, what's that for?'

'Meat, the roast beef, I think, or maybe the chicken.'

'One thirty-five for a chicken?'

She should know by now; no ifs or hesitations.

'No, you're right. It was the roast beef.'

'Ninety-nine pence, what's that?'

'Giant Daz.'

'Forty-two pence?'

'Teabags.'

'Fifty-one pence?'

'Oh, am… oh…'

For the life of her Eva couldn't remember what that was. Her brain raced along Quinnsworth's shelves. Garda Kojak's eyes didn't blink, oh very patient, like that cat in the garden this morning staring at the robin. Oh please, Jesus, what was it? Then she remembered and hoped this wouldn't be trouble, but she daren't delay any longer to think of a lie.

'Am… oh yes… yogurt.'

'What are you talking about?'

'I thought I'd give it a go. It's supposed to be very good, you know, after the baby.'

'Yogurt? Fifty-one pence?'

'It's six tubs attached. I'll show you.'

'Who's going to eat them? I won't be eating any yogurt. Will you eat six of them?'

'Well, if I eat one a day, they'll keep in the fridge until –'

'But what if you don't like it? You'll have to throw the rest out. What kind of waste is that?'

She knew she liked yogurt, but it was simpler to agree.

'You're right.'

'Fifty-one pence down the drain.'

'I see what you're saying.'

'Fifty-one pence you might need at the end of the week, yeah?'

'Yes. You're right.'

It was fine. He'd feel great now that he'd taught her a valuable lesson. Maybe that would be that, although he was having a good stare down the list. Then he picked up the other receipt from Mullaly's. Eight pence.

'*Titbits*?'

She was allowed that, even though he always had to tell her it was only rubbish.

'Pure rubbish.'

He took out the full set of receipts rolled up tight in a rubber band. Eva relaxed. Once today's receipts were added to the roll Garda Kojak would have finished this evening's investigation. He closed the tin and handed it to her. She returned it to the sideboard. What now? The telly clicked on. Something about the Spanish Civil War. Thankfully, he seemed to be interested. If she picked up *Titbits* now he'd only tell her to put it down, the programme was more interesting than that shit. He was a great one for knowing what was good for her. But Eva knew a way to escape this.

'Oh that's Cathal O'Shannon, isn't it? I like him, he's very good. Why is he doing a thing about Spain? When was the Spanish Civil War? Did he fight in it?'

'Jesus, will you let me watch the fuckin' thing in peace?'

'Sorry, sorry. I'll go see is Jean all right.'

She clutched *Titbits* out of sight as she went out. It was lovely sitting in the dark room, listening to Jean's baby breath, using the light from the landing to read like she had as a child.

'Shrink your own head - discover the real you.'

'Barefaced protest on SKINNYDIP BEACH.'

Catherine Schell was this week's *Titbits* cover girl.

'I'm not frightened of loving again.'

In the bottom corner there was a small picture of Phil Lynott.

'The Lizzy in a tizzy about his dad!'

Eva opened a drawer and rummaged under the baby clothes and nappies for the packet of Toffypops. She took three and, munching quietly, started to read about the rock star's search for his father.

Thirty-four: October 22nd

When Gráinne Kiely woke her first surprise was that she didn't feel too bad, considering the amount of drink she'd had. She lay still, breathing quietly so as not to disturb Francis. More or less twenty-four hours ago she'd been pelting down the AD concourse, late for her eleven o'clock lecture on The Novel, with no idea what a twisty turny day and night lay ahead of her. But wasn't that the best thing about college? First twist of the day: Dr White, no show. Some students were already leaving in a snot. Their loss, as it turned out, because a couple of minutes later an impressively tall man swept past Gráinne down the steps to the podium and delivered the most brilliant lecture. He didn't even bother to introduce himself. He just said that Dr White was unavailable this morning and he understood that the scheduled lecture was on *Mansfield Park*. And off he went. Despite not having read the novel yet and still suffering the last shards of a splitting headache, Gráinne was drawn into the compelling narrative the impressively tall man wove without notes or hesitations. His voice was even more impressive than his physical presence: seemingly languid but with precise cadences and a feather-light, but definitely deliberate, irony of tone which, it occurred to Gráinne, might be his way of forging a playful link with Austen herself, whose ironies, he said, were often as dazzling as Pope's. There was also the steel of a Northern Irish accent treading below the surface of his clean, clear received pronunciation. Though his lecture operated at what seemed to her a rich intellectual level, he also managed to convey the impression that there were far greater depths he might have plumbed were it not mere first years he was addressing. However, sufficient unto the day, they were still getting the good stuff. Miraculously, the narrative having built, climaxed and wound down, came to an entirely natural and satisfying conclusion at exactly five minutes to twelve. The impressively tall man then walked back up the steps and out, leaving Gráinne entirely convinced that *Mansfield Park* was the finest achievement of Jane Austen's art, a novel where Truth was at stake rather than Wit, where Austen had maturely and deliberately tempered the brilliance of her own ironic voice, in favour of a sterner ethic, in which 'charm' was viewed with a much more critical eye than in some of her other, more favoured novels. Forget Elizabeth, Emma and Eleanor – 'the E girls', Gráinne had scribbled in her notes – Fanny was a character woven with greater subtlety and moral depth by a writer of considerable literary courage working at the height of her astonishing powers. Gráinne left theatre M determined to start reading *Mansfield Park* immediately. It was unfortunate she didn't have the novel with her, but that was a minor blip easily sorted once she'd enjoyed a much-needed fag. Lighting up, she spotted a grey duffel coat amongst her classmates piling out of theatre M. Grey duffel coats weren't exactly a rarity in Belfield, but there was no mistaking the head on top of this one: Francis Strong, loping towards the library. He was always there, or at least if Gráinne didn't see him on the odd occasion she ventured in, she usually spotted the grey duffel coat hanging over a chair. He waved.

'Wasn't that incredible?'

'Fantastic. Who the fuck was he?'

'I heard someone say it must be the professor.'

Gráinne needed to let the lecture sink in, so she wandered over to the restaurant building for coffee and one more fag. She was really looking forward to getting stuck in to *Mansfield Park*. Her copy was in the halls of residence in Dartry, so the best plan was to head back there and spend the afternoon and evening reading. But before heading off for her encounter with Jane Austen's most profound novel, it occurred to her that, as it was gone half twelve, she might as well have lunch first, to get that out of the way. It

was in the queue for the upstairs restaurant that she met Susan
Breslin. A smirk shared with a stranger in a lunch queue changed
the day's plan and began, possibly, a whole new friendship. That
was college for you.

A student was paid to stand at the entrance to the restaurant
and shout out the lunch menu, so that everyone queuing up the
stairs could decide in advance what they would have. A demeaning
job, but he gave it great welly.

'NUMBER ONE, STEAK AND KIDNEY! NUMBER
TWO, CHICKEN CURRY! NUMBER THREE, SELECTION
OF SALADS! NUMBER FOUR, SPOTTED DICK WITH
CUSTARD, OR JELLY AND CREAM!

NUMBER ONE, STEAK AND KIDNEY!...'

Gráinne couldn't help muttering to the girl beside her that
she hoped they were paying him well for this daily humiliation.
The girl replied that the amazing thing was he seemed to relish
it, as if he saw himself as a sort of combination town crier and
circus ringmaster. It took off from there. Gráinne was relieved
that the girl, who sounded quite English, was also pigging out on
the glutinous steak and kidney pie, even though it looked 'like
shite' – according to Gráinne – and 'pretty gruesome' – according
to the girl. Without thinking about it, they sat together, babbling
away. They'd finished eating before it occurred to either to
introduce herself. Next thing they'd drank three cups of coffee
each and smoked Gráinne's pack of ten, with Susan apologising
and promising several times to get her back soon. It was only
when Susan looked at her watch and jumped up that Gráinne
noticed the restaurant was almost empty.

'Sorry, I have a half-three tutorial. Are you going to the L and
H tonight?'

Gráinne admitted that such a thing hadn't occurred to her.
She'd never been. Susan said it was a bit of a bear pit, but great fun.
She'd even spoken at some of the debates and her boyfriend was
on this year's committee. Gráinne had to come. Please! Tonight
especially the meeting would definitely be buzzing because

of the President's resignation. Gráinne had been aware of the controversy all week: a big barney with the government because the Minister for Defence had insulted the President in public, but she hadn't heard that he'd actually resigned. Embarrassed at her ignorance, Gráinne just nodded, thinking, why not? She'd taken an immediate liking to Susan, even though she was a Law student. The time had flown by talking with her. Growing up in her boring little city with two very old boring parents and six older brothers and sisters, Gráinne couldn't even imagine what it was like to have divorced parents, a brother in a swanky English public school, and a feminist mother who'd brought Susan with her to Belfast to buy contraceptives when she was only thirteen. Gráinne's mam would scurry off to confession if she even *saw* a contraceptive. Susan's mother was only forty-two – not much older than Gráinne's eldest sister, Iseult.– and she had a boyfriend. Ah Jesus! It was like *Rich Man, Poor Man*! And, to top it all, this boyfriend worked for the notorious CJ. If Susan hadn't been such an obviously straight-up, really sincere type, Gráinne would have thought she was taking the piss out of her, treating her like a big culchie eejit.

The wind scuttering up the steps from the arts block was icy. Nearly four o'clock. Gráinne thought that, rather than humping herself all the way to the halls of residence, she should box clever, stay on campus, go to the library, find *Mansfield Park*, read until nearly eight and then straight to the L and H. Much better use of time. First though, she needed to get more fags. The student bar was the handiest place.

'I RESIGN' – O'DÁLAIGH

A man in a dickie bow and linen jacket, obviously a lecturer, had the *Evening Herald* spread out on the bar. When he noticed Gráinne glancing sideways at the front-page story he asked her opinion on the President's shock announcement and insisted on buying her a pint. Had his manner been even a fraction less conspicuously lupine, Gráinne might have allowed herself to be charmed by him and settled in for a longer encounter, adding another twist in the road of this twisty day. Instead she invented a half-four seminar and made her escape. Still, she'd enjoyed observing his well-worn technique, as well as the free pint, and was now much better briefed on the constitutional *rí-rá*.

The long walk to the library proved a complete waste of time. This morning's lecture must have inspired other students too, because every copy of *Mansfield Park* was out. She wasted the guts of an hour, first searching for it, then thinking about something else she might read, while not actually reading anything – all the time surveying, with mildly despairing bitterness, the rows and rows of tables chocka with the organised focused ones, their heads bowed in devotional intensity over their studies. She spotted the grey duffel coat on the back of a chair, but there was no sign of Francis. By the time Gráinne hopped it out of there it was nearly six, which meant there was definitely no point now in spending half an hour going to the awful hall of residence only to come back again. Anyway, it was now officially Friday evening. Study time was suspended. Fanny Price would survive another day or two before Gráinne introduced herself.

She was more thirsty than hungry, but wary of returning to the student bar in case the wolf in the dickie bow loomed. She hesitated, then thought, what the hell! There were plenty of dividing walls and alcoves and it'd be more crowded now. It shouldn't be beyond Gráinne's wit to avoid him.

As she waited to order, a guy from her class she had thrown an eye over more than once but never spoken to, stood next to her. He caught her eye and nodded, unsmiling. Even though she already knew his name was Freddie and he was from Carlow, Gráinne just nodded back as if she'd never seen him before and resumed trying to catch the barman's eye. After a few silent seconds he spoke. 'Have I seen you in 1st English?' Gráinne did a big pleasantly surprised 'Oh yeah' and asked what had he thought of the lecture this morning? He said he hadn't been there. Jane Austen wasn't his bag.

'I'm a poet. Are you?'

Gráinne kept a straight face and said she hadn't really thought about it.

He said, 'You gotta, you gotta name the thing you are.'

He'd already completed his first collection, but was going to take his time before allowing it to be published. Timing was everything.

'Just because the poems are ready for the readers, doesn't mean the readers are ready for the poems.'

Gráinne would have liked to hear him say that after a few more pints. Still, he paid for her Harp and she found goatees quite sexy, and his spray-on drainpipes featured a promising bulge, so for the moment, she was happy to let him talk shite as much as he liked. But, during a pointless yet surprisingly heated argument about Ted Hughes' *Crow*, which Gráinne omitted to mention she hadn't read, and after smoking several of her fags and letting her buy the next round, the tedium of listening to Carlow Freddie sadly began to outweigh his attractions. Just in time, she remembered her promise to meet Susan at the L and H. And so, for the second time that day, Gráinne hared down the AD concourse to Theatre M.

Every entrance was jammed with students. She wriggled her way in but it was impossible to go any further, there were so many sitting in the aisles. Then she saw Susan waving at her from way down near the front. There was just enough time to step down around the sprawling bodies – whoa! Theatre M seemed even steeper than usual – squeeze in, thank Susan and forage for her fags, when the lecturers' door opened and the auditor of the Literary and Historical Debating Society trooped in with his committee. Sweet Jesus! Eight guys in monkey suits and one girl in a cocktail dress.

'Which is your fellah?'

'The blond.'

Gráinne was relieved that she could say, 'Mmm, tasty,' with reasonable honesty. Susan's boyfriend was the best of a dismal bunch: a neat boy, good-looking in a rich kid sort of way, nice healthy foreign-holiday glow about his soft face, and astonishingly clean nails. The outfit sort of suited him. The other guys on the committee were a disaster: pimples and glasses and terrible hair. A serious shortage of talent. Where were those fucking fags? Had she left them behind on the bar counter? Unlikely. Had Carlow Freddie pocketed them? Very likely. Oh, said Susan and reached into her bag. She took out a fresh unopened pack of Carrolls and slid it towards Gráinne. In that moment their friendship, like the lovely new pack of fags, was sealed. The auditor, standing at the podium, banged the hotel bell.

'Welcome to the third meeting of the one hundred and twenty third session –'

'Ngwaaahhh ngwaaahhh ngwaaaahhh!'

Whatever else he said disappeared under a deafening Donald Duck chorus. A bunch of lads cruelly mimicked the auditor's pronounced nasal tone. Gráinne was mortified for the poor eejit, but he didn't seem bothered. He rabbited on under the din. Suddenly, his tormentors stopped and everyone heard a few clear words, 'The first item on the agenda is –' before they began again. 'Ngwaaahhh ngwaaahhh ngwaaaahhh!'

Cruel and crude as it was, Gráinne couldn't help laughing. The voice really was a one-off. Vowels ground through his nose like meat through a mincer. Was the merciless barracking going to go on all night? And why didn't the auditor seem cowed in any way by so many fellow-students taking the piss out of him? If Gráinne was in his shoes, she'd either be out the door bawling by now, or shrieking tearfully at them to fuck off.

'Ngwaaahhh ngwaaahhh ngwaaaahh!'

Susan whispered, 'I told you, it's a bear pit. When he was running for election last year he spoke at every debate and this went on constantly. He's actually a really clever speaker.'

When the hecklers tired of their sport the auditor called on the correspondence secretary to read correspondence related to this week's debate. As soon as the girl in the cocktail dress stood up, the hecklers started whistling.

'Give us a twirl.'

'Nice knockers!'

The girl tried to look withering, but even Gráinne could have told her that what might be devastating in a disco when lasered at a poor cringing male hoping for a dance, would have zero effect on a howling pack of lads in an amphitheatre. She was only a few sentences into the first letter, from Ian Paisley, telling the society he had no interest in travelling to a foreign country to debate a matter which was none of their business, when the mob got restless.

'Boring!'

Then 'Get 'em off ya!' inspired a few to roar out the chorus of 'The Stripper.' The poor girl struggled on over the din. The auditor banged his bell a few times to no effect. Gráinne felt sorry for her, but wondered why did she do it? Every week? Was she a masochist?

'The next item on the agenda is motions for private business. Are there any motions for private business?'

The guy next to her stood up so suddenly, Gráinne got a shock. Susan whispered.

'Here we go. He's chairman of the UCD branch of Fianna Fáil.'

Gráinne remembered someone with a droopy moustache, trying to finagle her into joining during freshers' week. How much of a culchie did she look? This guy's moustache was neater, very Burt Reynolds. Was hair above the lip *de rigueur* for young Fianna Fáilers this term?

'Mr Auditor, I propose the following motion: That the society condemns the government's outrageous treatment of President Cearbhall Ó Dálaigh, which has forced his resignation, and calls instead for the immediate resignation of the Minister for Defence.'

The auditor repeated the motion and asked for ays and nays. No more than half a dozen said nay, but a heckler shouted, 'The nays have it!' and got a laugh.

'The ays have it. The motion will be debated. Mr Nolan will propose.'

Gráinne sensed real anticipation in the crowd as the guy called Nolan hopped over the bodies in the aisles and stepped onto the podium. Just as he was about to speak, a low, growling voice broke the silence.

'Hand out of your pockets.'

Laughter, then other fellahs joined in: 'What's that hand doing?…pocket billiards, pocket billiards, pocket billiards!'

Gráinne was mystified, then got it: the Nolan guy, trying to look casual, had one hand in his trousers pocket. Oh ha ha ha. The males in the audience seemed to find the chant of 'pocket billiards' hilarious. Susan looked around at them, contemptuous.

'It's so juvenile. This is supposed to be a serious debate.'

The Nolan guy removed the offending hand from his pocket. His tormentors cheered.

'Yeah, yeah, very funny, but let me say this. This issue isn't funny. Our President being insulted in public by a government minister is not funny.'

Now he got a round of applause. Gráinne had the feeling that there was real anger in the crowd.

'According to newspaper reports, the Minister called the President "a *thundering* disgrace."'

'Now whether or not "thundering" was the actual word –'

For days the rumours flying around college had been that the Minister had really said 'fucking disgrace', which was what Gráinne believed. Who ever used thundering as an insulting adjective?

'– he certainly said "disgrace". An appropriate word indeed – if applied, not to our distinguished President, but to the Minister for Defence himself!'

He paused and got the round of applause he expected. Gráinne could see he was very pleased with himself for thinking of that line.

'And here's even more disgrace. It is a *disgrace* that Taoiseach

Cosgrave didn't immediately demand the resignation of his Minister for Defence. I would go so far as to say that for a senior member of this *disgraced* government to insult his president in this way is much more than a disgrace. It borders on treason! But what does Cosgrave do? Nothing! Mr Law and Order can't be even bothered to uphold the dignity of the presidency. *That* is the greatest *disgrace.*'

Cheers and applause and pounding of desks. About a dozen more speakers followed, most of them laying into the government. Susan seemed to know everyone's political affiliation. 'Sinn Féin... Fianna Fáil... Fianna Fáil... Labour... Stickie... Fianna Fáil... Fine Gael... Students Union, a Trot... Fianna Fáil.' All guys, which didn't surprise Gráinne one tiny bit because, after less than an hour at her first L and H debate, she'd already decided that no woman in her right mind would face that crowd. Some of the guys would've been better off staying in their seats too. One poor misfortunate looked about twelve: he was no more than five foot tall, with glasses. What chance did he have with the mob? As soon as he arrived to the podium, the hecklers got going.

'Stand up!'

'Can't see you!'

It was relentless. With the face of an anxious child and a voice strangled with indignation, the guy insisted on explaining, chapter and verse, the precise legal situation. Not that anyone heard more than the odd phrase in the avalanche of heckles.

'The government's draconian Emergency Powers Act...'

'Who's talking, where is he?'

'Article 26.1 states, and I quote...'

'Stand up, whoever you are...'

'... the President shall decline to sign such bill...'

'Isn't this debate over 18's only?'

A neck like a jockey's bollocks; Gráinne almost – almost – admired how determined the little fellow was to say his say, even if most of it couldn't be heard. The next speaker was much heftier, wearing a thick greatcoat with a long red woollen scarf wrapped and dangling. His hair was lank and, behind gold-rimmed glasses, his broad face was cratered as the surface of the moon. Gráinne couldn't even begin to guess his age. It could be twenty or forty.

'Ladies and gentlemen, there has been a lot of PASSION in this debate, a lot of RIGHT-EOUS-NESS, or perhaps more accurately, SELF-RIGHT-EOUS-NESS...'

Gráinne thought, oh-oh, he's in for it. His voice was deep and languorous; he lifted and lowered it at will, lingering over certain words, then sprinting across whole sentences.

'I thought my dear little friend who spoke previously was going to COM-BUST such was his IN-DIG-NATION. I was very concerned that theporterswouldhavetocomeandscrapepartsof his BRAIN from the walls. Fortunately, he is still in one LITTLE piece and we hope his mammy will come and collect him soon.'

He gazed very directly at certain people as he spoke, gesturing with one hand while deliberately leaving the other hang limp. He looked like he was daring someone to heckle, 'Oooh duckie!' But, amazingly, no one took up the challenge. Gráinne began to wonder were they scared of him? There was something scary about him all right. And sort of mesmerising.

'On an issue so delicately poised we must, as Yeats advised, "be as cold and passionate as the dawn" and not become a HYSTERICAL lynch mob. Remember to whom the Minister for Defence was speaking on the ill-fated evening he uttered the phrase, that now seems destined to echo in infamy down the gyre of history. He was addressing an audience of SOLDIERS, ladies and gentlemen. That is very significant. That surely alters matters. Seated before this tattered, raddled old government minister – yes, tattered AND raddled, let us be honest even at the risk of being cruel – there before his eyes was the very FLOW-ER of Irish manhood: muscular, fighting fit, strapping sons of the Irish soil. And we all know what happens when soldiers come together. There are toasts and, amidst the clink of glasses and boisterous camaraderie, uniforms are unbuttoned... An air of manly relaxation ensues. I ask you, ladies and gentlemen, to consider the Minister's boorish outburst in that context. Is it not possible that in the overheated barrack-room atmosphere, he wanted to impress these virile young men? Perhaps he had one too many… young lieutenants hanging on his… every word and began to show off a little. If so, ladies and gentlemen, then his infamous remark was nothing more than a kind of ill-judged MACH-IS-MO. The kind of thing that would not have raised as much as an eyebrow at a reunion dinner for the SS or a Pinochet death squad. Perhaps our President should have been more understanding, as one generally is towards the bewildered, and accepted that the Minister for Defence was not a stalking horse for a *coup d'etat,* but merely an oaf, a moron, a neanderthal, a crude and brutish gombeen politician, and generously left it at that. I commend the motion to the house.'

He swept up the steps and disappeared out of theatre M, the crowd laughing and clapping and cheering him all the way. The auditor said the next speaker, would be the final one before the vote was taken. A bearded guy stepped up. Susan's whisper sounded very excited.

'He came first in History and Politics in first year and second year and he knows Dr Garret FitzGerald personally and he's such a brilliant speaker that everyone's saying he'll definitely be a TD in a few years time, or even a government minister.'

Gráinne thought having the future all mapped out like that sounded a bit freaky. She was happy enough to hide away in college for the next three or four years and then stick her head out and see what the real world was like. The guy who was going to be a government minister took some folded up pages from an inside pocket and read:

'The resignation of a president is a profoundly serious matter. Some might contend that planned assassination is even more so, such as the horrific explosion that killed Christopher Ewart Biggs and Judith Cooke, prompting the recent Emergency Powers legislation. The cowardly murder of 24-year-old Garda Michael Clerkin only a week ago might be seen by some as a far greater threat to our democracy than any off-the-cuff remark from a government minister, however crude. But, let us put the taking of innocent life to one side for now. Let us even ignore President O'Dálaigh's eccentricity, as evidenced by his peculiar behaviour during the Herrema kidnapping last year, when, in the hope of achieving Dr Herrema's release, he offered to take his place as hostage – a remarkably misguided proposal, which would not only have put his life needlessly in danger, but precipitated a constitutional crisis. Let us ignore all ancillary matters and, on the narrow point, willingly concede that the Minister's remark was entirely unacceptable. That being said, surely a president should seek not to make a drama out of a crisis by playing Salomé and demanding heads on plates. Would President de Valera have acted as Cearbhall O'Dálaigh has done? Or President Childers? I think even the Fianna Fáilers who spoke with such outrage earlier would agree that these former Presidents would not have publicly rejected the Minister's apology. They would not have confused proper respect for the office of president with the peremptory requirements of an eccentric ego. As a former chief justice, Cearbhall O'Dálaigh's rulings and opinions were always unquestioned. A whisper of dissent could easily become contempt of court. Could it be that, after so many years of speaking *ex cathedra* the subtle give and take of political interaction was beyond our president? Ladies and gentlemen, I hold no brief for a loutish minister whose attitudes and opinions are far removed from my own, but the motion as proposed fails to recognise that this unhappy controversy is not solely due to a minister's rudeness, but also to the overweening ego of a president, and so I must respectfully oppose.'

Susan mouthed, 'Isn't he fantastic?' as she applauded enthusiastically.

The crowd was not convinced. The vote went heavily in favour of the motion. Gráinne was glad. Not that she cared much, but as far as she was concerned the Minister was a big ignorant lump of a right-wing bully, who needed to have his arse kicked.

After the debate, Susan's boyfriend came over with one of the committee guys.

'Hi. Wasn't Fiachra's speech just brilliant?'

'Absolutely. Niall, this is Gráinne I told you about.'

'Hi, Gráinne, this is Rory. He's going to give you a lift to the party.'

It was the first she'd heard about a party. Or was it? Her plan had been to mosey on back to Belfield Bar. Maybe Susan had mentioned it. Where was this party on? Did she even want to go? When she saw Rory's eager smile and felt his oddly soft little hand shake hers, then grip an elbow to help guide her from Theatre M, she decided no thanks, absolutely no. But Susan seemed so pleased to have organised Niall to organise Rory to give her a lift to the party, it'd be hard to wriggle out of it.

'It's really good of you, Rory.'

'No problem, Sue. It's my pleasure. It's only Mum's runaround now, Gráinne, don't be expecting a Merc or anything. Heh-heh.'

What was the little laugh about? Did he think he'd said something funny or was it just some nervous thing? Niall and Susan strolled ahead arm in arm and Rory gently nudged Gráinne forward as if he was leading a blind person.

'Super debate, wasn't it? Really controversial stuff. Heh-heh.'

The little laughing sound again. Definitely nerves.

'I thought Fiachra really hit the nail on the head.'

Fiachra again. Which of the speakers was he? The last one, she guessed, not really caring.

'It's Garret I feel sorry for –'

Garret, which one was Garret? The little guy with the glasses everyone took the piss out of?

'I mean he's trying his best to change Fine Gael, make it more liberal, more modern, but he has to deal with the old guard.'

Gráinne realised that Rory was babbling on about Dr Garret FitzGerald, the Minister for Foreign Affairs.

'It's my strong view that if Garret was Taoiseach this Ó'Dálaigh thing would never have happened…'

Why was this eejit saying 'Garret' as if he knew him? But maybe he did. Hadn't Susan said that other guy, the last speaker knew him. Maybe they all knew 'Garret'. Maybe they had tea with him before tootling to the debate tonight. Gráinne didn't want to offend Susan, especially when she'd been thoughtful enough to remember to get those cigarettes and keep a seat for her at the debate and organise a lift to this party, but Jesus, was there any way to escape this?

She saw a grey duffel coat shuffle from the library tunnel and turn up the AD concourse. Was that Francis? Swotting at this hour? On a Friday? The head looked like him. The walk looked like him. Rory was still babbling and making that annoying laughing noise. The thought that the soft pale hand on her elbow might start to wander elsewhere inspired her to desperate action. As the grey duffel coat exited the arts block, Gráinne pulled away from Rory.

'Sorry, there's something I forgot. Where are you parked?'

'Near the Bank of Ireland.'

'Okay, do you mind waiting for me there? I'll only be a minute.'

'Oh, I can come with you. What do you –'

Gráinne galloped out of the arts block and down the steps turning this way and the other, first towards the bar, then the lake, then the library, before spotting a hooded figure bobbing towards the Clonskeagh Road exit like a grey duffel coat version of the dwarf in *Don't Look Now*. She hared after it, a bit panicky that she might make a fool of herself. What if it wasn't Francis? But when she shouted his name, it was he who turned.

'Oh hi.'

'Francis. Will you be my lifesaver? Will you do me a huge favour?'

'Depends. What?'

'Will you come to a party with me?'

'You're inviting me to a party? That's it? That's the big favour?'

'Well, more or less. You'd have to do one more small thing.'

'Go on.'

'You'll have to pretend we're an item. Please, look, it's a bit complicated but there's this guy giving me a lift to the party. I think he might be getting the wrong idea, so, if he thought you were my boyfriend, it'd put him off. Please! It'll be a good party. Free booze.'

'Okay, why not?'

Simple as that. As they approached the Bank of Ireland bunker, Gráinne saw the shape of Rory leaning his elbows on the roof of a little car. She felt Francis' hand catch hold of hers.

'We should look as authentic as possible, honey. Is that him?'

'Yes, I forgot to warn you. He's in a monkey suit.'

'What? Is it a formal do?'

'He's on the L and H committee. It's an L and H party.'

Francis suddenly stopped. 'He's looking towards us, isn't he?'

'I think so.'

'If we snogged now he'd definitely get the message.'

'Fuck off, politely.'

'Just a suggestion.'

'Hi, Rory! Sorry! I completely forgot I'd arranged to meet my boyfriend after the debate. This is Francis. Francis, Rory.' For some reason Gráinne was pleased with herself that she had managed not to say directly that Francis was her boyfriend.

'So, is it okay for him to come to the party too?'

'Oh, ah, oh sure. Sure, sure, sure, yeah. Yeah, sure. Of course. Why not?'

The absence of the little nervous laugh told its own story. If Rory hadn't been such a polite Southside boy he might have said, no, you were lucky to be invited to this party at all, so no, you can't drag along any stray in a duffel coat you pick up, now goodnight and fuck off.

The car was a little two-door job and Francis insisted on getting in the back. Then he sat forward, his head between them and plied Rory with questions for the whole journey, behaving as if everything he said was utterly fascinating. What year was he in? What course was he doing? – 2nd law, surprise surprise. – Had he a full driver's licence? Really? Already? That was very impressive, he seemed like a really confident driver. Francis said he wished Gráinne could drive so she could collect him when they went out on dates. He asked was it much easier to pull girls when you had a car? Rory seemed to get a bit flustered and the nervous laugh reappeared again. Where did he live? Rathgar. Where did he go to school? St Conleth's. Was he going to become auditor of the L and H? Again the little nervous laugh and a roundabout answer about how he couldn't imagine himself ever being as good a debater as, say, Fiachra, so he didn't really expect it to happen. Gráinne wondered if she, having actually been at the debate, wasn't sure who this Fiachra guy was, how the fuck was Francis supposed to know when he hadn't? Did this dope assume everyone in college knew his friend Fiachra?

The house was behind high walls and had a Georgian look about it, but had probably been built in the last ten years. Francis overdid the thank-yous.

'Thanks so much, Rory. Really. It's so decent of you. This is a delightful surprise. There was I, waiting for this minx in smelly old Belfield Bar, wondering where she'd got to. Thinking maybe she wasn't going to turn up. Again –'

He put his arm around Gráinne and nuzzled her hair. This was really taking the piss.

'– And now suddenly we're at this fantastic party. Thanks to you.'

'Sure, it's nothing, heh heh! No probs. Glad to do it. Any friend of Sue's, you know. Heh heh!'

Francis took Gráinne's hand and pulled her towards the door. He whispered.

'He's a nice enough eejit, isn't he? Why don't you give him a chance?'

'Are you serious?'

'Only saying. Some house, huh?'

The door was opened by a man in a pinstripe suit and red tie, with a great mane of brushed back grey hair. Gráinne detected a slight freezing of his big welcoming smile when he saw her and Francis.

'Hello, Mr Johnson. These are Niall and Susan's friends.'

It was obvious from Rory's words and the speed with which he moved past them to greet Mr Johnson, that the little lick-arse was washing his hands of them.

'Well Rory, by all accounts the debate was hot and heavy tonight. Fiachra the star of the show again, I hear. Some sparkling wine? Now I've been given strict instructions to say you can put your coats and accoutrements upstairs, first on the right. And the buffet is up and running in the kitchen, so help yourselves.'

Gráinne grabbed a glass of sparkly and made for the stairs. She had tossed her coat on the general pile and put her bag in a corner when she realised that Francis hadn't followed. She went looking for him.

The main lounge room was already crowded and everyone seemed to be wearing their party best, especially the girls. She felt like a complete peasant. Where was Francis? The duffel coat would definitely stick out like a wart in this crowd.

To her left she heard: 'Ford is so utterly hopeless all Carter has to do at this stage is stand there and smile that toothy smile of his. If the Democrats mess this up, then they might as well…'

On her right she heard: 'Well, if they're arresting Mao's widow, then the writing's on the wall for anyone who's associated with the old regime…'

A milkfed boy of fourteen or so was going round with bottles of red and white, topping up glasses. Gráinne caught his eye. As he poured, she asked, in a sarcastic tone, where the mad dancing was and, to her shock, was brought to a large cleared-out room where four girls in pretty cocktail dresses were doing their best to have party fun. The boy said that lots more would be dancing if his big sister had listened to him about what to put on the tape. Imagine, she claimed her friends wouldn't dance to The Ramones.

Wasn't that sick? His eyes were so vulnerably pleading that she couldn't shatter his dreams.

'Really? She hasn't a clue. But don't worry about the tape. Keep pouring the wine and they'll dance to anything.'

She was accepting a refill from the kid when Susan tapped her shoulder.

'So, where is this boyfriend of yours? You never mentioned him. Poor Rory's so disappointed.'

Though it wouldn't be kind to tell Susan how relieved she'd been to dodge that bullet, Gráinne couldn't not be honest with her about Francis. She pulled her into a corner.

'Can I tell you something? Promise you won't say anything to Rory.'

'Sure.'

'I don't have a boyfriend. The guy I told Rory was my boyfriend is just a pal of mine from home. His brother's married to my sister.'

'But why did you –?'

Then Susan's face cleared and Gráinne was relieved that she laughed.

'Oh I see, I see. Poor old Rory. Niall said when he pointed you out, he jumped at the chance to give you a lift. He is a bit of no-hoper. So you're free to roam after all. Well if you see anyone you fancy give me the nod and I'll introduce you.'

'Thanks, but I can't really shift anyone tonight. That'd be a bit too mean.'

'But there's nothing to stop you talking to someone you like, putting down a marker for the future. There'll be lots more parties before Christmas.'

Really? Susan had said it so casually. Was Gráinne suddenly in with a crowd? She didn't know whether she liked the idea or not.

'What about him over there? Is he your type?'

'No. His face, his nose… it's like it's pressed against glass.'

'All right. Him?'

'No. Way too sweet-looking.'

'Oh, I see, a bit rougher? Not a great selection here.'

Gráinne's thoughts exactly. But Susan was determined. Gráinne was familiar with this phenomenon: girls with boyfriends wanted their pals to have boyfriends.

'Ah. I know. Come here.'

She pulled Gráinne towards the hall. At the bottom of the stairs a group of three guys and two girls were yapping. It was obvious which one Susan wanted her to see. He was taller than the others, a strong face with a bit of a glint in his eyes. Gráinne liked the lazy way he gestured with his cigarette hand. And whatever he was saying, the others were listening and laughing eagerly. Definite possibilities. Willingly enough, she followed Susan to the group.

'… The simple fact is that the pound has collapsed and inflation is out of control, so Denis can bully his way through conference as much as he likes and sure, he'll win a pyrrhic victory, but sooner or later he'll have to face the reality –'

Appraising eyes registered Gráinne's arrival, but there was no pause in the monologue.

'When the hard left and the unions are asked to open their big mouths and swallow the kind of harsh medicine the IMF is inevitably going to insist on, and with no spoonful of sugar either, there isn't a chance that they'll accept it. The Labour Party is headed for a major split, simple as that and Denis knows it, but there's absolutely nothing he can do about it.'

Denis? Did this gobshite chat with the British chancellor on the phone every day? And the others nodding respectfully at him like this hole-talk was the beef? Gráinne wanted to interrupt and ask if someone could direct her to the PARTY, as she seemed to have stumbled accidentally into a SEMINAR on world affairs? Instead she quietly reversed out of the group and went in search of her fourteen-year-old best pal, who cheerfully refilled her.

'You didn't see a guy in a grey duffel coat by any chance?'

'Oh yeah. He's down in the kitchen talking with my mum.'

He said it like that was the weirdest thing ever. Sure enough, Francis was the buffet table simultaneously licking up to the mother of the house and wolfing into a ginormous wedge of pavlova. He lobbed a spare arm around Gráinne's shoulder.

'There you are, darling. I was just telling Mrs Johnson that I wished my girlfriend could make pavlova like this.'

Mrs Johnson had a merry laugh.

'Oh, I know cupboard love when I hear it.'

'Gráinne is always going on at me about over-indulgence, aren't you, love?'

'Oh, time enough to worry about that when you're my age.'

'You should have seen Mrs Johnson's poached salmon before the ravening hordes got at it. It looked amazing: a whole salmon, skinned and laid out with cucumber scales and mayonnaise. A masterpiece.'

Mrs Johnson tittered modestly. As they turned away from the buffet table Gráinne suddenly heard herself talking like a girlfriend.

'Are you sure you have enough? Look, you might squeeze another glob in that corner of the plate.'

'Nuts for the winter. I'm kinda low on pavlova back at the bedsit.'

Ah yes, the mysterious bedsit she'd hadn't seen yet. As far as she knew, no one had.

'I have to hand it to you, Gráinne, you know how to sniff out a party. Free transport, fantastic food, any amount of wine.'

'But what kind of party has Mammy and Daddy hanging around, doing the catering?'

'Fair point.'

'And not a sniff of weed.'

'True. Is it a bit embarrassing to admit that if you asked me to choose between dope and this pavlova, I'd go for the pavlova?'

'It's not embarrassing. It's tragic.'

'Shh, listen… Roxy Music?'

Throbbing down from the ceiling, Gráinne could just about hear the sax intro through the chatter and clink.

'"Love is the Drug?"'

'I think so. Come on.'

Shovelling the last chunk of pavlova down his mouth, he trolled out and upstairs. Gráinne remembered Francis in action at the Sunday afternoon discos. She was curious to see what Foxrock would make of the performance. Two boys had now joined the four girls, jerking awkwardly, not exactly Roxy Music cool. Even when supposedly dancing Gráinne noticed that the boys still seemed to feel the need to bellow things in the girls' ears. Could they not stop talking for a second even? When Francis made his entrance she wondered if the surprised faces were because of his moves, or because of the duffel coat? He could sway like Bryan Ferry all right, but looking like one of The Wurzels slightly spoiled the effect. He waved to Gráinne to join him, but the face she made was intended to convey that she'd sooner listen to the entire L and H committee discuss post-Mao China. Warbling 'Oh-Ohoh-Ohhhh! Love is the drug!', Francis began to peel off the duffel coat in a kind of striptease and finally flung it to Gráinne. She noticed Rory, staring from her to Francis and back as if he simply couldn't fathom the situation. A few others even stopped talking whatever shite they'd been talking, and were looking in the door at Francis. That was when Gráinne decided, fuck it, in for a penny, in for a pound, and she shimmied towards him, flicking the duffel coat like a teasing matador. With a big grin on his face he jiggled against her and next thing there they were, face to face, toe to toe, pouting lips and rubbing crotches. It was a great laugh.

Later, when Gráinne had collapsed on a sofa and wasn't really hearing what people were saying anymore – no great harm – Francis turned lifesaver again.

'Come on, fast. Rory's saying goodbye to people.'

'So what?'

'Remember he told us he lived in Rathgar. That's in my direction, and yours, right?'

'Oh yeah.'

'Well come on. Grab your stuff.'

As she was recovering her jacket and bag, it occurred to Gráinne that surely Rory wouldn't want his face rubbed in it again, but Francis seemed to know what he was at.

'I have to say goodbye to Susan.'

'You did. Susan and her fellah left ages ago.'

Gráinne tried to remember that as Francis steered her out. Rory was getting into his mum's runaround. All on his own.

'Night, Rory. Great party.'

'Oh. Hi. Yes. Brilliant, yeah, sure.'

Rory was slurring a bit. And no nervous laugh.

'Safe home. Oh and thanks for earlier.'

Rory just nodded and sat in. No lift offer.

'That's that.'

'Nah, don't worry.'

Gráinne half closed her eyes and let Francis lead her down the drive. They stepped aside to let Rory's runaround pass. Francis signalled him to stop.

'Will there be many taxis passing by here or should we go back and phone for one?'

'You might be better to phone at this hour.'

'Really, yeah? Maybe we'd be just as fast walking? Are we far from Clonskeagh?'

'About two miles.'

'Really? Definitely too far to walk?'

'Yeah.'

'Okay. So when we get to the main road, do we go left or right?'

'Ah, go left…'

Rory hesitated and then just gave up. Gráinne couldn't believe it. What a genius Francis was.

'Ah actually, I'm sort of going in that direction.'

'Oh man, really? That's fantastic. Where are you going?'

'Rathgar.'

Francis was already opening the passenger door and whooshing Gráinne in the back.

'Rathgar? Is that anywhere near Clonskeagh?'

If Gráinne hadn't been so wrecked she might have felt a bit sorry for Rory. An eentzy bit. The back seat was comfy, the car was warm. She could hear them blabbing away but just couldn't seem to make out what was being said.

'Sweetheart… Gorgeous… I'm getting out here, but Rory has very kindly offered to take you all the way. Can you direct him?'

Gráinne roused herself very fast. Where were they?

'No, no you're fine, Rory. I'm fine here.'

'Are you sure, love? Rory says it's no problem.'

'No, this is perfect. Thanks so much, Rory.'

Fucking little two-doors, how were normal-sized people supposed to get out of them! She tumbled onto the road. It seemed like Rory roared off very aggressively.

'You'd have got home in five minutes.'

'Yeah, and then another hour fending him off. Will it be easy to pick up a taxi on this road?'

'That trick doesn't work if the other person doesn't have a car.'

'No, seriously.'

'Don't you want to come up a have a look at the bedsit, now you're here?'

So she was being invited into the lair. And what a tiny lair. Well, maybe it was around the same size as her room in the halls of residence but she could use other shared rooms, a big kitchen and a library room and a parlour with a television. This was really pokey and stank of fried food. Francis turned on a two-bar fire. He pointed to the armchair and she sat down. He filled a pint glass of water.

'Take that.'

Gráinne sipped. She'd go spare if she had to live here. Or would she? In the halls of residence she spent most of the time in her bedroom, so same thing really.

'It's so small I can cook breakfast without getting out of bed.' said Francis. That sounded handy.

'Why bunks?'

'It's what was here. It means people can stay over and not have to sleep on the floor.'

That, Gráinne remembered, was when it occurred to her to stay the night. In fact, as she was so hanging tired and barely able to keep a grip on her pint glass of water, it seemed like an inspired idea, although how was she going to climb onto that top bunk was beyond her.

But she was lying there now, watching the morning sun creep along under the curtains that were too short, unable to remember anything much about the last bit of the night. Had the bathroom really been as freezing and as empty as she recalled, without shampoo, or soap or towel or even toilet paper? Jesus, how had she peed in there? She had a hazy image of Francis rolling out the sleeping bag, apologising again and again for not having any extra sheets, but she had no memory of actually getting into the sleeping bag, nor of stripping down to her knickers and bra, but she must have done and it must have been in front of Francis.

One thing she was sure about: he hadn't tried to paw or kiss her.

So Saturday quiet; being at the back of the house there wasn't even traffic noise. How long had she been lying here, half recalling, half dreaming ? What a day. What a night. It must be time to get up though, have a shower – then she remembered the bathroom. Oh Jesus. Absolutely nothing in there except flowery lino and the avocado bathroom suite. No, it was time to go home. Would she wake him, or sneak out?

She leaned her head cautiously over the side of the bunk and realised that, even though she couldn't see his face, it was fairly obvious that Francis was already awake, because there was a book in front of it.

How long had he been awake? From what she could see he seemed to have read quite a lot of *Mansfield Park*.

1977

Thirty-five: January 14th

The blackout caught Francis by surprise. With only the fast-fading glow of the electric fire for illumination, he spilled loose change from his pocket and found one 10p coin for the meter. The reading lamp flashed on and the bars glowed bright orange again. Francis sat down and picked up the single sheet on which a prose extract and a poem were printed. As always with the Practical Criticism course, there were no authors' names or any other information. There was only the text. Nothing else was important. The task of looking for meaning solely in the words and their arrangement made perfect sense to Francis.

The poem had been absorbing all his attention. He had quickly noted its modernity, obvious Englishness, directness, economy, and that its deceptive simplicity and apparent easy colloquialism disguised a careful structural formality, but Francis hadn't jotted down any of these observations yet, because 'Mr Bleaney' was speaking to him personally in a way that was unsettling, even frightening. Perhaps more so because he didn't know even the name of the author. It felt like a message scrawled on his wall by an anonymous hand.

The poet was looking at a room for rent. It could have been this bedsit. Francis had also said 'I'll take it' that evening last October. Mr Bleaney used to rent the room but it isn't clear what happened him. Had he died there alone? The poet lies on the same bed as Mr Bleaney and ponders the details of what seems a thin, fragile, dull, lonely existence. Did Mr Bleaney get what he deserved? Does a similar fate await the poet?

When the phone bell echoed down the stairs. Francis knew who it had to be. Allie would have been waiting in the foyer of the Irish Film Centre for at least twenty minutes. *The Tenant* would have started by now. Francis imagined her going out onto Earlsfort Terrace, searching for a phone box. Was she just puzzled, wondering had there been a mix-up, or was she angry at being stood up, or did she sense the bleaker truth? The ringing continued much longer than he deserved, more than he was worth. In some icy phone booth, her finger hovered over button A, She would know after four or five rings, that there wasn't going to be an answer – he used always race down and grab the phone quickly if he was expecting a call from her – but maybe she was hanging on hoping the guy in the bedsit next door might answer and pass on an anxious message from Francis: wait, he'd been delayed. Maybe she hoped he had fallen asleep and the persistent ringing would eventually wake him. Some such unlikely scenario.

How could he be so mean and cowardly? Just not turn up, not face her? He didn't know. The first time Allie had come here, she'd leaned against the bunk-frame, looking around, and said 'It must be nice to have somewhere all to yourself' just before she kissed him and he knew they wouldn't be going out anywhere that night.

Would she never hang up?

What was the matter with him? Barely three months ago it had felt wondrous just to be with her. Her nakedness had astonished him: so fleshy and unexpectedly real with little spots and creases and its paleness flushed in places. And despite revealing all this, she still seemed deeply shy. That had excited him most – how honestly she expressed pleasure. The smile in her eyes, her hands playing on his waist and bottom, sending signals, leading him, encouraging him to be more sensitive, more delicate. Even as he swelled he pressed no closer than to feel a tickle of hair. But as his fingers searched and suddenly sank into what seemed a peach or pear warmed in the sun, her sudden urgent breathing and clasping and whispered shrieks, shocked him. She gripped his wrist to make sure he didn't stop whatever he was doing. The entire weight of her lunged against him: teeth ground on his shoulder. When she shuddered and seemed to faint and gasped in his ear, repeating his name as if there was no other word, he had never felt so desired. He could see them both now: she impossibly suspended between his body and the bunk, her hair unspooling over both their heads, her arms and legs wound round him like vines. Still.

The phone stopped. The echo of the last ring took a long time to fade.

Pressing her down onto the lower bunk and entering and coming, in what seemed hardly any time at all, had felt good for sure – he had at last definitively lost his virginity – but even in that moment of crossing over, the achievement had seemed somehow beside the point compared to the miracle he had just been in some way a part of. Who cared as long as there were such moments?

But was that the problem, that everything they did together, every date on each longer chillier winter night, became, in his horny head, nothing more than a prelude to bringing Allie here to chase the miracle?

A door slam. Footsteps up the stairs. Logic told him it was the guy in the bedsit next door, but tension still made his fingers crumple 'Mr Bleaney.' The footsteps passed. A door opened and closed. Francis smoothed out the page. The night Allie had said she wanted to meet up with her pal Becky and boyfriend in the Long Hall he'd replied 'Sure', even though he had not wanted to really. Her pal was going through a bit of a crisis.

'She's wishing she had her virginity back.'

Allie wasn't someone who generally spoke in riddles, so if she'd been unconsciously sending a message, then Francis missed it. Becky's boyfriend was dull and ignorant. No wonder she wanted her virginity back. Francis wanted this night back, these hours. Resentment had thickened and squeezed like fat around his heart. Why had Allie dragged him here? Didn't she know he'd hate it? He never forced his college friends on her. Francis remembered his nausea when it occurred to him that she might suggest more of these foursomes. Had he behaved badly? Had there been petulant body language or a sarcastic tone? Certainly he remembered their silence on the 11A back to Clonskeagh that night. When Allie said she was wrecked and would go straight home, he hadn't argued, feeling, illogically he knew, simultaneously relieved and annoyed. When they'd next met, on the longest night of the year, and exchanged Christmas gifts and fucked, had he known already it was over? Surely not? He hadn't even known tonight, as the minutes crept towards eight o'clock. Was it possible that he might still have gone to meet Allie if he hadn't, by chance, been handed 'Mr Bleaney' today and enfolded himself in its frayed, frigid, fusty and dread world?

When the phone exploded in the silence again, Francis yanked out the electric fire plug and snapped off the reading lamp just in time before his neighbour's door opened and footsteps went by. The ringing stopped. The phone was too far away to hear what was being said, unless he dared open the door. Footsteps thumped back upstairs. Francis pressed tight against the wall, as if to make himself more invisible, and tried to breathe silently. Three knocks on the door. 'Hello. HELLO!' Three more knocks. 'Anyone there?' Like he knew there was.

The footsteps were quieter going down, and afterwards seemed to trudge back up. The guy passed and his door closed. It was over. Or rather, the tension of the moment was over, but shame and self-loathing flooded Francis. Had Mr Bleaney, pathetic as his situation was, ever stood in the darkness, pretending not to be there, when someone came knocking? Francis sank down against the wall. Next door opened again. Footsteps. Something stabbed under his door. When he was sure his neighbour had gone, Francis reached in the darkness for the folded scrap of paper and waited until it felt safe to turn on the reading lamp.

"Allie phoned. Ring her."

He knew he wouldn't. What was the matter with him? Was he someone who could never sustain a relationship? Like the poet and Mr Bleaney, would he always be alone? He didn't know.

Thirty-six: June 19th

'Alone, all alone, m-m-m-m-m-m-m.'

CJ hummed 'Slievnamon' as he rode. It must have been the rhythm of the gentle canter put the old song in his head. That masterful line 'alone in a crowded hall' described exactly how it would always be for him. Had Charles Kickham, one of the great old patriots, experienced such loneliness too? A profound song. 'Slievnamon.' The mountain of the women, which Fionn Mac Cumhaill had climbed. Another legendary figure, with his burden of great knowledge, also cursed to be forever alone in a crowded hall.

Holding himself even more erect in the saddle, CJ pondered the added misery that there was no one in his ambit who could even appreciate what it was like. Obviously not his family. He wouldn't want them to know anything of what he had to endure. He must always seem effortlessly strong for them. Not Terry who wasn't made for solitude, who needed company like oxygen. Certainly not the loyal party supporters who adored him, but expected heaven and earth. Liston? Perhaps a little. He certainly had the misanthropic streak. But he could live in the shadows, he never had to face the blinding lights, the accusing lens, the questioning eyes.

Last night CJ had endured the shock of the election result in a crowded hall. Like the sun, surrounded by his galaxy of true believers, he had had to shine brightly as he watched his party leader, his sly nemesis, Lynch, arrive to the election studio, looking as mournfully modest as ever, to claim his victory, savour his personal triumph. There had been no escape for CJ last night. He could not withdraw to howl and rave. The notion that these courtiers gathered round for his benefit and support was a lie. They fed off him. Their need of him was suffocating.

At first, he'd resented Liston's insistence that Lynch's record majority wasn't at all the disaster CJ was convinced it was. So it meant the Party was back in power and he'd be a minister again after seven lean years. That was no consolation if Lynch was untouchable, as he now seemed to be? Still in charge, stronger if anything, still blocking the way. His gilla had put a hand on his shoulder, intending to comfort and calm, but it only made CJ want to rip it from its socket and stuff his gob with it. But a little sleep and this solitary canter in the morning mist that drifted about his fields was allowing him to consider Liston's words more bloodlessly. To recognise their wisdom.

'On the surface Lynch is cock of the walk, gliding along with the wind at his back, but dive down, CJ, and who do you see feeding at the bottom? *Our* friends. The only reason Lynch has such a big majority is because *every single one* of our fellahs got themselves elected. It's better than we could have hoped. They're all there now… Flynn, Reynolds, Marky Junior… your own little party sitting on the backbenches… McCreevy, Cowen, Fahey… you broke bread with every one… Doherty, Leydon, McEllistrom… right now, they're all thrilled just to be elected, but these lads won't sit quiet for long… Burke, Lawlor, Ahern… It'll go sour for Lynch very quickly CJ, I'm telling you. And when it does, who will they turn to? Patience.'

Last night the word patience might as well have been poison. This morning, contemplating alone, he understood something very profound. He was in fact the master of patience. He had fallen far, and after seven years was back where he had been. Well not quite. Minister for Health was not and never would be Minister for Finance. But he was at the table again. That at least. He knew now he could wait some more. What was the alternative?

Through the trees he saw the house again. Someone was throwing open curtains at an upstairs window. Her bedroom. He thought: this prison where I live.

*

A £6,000 mortgage. Would she want to spend the next twenty or more years here? Marian looked through the front window at Stephen lounging against the Yamaha, happy as Larry, surveying the exterior, sizing up the whole estate. It would be wrong to say no. She couldn't do it to him. They were lucky to get approved for a mortgage. She was hardly in a position to be picky. From what she had overheard, other couples wandering around the showhouse seemed to be very impressed: great storage space in the kitchen, good-sized back garden, room for expansion. Marian looked again at the leaflet:

CLARE VIEW
A Guiney Development
Oil-fired central heating! Double glazing! Fitted wardrobes! Shower over bath unit!

Marian decided to be positive. She went smiling out to Stephen.

'So, what do you think?'

'It has everything all right, doesn't it?'

'Ah yeah, plenty of doodahs.'

'Central heating and double glazing. No danger we'll be cold.'

'You hate it, don't you?'

No, I mean… Well… I can see it has a lot going for it.'

'It's all right, I don't fancy it either. I've been sitting here, looking around, trying to think what's wrong with the place. And then it hits me. I'm in estates like this all the time on my rounds, right?'

He stabbed the leaflet with his finger.

Same crowd. Kerry View, Shannon View. Up and down every road, in and out to the front doors. I see in the windows. And… The thing is, Mar… I can never remember ever thinking, even once, God I'd love to live here. You know what I mean?'

Marian knew exactly what he meant and was very relieved.

'But whenever I cycle past somewhere like, you know the little cottages at the top of Edward Street or the old soldiers' houses in Rosbrien, nowhere fancy, you know, but they have a look about them, and I find myself wondering what are they like inside? I could be all wrong but it seems to me whoever built those little places didn't fling them up just to make a quick few bob.'

He jerked his head towards the long line of semi-ds.

'The only thing is, we're not likely to get the kind of place you're talking about before the wedding.'

'We could wait.'

'Rent?'

'I know, I know, throwing our money away. But it mightn't be for long.'

'Old places like that usually need a lot of work.'

'True. Yeah. It'd be a project.'

Marian knew by him that he loved the idea of a project. She quite liked it herself.

*

Tsh-tsh-tsh-tsh-tsh-tsh-tsh-tsh-tsh-tsh-tsh-tsh-tsh-tsh. Soft but incessant drizzle on the tent. Kerry water torture. Tsh-tsh-tsh-tsh-tsh-tsh-tsh. Grand soft day, isn't it, my friend? Every time Francis looked up from *The Reprieve* he saw a triangle of grey mist framed by the bright orange canvas. Tsh-tsh-tsh-tsh-tsh-tsh-tsh-tsh-tsh-tsh-tsh. It was still preferable to drinking in Begley's with the lads. He had to withstand some pressure: 'Ah Jesus, you can't stay here on your own.' 'Don't be doing the solitary poet now!' 'You're just trying to avoid your round.' But eventually his friends had given up and left him there. A man who'd choose reading over drinking mightn't be a proper man, but they were a live-and-let-live kinda gang. Tsh-tsh-tsh-tsh-tsh-tsh-tsh-tsh-tsh-tsh-tsh-tsh. Never go back. Never go back. Surely he'd known that coming to Baile na nGall again would remind him of Allie last year? Did he want to punish himself for being such a prick? Was he, in his way, as bad as cousin Eva's weird fucker of a husband? Francis laid down his book and stared out at the sodden gloom, thinking again what a coward he'd been the other day in Eva's. But what could he have said or done?

It had been a curious sequence of events that had brought him to his cousin's house. All because he'd finished his exams the day before the general election and been really annoyed it was happening two lousy days before his eighteenth birthday, which meant he didn't qualify to vote. The decision to get involved in some way and hop on the next train home and go to Jim Kemmy's election headquarters to volunteer had been pure impulse. But the end result was he'd found himself canvassing on St Brendan's Road, completely unaware that was where Eva and Mickey lived.

In his first burst of enthusiasm he'd been convinced that he personally would win lots of extra votes for Jim Kemmy. The signs had been positive. People had seemed to be well up for him – 'A decent man' 'He has my number one' 'Better than the rest of that shower' – until a woman opened her door and made a face when Francis held out the leaflet.

'Hold on now, isn't he the fellah insulted Bishop Newman?'

'No, he was only making the point that Church and State should be separate.'

'He insulted him. He made dirt of his eminence on his big day.'

Francis remembered the fawning report in the local paper about all the important people who attended the lavish ceremony to install the new bishop: the president, government ministers, TDs, the mayor in his robes and chain of office. It had made him admire Councillor Kemmy all the more for turning down the invitation.

'It wasn't anything personal. He was trying to –'

'Well why did he refuse him then? He must have some kind of a set against him.'

Jim Kemmy was the first elected politician Francis had ever heard accuse the State of being too subservient to the Catholic Church.

'No, his point is that politicians shouldn't be under the authority any one religious –'

'Bad manners is all it was. Pure ignorance.'

Francis should have known it was useless to keep arguing with her.

'But Councillor Kemmy was standing up for poor people. The church was having a lavish ceremony, with politicians queueing up to be there, while people living in areas like this are deprived of even basic toilet facilities –'

'Are you saying I'm deprived, youngfellah? The cheek of you.'

Francis saw cheap clothes and a worn face, but he also saw a big effort to look her best.

'No, no of course not. But I'm sure that some people on the road are very badly off.'

'Oh well, yes, I feel sorry for some of the poor women, barely able to feed their children.

'Well, Jim Kemmy is the man to –'

'But that's because their husbands won't get up off their backsides to do a day's work. You tell that Kemmy fellah it'd be more in his line to stop these latchikos drinking all their dole, than insulting the poor Bishop and he doing his best.

Tsh-tsh-tsh-tsh-tsh-tsh-tsh-tsh-tsh. By late afternoon Francis was raging at the lack of support for Jim Kemmy and frustrated by his own failure to change anyone's mind. Would these people not listen to reason? Some of them were so recalcitrant, mulish, stuck in a mire, brainwashed. Listening to them he had begun to fear that Jim Kemmy wouldn't get elected. Sure enough, 2,338 votes in the end. Not even close. And Fianna Fáil back with a bang. People voted for change all right. Back to the way it was before.

Why had St Brendan's Road somehow felt poorer, rougher than Rowan Avenue where he grew up? They were both corporation estates, and everyone was on the same housing list: luck of the draw where people landed. Yet, when he'd gone home later, the evening light had been golden and all the houses along his row definitely had more of a scrubbed look, softened by cut grass and trimmed hedge. In his mam's phrase, poor but respectable. Had the midday sun glared less forgivingly on St Brendan's Road, making the gardens seem more tangled, the paintwork more cracked, the clothes shabbier and faces grimmer? Francis had sensed distress peeling off the walls and smelt neglect in the damp hallways. Had the shock of cousin Eva's situation felt worse because she was living on this road?

Tsh-tsh-tsh-tsh-tsh-tsh-tsh-tsh-tsh.The front door of the last house in the row had been fully open. Francis had thought nothing of that, until he clinked the gate handle and a doberman pinscher lunged from the black hole of the hallway. As he sprinted toward him, Francis saw, like a camera crash-zooming, the creature's head and teeth magnify,

'Chop!'

At least it had sounded like 'chop!' Whatever word had been snapped out, the doberman had stopped instantly and sat, although his ravening stare was still aimed through the gate at Francis. A guy strolled from the gloom of the house into the sunlight.

'We don't want any of that election shite.'

There was something familiar about the odd combination of thin, high voice and muscled body. Then Francis recognised the smirky face.

'Mickey. Hello… I'm Francis Strong… Eva's cousin.'

It took Mickey Quinlan a few seconds to click.

'Ah yeah. How's it goin', head? Come on in. Don't worry about him, he won't touch you.'

Francis tried to look relaxed as he opened the gate.

'You're grand, come on. He'll only attack on my command. Who're you giving out leaflets for?'

'Jim Kemmy.'

Mickey was already walking back into the house, shouting. 'Hey! There's someone looking for you.'

The doberman's eyes stayed fixed on Francis as he walked sideways past him, not turning his back.

'I didn't know you lived around here.'

'Yeah. Got the kid, got the house.'

When Eva appeared at the top of the stairs, Francis sensed stare-eyed tension, just before the big smile spread across her face,

'Francis! You're back from Dublin?'

'Only since last night. We finished exams yesterday.'

'The fuckin' eejit's out canvassing. Who for?'

Hadn't Mickey paid attention when he told him? Or was he just being a prick? Tsh-tsh-tsh-tsh-tsh-tsh-tsh-tsh-tsh-tsh. 'Jim Kemmy.' 'Well, I've bad news for you, we won't be voting for him. But I've good news as well, we're not voting for any of them. Shower of fuckin' wankers.' Tsh-tsh-tsh-tsh-tsh-tsh-tsh-tsh. Mickey thought he was a gas man. Eva's laugh sounded forced.

'Will you listen to him? Just because he's not voting he thinks none of us should bother.'

Francis saw the way Mickey stared at her. Tsh-tsh-tsh-tsh-tsh-tsh-tsh-tsh. The questions – more like an interrogation – that followed felt more creepy and unsettling because they were asked so casually.

'You didn't tell me you were going out voting?'

'I thought if I got a chance later.'

'What time?'

'I hadn't decided.'

'Who for?'

'I thought maybe, this man Kemmy.'

'And here was I thinking she had no interest in the election. What party is he in?'

'He's… ah… he's Labour, isn't he?'

'Is he, Head?'

Eva's smile was attached to her face like joke teeth. Tsh-tsh-tsh-tsh-tsh-tsh-tsh-tsh-tsh. Francis felt nervous, as if there was a danger his answer might get Eva into trouble.

'Well he's – Eva's nearly right, he's an Independent Socialist.'

'That's not Labour though, is it? So are you voting Labour, or for this fucking eejit?' Then the smirk again. 'Sure she's only showing off in front of the college boy. She'd no intention of voting at all until you arrived.'

The way Eva tried to laugh it off reminded Francis of the

nconvincing bravado with which she used to give out about her
other.

'You see the way he can see inside my head. He knows what
'm thinking even. Gas, isn't it? Will you have a cuppa tea, Fran?
t's ages since –'

'He has no time for tea, he's too busy canvassing.'

The last thing Francis wanted was to stay in that house sipping
ea. On the surface nothing was awry. The place was spotless,
he hall and back room newly-painted, the furniture almost new.
There were no signs of neglect, no smells. A neat, pleasant home.
But the atmosphere was septic. Francis detected it in the sprawl of
Mickey on the couch, the doberman at his foot; in the way Eva's
yes, haunted behind the smile, seemed to plead with him to stay
and talk. He'd even started to feel afraid that something – he had
no idea what, but something bad – might happen if he didn't stay.
Tsh-tsh-tsh-tsh-tsh-tsh-tsh-tsh-tsh-tsh-tsh.

'Sure, yeah, thanks.'

'I'll put the kettle on.'

'I'll have a cup as well so. C'mere, have we any biscuits?
Toffypops maybe?

'No.'

'You're sure. You're sure there's no Toffypops. She loves the
Toffypops. None lying around anywhere, nah? 'No.' Ttsh-tsh-tsh-
tsh-tsh-tsh-tsh-tsh. It was the way his tongue clicked, 'Toffypops.'
Tsh-tsh-tsh-tsh-tsh-tsh-tsh. Like some secret conversation between
them. Tsh-tsh-tsh-tsh. Even after she went into the scullery,
Mickey kept staring as if she was still standing in front of him.
Had he forgotten Francis was in the room?

Yet, looking back, nothing had happened. They'd drunk tea and
Eva had taken him upstairs to see baby Jean, nearly a year old now.
He'd wondered if, alone together, she might whisper something
or throw him a meaningful look. But Mickey had appeared at the
bedroom door, asking was she going to the polling station before
or after getting him his dinner? Eva said she'd decided not to
bother voting after all.

Tsh-tsh-tsh-tsh-tsh-tsh-tsh-tsh-tsh-tsh-tsh-tsh-tsh-tsh-tsh

Francis was ashamed how he more or less ran out of the place
Had he left his cousin high and dry? But what could he do
People's lives moved along separate tracks, crisscrossing once in
a while, colliding on station platforms, before moving on; like
the characters in *The Reprieve,* scattered all over Europe on a
September weekend in 1938, waiting for war to begin. Without
knowing each other they shared a moment of history, but were
unable to do anything other than live through it, survive it
Anyway, what was so great about his situation that gave him the
right to improve the lives of others? He'd been thinking exactly
the same thing last night when Patch – having barely managed
to get his head outside the tent in time to puke – told them that
Cónal Collopy had gone totally apeshit in UCG last term, and
was constantly crazed from drink. He'd been arrested a few weeks
ago for causing criminal damage after dancing along a line of car
roofs singing 'God Save the Queen' – The Sex Pistols' version
obviously. Patch said there were rumours he'd joined the IRA as
well. Francis couldn't understand why he'd choose to do something
like that, although thinking about the oddness of his family, it
felt less surprising. Could it be called choice at all? Had Eva any
choice? And what about himself? Francis resumed reading *The
Reprieve.*

*

A hundred yards away on the pier at Baile na nGall, Gavin Bloom
was cursing his luck with the weather. Ten minutes of clear skies
– was that too much to ask, O Lord of the dance? Just a teensy
little break in the cloud? If he got enough sunshine time to snap
the relevant piccies, he'd fall on his knees in thanks. Well, let's not
go completely OTT, Gavin thought. It had been a long time since
he'd been on his knees. In prayer at least. He turned to the sky,
letting invisible rain spatter his face. No chance. The cloud cover
hung low, thick like granny's old blanket. Welcome home, Gavin,
aren't you thrilled skinny to have escaped filthy dirty New York?

No use in even attempting to take photos in this light. After even years working in American TV, he knew blue skies and unshine were the minimum requirements even when the scene vas a coffin ship setting sail. A soupçon of brooding cloud could lways be inserted with filters. Ah shag it! If there wasn't a clearance oon he'd have to stay the night and hope for better weather in he morning. This pier might be the one. Even in dire light and imited visibility it felt like the kind of location Mel would love. Ever since *Ryan's Daughter*, all American directors got a big hard-on at the thought of filming in the Dingle peninsula.

Gavin Bloom hopped over the pier wall onto the headland. He moved about, stamping his feet to test the ground. Not too boggy. Could be just the place to park the travelling circus: catering, costume and make-up, camera vans, generators. Yes, this location definitely had potential. If the owner allowed camping surely he'd be happy to take a fat fee from an American TV company. Gavin smirked at the solitary orange tent. Determined Germans, he guessed, camping and hill-walking, glowing in the exhilaration of mist and rain. He could see a body inside, stretched out, hand on head, reading. A quick peek through the Nikon's long lens confirmed it was male, but the face was unhelpfully angled towards the book and hidden by falling hair. Still, it would make a pretty photo. He'd spent so much of his life in performance, on display, rarely unaware, that someone absorbed and oblivious always attracted Gavin. In West Village bars the only time anyone was unaware was when they'd passed out. The young man might know about the owner of the field. It was as good a reason as any to come closer.

The sodden figure approaching was holding part of his sopping jacket up to protect a very fancy-looking camera. A German tourist, Francis figured. Who else would dream of slobbing around in this weather?

'Hi there. Looks like you picked the wrong week for camping, or are you a fan of rain?'

An Irish voice. With a touch of American?

'Not as much as you seem to be.'

The guy laughed and he rubbed his matted hair back into life.

'Me? Oh no, very much duty calling. Work, not pleasure, I can assure you. I was wondering who owns this… well… field, I guess you'd call it. Who do you get permission from to camp here?'

'People just come and pitch their tents. No one asks. Sorry, do you want to get in out of the rain?'

'Do you mind? Thanks.'

It was a big tent for one young guy. Gavin Bloom could see other sleeping bags and backpacks. He wondered what the skinny was.

'You like your space, I see.'

'Well, actually there's five of us.'

'Ah, much more Catholic. Family or friends?'

'Old classmates. We've come here before.'

'Where are the others? Off climbing Mount Brandon?'

Gavin enjoyed making a young man laugh, even a not particularly good-looking one.

'No. You'll be shocked to hear they're in the pub already.'

'Well, when in Rome. But not you?'

There was something self-assured about the headshake. And the book of course. Gavin wondered who he had here. A loner? A bit of an introvert? Enjoys his own company, as his mammy used to say.

'Are you thinking of buying the land?'

Gavin decided not to go into the whole working for TV bullshit, as least not yet.

'No, no dearheart, I'm a city boy, noise and smog. I wouldn't know what to do after five minutes in this kind of neighbourhood.'

'Drink your head off like the rest of them.'

In the West Village, Gavin's life-choices were so much more varied. Not only could he drink his head off, but he could at more or less any time of the day or night, get stoned out of his head and *give* head, which he suspected wasn't a big feature of life on the Dingle peninsula.

'Or I suppose I could spend time improving my mind, like ourself. Although, frankly my dear, it's a bit too late for that. A bit too late for a lot of things. Do you mind?' He picked up the book. 'Jean Paul Sart-ra? Hmm, we're not dealing with muck here, I see.'

Something in his voice, the way the guy gave everything he said an amusing *twist*, set off an echo in Francis' mind.

'My big problem with reading intellectual books is that I can't ask them anything. I can't say, 'Hold on now, Jean Paul, exactly what do you mean by that?' You know? We can't discuss it. I mean he could just be having a laugh at our expense, couldn't he? You're in college, are you?

'UCD. Just finished first year.'

'Belfield. Know it well, used to wave at it on my way to work. Never got near third level myself. I'm more gutter level.'

Francis laughed. There it was again – that *twist*. Though the face meant nothing to him, the voice teased him: its rhythms and tone and attitude. He passed Belfield going to work. The RTE studios were very close by. Did he work there? Could he be that guy, that brilliant funny floor manager he had met all those years ago?

'What do you do? Why are you wandering around a field in the rain with a camera?'

'Sounds a bit seedy the way you say it, dearheart.' Gavin felt embarrassed at his sudden desire to show off to the college boy. 'Actually what I do is almost completely semi-respectable, although, I grant you, it is the perfect job for a peeping tom. I'm a location scout for an American TV company.'

If Gavin was hoping for attention and interest, the widening eyes assured him he had it. Ah the magic of TV. It used to work all those years ago on outside broadcasts up and down the country and, even in the Eagle's Nest, it still worked now and then, with new meat. He sat up a little straighter and instinctively rustled his damp hair into a better shape.

'Oh yes, as you can see it's glam glam all the way. Basically, I trudge around in the muck taking pictures of potential locations. Weather like this is a problem because, even though this movie is set during the famine, they still want forty shades of green bathed in sunshine.'

'Is it about a starving Irish peasant who has to flee the evil forces of the crown, after stealing food to feed his wife and children?'

'I can see that university education isn't going to waste.'

'How long have you been in America?'

Francis wondered if his mounting excitement was becoming obvious. Could this really be that guy Gavin, 'the world is my oyster' Gavin?

'Too long, dearheart, believe me. New York is fabulous, but no country for old men, or even not-quite-as-young-as-they-used-to-be men.'

As soon as Gavin heard himself say that line, which he'd robbed from lovely sourpuss Jake, he knew he had belly-flopped into full-scale flirting. Why? He wasn't interested in the college boy that way. Or was he? No. Definitely not.

'I actually took this gig as a way of being paid to do a bit of personal location scouting. I'm thinking of clicking my heels and coming home, but I have to tell you – this weather. Sweet Jesus on the cross, I'd forgotten what it was like, or maybe just, you know, erased it. Who could live in this? And then I arrive to find there's a general election on and – I don't know if you've the remotest interest in these things? Did you vote, even?'

'Yeah, I'm interested, but I was too young to vote.'

Too young to vote? College boy had finished first year, surely he was at least eighteen.

'I missed it out by two days. Actually, yesterday was my eighteenth birthday.'

Francis didn't know why he felt the need to tell this guy something he hadn't even bothered mentioning to his pals. Gavin wasn't sure why he was so pleased to hear he was eighteen. As if that mattered. Eighteen, sixteen, twenty-seven? It wasn't something he ever asked. But St Mark's Place and a field in Kerry were very different worlds. What was underage anyway in a country where any age was illegal? But *he wasn't interested*, eighteen or not.

'Anyway I arrive at Shannon, and hear that Fianna Fáil are winning the election and I think, hold on, when I left here eight years ago they'd just won an election. I mean, come on guys! At least in the States they've managed to end a war and impeach a president in the meantime. And someone invented the Hustle, you know? Things changed.

Francis had to ask directly.

'So what did you do here before you left?'

'Oh, I did a stint in RTE. I was a child prodigy.' Gavin screamed at himself to stop. Age jokes were pathetic. 'The only twelve-year-old floor manager there.'

Yes! thought Francis, it was him, it had to be. So, was Gavin gay? At least that was the vibe he was getting from him now. At ten, he wouldn't have had the remotest notion of these things. And yet something about him had stayed in his head all these years.

'Then in New York I worked on the *Dick Cavett Show*. I don't think it airs over here, does it?'

'Don't know it.'

'How would I describe it? Dick Cavett is sort of the thinking woman's Gay Byrne. He'd have a great natter with your pal Mr Sart-ra for example, *loves* interviewing the smarter-than-the-average-bears. How he's lasted in American TV is a big mystery. I like Dick.'

The double-entendre was entirely unintended, but as soon as the words were out of his mouth Gavin found it very hard to keep a straight face. College boy didn't seem to pick up on it at all. He was too busy asking about the guests on the show.

'You want me to name-drop? I could name-drop for Ireland if you encourage me.'

'I do. I encourage you.'

Oh Christ! Gavin now felt the attraction of such eager, unvarnished fascination. In a tent on a dirty wet Kerry afternoon. Who'd have thought?

'Okay. Well I'll never forget the first show I did with him. Jani Joplin. It turned out to be only two months before she died.'

'Wow!'

'There was John and Yoko, George Harrison –'

'Wow!'

'Not the same night obviously, Orson Welles, Gore Vidal Woody Allen –'

'Seriously? Woody Allen?'

'Yeah, he and Dick are actually good pals.'

'Have you seen *Annie Hall*? I hear it's fantastic.'

'Yeah, it's great. In fact there's a New York city ordnance just passed. You're not allowed out in public in Manhattan if you haven't been to *Annie Hall*.'

Again the pleasure of hearing his laugh, the enchantment in his eyes, that crooked little smile… Steady on now, Gavin warned himself, steady on.

'What was Woody like, was he friendly?'

Gavin's instinct told him that college boy would appreciate irony more than bullshit. He wasn't an Eagle's Nest bunny.

'Oh yes, we had such a laugh. He took us all for cocktails and dinner in Elaine's after the show and later he and Dick popped back to my place and we shared a joint… No. To be completely honest, the way it worked – ah sorry, I never even asked your name –?'

Francis said 'Francis' and when he heard 'Gavin', felt the deep satisfaction of having reached a destination, by an unknown route, without a map.

'So, Francis, my interaction with guests would generally go along the lines of "Do you mind if make-up gives you a quick dab before we record, Mr Allen?" Or whoever. And the guest would say something like "That's fine." You see? The kind of dialogue that'll really kick-start a long-lasting friendship.'

Francis still didn't recognise anything about Gavin's face – although definitely he hadn't had a moustache back then – because his memory of that day was a lava lamp of colours, clothes, movement and voices. This face was much older and, just now, sadder than he would have imagined. Would he seem gay if Francis passed him on the street? He was no Clint Eastwood, but he wasn't Larry Grayson or Mr Humphries from *Are You Being Served?* either.

'Are you sorry you didn't, you know, get to know any of them better? Find out what they were really like?'

'No. The passing parade, dearheart. Showbiz. Hello, goodbye.'

It was getting uncomfortably confessional. Rein it in, Gavin told himself, aware now that he ached to reach out a hand and place it on a shoulder – cautiously – or thigh – recklessly. What would happen if he invited a kiss? It was very hard to tell with the college boy.

The flush of gold that suddenly lit up Gavin's face made Francis glance outside, only now aware that there was no longer any tap of drizzle on the roof of the tent. When had it stopped?

'Looks like you're in luck.'

'Sorry?'

'A break in the clouds. You can get those location photos now.'

For some reason, Francis was pleased that Gavin hesitated before responding.

'Yes. So I can.'

If there had been a moment it was gone now. Gavin knew about timing. Whenever it was a bit off, he was always ahead of the director with, 'One more take, dearheart?' Smiling, he offered his hand 'Thanks for the shelter,' and couldn't resist letting the handclasp linger a fraction longer than was necessary, though he had the impression that college boy didn't mind. Only an impression.

Francis watched Gavin stroll away, admiring the gaach, the traipse, the sway of him. How lucky that he'd stayed behind reading *The Reprieve*. Otherwise this little encounter, more intoxicating than pints in Begley's, would never have happened.

Time had flown by and there was some alchemy in the way the soggy, shrivelled stranger had moulted to reveal Gavin, the flamboyant, insouciant, free agent Francis had never forgotten. I had definitely been a good instinct not to mention their previous meeting. Gavin wouldn't have remembered it – why should he It had meant absolutely nothing to him. Besides, it would have made him think of Francis as a child, which might have altered everything, dampened the strange, beguiling, flirtatious mood He was more than startled to discover that having a man look at him with desire felt… agreeable. It was like that curious moment in the sea this morning: waking early, the stale smell of sleeping drunken boys had driven Francis out of the tent and down to the pier for an early morning swim. Joyce had got it spot-on; the sea was indeed scrotum-tightening, but he got used to it. Then having swum out for a bit, he was treading deep water when he felt a warm undercurrent swirl around his thighs. It shivered deliciously through him and then it was gone. Where had it come from? Was it something to do with the turning of the tide? He dived under but couldn't locate it again. The sea was chilly as ever. But it had definitely happened, mysteriously, sweetly: a liquid version of the gorgeous warming moment when the sun emerges from behind a thick dark cloud.

Thirty-seven: October 12th

Terry refilled CJ's glass. 'Oh darling, don't be so grumpy! It was funny! You have to admit that.'

From volcanic rage to adolescent petulance to grudging acceptance. It had taken a good half hour and plenty of Chev' Blanc and Terry energy to get CJ to this point. Still no smile but Ann Teresa chose not to let that worry her. She could see the funny side of the article even if he couldn't, and after all it was as discomfiting and cringemaking for her as for him. The description of the Gucci handbag incident made her seem like an utter cow and a monumental bitch, but it was so humorously done. Ann Teresa would love to discover who had written it and ordinarily would have gone to a lot of trouble to do so and probably even sent him – or her? No, this was unquestionably a male hand – a discreet note to express admiration while also letting him know that *she'd ferreted him out*. But CJ's reaction was a warning that it was probably safer if the identity of the witty scribe remained genuinely unknown to her.

How honest was CJ being about why the piece had riled him so much? Outrage at the British press poking cheap fun at Irish politicians might be superficially convincing, but *Private Eye* was hardly the *Daily Mail*. He could hardly claim to be hurt that ridicule had been heaped on his 'jogging for health' campaign when even he would admit it was just a way of linking his name to a popular fad. Ann Teresa had already poked fun at him about it Terry-style and he'd taken it all in marvellous good humour. Admittedly she hadn't thought of anything as inventively wicked as 'Horizontal Jogging'.

When Ann Teresa had first read the *Private Eye* piece and saw that their secret affair had finally been exposed in print via a very very good joke, she had *shrieked* with laughter, forgetting entirely that she was sitting in her car in the Setanta car park and that anyone passing might hear and see what would appear to be a crazy lady, rocking and chortling. Surely CJ couldn't *genuinely* be enraged that the anonymous *Private Eye* correspondent – who was he? It was unbearable not knowing – had described his sexual exploits with Terry as horizontal jogging. And aside from the adolescent cheek, it was, in its way, flattering.

CJ's close questioning – which persisted until, rather pointedly she referred to it as an interrogation – about who could have known all this detail, especially the Gucci handbag incident revealed something much more significant and true and sad to Ann Teresa: his distrust of her. She had always understood how extraordinarily difficult it was for CJ to trust anyone, but assumed there were exceptions and was exceptionally proud to include herself among them. But maybe at the core of that still, watchful hooded heart that she had almost penetrated, there was no room for exceptions?

This latest revelation of his distrust chimed with her sense that for quite some time, to keep him happy, she had to play Terry more and more. The truth was he preferred her to Ann Teresa.

Whereas the humour of loud hyperbole, the bitchy jibe and withering riposte was Terry's claim to fame, Ann Teresa enjoyed a finer, more private sense of irony. And it was neither pleasant nor amusing for it to dawn on her that the exposure of their affair in print had somehow made a fiction of it.

*

Had he let women down? What an idea! It really was quite the most exasperating question Dr Garret FitzGerald had been asked since being elected party leader. That it should be put to him in a forum that was very much home territory, a crowded theatre L in UCD, during a thoroughly stimulating and encouragingly enthusiastic student rally, only made it more irritating.

Naturally Dr Garret FitzGerald understood that as leader of

the main opposition party it was inevitable that he would face stiffer and more critical interrogation, even if some of it was of a trivial, inaccurate and occasionally mischievous variety, but there had been such a groundswell of goodwill towards him he had begun to believe that normal rules of engagement had been suspended and that out of the ashes of the humiliating electoral defeat in June, hope had sprung far more quickly than he would ever have expected. Indeed a path seemed to be clearing before him with astonishing ease!

Cosgrave, stoic, pragmatic old campaigner that he was, had recognised that, after such a dismal election result, he could not carry on as leader . That he had stepped down so quickly, without fuss and with some dignity, was a measure of the man, in Dr Garret FitzGerald's view. Though a leadership contest would been an excellent and proper democratic exercise and it was by no means certain that his almost embarrassingly overwhelming popularity ought to have persuaded all other potential candidates to step back from the fray, nonetheless Dr Garret FitzGerald accepted that it would be perverse to be other than pleased and flattered by such singular approbation from his colleagues. Even better had been the exhilarating response from the grassroots to his subsequent meetings and rallies up and down the country, culminating in a thoroughly delightful – until this precise moment of course ! – return to his Alma Mater. In fact, the frankly rather dour-faced student's question was revealingly misplaced. Amongst the gratifyingly large student attendance – his wryly self-deprecating, 'Far more than ever came to my lectures!' produced an appreciative ripple of laughter round the amphitheatre – he had already noticed that bright enthusiastic female students seemed to be in the majority! These splendid young women clearly didn't feel he had 'let women down' by not appointing any to his first opposition front bench.

The mildly embarrassing reality was that only one female candidate had been elected for Fine Gael last June! Dr Garret FitzGerald could easily explain to his interrogator that he had in fact offered this sole female representative a place on his front bench, but that – rather mortifyingly – she had turned him down. What more could he do! However, Dr Garret FitzGerald, friend of the media though he was, knew that a naively honest reply like this would only encourage further questions, such as *why* had she turned him down? He was also uncomfortably aware that, in truth, more strenuous efforts to persuade his female colleague might well have borne fruit, and he might also concede to his very closest confidants that this particular female colleague was from a very conservative constituency and not exactly the kind of progressive voice he wanted – very much wanted! – to see playing a leading role in the party and, indeed, looking to the future, in government.

But Rome wasn't built in a day so a New Ireland was unlikely to be created in a couple of months! Dr Garret FitzGerald could legitimately and in all modesty feel he had made a jolly decent start, although, not wanting to sound complacent, such an observation did not form any part of his reply:

'I couldn't agree more with the broad implication of your question and I am on record as saying that the present situation is unsatisfactory with regard to the position of women in our party and in politics generally, and a variety of circumstances have contributed to that, but I am looking to a future that will be decidedly different. On the way into the theatre for example I was introduced to some of the newest and most dynamic members of Young Fine Gael, and one bright, very impressive law student called Susan told me, in no uncertain terms, that she would never even have considered joining the party were it not –' Dr Garret FitzGerald realised just in time that what he was about to say, 'were it not for the fact that I had been elected leader', might sound unattractively self-aggrandizing. Rather neatly and without a stumble he revised the phrase – 'were it not that she fully expected me as newly-elected leader to crusade for change, the kind of change that will result in a far more significant role for women in our political life. I am delighted to say that I was able to assure Susan that was indeed my intention.'

1978

Thirty-eight: January 25th

It had crossed Gráinne's mind how unusually silent Francis had been for the whole bus journey, and when she and Susan stood up to get off at Suffolk Street, he still had his head stuck in the magazine.

'Francis, it's our stop.'

He continued reading, trailing behind them. Gráinne had to nudge him to pay attention as they crossed the road at Trinity College. It was only as they passed into the darkness of the front entrance that he looked up and said.

'And your mother wrote this?'

Gráinne could see that Susan was chuffed by his impressed tone.

'Yes. That's what she does.'

'Can I keep it?'

Gráinne was surprised. No little quip, no smart remark?

'You're honoured, Susan. He's allowing you to give him a free copy.'

No reaction to that even. The article seemed to have made a very strong impression, but surely it wasn't news to him that wife-beating went on in the country? Of course, knowing Francis, he mightn't even be thinking about the content, he might be just wowed at the quality of the writing. Whatever it was, he couldn't tear himself away from it. When they went into Players Theatre Gráinne had to nudge him again to stump up for his ticket and once they sat inside, he began reading again.

'Do you think he'll even bother watching the play?'

Susan grinned, but Gráinne had again failed to get a rise out of Susan's mother's latest number one fan. Then, as they were

discussing whether Players Theatre was 'intimate' or 'pokey', sh
heard a whispered 'Jesus!'

'What?'

'One woman says that after a beating her husband woul
throw holy water over her.'

Gráinne remembered that peculiarly repulsive detail.

'Tell him about your mother meeting her. It was like somethin;
out of a spy novel.'

Susan leaned across Gráinne and spoke very quietly.

'The poor woman was so terrified she wouldn't arrange
meeting anywhere in her own town – somewhere in the midland:
Mum wouldn't tell me where – so she took a bus to another tow
about thirty miles away and told Mum to wait in her car up a lan
beside a Quinnsworth's. Then she made her drive out of town t
this wooded area. And she was still nervy talking to her, lookin;
round all the time for fear someone would see them.'

'Wasn't she worried that the husband would read the articl
and recognise himself?'

'When Mum first got in touch with her she told her that th
article would be for *Hibernia* or *Magill* and she said – Gráinne
you can do the accent, tell him.'

'Da's alrigh', he wouldn' be caught dead reading dem aul
things.'

Zoo Story began with a character on a park bench, reading
He wore glasses and smoked a pipe. Gráinne nudged Susan, bu
she shook her head. This was not the guy she wanted her to see
the son of her mother's ex, who was more like a brother than
friend. Susan had told her – strictly between themselves – tha
he had recently drunkenly confided that, on the last day of term
before Christmas, he'd gone drinking in the Stag's Head with on
of his lecturers and ended up having sex with him. This bit o
goss, much more than his performance in a lunchtime play, wa
why Gráinne was dying to see the famous Matthew. Was he gay
Bisexual? Susan wasn't entirely sure of anything other than he
drank too much and loved to shock. Was his story even true

Gráinne hoped it was and would have loved to hear more gory details, but Susan had been all serious and concerned about it and wouldn't even say who the lecturer was.

The next character who came on had wild dark hair and the face of a starving angel, so Gráinne wasn't surprised to feel a poke from beside her. Ah! The famous Matthew. Within the first few minutes of his performance she was feeling that peculiar discomfort of being confronted by the weirdo in the park or the nutter on the bus. His character persisted in talking to the other guy whether he liked it or not. He said he'd been to the zoo, he asked if he was walking north, he commented on the other guy's pipe, he mentioned Freud. Already Gráinne was silently urging the guy with glasses and pipe to get up, walk away, run! Of course she knew if he did, there would be no play. They were all stuck here to the presumably bitter end.

Matthew Liston was scarily good. The other guy was more like an ordinary student making a decent effort at playing his part, which was fine as his character was the dull one who didn't get to say much. Matthew roamed about the stage, spitting out questions and firing sinister remarks like phlegmy gobs. His American accent was spot-on, and though under the heavy overcoat his frame seemed frail enough to pick up and toss across the stage, there was something unsettling, even dangerous about him. Was it all acting? Gráinne even began to wonder if Matthew might be a bit drunk. Whatever he was at, the effect was mesmerising. She couldn't take her eyes off him, although all her empathy was with the other guy. Eventually his character, Jerry, started into this long story about himself and a dog.

The curious surprise of Matthew's polite, shy-little-boy smile as he and the other actor took their bow, made Gráinne try to analyse where exactly in the story of Jerry and the dog she had forgotten that she was watching her friend's weird friend acting in a college play and instead had lost herself in the grimy urban miasma of trashy rooming houses and landladies who ate garbage, and women crying behind their doors and pornographic playing cards and poisoned hamburgers and bloodshot infected dogs with erections and, deep, deep in Jerry's eyes – or Matthew's? – a haunting, annihilating loneliness and spiritlessness. At the end of the play his desperate nihilistic need for contact was spine-tingling and surprisingly moving.

They waited outside. Susan looked anxious.

'He was good, wasn't he?'

'He was incredible. I won't be the better of that for a few days.'

Francis didn't comment. Off on another planet.

'Francis, what did you think of your man, Matthew?'

'Hm? Oh. Stunning.'

The other actor came out first. Even without the make-up he still had an older aura about him. As he passed, Gráinne said congratulations and he looked surprised.

'Oh, well, thanks. You liked it?'

'We loved it.'

'Good. Great. So you didn't notice ah… it didn't feel, I don't know… strange?'

'No. It's a strange play, obviously, but the acting was brilliant.'

The guy was probably used to everyone gushing at Matthew about his fucking amazing performance, so Gráinne added, 'Both of you.' Seeing him offstage, he was better-looking than she thought. The glasses and pipe definitely didn't do him justice.

'What's your name?'

'Derek.'

Matthew wandered out and Susan ran to embrace him. Arm-in-arm she brought him to the others. Gráinne noticed he shook hands without looking her – or Francis – in the eye. Then he hugged Susan again and kissed her on the cheek.

'You came on a really good day, didn't they, Derek?

Derek wasn't allowed an opportunity to answer as Matthew continued talking non-stop for a few minutes about how he'd been dissatisfied with his own performance until today when he'd tried something completely different, as Monty Python would

:ay, and it had worked really well. Then, out of nowhere, he said,
'Gotta go. Thanks again, Sue.'

Gráinne could tell that Susan was completely shocked as he
:ipped off towards Front Square.

'We were going to go for coffee. Do you want to come?'

Matthew spun as he spoke, but kept on the move.

'I'd love to, but no can do today. See you.'

There hadn't been any smell of drink that Gráinne could detect
and she was good at nosing out that kind of thing. Was he stoned?
Was that what he meant by trying something different? Maybe
:hat was why poor Derek seemed so ill at ease?

'Derek, will you come to Bewley's with us?

'Oh. Ah okay. Thanks.'

Bewley's! Jesus! It hit Francis what had been nagging at him
all through the play. This amazing guy was the one in Bewley's
:hat first day in Dublin. The one he mistook for a girl, passing
within inches without glancing in his direction, just as today,
:he dark eyes were averted even when they shook hands. Francis
stared, fascinated, after the sinewy, agitated body, darting round
:he corner towards the new arts building. So, his name was
Matthew.

'Francis! Planet Earth calling. Are you coming for coffee or
not?'

'Yeah, sure.'

'Are you all right?'

The question made him realise he felt fine. More than.

Thirty-nine: October 13th

CJ dared to hope again. Everything was working out exactly as Liston had predicted; such rich insight in that dark soul. Certain backbenchers were anxious to begin nudging Lynch to the exit door, but his gilla whispered that a kick-start was needed from CJ, some demonstration of his authoritativeness to reassure them that they were backing the right man.

CJ didn't care for the implication that he needed to prove himself. That wasn't it at all, Liston said. It was more about reminding everyone of his mettle; putting himself at the centre of things again, back on the front page. CJ understood. He accepted that a campaign to promote jogging, or giving schoolchildren free toothbrushes, or even banning tobacco advertising might be popular flourishes, but they were hardly the stuff of legend. Ideally, he wanted to launch an initiative to transform medical research in the country, make it a world leader in some important, headline-making area – cancer care would be perfect. CJ could see himself greeting international health experts, showing them round the wondrous facilities, graciously accepting their plaudits for Ireland's extraordinary achievement. Naturally there was no money available to make this happen. Money, always money. He'd go ahead and do it anyway if he thought for a moment that Lynch and his cabal in the cabinet would let him away with it.

But the immediate reality was that, as Minister for Health there was only one issue in his control that would cost nothing and yet guarantee the attention of the entire country: contraception.

If he could succeed where the previous coalition had failed so ignominiously, sort out a legal mess that had been lying around since 1973, delicately guide controversial legislation through the ouse, that would send out a clear message about his political kill and leadership. But how soon could he have the necessary egislation ready? If it meant helping to hasten Lynch's departure hen as quickly as possible. Early New Year? CJ liked the sound of hat. The quest was becoming real again. He saw himself presenting he bill in the chamber, heaping derision on opposition members, astrated by their own pathetic failure to legislate when they had he chance. The eyes of the nation on him once more. He would be the man who finally ended the ban on contraception.

CJ wondered at Liston's long silence after he proposed the idea. Didn't he like it? Eventually he nodded. But there was a 'but'.

'As you can imagine, CJ, some of our favourite backbenchers will be nervous. They understand about the Supreme Court and that there has to some kind of legislation, but not the kind you or I would want. Remember some of them rely on votes from people who think that artificial contraception is a mortal sin. They'll want you to sort it with no fuss and no grief for them.'

'What the fuck is that supposed to mean?'

'Ah Jesus, you know what it means. If the things have to be legalised, well and good, but it can't be a free-for-all. Definitely married couples only. And it shouldn't be too easy for them to get their hands on them either.'

Despite a snarl and a contemptuous wave of the hand, Michael gauged that CJ understood how it would have to be. The lesbians in the *Irish Times* would flay him alive but he'd have to live with that.

'It won't be popular like the free travel, CJ, but put this to bed without frightening the horses and you'll remind everyone that you're the man to get things done. It'll be the signal to the country and western gang to start moving against Lynch.'

Driving home, Michael Liston couldn't help thinking about her though he didn't want to. He'd managed to ignore the effect of her departure for a long time now and it had been better that way. If he'd got drunker at CJ's it might have helped get her out of his head now too, but thanks to all that fucking talk about contraception she was still there, reminding him of how he'd once boasted that he would make them freely available and tax them big, same as fags and drink; every budget slap another tuppence on a three-pack of Johnny's, a cast-iron revenue stream. What if he persuaded CJ to go for a bill like that? Would she contact him then and say, well done, you were as good as your word? Michael doubted it. Anyway, she was the past. All women were the past now.

The house was empty as usual. He couldn't remember the last time Matthew had been there when he came home. Michael couldn't face bed because she still hadn't vacated his brain and the bedroom would only remind him of the morning he woke up to find her gone. Why had she snuck away in the middle of the night? Should he have seen it coming? No warning, no explanation. Then that cold crabby phone conversation, those deadly pauses, her 'Let's just leave it for a while.' That was all he got. Naturally he hadn't begged for explanations. Fuck that. Let her call me, he'd told himself. And that was that. Nothing more to think about. There had been good and bad in the thing and now it was no more.

He'd have to be patient. Sit down, have a malt and wait it out. Would music help? But he couldn't think of anything he wanted to listen to and couldn't be bothered searching. No other option but to put up with her a little longer. Soon his brain would drift on to something else, or he'd grow tired and just conk out where he sat.

*

The heat in the little cottage on the South Circular Road was becoming stifling. On such a cold foggy night it had seemed a cracking idea to have a big blazing fire in the main room, and the first few to arrive at the party had dived at it and rubbed their hands and gone 'ooh! aaah! lovely!' But now, with more than fifty crammed in, no one could even see the fire. Gráinne, sweating already, spotted Susan with bucket and tongs and, realising she hadn't a hope of being heard over the din of chatter and Blondie, waved frantically to stop her piling more coal on. She looked uzzled for a second, then somehow understood Gráinne's idiculous mime and nodded. Housemates barely a week and lready they could interpret each other's nods and winks. Leaving alls of residence was a jailbreak for Gráinne, but she had the mpression it might take Susan longer to get used to not living at ome.

'Best party I've been to since I started college', Derek whispered, uzzling her earlobe, and she knew he meant it, although he vas ever so slightly partial. It wasn't a bad do if dozens of bodies rushed together waving plastic cups in the air and roaring *ha-a-ngin' on the telephone* was proof of success. Right behind her, she ould hear Francis going on about his InterRail holiday.

'We were expecting topless girls, but a fat, middle-aged Spaniard wearing what looked like a bit of string and nothing else vas a shock to the system.'

Gráinne had heard all about it. The magic of European train tations, ten countries in thirty days. A bit exhausting as far as she vas concerned. Holidays were for lounging, but he'd obviously oved it.

'Right in front of us, he stops to survey the scene, hands on hips, so now we're treated to a close-up of a droopy hairy arse with string going up the crack. And I think – you know the way thanks to the EEC we're drinking more wine now and eating fancy cheese? Well what if this beach fashion finds its way from Barcelona to Ballybunion, imagine the likes of your dad or mine strolling around in a little pouch and string, goose-pimpled in the breeze. No, no please.'

Gráinne stuck her head over his shoulder and said,

'Did you tell them about Morocco and the two American "gurls"?'

'Oh right, yeah. We're on the slow train to Malaga and we meet these two New York women. Middle-aged, you know, but good fun. And when we tell them we're headed for Morocco they make these faces and one of them says, "Take our advice, guys. Bring sandwiches."'

Though wallowing in the laughter, Francis was consciou. of not mentioning his happiest memory of that same journey After the 'gurls' had left the train, Andrew Liddy and Patch had fallen asleep on either side of him, Patch slumped, his cheek pressed against the carriage window, but Andrew dozed or Francis' shoulder, then slid onto his chest before finally Franci eased his head onto his lap. A Spanish mama sitting opposite smiled and made the sleep gesture. Francis nodded, trying to look like the long-suffering friend. The Spanish mama had been producing miraculous quantities of bread and cheese and chorizo from her bag and giving them to her little chocolate-eyed son, who delivered the offerings to the corridor where his papa was smoking, shouting and gesticulating with several other men. Now she gave him more bread and cheese and pointed toward Francis. The little boy handed over the food and, staring solemnly at sleeping Andrew, put his finger to his lips. *Shhh* Francis smiled his thanks and, as he munched, allowed himself do something he would never have done in Ireland: he rested a hand on Andrew's waist and, feeling his easy warm breath against his thigh, was utterly content even though he had to sit still for over an hour until Andrew woke and jolted up, dazed.

But the partygoers wouldn't be told any of this. The anecdotes had already moved on to Morocco.

'There's no embarrassment, the guys just kneel down, dig a hole in the sand with their hands, whip the lad out, cool as you like, piss in the hole and fill it again. I swear. I saw it happen again and again in Rabat and in Fez, so it must be a thing. Well you know, is it any worse than pissing in the sea?'

'And do men really go round holding hands?'

'All the time.'

'But they can't all be queer, can they?'

That had been Patch's observation too. Another thing Francis didn't tell his grinning audience was that, on Rabat beach, walking with Andrew to the sea, he had briefly but vividly imagined holding his hand. There were so many unrevealed moments, a whole other holiday in his head, turbulent and confusing, but potent too. Memories that might never be commemorated with words. From the very first day more or less. In Paris, having found a cheap hotel on rue Cujas, they sat outside Le Depart St Michel, drinking beer slowly because it was so expensive, loving the buzz at the fountain and astounded at so much casual, elegant beauty. Patch had been the first to speak.

'How many hours did we waste outside Todd's and never had a hope of seeing anything like this. It's a cornucopia of talent. What is it about French girls?'

Andrew always had the expert eye in these matters.

'They just don't seem to try so hard. You know the way girls at home plaster the make-up on? Well, see your one passing now, look at her skin. Totally natural. And her clothes seem like she just threw on whatever was handy and ran out the door.'

'So that's *chic*, is it?'

Francis thought he'd better join in.

'Is a *flâneur* the one who sits watching the passersby, or the one who passes by?'

'Who cares as long as her arse is as shapely as that. Look at those contours. Art in motion.'

But Francis never mentioned what was actually on his mind: why did all the young Parisian men carry little handbags? Weren't they awkward, dangling by a strap from their wrists? A bit girly too. He had a theory about why the things were such a fashion item. They wore trousers so tight nothing could fit in the pockets, at least not without creating bulges, and there was only one bulge these guys wanted to show. Francis wasn't sure why he kept these thoughts to himself and didn't even make even some jokey reference: 'What do you make of the lads with the handbags? Can't see it taking off outside Todd's, can you?'

Weeks later, after France and Spain and Morocco and Switzerland and Holland and Germany, on their way to the Ost Bahnhoff for the Athens train, they'd heard that the new pope had died suddenly. What had made Francis suggest going to Rome instead to see the body? Wasn't that the beauty of InterRail, he'd argued, they could change plans anytime; just hop on a different train. But Patch and Andrew were focused on Greek islands and nude beaches, not dead popes. When Francis suggested splitting up, the discussion got a bit heated and hurtful, but eventually they agreed to meet up in Naxos in a few days. Later, on the train to Rome, reading *Portrait of a Lady*, he smiled when the man opposite pointed and said something in Italian about 'Chenery Chames'. It was then that Francis comprehended more clearly that the dead Pope was just an excuse. What he wanted was to travel alone, at least for a while, though he wasn't sure why. Much as he'd loved being with his friends, now he sensed some burden lifting. He could look at anything he liked and think anything he liked and wouldn't have to join in some other conversation that was not his.

Yet tonight at this party he was uncomfortably aware that he was doing exactly that, playing the role of someone who had taken a six-hour train journey in order to queue in St Peter's Square and file past the holy corpse, because he had felt some urge to see a moment in history unfold.

'I mean I had to. After all, how often does anyone get a chance to look at a dead pope? Well, twice a year, it seems.'

The joke sounded stale in his mouth. The laughter didn't help him shake off the scratch of unease, the whisper of hypocrisy.

When the front door opened Mags Perry felt a welcome blast of heat and saw a pretty young face looking puzzled at the old lady's presence on the doorstep. Behind her, the hall was crammed with other young faces paying no attention at all.

'I'm Susan's mother.'

'Oh right. Hi, Mrs Breslin.' Mags didn't bother to correct her. 'Susan is around somewhere.'

Pushing through the crush in the hall, she was preternaturally aware that hardly anyone was over twenty, let alone forty. She smelled pot and quelled a hypocritical twinge of maternal disapproval. In the main room Gráinne was the first person she recognised.

'Mags, brilliant! We were wondering what was keeping you.'

Mags stopped herself from saying surely no one arrived to a party before midnight, in case it would sound like she was trying too hard to come on like an old hippy. Gráinne's boring boyfriend, whose name she'd forgotten again, said hi.

'I've no idea where Susan is, she was dancing a second ago. Let me get you some plonk?'

Gráinne guided her through another blur of baby faces to the kitchen.

'Will I open your own bottle?'

'No, just throw it in with the rest and give me what you have.' Mags liked Gráinne. Was it her brazen, country-girl style? No one's fool.

'So will it be parties like this every other weekend?'

Even as she said it she cringed. Where had that mother tone come from? She'd have to be more careful, although it would be even more pathetic if she demanded a joint and started flirting with one of Susan's classmates.

'No way. This is it. Get it over with in one go. Jesus, Mags, you'd only clean up after something like this once. I'm not looking forward to tomorrow, I can tell you.'

'I'll help.'

How had the dull boyfriend managed to make two words sound so irritatingly sensible? Mags wondered why someone like Gráinne had gone for that type. She'd heard him explain how he saw his future unfolding. Phrases like 'career trajectory' and 'forward planning' featured. She understood Susan's choice slightly better because the child was so intense and idealistic, someone like Niall suited her, even if he was a fraction on the wrong side of bland. When Susan had first coyly mentioned the possibility of *maybe* moving out, Mags knew she was worried about her poor mother being lonely, so, remembering the swan she'd watched one day on the canal near Ranelagh bridge, flapping and biting and forcing her reluctant little ones out into the scary world even though the poor little things kept gliding back, Mags did the sensible thing and encouraged Susan, helped her look for a place, disguised her own fear. Except it wasn't really fear, was it? Worry? Concern? No. It was – slowly she'd realised it – envy. It was impossible looking at these kids not to feel it. If only, if only… Margaret Perry at twenty, shy and swooning because a young dentist had smiled in her direction. What a waste of youth. But, getting better, getting better all the time. Her generation and Michael's had never had a hope really of knowing how to get it right. Too much poison in the culture. But there was a much better chance for Susan and Gráinne's generation. As long as they realised there was a long way to go yet, always a struggle, with plenty of roadblocks. Oh Christ, sounding like a mother again, or worse, one of those mealy-mouthed censorious feminists. *'They don't appreciate what we've done for them.'*

Susan's hug felt lovely and Niall asked her, just like a son-in-law, to dance. She said maybe later with enough drink on board. He offered to take her coat and put it somewhere safe. Gráinne brought a friend over.

'This is Francis. He wanted to meet you. He was in Rome for the Pope's funeral.'

Mags wondered was he one of those Charismatics, although he looked a bit too shaggy and unkempt for that.

'I'm really glad to meet you. Your stuff is great. Really great.'

Her stuff? Her writing, presumably. Definitely not a Charismatic then. Although he had something of that light in his eyes. She was distracted by Niall at the entrance to the hall, gesticulating, looking unusually disturbed. When Susan reached him, he bellowed in her ear and they disappeared up the hall. Gráinne said, 'I'd better see what's going on.'

Matthew wasn't sure of the house number. Why was 63 in his head? 63, 63, 63. Where was he now? Why didn't they put fucking numbers where people could see them? And the fog didn't help. Was it possible to suck in fog? Big breath, whhhhhhhh! No. Just cold. He looked up the road and down the road and up the road and down the road. A long long way from home. Had he enough or a taxi? But hey, he'd hear a party, right? Yes of course. He might even see it in a window. Okay, let's do it. No… No… No… Ah, a number. 45. Okay, 47… 49… 51… 53… What was the last one? Fifty what? Wait. Shh! The Boomtown Rats, definitely. Follow the Rats. This had to be it. Bodies against the window. Boomtown Rats. She's so boom boom boom! Matthew bent over and stuck a finger down his throat. Ughhhghgghg! No. Nothing doing. He went boom boom boom on the door. Faces stared. They all had the same hair. A little smile, a little cute wave. Only pretty me, let them see I'm harmless. Say the password. Susan's friend. Jesus, the heat! The stink! Sweat and breath. Smelly party. Hey! Sorry, sorry about that. The lino is kinda slippy, Eugh! Ah! Here it comes. Eeuuugghgghgheeeuughghghghggh!

The crowd in the hall had pulled back and Gráinne recognised the black tangle of hair even though the face was buried in his own puke. Where had he appeared from? Susan, on her knees next to him, was frantic.

'Let's get him to the bathroom, Niall.'

With Niall and Susan taking either side, there wasn't much Gráinne could do. He was no great weight anyway. Everyone else was tiptoeing round the puke, escaping into the main room. Someone would have to clean up the mess and Gráinne had a horrible feeling who that would be. The little fucker! Had he only just arrived? Just popped along to vomit all over their party, had he?

'Oh Jesus, what happened?'

Some instinct told Gráinne it might be better if Mags didn't know that the puke belonged to Matthew.

'Oh some guy's after getting sick. It's fine. Niall and Susan are looking after him in the bathroom.'

'Is he all right? I should go in.'

'No, he's fine.'

'We'd better clean that up.'

Much as Gráinne would have liked to hand Mags a bucket and mop and go back to the party she knew that wasn't on.

'Mags, Mags. Get yourself another glass of wine and have a dance.
But someone has to –'

'What would we do if you weren't here?'

Whatever way Gráinne said it, she got through to Mags. Of
course. Let them sort these things out themselves. This was their
world. BOY THROWS UP AT STUDENT PARTY. Not an
arresting headline. Best to be a guest, step away, go back into the
maw of the party. Why not dance? She didn't recognise what was
playing, but never mind that.

Gráinne was relieved that Mags nodded and said, 'You're right.'
Fair dues to her. A top woman. Now only Derek and Francis
remained, staring at her, then at the vomit.

'It's Matthew.'

'Oh no. I didn't even know he was here.'

'He arrived just in time to throw up. Get me a bucket of water
and a mop, will you?

When Derek left she turned to Francis.

'Matthew was that weirdo in the play with Derek. Susan's
friend, remember? I don't want Mags to know the state he's in.
His father is her ex-boyfriend, long story, very complicated, okay?
Will you keep her chatting in there until we can get him out of
here, into a taxi, whatever?'

Susan stuck her head out the bathroom door.

'How is he?'

'He's all right. Niall will drive him home. Where's Mum? I'd
prefer if –'

'Sorted. She came out, but I made her go away again. Francis
is going to keep her talking.'

Gráinne realised Francis was still there, staring in at Matthew
on his knees, head in the toilet bowl. For crying out loud!

'Is there anything I can do to help here?'

'No. You can help by distracting Susan's mother. Go!'

Derek arrived with bucket and mop and Fairy Liquid. Francis
got to the main room just in time. Mags was coming back to the
hall.

'Oh, hi. They're loading him into a taxi. He's feeling a lot better... Listen, can I ask you something? It's about that amazing interview you did a few months ago, with the woman who wouldn't leave her abusive husband... Actually, I need your advice.'

Not really the perfect time to bring this up, Francis thought. But he'd done it now and at least he had her attention.

'It's about a cousin of mine. Do you mind me asking?'

'No, but isn't it a bit noisy here?'

He led her through the dancers to the kitchen.

'The thing is, I've no proof, but the woman you interviewed made me think about my cousin.'

'Because?'

'Well... I have a feeling she might be in the same sort of situation.'

Now Francis heard a different tone in Susan's mother's voice: something clear and penetrating.

'You mean abuse, domestic violence?'

'I think so.'

'But if you say you've no proof, what exactly makes you think there's something going on?'

And Francis told her about Eva's staring eyes, he described how Mickey spoke, the shapes he threw. And the doberman of course.

Gráinne at the front door lit up as she watched Susan and Niall pouring the little fucker into the car. Derek, behind her mopping up the vomit, was saying it was such a pity because Matthew was a brilliant maths student. First-class honours two years running. Susan had said it was very complicated with his dad and other stuff, whatever that was supposed to mean. Right now Gráinne was inclined to say fuck him. Maybe she'd feel more understanding in the morning.

1979

Forty: February 28th

Last summer in the great rail cathedrals of Europe, Gare du Nord, Gare de Lyon, Hauptbanhoff Munchen, Roma Termini, Wien Sudbahnhof, he had loved the flurry and flow the stench of suspense, the feeling of being on the set of a cold war thriller. He never expected to experience the real thing stepping off the Dublin train onto shabby platform three in Colbert station, but he did. He'd agreed with Mags Perry a simple cover story in case somewhere between here and Café Capri they encountered any old acquaintances. Mags was a lady he had met on the train and, being such a well brought up lad, he was guiding her to a hotel. They walked in the grey air down Wickham Street. A geezer lurching out of Sadlier's bar looked shifty and he was sure he recognised another fellah ambling towards them from William Street, but he swung right into Cahill's tobacco shop before their eyes met. He wondered if the town looked shabbier and the people sadder because of the Ferenka closure, or had it always been like this? He was seeing it through the eyes of this sophisticated female journalist walking beside him. Presumably she was absorbing it all, composing a grim scene-setter for her article.

As a rendezvous, the Café Capri was definitely more le Carré than Fleming. A takeaway with a few tables attached, hard plastic and chrome; brown vinegar bottles with the screwtops speared. He hadn't been inside it since that day with Gráinne. That had been a good laugh.

They sat in the furthest corner, even though the place was empty apart from a couple of old ladies sharing a pot of tea and bread and butter. Almost immediately, as if she'd been watching for them – maybe she had – Eva pushed the door open with her

back and pulled a buggy in. He sensed nerviness in her movemen
as well as in her eyes. But her smile was big and an unexpecte
reminder of a younger girl, full of mischief and fun. He stood
and was about to embrace her, but remembered that was a colleg
thing. Instead he looked towards Jean and said how big she'd got
a proper little girl now. He introduced Mags and she hunkered
down and said, 'Hello.' The child looked away shyly. Though he
would have given anything to stay – not interfering, just listening
observing – he knew the go-between had to exit now.

'So, I suppose I'll leave you to it. Will I meet you back at the..
station?'

He wanted to say rendezvous. Mags suggested six o'clock
Hopefully she'd confide in him on the journey home. Home
Dublin? Yes, he realised. He had merely ducked back over the wal
on a secret mission, undercover, not even contacting his family
He'd hole up somewhere, at the pictures or the library and, in a
few hours, slink away again. Home.

Mags decided it was the tense staring eyes that made Eva look
older than twenty-three. She wouldn't take out her notepad and
pen yet. That was when the penny usually dropped about what
the interviewee had agreed to. Time enough. A pot of tea first
some casual chat. The smell of chips was actually making her
hungry.

'You and Francis are good friends as well as cousins?'

'We were always in Ballybunion at the same time every year.
The whole gang of us in Brosnahan's. It was a great laugh. Francis
told me your marriage broke up.'

Mags was surprised. This must be important for her if she was
bringing it up so soon.

'Yes. In England. Eleven years ago now.' Mags chose her next
words deliberately. 'I walked out on him, took the children. Came
back to Ireland.'

'And he never came after you?'

'No. He was more the self-pitying type.'

Eva stared at her for a few seconds. When she said, 'Would you

ind coming back to my house?' Mags thought she hadn't heard
er right.

'Your house? Are you sure you want to?'

'I do, yeah. I want you to see how mad he is.'

Surely her husband wasn't at home? Eva had stood up already.
As they left, Mags heard the woman behind the counter mutter
omething about nerve. Out on the street, Eva raced ahead with
he buggy. Mags trotted to catch up.

'You know he's never hit me? I told Fran to tell you that?'

'He did. Is it true?'

'Never laid a finger on me. It wouldn't suit him. He knows I'd
be gone like a flash if he did.'

Mags hoped she'd remember all this without the benefit of
notes.

'I should explain, Eva – if you say anything that you don't want
me to use, just tell me, okay?'

'Use whatever you want. I don't care. Wait till you see the
house, wait till you see the way he has his stuff all laid out. And
the dog of course, you have to see him. It's the dog made my mind
up. Only I had no one to talk to. I still can't admit it to Mammy.
She was right, she hated him from the first day she met him, but
of course that only made me fancy him more just to spite her. I
suppose I thought he was on my side.'

They crossed over the river. Mags didn't interrupt even to
ask how long it would take to get to the house. She just tried to
remember everything Eva said and let her talk now that she was
talking.

*

CJ breathed in the silent expectancy of the chamber. He was back
at the centre of things, very close now. Not many trials of fire to
go. In front and around and above him they leered, waiting for
him to trip up. They'd be waiting.

'We have here the first real Family Planning Bill to be introduced
since this matter first became the subject of controversy in this
country. The bill introduced by the last government in 1974

specifically related to the control of the importation, sale and manufacture of contraceptives. The bill now before the House genuinely merits the title of family planning. Its emphasis is primarily on the provision of family planning services and it deals with the control of contraceptives as something which, apart altogether from the 1973 Supreme Court decision, must be dealt with in the context of a comprehensive family planning service. It is because this bill is a Family Planning Bill in the full and proper sense of those words that I am commending its provisions to the House. I hope that when it has been fully considered and discussed, its enactment will bring an end to the controversy about what we should include in our family planning legislation…'

*

Mags guessed the houses on St Brendan's Road had been built in the thirties, during that first enthusiastic phase of public housing undertaken by de Valera. They must have been such a step up for so many poor people then, everything new and freshly painted, a room for Mammy and Daddy and a room for the kids. A flush toilet. Luxury. People were happy with so little then, or at least that's what they told themselves. Eva had not stopped talking since leaving Café Capri. Mags needed to take notes soon or she'd forget a detail or a turn of phrase.

At first Eva said she'd paid no attention to his questions: 'Just a bit of goss when he came home from work', she'd thought, just filling each other in on what had happened that day. 'I never noticed it was all one way.' She'd tell him lots of bits and pieces, but when she asked him anything it was 'a grunt or a couple of words and a question back.' It was ages before she put a word on it: 'I thought of it as a joke one evening, God what's this, an interrogation? In my head, you know.' She hadn't said it out loud.

When they arrived at the house Eva said, 'Shh, wait now till you hear what happens at the click of the gate.' She lifted the handle and Mags heard ferocious barking. 'Don't worry, he's tied up round the back.' Inside, the place was spotless. 'Come here,

ake a look.' There was something elated in Eva's manner now,
ike someone on a dangerous funfair ride. Mags followed her
nto the scullery. Through the little back window she saw the
lobermann jerking on his leash, teeth bared at the unseen threat.
'Come upstairs.'

This seemed a good moment to take the notebook and pen
from her handbag.

'Do you mind if I take notes?'

'No. Wait till you see this. This'll give you an idea of what I'm
dealing with.'

She trotted upstairs. Mags hurried to keep up. Into a neat
bedroom. New cream wallpaper with a yellow tree, flowers and
birds.

'Take a look at this.'

She opened the top drawer of a formica chest of drawers. Inside
nine shirts were laid out, folded and layered three by three.

'And this.'

She opened the second drawer. On one side white underpants
were neatly folded and laid out in layers. On the other side were
vests, also folded and layered. It was like a display in an old-style
gentlemen's outfitters.

'He has to have it that way. He goes into a sulk if it's not
exactly right. Look.'

The third drawer had eight pairs of men's socks, laid out, neatly
spaced apart.

'He's mad in the head, isn't he? His clothes take up twice
as much room as mine. It's not normal, is it? Tell me it's not
normal.'

Mags sat on the edge of the bed. She wondered would the dog
ever calm down. 'No, it's not normal.'

*

'The effect of the bill, which I am now introducing, is generally
to control the availability of contraceptives and restrict effectively
their supply to certain authorised channels for family planning
purposes. Before introducing a major bill of this nature, dealing

with a matter which has been the subject of concern and controversy for so many years, I deemed it prudent to make every effort to inform myself, insofar as this could be done, of the views and attitudes of those professional bodies who would be affected by the provisions of family planning legislation, the health boards, Church leaders, and all those community organisations, vocational bodies and individuals who could help to convey to me the range of views held throughout the community on this important issue. It should first be made clear that there is a general consensus that family planning, in the sense of deciding upon the number and spacing of children, is regarded as being highly desirable. All the bodies consulted by me agreed that there was a need to legislate in relation to family planning and contraceptives. Most of them took the view that the present position, which allows any person to import contraceptives for his own use, but in which they cannot be sold, should not be allowed to continue. It emerged clearly that the majority view of those consulted was that any legislation to be introduced should provide for a more restrictive situation in relation to the availability of contraceptives than that which exists by law at present. The general view was to the effect that the availability of contraceptives through a large variety of sources and, for example, from slot machines and similar dispensers, should not be tolerated…'

*

'One day it just came out. "What's all the questions for?" I said. "What do you want to know every detail for?" And he looked at me. Of course he didn't answer, he never has to answer anyone's questions. Do you know what he said? "I worry about you"! Can you credit that? "I worry you'll end up like your mother." says he, "gallivanting around the town all day, gossiping, sticking your nose in where it's not wanted. You know what she's like. Would you blame me for wanting to make sure you don't go the same way?" Next thing, I don't know how it happened, but I'm apologising to him. I'm saying I'm sorry for snapping at him and he's saying it's all right. "I forgive you," he says.'

It was her first pause in ages. Mags' tea had gone cold she'd
been so busy taking notes. She looked up, aware of the barking
for the first time in a while. The child stirred in Eva's arms and
sleepily poked her fingers towards her mother's nose and mouth.
Eva said *shh* and brought her to her cot, laid her down gently and
watched for a few seconds to make sure she was asleep.

'Do you want to hear about the shopping receipts? That was
the next thing. See that tin over there? Take a look.'

Mags crossed the room and picked up an old cocoa tin. 'I was
short one week to pay the insurance man. Fifty pence. So he says,
"I'll help you sort that out." He brings home this tin and tells
me to put all my receipts in it so that I know exactly what I'm
spending. Go on, take a look, it's all right.'

Mags pulled out the tight bundle of little papers. There had to
be hundreds of receipts.

'So then it's every evening, going through the receipts. I swear,
if you only saw the face on him you'd laugh, questioning every
item, like he was an accountant.'

There was no danger of Mags laughing. She felt tense looking
at this hard crush of paper crammed with figures, listening to this
nervy young woman describe their role in a torture that broke no
bones, left no visible bruises.

*

I propose to work closely with NAOMI and with the Catholic
Marriage Advisory Council and to obtain their assistance in
providing a comprehensive natural family planning service
so that couples have available to them appropriate advice and
information on this method of contraception in addition to
other methods and that there will be available to them, if they
desire to utilise this method, informed guidance and assistance
in doing so. Where instruction or advice in relation to methods
of family planning which involve the use of contraceptives is
given, this can be done only under the general direction and
supervision of a registered medical practitioner. Contraceptives
shall be sold only by chemists in their shops and that they shall

be sold only to persons named in a prescription or authorisatio
given by a registered medical practitioner. The section require
that the medical practitioner be of the opinion, when givin
the prescription or authorisation, that the person requires th
contraceptives for the purpose, *bona fide*, of family planning c
for adequate medical reasons and in appropriate circumstances. I
is clear to me from my consultations that majority opinion in th
country does not favour the widespread uncontrolled availabilit
of contraceptives. The view was also expressed frequently tha
the existing position in relation to the supply of contraceptive
is unsatisfactory in that it makes contraceptives available withou
any form of control to anyone, child or adult, single or marriec
who wishes to write away and import any form of contraceptio
they wish.'

*

'I didn't tell you about the Toffypops yet, did I?'

'No'

'Oh that was the best yet. Kojak I started calling him in m
head after that. I used to get a packet of Toffypops when I did th
big shop in Quinnsworth's. Of course he never eats biscuits bu
he was very generous about it, oh yeah, awful generous. As lon;
as I didn't go short again, he said, like that time. He was alway
reminding me about it. Remember that time, he'd say. Sorry
where was I?'

'Toffypops, he didn't mind you getting them.'

'Oh yes. Anyway one day I got home from Quinnsworth's,
don't what was the matter with me, it must have been something
I suppose, but I arrive home and put Jean down for a nap anc
I make myself a cup of tea and… and I eat the whole packet o
Toffypops. I don't even realise I'm doing it.'

'I've done that many times – not Toffypops, mind you
Cadbury's Snack is my downfall.'

'But I'd never done it before and I don't even notice until there'
only the last one staring at me. So I think, what the hell, and finish
it off. I feel a bit… Well, a bit strange. Guilty, I suppose. Anyway

put the wrapper in the bin. When he comes home he's delighted
have the big receipt for the weekly shop to get his teeth into
nd that's all grand. But then a few hours later he's in the kitchen
nd next thing he comes in holding up the wrapper and a big
mile on his face. "Lucky I found this. I thought you told me a
e," says he. "I couldn't see any sign of Toffypops, but you'd said
ou got a packet today." And this smile on him, you know. But
was – I don't know what I was, but I wanted to box his face or
omething to take that look off it. Then he stopped smiling. "You
te the whole packet," says he, "and then you hid the wrapper."
I didn't hide the wrapper," says I, "I threw it in the bin." "Didn't
ou feel sick after it?" says he then. "No wonder there's no weight
oming off you after the sprog, eating a whole packet in one go
ke that." And every day after that he brings it up. Every time
re eat, every time I make a cup of tea. And the next time I'm
oing the big shop he says to me, "I think you should lay off the
offypops this week. Just to see if you can do without them." Like
nere was something wrong with me. So I didn't buy them, but
nen the next week, to get him back, I bought two packets and
id them upstairs and pretended the price on the receipt was for
omething else. There were things he didn't know the price of and
ouldn't keep track of. I started doing that every week. Sometimes
'd get three or four packets, just to spite him. But one evening,
e found them.

*

It seemed to me most appropriate that the responsibility for
providing guidance and assistance in relation to decisions on family
planning and for authorising the provision of contraceptives,
where these were appropriate in the family planning context,
hould reside with the family doctor. He is the person who most
ppropriately can give such advice and assistance, since he is the
professional person who knows most about the physical and
psychological characteristics of the couple seeking his advice and
who is also aware in a general – or frequently in a very specific
– way of their social and financial circumstances. No other

single professional person is as well qualified as he to advise o
appropriate methods of contraception. The bill, therefore, plac
family planning firmly in the context in which, I believe, it shoul
be placed, that is, in the context of family medical care provided l
the general practitioner. This seems to me to be a wise and sensib
way to ensure that the making available of contraceptives will l
for family purposes and will be accompanied by advice regardir
the merits and the hazards of different forms of contraception.'

*

The doberman had finally given it a rest. More or less. Mag
thought she could still hear a low persistent growl. Did he kno
they were talking about him?

'He never gave any reason why he got the dog?'

'Reason? Mickey never has to give reasons for anything. H
just arrived home with it. For a while, every evening after h
dinner he'd be out training him. He put up that fence out th
back. At night he'd have him in here at his feet watching the tell
I think the dog thinks I'm a sort of a slave. He doesn't budge whe
I call him, just stares at me. Sometimes, when I leave the roor
he follows me out to the hall and watches me going upstairs. A
least during the day he's tied up outside. I know how to ope
the gate without making any noise so he doesn't know I'm gone
Anyway, one night Mickey came home very late, drunk. Oh,
forgot to tell you that he'd started bringing the dog for a walk ver
late some nights. I don't know if he was stopping at a pub or...
or somewhere else, but he always arrived back with the smell o
drink on him. Usually I waited up because I hate going to bee
and then being woken as soon as I'm asleep.'

She stopped. Mags wondered was she getting tired now. Hov
long had she been talking? What turmoil was filling her head? A
least some of it had gathered and rolled, a great swirling, crashin
wave of revelation. Had she ever said anything to anyone? A hin
even, to a priest? Although she hadn't mentioned religion at all. A
doctor? Mags doubted it. Doctors kept well away from this sor
of situation, apart from doling out the Valium.

'He was drunker than usual and with a smirk on his face. You now that really annoying drunk mood when someone thinks e's great gas. It was after one o'clock. "Look at you with the ong face," he says to me. "I'm going to bed," says I. "Where's the prog?" says he, out of nowhere. "Where do think she is at this our, out at a disco?" So, I'm upstairs, just getting into bed when e arrives. I see him heading straight for the cot, so of course I now he's going to wake her up and, without even thinking, I take mad jump of the bed and get between him and the cot. "Leave er alone, you'll wake her." And he says, "Yeah? And? I'll wake her f I want. I'm her father." "No, you won't, now get away." And his is all whispering. Even he's whispering. Well! He looks at me ike he can't believe what he's hearing, like he can't believe I have he cheek to give him backchat. For a second I think he's going o hit me at last. He might be drunk enough. I want him to hit ne so that would be that. "You're not going anywhere near that hild in the state you're in, so you might as well forget about it."

don't know where all this is coming from, except I'm sure I'm ot going to let him wake her up. Well. He stares at me for I don't now how long and then he just turns and goes downstairs. Jesus, Mary and Joseph! I was shaking. I remember I put my hand on he side of the cot wondering what would happen now. Would ne come to bed, would he sleep on the couch, would he go off to vherever he walked the dog? I knew it wouldn't be the end of it, out it never crossed my mind that he'd... Even when I heard his ootsteps coming up the stairs again I didn't notice the sound of he paws. He comes in holding the dog by the collar. He gives one of his stupid commands and the dog sits on his hind legs, head up, all alert. Then he says, "Move away from that cot or one word from me and he'll rip you open. You'll move then all right."

'Jesus Christ.' Mags couldn't help herself.

'I still don't move, so he goes down on one knee and hisses in he dog's ear and he starts growling and dribbling and pulling on he collar and Mickey looks at me. "Last chance."'

Mags saw the poor girl's eyes fill up. She looked at her sleeping daughter and, when she spoke again, her voice shuddered at the memory of it.

'So I get out of the way and he says something else to the dog and he sits, all quiet again, and he lifts Jean out of the cot and of course she starts crying and he lifts her high and brings her downstairs and I can hear her crying and him getting annoyed because she doesn't want to play and the dog sits there staring and, every time I move towards the door, he bares his teeth.'

*

'I know at this stage that there is throughout the country as a whole a wide general acceptance of the desirability of family planning and of the need to have available for families a satisfactory family planning service. The majority of couples consider it necessary to have at their disposal up-to-date and comprehensive information about the various methods of family planning and, relying on that information, to decide on the means of family planning which is most appropriate to their circumstances. There are many others who, while they accept the desirability of family planning, would not in the determination of the size of their own families wish to avail of any other than natural methods. Similarly there are those employed in the health and ancillary services who would not wish to be associated with either the provision of information or with making available any means of family planning other than natural ones. There will be no compulsion on anybody to use any part of the family planning service to which they have an objection or to be involved in the provision of information or advice about any aspect of family planning to which they have a conscientious objection.'

*

'Eva, it's not my place to say this, but I will. You have to get away from this man.'

'I know. Thanks.'

'What are you thanking me for?'

'Just 'cause… 'cause I wanted to hear someone else say it to me. I was hoping you would.'

'I'll help you in any way I can. It sounds awful, but you might
e glad in the end about what happened with the dog, because
's the thing that might be the difference between you getting a
arring order and not.'

Mags knew that a barring order only lasted three months, but
would be something. A breathing space. It might allow the
oor girl to start the process of separating herself from this lunatic
ho'd never laid a finger on her.

*

J lifted his head and his fine nose detected the scent of victory.
Ie had heard it already in murmurs of approval behind him and
ensed the warier backbenchers relax as time and time again he
ffered them the balm, the soft *f* and *m* and *l* of *family* and the
olid reassurance of *planning*. A warm phrase to use and re-use
mongst their suspicious voters. He had avoided inflicting on
heir sensitive ears the harsh aggression of *contra-contra-contra* –
oo like contro-versial – *contraceptive*. His strategy had worked.
ll the earth's fair treasures were back within his grasp and, beside
im, Lynch's bald head was bent low in sullen acknowledgement
f this political miracle.

'I recognise that this legislation will not satisfy everybody.
here is no legislation which would. There are diametrically
pposing views sincerely held on practically every aspect of this
ssue. There are powerful lobbies ranged on different sides. There
re many people around who want to impose their views whatever
thers may think or whatever the consequences may be. There
re commercial interests seeking their own ends. I think the time
as now come when the parliamentary process should prevail.
Everybody has had his say. It is now a matter for the elected
epresentatives of the people to decide.

'This legislation opens no flood-gates, but it seeks to meet the
equirements of those who either have no objection to the use
f artificial contraceptives or who, having found other methods
nsatisfactory, wish to utilise means other than natural family
olanning methods. It invokes the co-operation of the medical

profession whose involvement in the provision of family planning services is the best guarantee of their availability and the successful implementation. It provides that those who find the provisions unacceptable need not involve themselves in any way.

'This bill seeks to provide an Irish solution to an Irish problem.'

*

Francis hadn't been in the local library for years. He remembered Marian bringing him here for the first time when he was seven. It seemed funny now that he hadn't been able to believe that all those books could be borrowed free of charge. The last time was the day of the Herrema march, when he'd sat on the steps waiting for everyone, and Gráinne was the only other person to turn up. That was the day he discovered just how funny and cynical she could be. She could nail things much better than he could. She'd done it a few days ago when they'd noticed a crowd gathered to watch the porters remove the condom machine from the Student Union offices. A crew from RTE was filming as the machine was unscrewed from the wall and carried away like a coffin. Francis had been amused when a bunch of smart lads standing behind the camera started sarcastically roaring out the old hymn.

> 'Faith of our fathers living still
> In spite of dungeon fire and sword
> Oh how our hearts beat high with joy
> Whene'er we hear that glorious word
> Faith of our fathers, Holy faith
> We will be true to thee till death.'

He'd been about to join in himself, when Gráinne whispered in his ear and her words made him think again. 'They sound so brave, don't they, but you notice, they're keeping well behind the camera, so their mammies won't see them.'

'Kennedy', called twice, made Gráinne realise she'd hear her own name soon. She told herself to snap out of it and stop bemoaning the conferring ceremony's lack of even a basic sense of occasion, let alone grandeur, rarified air of academe or historical splendour. The name of the venue for the great occasion said it all really: 'Lower Ground Floor 1 and 2'.

'Kenny.'

A windowless bunker. Brick walls charcoal-painted by Dramsoc to create a black space for their shows, the grey partition between LG1 and LG2, accordioned against the wall to open up the larger space needed to cram in all the lucky new graduates and their proud families.

'Keogh.'

So this was it. The culmination. A backdrop and some flowers on a makey-up platform lit with a few spotlights. Whatever qualities UCD had – and Gráinne had had a ball, she wouldn't deny that – it didn't have class. It urged its students *ad astra,* but conferred degrees in a basement.

'Kerrigan.'

Thank Christ she and Derek had decided to be sensible and keep their conferring ceremonies family-only. Gráinne would have hated him to see this penny ha'penny effort compared to the opulent and ancient Exam Hall where Derek had been conferred. At Trinity anyone could meander through a degree, majoring in coffee and chat, and still end up part of a glorious pageant in an historic setting.

'Kettle.'

Kettle? Who? Surely she'd have noticed that name before Didn't recognise his face either.

'Kickham.' She must be next.

'Kidney.' Ah Jesus!

At last. She settled the cap and stood, telling herself to straighten up.

And amazingly, for however long it lasted, it felt special after all, like a cherry bun in Bewley's: the tingle of applause, the blur of smiling faces from which Francis emerged into clear focus, his fingers waving. Up the steps without a stumble, thank Christ. The handshake. The smile even looked genuine. 'Congratulations.' The scroll. BA. The smile out into the glare and beyond, to the shadowy heads and hands. Then off the other side.

'Kirby.'

Francis grinned because Gráinne had managed to keep her shoulders straight until she stepped off the platform and then became her slopey self again, searching for her row in the dark. She could relax now. He had a long wait for the 'S's.

Thankfully his mam next to him had recovered from the shock of Francis booking them into brand new Bloom's Hotel. 'You shouldn't be spending your money on a place like this.' It had been a special opening offer, but he didn't tell her that.

'Never mind the cost, it's a treat.'

But a B & B is all we want. We'd have been perfectly happy with a B & B, wouldn't we Fonsie?'

'Well you'll enjoy this more.'

'No, no we can't let you spend all that money. Can you cancel it? We'll find a B & B easy enough. Where's this we stayed that time, Fonsie, before we got the boat to Liverpool?'

'Mam, it's paid for. It's fine –'

'Don't be wasting your money.'

'It's not as dear as you think –'

'Tell them we have to go home. An emergency. They'll refund you.'

Francis could no longer keep the frustration out of his voice.

'Mam, I wanted to give you something, can't you just enjoy it!'

He was determined to halt ridiculous tears. Finally, his mam emed to realise there was something upsetting him.

'I'm only saying there was no need. Surely you know we'd ver have booked an expensive place like this, that's all I'm ying.'

His dad brokered the truce.

'Well sure, we're here now and we're booked in. We might as ell make the best of it.'

So they had rested last night in unhappy comfort in Bloom's nd here she was now, loving the comings and goings of every esh graduate. Isn't she lovely? He's very tall. Would he not have ut his hair for the ceremony? That's a lovely smile. He has a great elcome for himself, I'd say. Oh she's very serious, those glasses on't suit her at all. All lovely young people with lovely parents n a lovely occasion.

Ford Madox Ford may have taught Francis how impossible it vas to fathom the heart and mind of another, but when it came o his mam he thought he could make a stab at it. Today she was n her element. And if she was happy, his dad was happy and the ame with Ritchie. Little Eugene was no book of secrets either: pen-mouthed at this glimpse into his big brother's curious world, is face was his soul.

Francis thought of Marian, at home with her new baby. More amily excitement. If she was his age, would she be here with Gráinne and all those other girls? Was timing the only difference? f it was better to have been born at the end of the fifties than at he start and Francis was sure it was – then was the next generation lways luckier? Was Marian's little fellah, born two weeks ago, he most fortunate of all? Were things always getting better as he world turned? Had his sister been a victim of that? Francis vould love to know what she really thought and felt. Marian was . placid pool, but deep. 'It'd be more in your line to take a good ook at yourself first,' his mam might say, 'before you go passing emarks on others.'

'Francis Strong.'

He smiled at his mam as he stood. This moment was happ
for him, for her. Let that be enough.

*

CJ would have preferred not to have blissful thoughts interrupte
but his loyal lieutenant had been speaking for some time now ar
he should allow him an ear. His wise ancient: a wonderful titl
What play was it where the prince had an ancient? He must loc
it up.

'Sorry, I was distracted for a moment. Again.'

'I was only saying that O'Kennedy opting to support you ca
only mean one thing. The slimey fuck thinks you're going t
win.'

'Yes. Actually it means three things. One, I finally have a membe
of the cabinet voting for me. Two, as you've said, O'Kenned
has sniffed which way the wind is blowing and decided to clim
aboard. And three, for this he'll expect promotion when I tak
charge. Why don't we just tell the amoeba to go fuck himself?'

'I'd like nothing better, CJ, but the numbers are too tigh
The margin will be somewhere between two and six. Can't tak
chances with that and anyway, being able to put the word ou
that O'Kennedy has shifted your way is useful for settling an
nerves.'

A wise ancient.

'Between two and six? I say eight or ten.'

'You can say it, CJ. But bear in mind that it's a secret ballo
and some of these fellahs are not exactly the most trustworthy. A
poor old Colley is about to find out.'

Trust. CJ tried to remember a time when he'd trusted people
Had he ever? Long, long ago.

'The first time we met, you were the bearer of bad tidings, yo
bollocks. Lynch couldn't be beaten you told me. You came all th
way out to the house with Dom to persuade me not to contes
the election.'

Michael wondered where that had come from all of a sudden

sus, thirteen years ago. And it wasn't the first time he'd met
J. They'd been introduced a few months before that and had
ɔoken on another occasion. Michael didn't bother correcting
ᴖese details.

'I didn't think it would take so long to get you here.'

'Thirteen fucking years. But I'm here now. We're here. Who
as it said the true measure of a ruler is the quality of the men
round him?'

Michael didn't know or care. This was in danger of getting a
it mawkish. There was a vote to manage.

'I have to go talk to a few people. Make sure there's no slippage.
pread the word quietly about O'Kennedy.'

'Of course. Of course. Oh, in case I forget later, Terry wants to
ome to the House. You'll look after her, won't you? Don't worry,
ᴖe won't overstep the mark. She'd just love to be around after the
ote. Savour the atmosphere.'

'I'll sort it.'

*

ᴄva Durack stayed sitting, Jean on her lap, watching everyone
et off the train, still half-expecting Mickey's face to appear out
f nowhere, like that day on the bus home when she'd barely sat
ᴖown and, next thing, he appeared at the top of the stairs and
trolled right past without as much as a glance. He could have sat
ight behind her for all she knew, not daring to look back.

Despite the barring order, everywhere she went, he'd pop up
n the vicinity: in Roches Stores on the top floor when she was
ooking at hair dryers; in the Stella Café sitting a few tables away
ᴖever looking at her; at the traffic lights on Catherine Street,
tanding on the other side. When she'd brought Jean to see the
ᴖope she'd begun to feel jittery during his homily:

'Divorce, for whatever reason it is introduced, inevitably
ᴖecomes easier and easier to obtain and it gradually comes to be
ᴁccepted as a normal part of life.'

It had felt like the Pope was wagging his finger at her.

'The very possibility of divorce in the sphere of civil law makes stable and permanent marriages more difficult for everyone.'

'Why had she felt the need to look around? Had she onl
imagined Mickey's face gazing up at his Holiness no more than
few feet behind, amongst the kneeling crowd?

'May Ireland always continue to give witness before th
modern world to her traditional commitment to the sanctity an
the indissolubility of the marriage bond.'

Pure panic had made her hoist Jean into her arms and ru
from the racecourse, bumping through the crowd, not carin
what dirty looks she got.

Mickey's cleverness was that no matter where she saw him, h
never actually came up to her or spoke to her or even looked
her. It was all just coincidence. How well he knew how to get a
her, punish her for daring to defy him.

'Mammy, they all gone.'

The carriage was empty. Imagine if it pulled out now and the
were left on it like eejits? She grabbed her luggage and, takin
Jean's hand, went to the door.

Behind the barrier at the end of platform two, Mags wa
trying to stay calm, even though her professional instincts wer
signalling danger. Had Eva simply changed her mind or ha
something happened? The poor woman had been so distraugh
when she'd phoned. Though the invitation had been impulsive
Mags hadn't regretted it and was now alert and worried. Hundred
of passengers had passed. The platform had more or less emptied
What should she do? Take the next train and go in search of her
Go home and wait for a phone call?

When she saw the distant figure step down and lift a chil
onto the platform, Mags surprised herself at the surge of relie
and delight that tingled through her. She waved with both hands
Eva, clasping Jean's hand and dragging a bulging suitcase with th
other, couldn't wave back, but even far down the platform, Mag
could see her big big smile.

*

Ann Teresa signed a brash 'Terry' and allowed Liston to guide he from the porters' hut towards the entrance to Leinster House. Were those porters now staring in startled recognition at that signature? Did they read *Private Eye*? Passing through the main door, Ann Teresa saw a couple of glances flick her way. Curiosity, perhaps, at seeing CJ's hatchet man stroll about the House with an attractive younger woman. Over the years Ann Teresa had learned to appreciate this blank man, though she hardly thought of him as a man in the physical sense at all. She could not imagine him in an actual human relationship. What had Mags Perry ever got from it? Ann Teresa had never been interested enough to inquire, but the thing had gone on for so long there must have been some spark. Had it been an ugly, messy end, or had she simply woken one morning to find that there was nothing of flesh and blood there? Terry preferred constructing a more amusing and mildly demeaning burlesque of Liston as that perfect butler in *Upstairs Downstairs,* the silent, utterly trustworthy retainer now serving his master by spiriting the lady through a bewildering maze of secret passages to where she could observe, from afar, her lover become the cynosure of all eyes.

Whatever Liston was, one thing was perfectly clear to Ann Teresa: he knew how to keep the wolf from CJ's door.

'I don't know how long the meeting will be. You know yourself, points of order, procedure, speeches and so on.'

'But you're confident?'

Though the shrug was meant to be non-committal, Ann Teresa detected unruffled certainty, as if the outcome was already arranged.

Michael paused at the turn of the stairs. It was straight ahead for the chamber, right for the Dáil bar and left for the party rooms. Where should he position Terry so she'd get a good view as they piled out after the party meeting, while also keeping her in the background? And what should he do with her in the meantime? His head was too full of CJ just now, mentally tracking his every look and thought in there, second by second. So close now. Michael knew exactly which of their potential supporters got on

CJ's nerves, who filled him with contempt, who bored him, who turned his stomach, who he sneered at, who – only one – he had a sneaking regard for. What Michael admired more than anything was how, when it came to it, CJ had been able, time and again over the years, to prostrate himself before so many trogs, as he called them, in order to achieve this moment. He deserved the leadership for perseverance alone. Michael could never have eaten shit and smiled the way CJ had. He didn't mind not being at his side now, because a party meeting was CJ's playground. He would be utterly in command of the room. Let his enemies make weasely speeches: not a glance would be aimed in their direction. Only supporters would get his attention. He would remember every name and each one would be favoured with the gaze that would recall to them a pat on the shoulder, a press of the elbow, a special smile, a whisper in the ear, warm words and hearty laughter, some timely public gesture of approbation. Michael knew that these supporters would also sense an icy undercurrent, the merest tremor of unease that a change of mind would undoubtedly be unmasked and avenged. He was confident that CJ would, in particular, eyeball the four who Michael had specifically named and warned might need last-minute encouragement.

In the party room, CJ, with modest murmurs, accepted handshakes and smiles, anticipating how many more were gathering outside with cameras ready to relay the news to countless more beyond. He could see the mouths and hear the whispers. 'CJ's done it!' 'It's CJ!' 'CJ's won!' '44 to 38!' The moment was so near. The doors would open and the new Leader would present himself. Behind him, frantic to be in his aura now, many more than forty-four would scurry and stumble in his wake.

He spotted Liston immediately. He knew where to look, deep in the background. Not smiling of course: contrary as usual. Had he managed to –? Yes, there she was. He met Terry's eyes, but couldn't halt his momentum down the stairs, the thrust of bodies propelling him on. He held the secret gaze as long as possible, then her face disappeared behind wildly grinning jack-in-the-box

eads as he tumbled down, down. He hoped it was enough for
er. It would have to be.

In Terry's eyes, CJ's look had halted the mad parade. The tumult
ubsided and the flunkeys stumbled back, as his gaze wafted her
o his arms. Respectfully, the photo boys dropped their cameras,
he political correspondents averted their eyes. Only those few
ortunate enough to witness the moment would know it ever
appened and carry the memory. The kiss was exquisite, her
whisper perfect in its simplicity. 'Congratulations, darling.' Her
owsie had become the boss. Terry sent him on his way to wallow
n his giddy success. The cameras clicked again. The journalists
cribbled. The amusingly red-cheeked men who adored him
lmost as much as she did enveloped him and swept him down
he stairs.

*

Ann had thoroughly enjoyed the meal in the Anna Livia restaurant
t Bloom's. Everyone had. A starter *and* soup. She'd had the mixed
egetable but didn't touch the bread or she'd never have been able
o enjoy her main course. Lamb. It was gorgeous and no dearer
han anything else because they were on the fixed-price menu.
The whole day had been gorgeous. All the young scholars so
oright and smart in their caps and gowns. She had to admit that
he dickie bow had looked very well on Francis. One of his mad
deas of course, but still. And Gráinne had looked so serious and
ntelligent collecting her scroll. Her hair was absolutely beautiful.
t really was the making of her.

Ann sat back, satisfied with just a tiny mouthful of black forest
gateau even though it was lovely and moist, taking in the scene
around the table, the Strongs and the Kielys, all noise and chat, all
getting on. Cormac Kiely clinked his glass with a teaspoon. Ann
ooked at Fonsie. She'd warned him to have his money ready to
pay their share. Knowing Cormac, he'd try and foot the bill for
everyone.

'I couldn't let the occasion go by. Ideally I'd mark it with an
appropriate song, because a song is always worth a thousand words.'

Ann couldn't agree more. She was delighted Cormac ha decided to make a speech. He was such a lovely speaker.

'A chorus of "Gaudeamus Igitur" from the *Student Prin* would be just the thing for the day that's in it, but I don't thir the other diners would appreciate us intruding on their night ou so I won't stand up either. First of all, obviously, I'm sure I spea for everyone when I say how proud we are of our two scholar Gráinne Kiely, BA and Francis Strong, BA.'

Everyone murmured, hear hear. Ann saw Francis tryir to distract Gráinne. Why did he have to make a laugh everything?

'As to those degrees of yours, I'll only pass on the advice the old Gospel parable: use your talents wisely, don't go buryin them in the ground. Now, while you two are the main excus for this delightful gathering, I shouldn't neglect to mention tha congratulations are in also order for the new arrival on the Stron side of the house. A little boy, I hear.'

Well, wasn't that lovely? Ann was delighted he remembere Marian and Stephen. Only right too. Wasn't a new baby mor important than any degree?

'And of course Áine and Ritchie have recently passed the ten year milestone. Thanks to them, the Kielys and the Strongs hav been very pleasantly entwined, and as time, like Old Man Rive just keeps rolling along, it seems that our connections grow alon with our children, and our friendship becomes ever closer, an that is what we should celebrate tonight...'

How right Cormac was again. He had such a knack wit words. It was lovely that Francis and Gráinne were good pals Like twins today in their caps and gowns. Ann had spotted th way they glanced at each other as if they knew what the othe was thinking. Imagine if...? She never knew what to think wit Francis. Too independent, always had been, wouldn't even hol her hand taking him to school that first day. 'Will he be all right? she'd asked Fonsie, not able to sleep last night for all the big fanc bed they were in.

'Sure hasn't he been all right so far? He'll go his own way and e'll be grand. What harm can come to him?'

Sometimes Ann found Fonsie's way of looking at things a bit oo easygoing and lackadaisical, but sometimes he was right.

'A favourite old march of mine – you'd know it if I hummed t – is "Alten Kameraden." Old Comrades. Well, I can't think of better toast than that. Let us raise a glass to the Kielys and the trongs – Old Comrades!'

It took Francis all he could do to keep a straight face as everyone lutifully muttered 'Old Comrades', followed by a flurry of glass linking, during which he tried and nearly succeeded in making Gráinne laugh.

*

Or Garret FitzGerald was utterly despondent. This was one of he most difficult speeches he had ever written. It was slow work ind thus far quite uninspired. Yet there was no question of him leeping until it was completed.

Though he had spent much of his political life decrying the ethos and mind-set of Fianna Fáil, he had never been unwilling o show due courtesy and respect for the minds and talents of a number of individuals in that party, and certainly never questioned or a moment their honourable motives as servants of the State. They might be misguided in their policies, myopic on many vital ssues, with a penchant for tribal politics that frequently retarded them from recognising the correct course of action, simply because someone from the opposition – frequently himself! – had first proposed it. But by and large they were decent people doing their best by their – it had to be said, not very bright – lights.

But this was not true of everyone in that remarkable party.

Despite his rule of thumb that, given a choice between the right and wrong thing to do, Fianna Fáil would almost invariably choose the latter option, it came as a staggering shock that they had elected as their leader and therefore Taoiseach-designate, the man least deserving of such a signal honour. George Colley would have been a decent and perfectly serviceable choice, but instead,

the party had with – in Dr Garret FitzGerald's considered vie
– quite staggering recklessness and breathtaking disregard for th
good of the nation, chosen someone who might well be describe
without hyperbole, as –

Dr Garret FitzGerald stopped himself before he went too fa
even in his thoughts. He could not afford to let bile infect his moo
because, if he did, his formal task, as leader of the oppositio
of wishing the new Taoiseach well, would prove utterly beyon
him. Instead he would hunch at his desk all night, metaphorical
foaming at the mouth and consigning page after crushed page t
the bin. The dignity of the occasion deserved better.

He had managed some sentences of vaguely generous impor
'For more than 35 years I have never suffered insult or injur
from him nor exchanged with him bitter words at any time.'

His last sentence had been a real effort to be positive: 'I mus
recognise his talents, his political skills and the competence he ha
shown in the past in the administration of departments. Thes
are important qualities in a taoiseach…' But reading it back, D
Garret FitzGerald found himself unable to continue until he ha
added, '… but they are not enough.'

Moving swiftly on to the previous six heads of governmen
it was a relief to write warmly of the honourable men who ha
served before. But the issue of CJ's suitability for the role coul
not be avoided entirely.

'He presents himself here, seeking to be invested in office a
the seventh in this line. But he –'

Dr Garret FitzGerald paused. But he what? He is corrupt an
dangerous. He is a serpent lurking in the nation's garden. He is vena
and treacherous. He is ostentatiously and suspiciously wealthy?

Oh to let rip! Instead, for several minutes, he stared at th
page, gulping back the bitter gall.

But he what?

Conscience insisted that he not be cowardly. Yet on such a
occasion there should be no petty partisanship. Finally Dr Garre
FitzGerald wrote,

'But he comes with a flawed pedigree.'

It would have to do, or he would get no sleep tonight.

*

eing as Mags said there was no point in coming to the Coffee
n and not having the spaghetti bolognese, Eva decided to give
a go. She was feeling embarrassed at her stupid answers to the
ings Mags' friend was asking. Trish was only being friendly and
as from the country too and not much older than Eva, so there
as absolutely no reason not to able to chat away with her, but it
as strange and a bit unnerving to be out at this hour at all and
a place like this, smack bang in the middle of Dublin, with a
oman she barely knew and another she'd only met a few minutes
;o. Trish started giving out yards about CJ becoming Taoiseach
d asked Mags if she was sorry now that she'd missed out on
:ing so close to the centre of power? Whatever that meant, it
ade Mags laugh, and she mentioned someone called Michael,
it Eva didn't really follow the rest of the conversation because
r mind drifted back to Jean again.

It wasn't that she thought Mags' mother wouldn't be well able
mind her and she was fast asleep before they left, but still, Eva
dn't feel right about leaving the child in a strange house – in
strange city! – and she out enjoying herself. Except that she
asn't enjoying herself, which was a pity, especially because the
offee Inn was much nicer than Café Capri or the Stella – and
ot because it was fancier, which it wasn't. Most people weren't
en eating: they were just drinking coffee and smoking. It was
acked and noisy, but no one was aggressive and everyone seemed
be talking with smiles on their faces.

When the spaghetti bolognese arrived Eva made a real effort
ot to be such a mope. She asked Trish what was it like when she
rst came to live in Dublin.

'I thought I'd died and gone to heaven. A pure eejit, of course,
it no one to mind only myself, as free as the breeze and a few
ob in my pocket.'

Eva thought it sounded great. Too late for her now. Maybe

coming to Dublin was the wrong thing to do in her situatio
nice and all as Mags was. Even though she kept saying she cou
stay as long as she liked, it would be wrong to take advantage. T
thing was to make up her mind and either start looking for h
own place, or head back home and find some other way to de
with her situation.

'Don't you like the spaghetti bolognese?'

Eva realised she must have some sort of a moany look on h
face. She made herself smile.

'No, no, really it's lovely.'

Mags stood up

'Come on with me. We'll only be a couple of minutes, Trish

Feeling like she'd done something wrong, hoping she wasn
going to be given out to, Eva, squeezing between the table
followed Mags outside and across the road to a phone box.

'You're worried about Jean, aren't you? We can go home straig
away if you like, or you can give my mother a ring and see
everything is all right.'

Eva was already feeling better as Mags called out her numbe
Mrs Perry's Dublin accent sounded down-to-earth and war
as she reassured her that Jean was still fast asleep, not a pee
out of her, a little angel. Eva put down the phone, relieved b
mortified.

'I know exactly how you feel. You can ring again anytime or v
can go home straight away, whatever you want.'

Eva couldn't really tell from Mags' voice or face what she wante
her to do, but guessed she'd prefer to stay out on the town.

'Well, I suppose it would be unfair on Trish if we –'

'Don't worry about Trish, she'll either come back with us, or g
off and do her own thing. Honestly Eva, we're all easy.'

That sounded really nice. It sounded like she meant it. Wha
harm would another hour do? Jean was exhausted after the lor
day and if she hadn't woken so far…

'No, we'll stay. Sure I have to try this coffee you've been goin
on about.'

It was strong and frothy and felt good. Trish asked Mags to
an forward and cover her. She took out tobacco and cigarette
pers. Eva was puzzled why she didn't want to be seen but when
ish revealed the little brown lump, she copped on.

'But, won't there be a smell?'

'Sniff.'

Eva sniffed the air and only now noticed a sweet smell from
mewhere else in the café.

'They ignore people smoking, but they have a thing about
em actually rolling joints here. Don't ask me. Just enjoy.'

Trish lit and took a long drag, then handed it to Mags. Eva
new what was coming next, so, she quickly said,

'I've never even smoked cigarettes, let alone pot.'

'From what I read about what a little fucker your ex was, you
uld have done with the occasional toke to take the edge off.'

Eva couldn't help giggling. Trish had a point.

'Would you not give it a go?'

'Don't force her.'

'I'm not, I'm only saying one little toke to celebrate your return
the single life.'

The single life. It was strange hearing it said like that. Was
at what she'd done? Was that possible? Was it something to
lebrate? Eva, smiling, shook her head.' No thanks. I'll chance
other of these lovely coffees though.'

*

le'd got it now. This was perfect. It was a circus he'd seen
mewhere down the country, years ago when he was a kid, and
ow, out of the blue, it had materialised in the Russell Hotel,
nly bigger and noisier, with loads more clowns. It was all familiar
Matthew, but exaggerated, heightened in his memory. He
efinitely remembered the clown on stilts. He'd never forget him,
wering over everyone, more scary than funny. There was the
nart-alec clown with the joke teeth, and the fattest clown ever
ith a big red balloon instead of a head, with cross-eyes and huge
lasses drawn on it, and the melancholy clown with the mournful

mouth and crying eyes who followed him around the roo[m]
waiting for the chance to slam a pie in his face, and a troupe
identical clowns who just pogoed up and down and went yo-
all the time. And it was all for free, with free drink. Why had [h]
father left that note on the table this morning? 'Win, lose or dra[w]
we'll be in the Russell tonight. You're welcome to come alon[g]
They never informed each other where they'd be or what the[y]
be doing. Often they didn't even know that the other was in t[he]
house. On the day of the Pope's mass in Phoenix Park, Matthe[w]
had just assumed, as he crawled out of bed, that his father w[as]
up there, head bowed, on bended knee, along with the rest [of]
Dublin. He'd run a tepid bath and got in wearing nothing b[ut]
his new pair of drainpipe jeans. Once he'd got over the glu[ey]
discomfort of wet clothing, the slow squeeze of shrinking deni[m]
around his thighs and the sight of puff-clouds of blue dye curli[ng]
through the water was quite relaxing. So when the unlocked do[or]
had swung open and Matthew discovered that his father was n[ot]
in the Phoenix Park, but careering to the bathroom for a pis[s]
wearing nothing but sagging Y-fronts, there was a second – [or]
was it several hours? – of ossified silence. One of his father's le[gs]
danced spasmodically to stop himself pissing there and then. It fe[lt]
like the moment they had striven to avoid all their lives togethe[r]
Matthew had mumbled something apologetic and, rising fro[m]
the bath, dripping blue water, had slithered to his room.

They had managed not to see each other since that morning ov[er]
two months ago, and Matthew still hadn't spotted him tonigh[t]
although when he dropped his name to the gentlemen guardin[g]
the entrance to the circus they had practically prostrated themselve[s]
on the carpet and begged him to walk all over them on his way i[n]
How long had he been here? At this stage Matthew could only cou[nt]
in drink time: most of a bottle of wine, a pint of Harp, some shor[ts]
– though he couldn't remember exactly what they were. He'd ju[st]
picked them up from tables as he passed. Drink was everywhere f[or]
the taking, and he kept roaming around and taking, as the circ[us]
got louder and gaudier and funnier the more he guzzled.

But where was his father? For once he wasn't anywhere in CJ's vicinity, who was seated formally next to a woman, with a grown-up boy sitting on his other side and a girl sitting with the woman and another boy standing behind them. It looked like a portrait of a family. A never-ending line of clowns queued up to meet CJ, but they didn't play little clown tricks, finding a coin behind his ear, or holding something that squeaked as they shook hands or waggling their fingers at the last second. They were all bowing-and-scraping clowns.

His father was surely hovering somewhere? Matthew steadied himself and focused and slowly scanned the shadows, the darkest corners, the gaps between the boisterous clowns.

And there he was.

The shape of him emerged, through layers of waving arms and technicolour faces. It occurred to Matthew that he was so drunk there was every chance he was hallucinating, because his father's head seemed disembodied and the features were shadowed and expressionless against the kaleidoscopic jubilation around him. Matthew closed his eyes and slowly opened them again. The face was still there. His father really was at the far side of the room. His presence, embedded deep in the madness, so still and watchful, reminded Matthew of how old Dutch masters used to bury in their paintings tiny self-portraits, teasingly reflected in a mirror or glass. Though the placing was always discreet and modest, the image itself was usually of the artist standing at the easel, in full control of the canvas, pondering the next brushstroke, deciding whether or not the masterpiece was complete.

*

After the feasting and drinking and the joyously rowdy twenty-minute goodbye in the foyer of Bloom's, Francis liked the way the noise of the night faded to a gentle clack of bicycle chains as he, BA and Gráinne, BA pedalled up silent, shabby, rickety Camden Street. The old country mice had finally been dispatched to their special-offer hotel beds and the young mice owned their city again. Gráinne had drunk a lot more than Francis, so everything he said made her laugh and wobble. They stopped at the crossroads nea the Manhattan and Francis said wouldn't a big dirty fry be jus the thing now? Lovely pink sausages deep-fried and dripping i dripping. Black pudding impregnated with dripping, fried egg floating in dripping. Gráinne said if he was trying to make he puke he was wasting his time.

This crossroads was their parting spot, she down the Soutl Circular Road, he across the canal to Ranelagh and Clonskeagh Each rested a foot on the ground and Francis noticed the fron wheels of their bikes kissing softly. Not sure if he was reluctant t let go of the night, or of Gráinne, he reminded her that that thi was where they'd met up that mad morning to cycle round th empty city centre during the Pope's mass. Gráinne remembered how funny and freaky it was, whizzing around in the unrea silence, waving at the odd passing car and shouting hello to an other refuseniks they met, like they were members of some specia club. From the way Gráinne kept talking and recalling more college yarns, it seemed that she didn't want to say farewell either Occasionally Francis' fingers on the handlebar reminded him jus how uncomfortably cold the night had become, but then anothe recollection would happily distract him. Every now and then, ir a brief moment of pause, their eyes would meet a certain way until some incident or character would ignite the babble and the laughter again. Francis had the feeling that Gráinne, like himself was remembering their drunken French kiss a year or so ago tha they had never mentioned since and probably wouldn't mention tonight either. There was definitely something she kept nearly saying. He had no idea what it might be but it made him curious and fearful at the same time, drawn to hear it, but instinctively avoiding it.

Who knew how much time had passed before, chilled to the bone and with nothing left to say except, finally, goodnight, Gráinne said, far too casually: 'Derek has been offered a job with Deutsche bank. In Frankfurt. He's asked me to go with him. Actually he proposed to me.'

Every instinct and urge in Francis strained to scream: What! No! Are you off your head? Don't even think of it!!

'I mean obviously that's a bit mad and I sort of wanted to tell him that, so I said woah, hold on, Jesus! I'll have to think about that one.'

What did she mean, think about it? Was she seriously going to think about getting married?

'And he was fine. I mean, you know Derek, he doesn't lose it, you know, so he said okay. So. There you go. Anyway. I mean there's no danger I'll be giving everyone a big day out anytime in the near future, but… but…'

And the way she looked at him, Francis felt like she wanted him to interrupt her, not let her finish.

'Yeah… I think maybe I'll go with him all right.'

She hadn't asked a question, but Francis had heard the whisper of one. He still wanted to shake her and shout. No! No! Derek is boring. He's not for you! But he didn't. Because what would he say after that? He had no right to speak at all if he had nothing else to offer? And had he? Francis wanted more than anything to be able to tell himself 'yes, of course', or even 'maybe'. But he could also hear an urgent whispered 'no'.

His voice sounded shamefully careful and dull. 'Wow. That's big news all right.'

'Yeah, I mean, well, you know… The country's a disaster, right, Fran? I'm as well out of it for a couple of years. They're paying him shitloads. They're giving him a car. We can drive all over the place. I'll be like you on InterRail, only more comfortable.'

They laughed and Francis thought about the young Austrian couple in love on the train to Athens, and recalled the day and night he spent, sharing a carriage with them, rolling through the surprising beauty of Northern Yugoslavia. They'd looked so young – younger than him – that Francis had guessed it must be their first time away together. As they'd whispered and pecked and curled into each other he'd been charmed by how surprisingly sweet and childlike German could sound. He'd pretended to be

engrossed in *Portrait of a Lady* so he could watch without seemi
to. All the pretty murmuring had been getting a bit borir
when something had changed. Francis wasn't sure exactly why
happened, but dusk was setting in when he'd first noticed harsh
sounds, angry words, then pouting and silence, then partin
The boy had flounced out of the carriage and, left alone with
shocked tearful girl, Francis had buried himself deeper in *Portra*
of a Lady, turning unread pages far too quickly. It had seeme
a very long time before the boy returned and launched into
mighty *schimpfkanonade*, but he hadn't had it all his own way an
soon there was a full-scale screaming match. Francis had bee
able to observe openly because his presence was so irrelevant t
them. This time it was the girl who flounced out. Francis ha
already thought how alike the lovers looked in jeans and t-shirt
with the same flyaway mousey hair, skinny frames and pale high
boned faces and, in their hysterical rage, effeminacy in the
gesticulation. But now alone with the boy, their eyes had me
briefly, and there'd been no mistaking his intensely masculin
shame that another male had witnessed his ignominy. A momer
later he'd exited again.

Francis had felt amused and touched, but envious too. An
lonely. For the first time since separating from his school pa
nearly a week before, he didn't like being alone and wished h
could share this teenage melodrama with someone else who woul
appreciate, in the same way he did, how laughable and beautifu
such high passion could be

Outside, the gorgeous forest-filled mountains darkened to hug
shapes against a deep deep night-blue sky. Using the little overhea
light, Francis was genuinely giving *Portrait of a Lady* another g
when he heard the carriage door rattle. The young Austrians wer
holding hands, their eyes rubbed red, their pale skin tear-stained
How disappointing that a vital scene had happened elsewhere
Somewhere along the corridor, perhaps even locked away in th
toilet, they had talked and cried and kissed and made up. No
cuddling and whimpering, once again Francis did not exist fo

em. After a few minutes he closed the book and switched off his
ght, the better to observe how beautiful they looked in the blue
ash of the nightlight, stretched along the seat across from him,
folded into each other, making low pretty noises.

Right then Francis had wished Gráinne was with him.

'Jesus, we'll get frostbite if we stay here any longer.'

As they warmed each other's fingers by way of saying goodbye,
once again imagined Gráinne's eyes were pleading with him
say something. Did she want him to persuade her not to go to
ankfurt? They both pointed their bikes towards home, but as
ráinne cycled away down South Circular Road, Francis didn't
ove. One glance round and she'd catch him. Soon she was no
ore than a fuzzy black spot bobbing under a distant streetlight,
ut the effect of her laughter, her warmth, still lingered, curling
und him, a protection against the bitter night. He turned his
ike round towards the city centre and stared back down Camden
treet.

Some instinct had warned him not to beg Gráinne to give
p her plans. He was relieved it had kicked in before he'd acted
lfishly and ended up, as he inevitably would, hurting her just
ke others. What was the thing, the instinct, the voice? What did
mean? Was he afraid to find out? For a few months he'd been
utting if off, avoiding it, ignoring it, disbelieving it. Maybe the
ull truth was that he felt embarrassed. Smart boy though he was,
ad something obvious passed him by? Something a Bachelor of
rts should surely have spotted?

Francis set off down Camden Street towards the city centre.
Once he got going he began to pedal very fast.

*

When the screaming stopped – entirely at his whim – the
ontented little mewls as he fed were such a relief. Marian now
nderstood why her mam always went on so much about Francis
ever sleeping. Was little Stephen going to be the same? Her eyes
losed and she jerked them open immediately. Careful! She fixed
er gaze on the far wall. The plaster would be dry soon. Stephen

would have to do all the painting himself now. And the tilin
behind the sink. That would be the kitchen more or less don
Bit by bit. She noticed a hefty book on the worktop. She kne
exactly what it was but her brain was too tired to remember th
title or author.

Stephen appeared in his boxers, barefoot.

'Tea?'

'Will you go back to bed. You have to be up at half six.'

'When he went quiet so suddenly, I thought I should mak
sure you hadn't killed him.'

Marian watched him fill the kettle. Wasn't he freezing in h
bare feet?

'He turns it on and off like a tap. At least with the screamin
there was no danger of me falling asleep, now I can barely kee
my eyes open.'

'Biscuit for energy? Sandwich?'

'No, tea's fine.'

She stared again at the book. Stephen was standing next t
it buttering bread and slicing cheese. He'd be able to tell he
the title, but now she was determined to remember hersel
Medieval... The Black Plague... Barbara... yes, Barbara..
She got it. Tuchman, *A Distant Mirror.* Good, not completel
gone to mush yet. How could he eat that at this hour? Woul
he get any more sleep tonight? At least she could lie on. No
having to get up early for work had seemed like one of the grea
compensations of motherhood and, while not fooling hersel
about how exhausting it would be, Marian had imagined that
being home all day, she'd have plenty of lovely reading time whil
little Stephen fed, or slept in her arms, or lay in the cot. A seven
hundred page doorstop about Europe and the Plague? She'd fl
through that. Marian could see the bookmark sticking out of
Distant Mirror, still at page eighty-something, where it had been
the day she went into labour. Even holding the book open woul
be an achievement now, let alone reading it. When would sh
ever finish it? Or any book? When he stopped feeding? When h

tarted walking, or talking? Maybe she wouldn't read again until
e went to school?

Stephen put the tea in front of her and started into his sandwich.
Ie seemed to like just sitting there, nibbling silently, not exactly
taring, but watchful, making himself part of this feeding time
1 some way, an eager witness, storing memories. Was it cycling
round all day, alone with his own thoughts, that made him so
atient and considerate?

'I've been thinking.' Until she spoke, Marian had no idea that
ıe was about to. The physical sensations she'd been experiencing
ver the last week had been dizzying and intense, but it had been
o hard to hold onto even a simple thought for any length of time.
'he thing was, Marian didn't want her brain to shut down.

'When all this settles a bit, you know, when things get a bit
nore normal.'

'Which will be?'

'Well, in a few months I suppose. That's what I'm told. It'll
ιecome more of a routine . Anyway I was thinking, you know,
ıext September, October say…?'

It was really hard to keep talking, to connect the thoughts.
And from the way he was munching and looking, it was obvious
tephen hadn't a clue where this was going. How could he when
he'd never ever mentioned it before, even though it had been
n her head since… well, since before she got pregnant. Was it
nsane to start talking about it now? Did it sound like babbling?
Would Stephen just laugh and say it was a ridiculous idea?

'What were you thinking?.'

'Oh, I was thinking… I was thinking…'

If she didn't say it now, she mightn't say it at all. The little
ips and gums caressing her nipple seemed encouraging. Go on,
Mammy.

'Maybe I could apply for an Open University degree.'

'A what?'

'It's a degree from England, but I can do it at home.'

'Really? Are you serious?'

At least he was still munching and sipping. He didn't look hugely put out.

'It's called distance learning. I've ah… I've been thinking about it for ages.'

'Won't it be a ferocious amount of work?'

'I know. I know. I mean it's part-time, but yeah, six years is a long –'

'Six years?'

'I suppose that's why I'd like to start… well, soon… soon as I can. I thought by next October… I don't know, maybe that' mad, but… it's been in my head, you know…'

'Well, sooner you than me.'

'But if… okay, if in a few months time things are a bit more… like I said, routine… and if I still really wanted to?'

'Yeah? What?'

'What would you say?'

'Me? Oh. Well… I'd say, work away.'

'Really?'

'If it's what you want, why not?'

Exactly, Marian thought, why not? She kissed the top of little Stephen's head.

*

As Francis locked his bike to a lamppost at the new Central Bank Plaza, he was thinking about his first year history tutor, Liam De Paor: those nervous eyes that seemed to evade engagement, the diffident tone that quite misleadingly implied lack of interest, the discomforting silences that punctuated his tutorials. Crammed in the long narrow space between bookshelves, the group would wait uncertainly. Had he lost his train of thought or was he waiting for some response from them? It was a particular tutorial that Francis was remembering now: the day Liam De Paor had asked if there was such a thing as an objective historian. Naturally the group had been unanimous that there was, so he'd asked them to pick from the shelves any work by such an historian. And when *The Fall of Parnell* by FSL Lyons was chosen, he'd requested one of the group to open a page at random and choose a passage. Then he'd read it aloud, and re-read it more slowly, dissecting each word this time, noting cultural bias in the language, painstakingly teasing out political and social assumptions underpinning the shape and tone of the narrative. Though his delivery was hesitant and pedantically precise, the effect was of an amazing conjuring trick. Before their very eyes he had made objectivity disappear. But he assured them that subjecting any passage of any book by any historian to such rigorous analysis would produce a similar result. His point was different: 'Never pretend you are being objective. Of course work hard to understand your chosen area of study as widely and deeply as possible. But, more important than that, you must understand yourself.'

Even at the time, Francis had felt the significance of these words. Yet for all his study, all his fascination with the subtlety and texture of language, all his exploration of characters and their relationships, his enthusiasm for critical analysis, he had failed to recognise a free radical coursing through him, invisible to the naked eye but as real and present as a shiver or a heartbeat. He had rattled on, his own unreliable narrator. That had to stop.

Fownes Street was somewhere behind the new Central Bank Plaza. When he found it he was shocked at how grim it looked, but relieved it was empty. He walked slowly past the locked-up, barred-up buildings, eyes shifting left and right. According to *In Dublin* a place called the Hirschfeld Centre had opened somewhere on this street and in it was a gay club, Flikkers. But Francis had read that months ago. Maybe it was gone already, maybe the cops had closed it down. He heard a disco beat, distant but unmistakeable. He listened trying to locate it. 'On Your Knees.' His eyes followed the sound and saw a small pink triangle above a locked door. There were security bars all along the front of the building. It didn't look much like fun. Francis hesitated, then walked on to the bottom of Fownes Street. He stepped into the shadow of a shop porch and stared back. So, what now? He told himself not to be so dumb. Knock on the door, someone would open it. Then go inside. Buy a ticket, presumably.

Still Francis did not move. Could not. He felt intolerably foolish. The door opened and two men lurched out. He heard goodnights, the door closed again and the two men swung in his direction, talking loudly, He pressed himself deeper into the shadows. They passed by, too drunkenly, happily horny to notice him. Francis peeped out. He could just about hear the thump of music. Still he did not move. For minute after cold petrified minute his brain just kept repeating, 'Well, are you or aren't you?' Then he heard footsteps approach from the top of the street. It was too dark and distant to see anything other than a shape and movement, yet the bounce of hair and the sinewy walk felt instantly familiar. Even the arrogant swing of the hand as it banged on the door of the Hirschfeld Centre seemed a memory of some gesture he'd seen somewhere. The guy's back was turned but when the door opened the light from inside fell on gracefully ruffled ebony hair and a bum-freezer bomber jacket. Francis knew it had to be him.

Now he couldn't stop himself moving. Like a creature unleashed, he reached the door just as it closed behind the guy he was convinced was Matthew Liston, and didn't know or care if he knocked loudly or quietly, and had no idea what he babbled to the guy who opened the door, nor what form he signed, nor how much money he pulled from his pocket, except that it seemed to be enough. The music was much louder now and the beat propelled him up the stairs, but his brain didn't register singer or song. He fought a crush of men and along with their sweat and deodorant, some other unfamiliar abomination assaulted his nose. Rubbing against clammy bodies, he saw no faces because he was searching for one only.

There it was. That haunting face. On the dancefloor, lost in himself, Matthew Liston scarcely moved, just jerked his head from side to side, occasionally swigging from a bottle hidden inside his jacket. A guy loped up. You fucker! Francis thought. But it was okay because when he leaned in close and spoke, Matthew Liston

idn't even look at him. He just kept jerking his head, like the guy
asn't there. No pretence, no acting nice, no wasting time. The
uthlessness of it excited Francis. The poor mope was left with no
hoice but to try and dance away casually, hoping his humiliation
adn't been noticed. He'd get over it.

Francis noticed his own body swaying to the music. He even
ecognised the song: 'I Need Somebody to Love Tonight.' Now
e began to take in the different shapes and ages of the men who
assed in front of him, invading the space between himself and
Matthew Liston. And what *was* that obnoxious, stinging *pong*?
He wondered if, seriously, there was any chance of shifting the
eautiful, ruthless boy.

A prodding finger. A voice bellowing in his ear.

'I knew it. I knew it!'

A face obliterating his view of Matthew. A stupid, pouty
mile.

'It's you, isn't it? Kerry? The big orange tent?'

The face came so close, Francis had to shift back to focus
roperly. Now he recognised Gavin. He had aged surprisingly.
The moustache was gone, but the rhythm of the voice was still
unmistakeable.

'Tell me it's you. Unless I'm going completely gaga, dearheart,
t has to be you. Rain pissing down? We had a great chat?'

He looked so eager to be right, it would be lousy to deny him.
But what if he wouldn't go away?

'Yes, I remember.'

Francis shifted position slightly to keep Matthew in his eye-
ine over Gavin's shoulder.

'I knew it! And you know something? Uri Geller how are you,
but I felt it at the time. I saw it in you. You know the way.'

Was that true? Two years ago? If he'd seen it, had others?
Francis wanted Gavin to stop being so pleased with himself. But
more than that he wanted him to *go away*! So they'd met in Kerry,
so he'd talked to him in a tent, so he'd spotted the gay in him –
did that give him the right to monopolise him like this, stand too

close, be so gleeful, touch him lightly on the arm? Matthew w:
still on the dance floor, but he might walk away at any momen
What then? Now Gavin was saying something about New Yor
and Francis thought, why don't you fuck off back there, why a
you still hanging around this backward shithole of a place?

Gavin suddenly stopped talking. He turned, following Franci
gaze.

'Ah I see. Can't say I blame you, dearheart, but I have to war
you all the same. Dangerous little beauty, that boy. Believe m
You're too nice to tangle with that.'

Francis hated Gavin for making him flush so uncontrollabl
He could only hope that it wouldn't show in the cheap flashin
lights.

'The mystery is why we never bumped into each other her
before. It isn't as if there's anywhere else. You've blossomed, you'v
a bit of an air about you since that time. All grown up. Honestl
now, I'm really chuffed with myself I spotted you that time.'

Did he have to keep on about that? As if Francis was som
kind of lab rat.

'So, you're probably wondering why I'm still in Dublin?'

'No.'

'Oh the lash, you cheeky little fecker. You showed a lot mor
respect a couple of years ago.'

Gavin talked on, something about John McGahern, but Franci
stopped listening because Matthew Liston had disappeared from
his eyeline. Fuck!

'It's called *The Pornographer*. Have you read it?'

What was he talking about? Where was Matthew gone?

'It's urban, it's Dublin now. People actually having sex…'

Francis' eyes darted every way. Why wouldn't he stop talking
There! A bounce of black hair going towards the stairs, the exit.

'I said to myself, get the film rights, produce it yourself, Gavin
Why not? I mean some of the –'

If Francis hadn't just walked away, it would have been too late
As it was, Matthew was out of sight already. Fownes Street wa

mpty. Francis looked up and down, not knowing which way to
earch. It was too late. He cursed Gavin.

Matthew, stretched on the steps of the new Central Bank
laza, stared up, mesmerised by the enormous concrete overhang.
: looked askew, awry, out of kilter, as if the thing was tilting over
nd would collapse and crush him. But he knew that wouldn't
appen because his father had told him the architect was a genius.
Matthew understood how it was built, the physics and maths
f it, the twin cores and the trusses and each floor cunningly
uspended from above. But he also understood how it was really
uilt: *money* had built it. And money would sustain it. It would
ever be allowed to topple over.

Matthew wondered why a face was looking down at him. A
oung face, not particularly attractive. Pity. Not ugly though.
omewhere in that vast human hinterland between, where the
orgettable live.

'Are you all right?'

Ah, thought Matthew, here we go. The old, 'Are you all right?'
ine. 'I want to help.' 'Take my hand. Come with me.'

'I saw you in Flikkers.'

But I didn't see you, Matthew thought, or maybe I did and
've forgotten you already. Then, unexpectedly, the face from the
interland lay down next to his.

'Ah, I see now. It looks like it's going to keel over. Weird. Aren't
ou freezing?'

The smile had something. Yeah, the smile was a bit of a surprise.
Matthew began to wonder if the face from the hinterland had
noney for a taxi?

'Do you want to go to a party?'

'With you?'

'Yeah. There'll be loads of free drink.'

'Where?'

'CJ's place.'

'You mean…?'

'CJ. Our new leader. Haven't you heard of him?'

'Okay, sorry, I don't get the joke.'

'It's no joke. CJ's victory party. Out at his place. They'll b drinking all night.'

'Somehow I don't think he'd be interested in having us at h party.'

'No, you see. No, no, no, no. That's where you're wron Totally wrong. You see, I'm in the know. I'm in there. My ol man works for CJ.'

'For real? What does he do?'

Yeah, the smile was surprisingly cute all right. And somethin else. Matthew liked the voice. It was… what was it? What was th word? Sceptical. Suddenly he really wanted the surprising smil and the sceptical voice to believe him.

'What does he do? What does my old man do? He stands i the Presence. He whispers in the ear. He's the lightbulb over CJ' head and the apple falling on it, he's his right ball, the *eminenc grise,* the *consigliere,* the bagman; he's an alchemist, he's the mar who puts the figs into the fig rolls. Come on, let's go to CJ' party.'

Francis stood. He didn't want to go to any party, but he knew now if it meant being with Matthew he'd go. Matthew grabbec his outstretched hand and allowed himself to be hoisted up anc let his body fall against Francis who held him and pressed the hard thin frame closer. It felt right. He could stay like this for : long time. He whispered: 'I can think of better things for us to dc than hang around with that bollocks and his gang.'

Matthew's hands, which had hung limp, now squeezed hi waist and slid upwards until Francis felt thumbs caress his neck He ached to taste the alcohol and cigarettes on Matthew's lips.

'You're right. Fuck CJ and his free drink. Do you want to take me home?' The way he said it like he didn't care much either way made Francis want him more.

'Yes. Where's home?'

'Clontarf. Not far, as long we don't have to wait forever for a taxi.'

'Ah.'

As well as the cute smile and the surprising voice, the guy omehow knew how to hold him, those hands were boss. But hat still didn't explain what had made Matthew suggest going o Clontarf. He'd never brought anyone there before. Just for the ree taxi ride? He wasn't so sure about that. What was the sceptical voice saying now? Why was he showing him a bike chained to a amppost? As he unlocked the bike, Matthew understood, and it struck him as the funniest thing. It was really funny.

'That's brilliant. I sit on the bar?'

'You're fairly light. It should be okay. You've done it before, haven't you?'

'No.'

'Never? Even when you were small.'

'Never.'

Matthew was laughing his head off now. Ah! The bar felt hard and cold and slippery under him, but once he leaned back and rested against the comfy body it was fine. After a bit of a wobbler taking off, they speeded up. Matthew couldn't stop laughing. Now he really was looking forward to bringing the face from the hinterland home. He hoped his father would be there in the morning and meet them on the landing arm in arm, or find them sucking face in the kitchen. What would that do to his day?

'My father drives a Mercedes.'

'Sorry about that – this is the best I can do.'

'No, no believe me, this is much better than a Mercedes. My hands are freeeeezing!'

Francis felt the shock of icy fingers thrust inside his shirt.

'This feels nice. So warm. Mmm, lovely hard nipples. Can I have a suck?'

'No, you'll fall off.'

But he sucked anyway, which didn't surprise Francis because he already knew Matthew Liston was someone you couldn't tell what to do. He shivered with cold and exhilaration and arousal, but made sure they didn't fall over. He pedalled hard over the river and round Busáras. It struck him as strange that it didn't feel strange to want nothing more than this. He asked, 'Where next?' and from inside his shirt heard, 'Straight on!' Straight on he sped until they wobbled going over the filthy canal. 'Where next?' Matthew's cheek was now relaxed against Francis' shoulder, his fingers felt warm, his voice sleepily unconcerned: 'Straight on.'

Francis flew past Fairview Park and burst suddenly onto Clontarf seafront, where he couldn't help howling delightedly into the fresh freezing air.

'WAAAAH! AAAAAAAAAGH!! WAAAAAAAAAA–AAA–AAAGGGHHH!!!' Beyond the streetlights, he could see the dark triangle of Dublin Bay open out and out and out, as unknowable as what was to come.

Acknowledgements

Invaluable reading from the period includes the *Magill* magazin
archive, *In Dublin*, *Hot Press*, *Hibernia* and June Levine's *Sister*
Diarmaid Ferriter's towering *Ambiguous Republic* offers contex
and insight.

Personal thanks to Anna Austen, Anne Bergin, Edward O'De:
Chantal Barry, Anne Richardson, Kevin Thornton, Olivia O'Lear

To Ben for making it such a positive experience, and especiall
to Gráinne Fox for her insight and untiring support.